M000211387

INFLAME

The Completionist Chronicles Book Six

DAKOTA KROUT

MOUNTAINDALE
PRESS

Copyright © 2021 by Dakota Krout

All rights reserved.

No part of this book may be reproduced in any form or by any electronic or mechanical means, including information storage and retrieval systems, without written permission from the publisher, except for the use of brief quotations in a book review.

This is a work of fiction. Names, characters, places, and incidents either are the products of the author's imagination or are used fictitiously. Any resemblance to actual persons, living or dead, businesses, companies, events, or locales is entirely coincidental.

ACKNOWLEDGMENTS

As always, it is a true delight to release a new novel into the world. It looks good and is on time only ever thanks to my lovely wife, boss, and best friend: Danielle Krout.

I would like to make a special thank you to a few groups of people, as well as a few spectacular individuals. My followers on Facebook, thank you so much for sticking with me and getting as excited about the process as I do! My Patreons, thank you for wanting to be the first to have eyes on the work, and for giving me tips to make it all better.

Finally, to Aaron Walker, Jim Eleven, Mike Hernandez, Michael Pregler, Kyyle Newton, Garett Loosen, Chioke Nelson, John Grover, William Merrick, Justin Williams, Samuel Landrie, and Karnnie... thank you for doing so much, and asking for so little in return.

PROLOGUE

"Hello," a musical voice called over as Joe peered around from the fluffy chair that he found himself in. He blinked as he locked eyes with an Elf. "Welcome to Alfenheim. You have a choice to make."

"Welcome to *Svaltarheim*, and the choice should be an easy one!" the Dwarf on the other side called out. "Join the snooty Elves, and become a sworn enemy of the Dwarves-"

"Or join the unruly mob that is the Dwarves, and become the sworn enemy of the Elves."

Joe tried to catch his breath, but every single moment felt like standing in the presence of King Henry. The Dwarf narrowed his eyes as he watched Joe struggle to breathe. "You... celestials above, human! You didn't wait to break the mortal limit before you came here?"

"This one is clearly going to join the Dwarves; he must have no intelligence at all. I'm pleased to see that not every human that comes to this plane is going to be as talented and impressive as all the other ones that already arrived and joined *us*." The Elf scoffed as Joe fully collapsed to the ground. "Look at him. This is a joke, for sure. Dwarf, you may as well leave; he has no physicality at all. He's all mind characteristics, so there's nothing he will want from *you*. Even if we have no choice but to accept him, he'll certainly want to join the group that can actually *help* him."

"Pah! That's exactly *why* he'll join the Dwarves!" The stocky recruiter stepped forward and reached out a hand to help Joe up. "He needs to beef up! Focusing on his mind above all else has made him as weak as a kitten, and he's getting a chance to rectify that. Come on, lad, as soon as you join up with me, we'll go get a steak together!"

"Touch him…" The Elf threatened softly as the Dwarf reached out, "…and this is the last time we will see a peaceful recruitment. You know the *rules*. They have to make their choice alone, and *anything* we do besides informing them of their options will be seen as an act of aggression. Help him or hurt him before he chooses, and all potential recruits start spawning into a dungeon."

A look of sorrowful hesitation crossed the Dwarf's face, and he reluctantly dropped his hand. "I'm sorry that I cannot take this moment to do right by you, human. Arrow-Head over there has a point. There are precious few places where we can be in the same area without killing each other directly. If one of us messes this up, it will mean a demotion, at best."

The Elf turned on the Dwarf and spat to the side. "Arrow-Head? Ah, my ears; I see. Yes, personal attacks are exactly what I expect from rabble such as you. Eventually, we will meet on the field of battle, and I will teach you that there are people beyond people, and heavens beyond the heavens. Your secular ways truly shine through with everything you do."

Joe wheezed, but only frothing bubbles came out of his mouth as he tried to force his lungs to voice the words he wanted to speak. He couldn't get out more than a pained grunt, and the Elf and Dwarf were forced to watch without helping as the energetic environment of the second Zone slowly crushed and suffocated him over the next hour.

There was only one benefit to this terrible pressure: it counted as characteristic training all by itself.

Characteristic training complete. +1 Strength, Constitution, Wisdom, Perception. Caution: there appear to be massive downsides to training in this style!

You have died! Calculating: you have lost 4,400 experience! You will respawn in 12 of Zone Two's hours!

Joe blinked and found himself in his respawn room. He sank into the giant bean bag cushion that appeared in the center of the room, rubbing the center of his forehead. "Well, that did not go nearly as well as I had hoped it would. I need to figure out how to break the Mortal limit within an hour of respawning? Can I study that here? Maybe my 'mortal mind' just won't be able to comprehend it?"

He smirked at the thought, but the smile faded as he realized that he was actually probably correct about that. "System, can I inspect the items in my storage even though I'm dead?"

Joe wasn't expecting a response to this, and was pleasantly surprised when his inventory opened up. He received a notification immediately afterward, letting him know that he would not be able to interact with any of the items in his storage. He could only inspect them, though he could read over the books or data that was stored within. Joe pulled out the... scroll? Book? It was hard to tell exactly what this document was, as it shifted to a new form every time he blinked. "Thank you, System, that's exactly what I was hoping to see..."

Those were the last words he spoke over the next few hours, as he read over 'Breaking the Mortal Limit'. The document itself was not difficult to understand; it was instructing him on how to create certain permanent patterns within his mana— and therefore, his body as a whole—and luckily had been tailored to his particular case. His mana was unrestrained and rampaged through his body at all times. The most difficult portion of study was the fact that there was no way to *test* his knowledge. While he was in his respawn room, he could only try to memorize the patterns as perfectly as possible.

At some point, the portal reopened, but he ignored it; for a day, then two, but just as the timer showed that he had been in the room for exactly forty-eight hours, Joe got to experience something absolutely brand new. He was violently and unceremoniously ejected through the portal at speed.

You are not allowed to stay in your respawn room for more than two days now that you have reached Zone Two! You have gained a debuff: Weakling. Avoiding your duty for two whole days has reduced your maximum health and mana to one quarter of its normal pool for the next 12 hours!

The debuff, coupled with the fact that Joe hit the floor *hard* when he came out of the portal, meant that the Reductionist nearly died by *respawning*. That would have been completely humiliating, but his current state of being completely unable to move beyond spastic twitching wasn't much better.

"Oh look, that human is back." The Dwarf immediately put on a greasy smile, moving into full salesman mode as soon as his target arrived. "You've been gone so long; you must have gone back to the previous Zone? Did you take the time to break the Mortal limit? That was very quick—what the abyss?"

A wave of healing water washed over Joe, bringing his health up to its current maximum. However, Joe did not stand up, nor did he move. He was stuck to the floor once more, slowly being crushed to death. The Elf scoffed at the sight, doing his best not to laugh aloud, but didn't bother to comment about the weakness; instead making an astute observation. "He must have been banned, exiled from the previous Zone. Human, make sure to study and prepare during your time dead, else you will eventually return to the moon."

The Dwarf winced at that, slightly sneering. The reason became apparent with his next words. "I hate to agree with this poetic fraudster, but if you die even a couple of more times, you are going to start losing ground faster and faster. You begin racking up debuffs, penalties, and you might just start respawning over and over. You will be level zero in no time...

and your only hope will be returning to the previous Zone when your ban is over. For your sake, I hope that there is a time limit."

"Either way, can you be quick about it?" The Elf sighed and picked at his nails. "Until you either leave for good or pick one of us, we are stuck without new recruits. This position and all bonuses are based on turnaround time, so…"

The fact that this was something they agreed on made Joe suspicious. They *acted* like mortal enemies, but they seemed to be getting along pretty well… or it *might* just be that important. Joe opened his status sheet and looked at the countdown timer. Three hundred and sixty-one days remaining on his exile. He swallowed, feeling like he was trying to get a ball of lead down his trachea.

Joe really needed to figure out this Mortal Limit thing.

CHAPTER ONE

"Four more deaths, and five days lost in Zone Two." Joe sighed as he checked the countdown for his exile. That was the most accurate way for him to track how much time he was wasting due to failing to break the Mortal Limit over and over. Three hundred and fifty-six days of exile remaining meant that there was exactly one way forward. "I have gained four more characteristic points during each of those suffocation training sessions, and lost twenty-two *thousand* experience. I'm back to level twenty-one today, and if I can't figure it out this time around... I don't want to prove those two right."

Joe decided to peruse his status sheet while he waited for the portal to reopen. He had learned that the weakling debuff increased in potency every few minutes that he waited to exit after the portal opened, culminating at the forty-eight-hour mark. That meant that the only way to maximize his chances of successfully creating the necessary mana patterns was to get out of his respawn room as soon as physically possible.

Name: Joe 'Tatum's Chosen Legend' Class: Reductionist
Profession I: Arcanologist (Max)

Profession II: Ritualistic Alchemist (1/20)
Profession III: None
Character Level: 21 Exp: 248,820 Exp to next level: 4,180
Rituarchitect Level: 10 Exp: 45,000 Exp debt: 14,714
Reductionist Level: 0 Exp: 0 Exp to next level: 1,000
Hit Points: 0/787 (Currently respawning)
Mana: 0/2,152 (Currently respawning)
Mana regen: 44.54/sec
Stamina: 0/781.5
Stamina regen: 5.97/sec

Characteristic: Raw score

Strength: 76
Dexterity: 93
Constitution: 77
Intelligence: 138
Wisdom: 118
Dark Charisma: 80
Perception: 93
Luck: 59
Karmic Luck: -1

"I don't even remember getting to level twenty-two. Did that ritual wipe out a monster population when it hit them? Did I get experience for that?" It had been an astonishingly long time since Joe had looked over his entire status sheet, and frankly, he was surprised to see how much it had changed. The final battles, changes, rituals, everything that he had done had apparently shot his level skyward.

However, now that he was *losing* levels, Joe had another concern. When he had gained the Reductionist class, there had been something in the description about not gaining characteristic points by leveling. If he continued to lose levels, was he going to start losing the characteristic bonuses that he had gained? When he *had* been able to get the little extras, it had always felt like an awesome reward, and losing them would feel like a double defeat. The whole situation was a little frustrating, but hopefully… that would all end today.

"I think I'm finally ready." Joe had memorized the entirety of the mana flows, and he was about eighty percent certain that he could get them in the correct configuration today. The first time he had attempted it, he had only hastened his death, causing his body to implode and leave behind a puddle on the ground that neither the Elf nor the Dwarf had bothered to clean up. He had nearly drowned when he respawned the next time around. Who could have guessed that shifting energy that was as potent as unbridled lightning around in your body could have negative effects?

The Reductionist closed his eyes and tried not to give into frustration. He needed to be as balanced mentally and physically as he possibly could be if he wanted to have a shot of breaking through the Mortal Limit during this life. The portal opened, and he fell backward through it. Oddly, he came walking out the other side, just like every other time—except for the first, when he had been forcefully ejected. It was a truly strange phenomenon, but he did not have time to dwell on the mechanics of resurrection right now.

"An oligarchy is the only way to have a fair society based on the merit of the individual!" The long-bearded Dwarf was apparently making a case that was falling on deaf ears, because the Elf cut him off right away.

"Yet nothing ever *really* changes for your people, does it? That is why our *theocracy* is the best path. Our rulers are mandates from above!" The Elf's voice was an unusually soft countertenor, and could have easily been mistaken as tenor, something Joe hadn't really thought about before.

"*You* have the gall to talk about nothing changing? Your leadership has literally *never* changed without death involved."

The Elf returned a simpering smile. "Mandated from above means permanency."

Ignoring the caustic bantering of the recruiters—just as they ignored his body arriving and dropping to the floor—Joe got to work right away. He directed his energy back and forth, creating swells, tides, whirlpools. He had a strange crystallizing moment of realization that if he had kept his mana within a core like *everyone else* in the Mage's College, this process would have been much easier; far more streamlined, at least. Joe could feel it, he was *almost* there. Just a few more whirlpools, another few seconds…

He lost it. While he was mentally groping for a thread of power to tie all of his effort together in a pretty bow, Joe *slipped*. Instead of pulling away a tiny stream of mana, he *slapped* his mana pool like he would a bag of mulch in a supermarket; dispersing a massive amount throughout his body. Everything that he had put together washed away in the face of that tidal wave… on the positive side, his body didn't explode. Or implode. That was nice, too. Yet, he was back to square one with only a few minutes of oxygen remaining. He could practically feel the carbon dioxide building up in his blood, poisoning his organs and reducing his vision to a dark tunnel…

"Poisoning…? *Poisoning!*" He gasped the words out, attaining a queer look from the recruiters at the non sequitur. It took a mountain's worth of mental energy, but Joe activated 'Neutrality Aura' and hoped for the best. It started without a hitch, and he could feel his body getting cleaner… but only the outside. Joe was still suffocating, and the spell was doing nothing to alleviate that fact. Unable to speak his frustration, Joe simply closed his eyes and thought, "Well, at least I tried. I guess this just isn't powerful enough-"

His eyelids slowly pried open, the gravity making them feel as if they were tied down. He didn't care; that was only a reflex. What he wanted to see wasn't something he needed his eyes for. Joe's status sheet appeared in front of him, and he searched desperately for the *one* thing that might help; might allow him to survive this situation. *There.* He had been correct: there were nine free skill points remaining for him to allocate. He had just… never gotten around to it. Right now, all he could do was thank his younger, less focused self.

One point dropped into his Neutrality Aura, bringing it up to Apprentice nine; then the second one was allocated. Joe accepted the changes with a desperate hope in his heart and tunnel vision closing in. With only seven free skill points remaining, he wouldn't get another shot at upgrading the skill tier.

Skill increase: Neutrality Aura (Student 0): By relying on this skill far too often—for everything from showering to staying hydrated—this skill has increased far beyond what it was ever intended to be. Bonus added due to usage: this skill will now act as a gas exchange, directly exchanging the harmful gases in your blood for the helpful gases surrounding your body. While not as effective as breathing, you will be able to remain underwater or in toxic environments for a significantly longer time without inhaling.

"Intent matters. I *knew* it mattered." Joe's lips twitched upward at the thought, as clarity started to return to his vision. His eyes, which every time before now had become painful and dried out, were remaining nicely hydrated, even though he could only blink once every few minutes with great effort. If he physically could have facepalmed, he would have. Joe had no idea why he hadn't thought to activate this skill previously. Panic, perhaps? Lack of oxygen to the brain?

He was still struggling to breathe, only able to pull in one lungful every fifty seconds or so, but it did not feel nearly as terrible as it normally did. Beforehand, he'd had to focus at least half of his attention on making his chest rise and fall. With his skill reducing his need to breathe by… maybe a quarter? Joe started to feel real hope. His characteristic training notification went off, he stayed alive, and *kept* staying alive. Eventually, even the recruiters started to take note at the greatly extended time-to-live he was showcasing.

"Did you do it? Did you choose Mind Over Matter?" The Elf stepped forward excitedly, the first time Joe had seen something other than vague disgust on his androgynously 'pretty' face. "Work with us, and I promise that you will reach heaven in a single bound! You can start directly in the Officer track. I have seen you go from not even understanding that you *needed* to look at the Mortal Limit, to breaking it in under five full days of attempts. I'm not one to have eyes and fail to recognize Mountaindale!"

"Ignore the pampered twig, human!" The Dwarf cut in, panic filling his voice for once. "I've recognized your talents ever since you arrived. Were it not for this... *thing* stopping me, I would have been working with you to improve and reach this stage the entire time. I would have been able to keep you alive; we would have... hold on one abyssal second... why aren't you getting up? What did you choose...?"

At practically the same time, the two recruiters realized that he had not actually broken the Mortal Limit. The Elf only deigned to shrug, then went to sit on an intricately formed tree stump. "It appears the carp did not jump over the dragon gate. It appears that sometimes a fishy is *just* a fishy. It appears the Celestials don't smile upon this one. No talent, no luck. Cast off even by his own Zone."

"I still... believe in you. You can do it. Take the chance to grow and better yourself," The Dwarf promised very unconvincingly, before he too went and sat down in a meditative pose on an anvil that had been repurposed as a chair. "If *only* I knew what you were going to decide."

Joe's eyes moved between the two of them, frustration mounting in his heart. Neither of them would help him because he might choose to work with the other? Because they had a *deal?* So, helping a potential enemy was worse than rescuing a potential ally? Joe wanted to spit at both of them, but ended up only drooling out of the side of his mouth.

Right then, he resolved that if he didn't need to make a choice between the two, he *wouldn't.* When Joe was strong enough, when he broke the Mortal Limit, he was going to get out of here on his own terms.

CHAPTER TWO

Almost... *almost.* Joe broke his concentration to heal himself, and the *almost* complete structure for his mana circulation pattern shattered into motes of light that faded away like a handful of glitter thrown in the air. Gasping in a long breath, he let his face fall to the side and tried to throw up from the pain.

Luckily, or unluckily, depending on how Joe thought of it, he had not had anything to eat for days and days. The healing water washed from his hands, traveled along his body, and brought him back up to his maximum health. He was lucky that Lay on Hands did not require him to physically touch himself on the chest, or some other strange somatic gesture. He still couldn't raise his arms, after all.

"You can do it," the Elf called over, pretending to speak with affection for the human that was keeping it from gaining boons and sleeping well. "It won't take *you* weeks or months like it does for *everyone* else. *You* can do this very easily. Perhaps if you just give it your best shot-"

"Stop pretending that you care about anything a human would be able to accomplish." The Dwarf growled at the simpering Elf, obviously missing the sarcasm. "All you want to do is pad your bottom line, get a bonus for convincing the humans to join your race over mine. A foolish choice, and we both know it. The winning side is ours, and it always will be. I look forward to seeing your new face after our first battle."

That final taunt made the Elven liason's face contort in rage, but he replaced it with a sneer a moment later and launched his own verbal offensive.

Joe stopped listening; he wanted to get this process down. He focused, putting all of his mental energy into holding the mana weave that was propagating throughout his body. The voices of the squabbling recruiters faded into background noise once again, and Joe pushed on his free-formed mana, again, *again*. This system was built with him in mind, which meant it was something perfectly structured for himself. Joe knew that if he could not make this work, there was no way to progress in this Zone. There was no other option—there was nothing beyond success—that meant that he *would* succeed. Now, or... maybe after he had a few more tries.

As that mindset solidified within him, Joe heard a distinct **click**. The weave that he had been creating, the circuitry throughout his body, solidified. His mana began rumbling along the new pathway that he had created, and contrary to his expectations... the feeling of freedom that his mana was steeped in did not go away, but instead *increased*. It was strange, because all of the power was moving, but there was a feeling that it didn't need to move if it didn't *want* to do so.

As if it were... a different kind of non-Newtonian fluid? Gaseous and free-floating, but flowing along the channels created like a liquid while also carrying the potential to be structured into the 'solid' feel of a spell, the circuit revolved in his body. There was a clear starting point in the center of his heart. From there, it traveled down his legs, then up his body. When it got to his brain, time seemed to freeze for a long moment, and Joe *felt* a question coming. For the first time ever, he instinctively knew the system was about to speak to him, and was prepared.

You stand at a crossroad that loops upon itself and must directly choose the path you will walk upon. For the first time, you will know what lies at the end of each path. Do not be afraid to make a choice now. At your next specialization, you will need to walk the opposing path if you wish to progress further upon the road.

1) Mind over Matter. (Most suitable for your current characteristics) By breaking the Mortal Limit using only your mind, you will learn how to survive in energetic environments by simply reaching a state that allows you to move through the energy like a leaf in the wind, catching the gusts that you need in order to progress. As a fringe benefit, the mental characteristics (Intelligence, Wisdom, Charisma, and Luck) will be trainable twice per day.

2) Matter over Mind. By breaking the Mortal Limit using only your raw physicality, you will learn how to survive in energetic environments by smashing through the barriers that would keep you in place, surrounding yourself in that same energy and cutting through the energy like a ship sailing upon the sea. As a fringe benefit, the physical characteristics (Strength, Constitution, Dexterity, and Perception) will be trainable twice per day.

Joe looked at his stats and tried to make a decision. He did not know if choosing one over the other would allow him to get up on his feet right away, but he did know that his mental characteristics were far and away higher than his physical ones. If he took Mind over Matter, he was certain that he would be able to get up and get going much faster. However… the only time he had seen excitement on that Elf's face was when he thought he was going to get a new 'acquisition'. Joe didn't want to admit it, but he was a *teeny* tiny bit stubborn and potentially—just maybe—a *little* spiteful.

With that self-realization at the front of his thoughts, he chose Matter over Mind. The weave of power that was moving through his body shifted slightly, though it took him a few moments to realize exactly *how* it differed. The knots and whirlpools that had been created had shifted inward, no longer floating over the surface. Mana was sinking into his muscles, bones, tendons, and organs.

Matter over Mind has taken effect! This is not an active effect or title, but a state of the energy that flows through you. Checking for traits to absorb... one trait found!

Trait: Suppression Resistance. Current effect: Will grow as your power does and gives you a 50% resistance to stun, silence, and paralytic effects. Your mind has always been striving toward freedom, and your mana has taken on a bit of your resolve.

This trait will be absorbed into your matter. You can only choose how it evolves:

1) Suppression Resistance (mind and body). This will grant you 70% resistance to hostile stun, silence, paralysis, illusions, ensnaring sounds, and formations of the Journeyman rank or below.

2) Unsuppressed Growth. Choose one characteristic set (mental/physical) to feed into the other. The fed characteristics will gain floor(10%N) where N = the feeding characteristic.

Joe's eyes widened fractionally, and he almost mentally slapped option two... but stopped himself. The system typically did not give two such wildly differing reward tiers. It seemed almost like this was a bait and switch, where the second option seemed incredibly better than the first. But, if he was correct in his assumption, the mind and body suppression resistance was being shown as *equal in value* to the unsuppressed growth. Joe realized that he did not know what the feeding or fed characteristics would be, or if he would get to choose them.

Once more, he was faced with a choice that could have long-term benefits, or something that would give him great power in the short-term *and* long term. He needed more information! How was he supposed to know what to do without proper time to go over the options, the pros and cons of both? With a mental shrug, he tried to boil it down. The question really became: which one would be better *forever*? Having ten percent of his intelligence added on to strength right now would take it from seventy-six to eighty-nine, and only ten—no! *Five* days of training would bring the stat to the next threshold!

But the things that had been added onto the suppression resistance... Joe had an intense gut feeling that 'formations', like those the Jester Assassins used, were something that the

Dwarves would have in spades. Ensnaring sounds? That sounded distinctly Elven, if Joe was going directly by mythology. Either way, if he ended up facing off against one or both of these groups, he was certain that the suppression resistance would remain useful.

Joe had one final thought, one that made the choice for him. The fact of the matter was that, *eventually*, he would be past this Zone. He would not be fighting Elves and Dwarves forever; in fact he was certain he would not be *fighting* forever! Yes, he would be seeking power, but that was not the same thing as attaining power. Eventually, as he gained in experience, there would be fewer things that could challenge him and what he could do. There could only be a few individuals at the peak, else it wouldn't *be* the peak. Frankly, there would ultimately be very few things that could suppress him.

At the highest ranks, Joe was certain that pure stats would already let him disregard almost anything that people of a lower level could throw at him. His mind came into alignment with his personality, and he went with his initial choice of choosing the second option. In an instant, Joe was shuddering on the ground as power started to flow into every cell of his being.

Character trait updated! Unsuppressed Growth added. Mental stats feeding physical stats has been chosen. Intelligence is feeding Strength. Wisdom is feeding Dexterity. Dark Charisma is feeding Constitution. Luck is feeding Perception.

Characteristic: Raw score

Strength: 76 -> 89
Dexterity: 93 -> 104
Constitution: 77 -> 85
Intelligence: 138
Wisdom: 118
Dark Charisma: 80
Perception: 93 -> 98
Luck: 59

Karmic Luck: -1

You have reached a threshold for Dexterity! Upgrading nervous system!

Joe twitched uncontrollably, only the massive pressure of this Zone keeping him from flailing wildly as his muscles swelled slightly and his nerves were remade. His health increased, and he could feel his self control becoming finer.

Stamina now regenerates at a rate of .3*Constitution+.3*Dexterity instead of .275*Constitution+.275*Dexterity. Stamina regen has moved from 5.97/second to 6.05/second! Congratulations on reaching this threshold!

"Yay... so worth the pain," Joe muttered into the air, not realizing that he had managed to actually *speak*. "Hey, at least I can think my way into muscles now. I've always dreamt of reading a book and getting fitter; maybe I can walk into a library and come out a bodybuilder? That's how it works now, right?"

"*What!*" The Dwarf was on his feet in a second, inspecting Joe excitedly. "You actually managed it! You improved yourself to such a degree in this short time! You're an abyssal *genius*! I *knew* it!"

"From the look of you, more changed than just a simple crossing of the Mortal Limit." The Elf's already huge, moist eyes widened even further. "A crane in a flock of chickens, indeed...! You had a character trait. A bloodline. Literally one in one hundred thousand. Human, I can tell you now that the advancement opportunities I can offer you are limitless."

"Quiet, twig! To use your overblown and overused sayings, 'you are just trying to fish in troubled waters'. You can't even give promotions; those are *mandated*." The Dwarf didn't even bother to look over at the Elf as he dismissed him, which was too bad, because it was the first time the Elf really reacted *truly* furiously. The expression faded from the perfect face after a few long moments of struggle, but if the Dwarf had seen it... he would have gloated for the next decade.

"Both of you. *Stop. Talking.*" Joe still couldn't sit up, but he could speak with only moderate difficulty. "I've wanted an answer to this for *days*, and this is the first chance I've gotten. Don't deny me, I've waited too long."

"Go on, lad." The Dwarf waved at the human encouragingly. "You've got your chance now, and you should walk the path of rewards for your actions."

The Elf slightly turned his head to the side in an inquiring manner, "What is this burning question that you have for us? I am sure that both of us would be happy to expand upon the benefits of joining us."

"You sit across from each other, you talk to me and bicker constantly, and not *once*..." Joe stared at one, then the other. "... have either of you said your *names*. Do you know how *annoying* it is to call you only 'Androgynous Elf' or 'Beardy Dwarf' in my head?"

CHAPTER THREE

"Names? You want to hear our *names*?" The Elf shook his head at the thought, and even the Dwarf started chuckling. "You may refer to me as 'Enlightened One'."

"Call me 'Captain'," the Dwarf volunteered easily, reaching out for a fist-bump, only to drop his hand when he remembered himself and the current situation. "I was really expecting that you would ask about our offers before anything else. That's what everyone else has done."

Joe shook his head, albeit slowly. His words came out breathlessly, since he needed to stop and suck wind every few words. Luckily, he was used to this; when he had first entered Eternium, his stats hadn't allowed him much freedom of motion. "I have no... intention of joining... either of you. In my mind, you have already proven... that you can't be trusted to help people when they need it. You are only after the largest benefit to yourselves. I just wanted the names... of the two people who so drastically disillusioned me as soon as I got to this Zone."

Captain's face darkened, and veins began to pop out on his forehead. Before he could start shouting, 'Enlightened One' spoke up. "One of *those* types, huh? Well, human, I can tell you right now that *not* choosing a side means that you have chosen *both* of us as enemies. I can tell that you have the favor of a deity; I can also tell you that here... neutrality means *nothing*. You walk away with one of us, or you never leave this room."

"That would be quite the shame after you spent so much time just figuring out how to survive long enough to *breathe*," Captain growled at Joe, his already deep voice going so low that Joe practically vibrated with the sound. "Hear our abyssal offers; choose to join one of us, or-"

"We will kill the chicken to warn the monkey," the Elf finished, cutting off the Dwarf; much to his displeasure.

"Celestial's sake, can't you just say the words 'use you as an example for others'?" Captain turned to glare at the Elf, then back to Joe. "This is why you don't want to join them; every conversation is doublespeak, and you have no idea what the real meaning behind their words are."

"Just because your race panders to, and even *elevates*, the least intelligent beings doesn't mean everyone else does, or *should*." The Elf turned his mesmerizing eyes on Joe, allowing a hint of a smile to appear. "I can tell you this, *Captain* is likely the most intelligent Dwarf that his race could possibly afford to send to this incredibly important recruitment position. You see how angry he is getting? Right now? It is not because I am saying something negative about his people, nor that I'm calling them dumb; it is because I am calling *him* smart."

"You watch your mouth!" Captain snarled practically animalistically at 'Enlightened One'.

"There it is," came the smug reply. "Imagine joining the Dwarfs, and being surrounded by thousands upon thousands of beings that only listen to their... the human equivalent is testosterone, I believe. Male and female alike, I'll add. Instead, you could join a refined culture, one where advancement is predicated upon your ability to think through situations and gain the favor of those above your station... not punching enough people in the face that no one can tell you 'no' anymore."

"A place where you become stifled by bureaucratic *nonsense*! A place where you have to fill out a form in triplicate so you can join combat when your people are in danger!" Captain spat on the ground between them, but the Elf simply raised an eyebrow and caused a flower to grow out of the tiny puddle in retaliation. "You join them and it is not a death sentence... it is a guaranteed life of boredom and frustration."

"So this is a choice between joining the Marines, or the Air Force. There was a reason I joined the *Army*," Joe muttered with his eyes closed. "Actually, less joining, more being drafted. Fine. Tell me why I should join you. Enlightened One, please start."

"A wise choice." The Elf unfurled from his lotus position and rose to a profound stance, hands clasped behind his back. "You are clearly a human that uses his brain. You have immense talents with internal mana manipulation, and even appear to be mainly self-taught."

"How can you-" Joe started, only to be cut off by the Elf's careless wave.

"Your mana... *suffuses* your body." A slight twitch accompanied Enlightened One's words as he said this, but he didn't comment on it further. "If you were traditionally trained, your mana would be well on its way to forming a central core from which you direct all mana. Your current state will make it harder for you to learn in certain ways, but likely allows you to cast the spells that you *do* know much faster. We can teach you, train you, in all the things you need to learn. You can grow so quickly, and become a powerful force by working with us; especially on the Officer's track."

Seeing that the Elf was done, Joe turned to the Dwarf. "Captain? How about you? Can I get on the Officer's track?"

"Ya don't know what you're asking for, lad." Captain wiped sweat off his forehead and shifted uneasily. "You don't 'get in' to the Officer's track; you need to survive Candidacy and selection. I *can* tell you that our area is more fun. You'll grow in the ways you want to grow; not be forced into small rooms and told what to learn for the next decade. You'll get into the mix, and learn in a hands-on environment."

Joe tried to escape one last time. "Just to be sure, there is no way either of you are going to just... let me out of here? I'll just go do my own thing and leave you both alone?"

"You get near that door, and I will turn you into fertilizer," Enlightened One stated serenely.

"Every single unit of land is constantly being... contested." Captain chose his words carefully. "If we let another person onto our land, and just let them do their own thing, we are essentially creating competition for ourselves. We will not let that happen. Neither of our people will."

Joe rubbed his bald head, even though it felt like lifting a boulder and dropping it on his skull. He resolved not to do that again. "All right, fine. I'm joining the Dwarves."

A blast of mana sent him skidding across the floor, tumbling until he hit the wall of the strange cave they were in.

Health: 200/875. Burning, -20 health per second for 12 seconds.

The Reductionist hadn't even seen what had happened. One moment, everything was fine and calm. In the next instant, the world had been washed out in white light. Captain's deep laugh echoed through the area, along with the sound of metal hitting wood. "I got one! Sod off, twig!"

"He *dies*! How *dare* he turn down the Elven Theocracy?" The Elf's voice was no longer calm or cool; it was instead... a Boston accent? What? "Show *me* disrespect? Your intestines are gonna turn green from regret, then black from rot, you get me?"

Faction joined: Dwarven Oligarchy.

"Buzz off, Sparkle Bro!" Captain did *something* with his hammer, and the Elf was blasted out of the room—through the stone wall—by a torrent of fire and steam. The Dwarf turned toward Joe with a wide smile as a large top hat appeared in his hands. He put it on, and unseen mechanisms *whirred* to life. Thick sunglasses that could easily be used for welding dropped over his eyes, and the Dwarf took a step forward. "Recruit, let me officially welcome you to Svaltarheim, Dwarvenheim, Deepvenheim. Take your pick; they mean the same thing: Home of the Dwarves."

"Not... Nidavellir?" Joe was wracking his brain for all his old mythology. "I thought *that* was the land of the Dwarves."

"Once upon a time, lad." Captain winced and looked away at Joe's comment. "I wouldn't mention that name to anyone else. Anyone who knows about the ancestral home is... salty about it. Abyssal long-form *dragons*. Let's... let's talk about *you*. Take a look at what you got before that maniac tried to bring down this entire spawn point, and then we will talk about your future in the Legion of Silver, the Dwarven Legion."

"Sounds very rock and roll."

"...what?"

"Forget I said anything. Did you say something about dragons?" Joe sighed and read the blinking notification tab.

Faction Bonuses gained:

Dwarven Superiority. You have chosen to join the Dwarven Oligarchy and now understand that they are superior to Elves in every way. You will see them in a favorable light, and Elves unfavorably in every situation. This is a perception shift, and cannot be denied or changed without leaving the Dwarven faction.

Dwarven Currency. You now have access to the Dwarven currency system. Precious metals? Beautiful gems? None of that matters here. All that matters is your word. You are now able to trade reputation points gained from Dwarves for goods and services. Note: Any skills, titles, or classes that grant reputation bonuses will not function within Dwarven society.

Faction Quest Gained: Shatter the Elven Theocracy. Completing this quest will break the Elven Theocracy, leading to their eventual eradication or subservience to Dwarves. Reward: The Zone gains the designation 'Svaltarheim', Variable (Based on contribution). Failure: The Dwarven Oligarchy is shattered, leading to the eventual eradication or subservience of all Dwarves to Elves.

"Oh, come on!" Joe waved a hand at the faction quest. "Not *this* again!"

CHAPTER FOUR

"Don't worry about dragons. There aren't any in this Zone." Captain pulled Joe up from the floor and brushed off his charred shoulders. Skin sloughed off, and Joe let out a sharp gasp of pain. "Yikes, that light magic really did a number on you. Gotta watch out for that; Elves are known for their 'impressive' ability to manipulate light, sound, and sensory input. Just one more reason you can never trust them."

The Dwarf snorted, half-turned and took a few steps, then waved at Joe to follow after him. "What's all that impressive about creating things that aren't real? Solid? 'Oh look, I tricked this person into tripping over their own feet. Look at how witty I am'. Ridiculous. What a waste of an existence."

Joe healed himself with two spells in quick succession, then started to follow after Captain. A thought crossed his mind, and in the next instant, he activated his Exquisite Shell. It appeared that they would be walking for quite a while, so he was not worried about having to use his mana anytime soon. As soon as he could, Joe toggled Retaliation of Shadows to be on as well. He was almost kicking himself for not having these active, but to be fair, he *had* been devoting all of his mental energy to breaking the Mortal Limit. "Where are we going, Captain? What is going on in this Zone, and how can we move it along so that I can start doing what I *want* to be doing?"

"We are going to the spawning grounds of a minor fort," Captain told the human without turning back to face him. Joe hoped that he was just focused and not nervous about what might be in the area. "As for what is going on? War! I'll tell you now, human-"

"My name is Joe."

"I'll remember your name when it *matters*." Captain spoke the words with the same inflection as a hardcore gamer casually promising to do the dishes 'later'. "Let me explain the rules of Svaltarheim for you. Reputation is everything. You buy things *with* it, sell things *for* it, you gain reputation for completing quests and for acts of service for all of Dwarvenkind. Things that will get you the most reputation: capturing minor forts, capturing major forts, and doing what your commanding Officer tells you to do."

"What is this about forts? I don't have any idea what that means." Joe was starting to get grumpy; even though this Dwarf had much shorter legs than he did, his physical stats were likely *insanely* higher. He was practically running just to keep up, and still trying to ask questions? It was starting to become frustrating.

"Right, well, you know what happens when the people of Eternium die. It's a little different here, because of the constant war. If we all respawned with opposing viewpoints every single time we died, we would have-"

"*Wait.*" Joe cut Captain off, his eyes wide. He had been seeking out this information, subconsciously or not, since he'd started the game. What *did* happen to NPCs when they died? "Captain, I don't know why you assume I would know what happened to the people of the world. Could you give me a quick rundown?"

"What?" Captain actually came to a halt, surprise clear on his face. "But you are *here*? You won the war for your Zone already; we all got the notification. Don't tell me you won your war, and you didn't even know what you were fighting for? *Celestials*, humans are kinda messed up… that means…"

"Your people are going to fit in with us *just* fine!" Unexpectedly, Captain burst into laughter. He clapped Joe on the shoulder hard enough to knock the man to the ground and got slapped by a shadow for his trouble, then continued walking, still chuckling. "Pretty big mosquitoes in here. Listen up, human. When a native of Eternium dies, they come *back*. Problem is, all of us made a deal so that we could live here. Part of the deal was that we would always come back. And…"

Captain hesitated for a breath of time, but he pressed forward after a long pause. "It was a dark time in our history. We had the option to live in peace and grow together, but too many people clamored for war. *The System* decided that if we were going to be at war all the time, we needed to really *understand* what we were doing to each other. Every time one of us dies in enemy territory and the fort isn't captured by our people in time, our memories of living as that race are saved and locked away."

"Then, we come back as a member of our opposing race, losing all the memories of that life. By regaining levels, or by increasing certain characteristics to a high enough point, we slowly unlock the memories, skills, or spells that we have stored away. It's all race-specific. For instance, if I died, I'd come back as a low-leveled Elf. If I got to the level I am now, as a Dwarf, I'd start to remember my life here, as a Dwarf. I wouldn't be any good with a hammer, but I'd understand it better. Just like I understand illusions, and how *nasty* they are."

"The war… is still going on? Even with all that? *Knowing* that you were an Elf at some point?" Joe couldn't comprehend what kind of twisted mindset was required to be literally at war with yourself for hundreds of years.

"Aye, that it is." The Dwarf nodded sagely, a lopsided grin almost hidden by his thick beard. "The only way to stop the cycle is to shatter the other race. Then, if and when we die, we will at least come back *only* as Dwarves. That's also why we defend ourselves more than we attack; every soldier that we lose means another enemy we will have to face. That's what I was saying when I said that things are a little different on this Zone. Here is where the forts come in."

"Now I understand why humans had been reduced to one single City, and were so reluctant to launch an attack against the Wolfmen. At least until they were almost positive they would win in a single strike. As for here..." Joe prodded Captain after a few long moments in which neither he nor the Dwarf were speaking. "Please go on."

"Huh?" Captain frowned at him in confusion. "Wait, you actually *want* to hear about this? History and such? I kind of figured that you had zoned out, so I just... yikes, you might have a harder time in the Legion than I was expecting. Alright, listen. There are nine *minor* forts that surround almost every *major* fort unless something wonky is going on. Anyone killed in the territory of a minor fort will respawn at that minor fort after a day, so long as we retain control of it and pay the fees for the Ledger of Souls. The Ledger is commonly known as 'the rolls', while respawning is referred to as 'roll call'. Any enemies we kill will come in as low-level Dwarves after that same amount of time."

Joe was starting to see what Captain was getting at, "I'm guessing that if they took the fort, the Elves would be able to recoup any of their lost troops? They would also gain any Dwarves that fell in that area?"

"Yes, and no." Captain nodded approvingly, though there was a slight hint of disgust on his face. "They would get their troops back, but the second part is where major forts come in. If we lose a minor fort, we can pay a certain amount of resources to bring back a portion of our fallen, as I said. It is random, so we can't always bring back the best of the best every time, but it is still a costly gamble we are usually willing to bear. The major forts allow *specific* people to be brought back using the Ledger of Souls; they also act as rapid transit systems. So long as they are not under attack and can pay the cost, minor forts can transfer their people to major, and major can transfer to *other* major. Gotta hoof it from major to minor forts, unfortunately."

"I'm betting that skirmishes are really frequent, but all-out attacks are crazily rare?" Joe nodded at his own logic. "That's why you are so excited to take on whatever human arrives? Because they can throw themselves against your enemies again and again without a cost to you, and they'll always come back on your side? This... this is going to change the face of your entire war, isn't it?"

"Got it in one. Lad, you contribute enough to the war efforts, and you'll be a hero in no time. But we are here, and it is time for you to join the Legion and the blood games." The two of them emerged from a tunnel and were met with an assortment of weapons pointed directly at their faces. Captain grinned, then screamed an incoherent stream of expletives at the Dwarves threatening them. So foul were the words—and so potent was his voice—that the air in the vicinity actually started to turn light blue. Captain paused to take a breath, and another Dwarf stepped forward with a smile.

"Captain Bro!" He slammed his forehead into Captain's, and the two bounced away with grins on their faces and blood dripping down into their eyes. "Welcome back! It so good to see you, haven't had proper spotter in days!"

Joe watched the odd social interaction, trying to figure out if they were speaking his language so poorly. Was there a different language, a Dwarven language, and they were speaking human just so they could be friendly to him? If that were the case, he decided not to judge their poor grammar and sentence structure. The Dwarf turned to face him, and an even wider smile appeared on his face.

"*Human* Bro! You joined up! Dudemeister, I gotta know... how many plates you squat? Feces, look at the way you stand! Your form terrible, thin Bro. No worry, we fix!" He grabbed Joe's shoulders and slammed their foreheads together, creating a shower of sparks and a dark version of Joe that slapped him in the face.

Joe stumbled back as all of the Dwarves in the area laughed in excitement. Another, this one without a beard but sporting a glorious mustache, jumped forward and slammed their heads together. "Ha! Sparks and funny feel! Dudes and Dudettes, try this out!"

Wham.

Every Dwarf in the area raced over to bash their head against him, and Joe began to despair. "I was wrong. They're speaking as well as they *can*. They're idiots."

CHAPTER FIVE

"*Wake up*! It is already four in the morning! Why're all of you lazing about instead of getting ready to go kill Elves?" The explosion of the amplified voice literally knocked the Dwarves closest to the door out of their beds. Joe only managed to stay in his because his blankets had been tucked in on the edges, and he was able to use them to hold himself down.

"We're *ready*, Drill Instructor!" the reply boomed from every single person in the barracks. It was true. Since they never knew what time they were supposed to be getting up, everyone slept in their clothes and armor, as well as keeping their weapons handy.

It was the start of Joe's second day with the Dwarves, and his first morning. He had never gotten the steak promised from Sarge for joining the Dwarves, but that was the least of his worries at this moment. Joe wasn't exactly certain what he was supposed to be doing, but it appeared that the Dwarves weren't going to make him choose for himself.

They had tossed him into Legionnaire training, along with the new batch of Dwarven 'recruits'. It was somewhat telling that there were only thirty people total in this group, but apparently the training started on Monday each week. He had just gotten 'lucky' enough to get in this batch as soon as he joined up. Besides the voice waking them up, Joe had another surprise waiting for him.

Characteristic training complete. +2 Strength, Constitution.

Just being in this environment was enough to train his strength and constitution, which meant that by the time he woke up, he had already trained the maximum that he could. That was unfortunate, since he was already exhausted, and the training day was just about to *begin*. Maybe he could convince them to let him train other characteristics?

Moving as quickly as he could, Joe still found that he was the last person getting out the door. Concerned that he would either be punished, or people would try to 'greet him' again, he activated Retaliation of Shadows and Exquisite Shell. Both had gone up a skill level the day before, a direct result of so many people bashing their head against his to say 'hello' and test the strength of their forehead against his shielding. Remembering the upgrade he had gained, Joe smiled and checked it one more time.

You have reached the Journeyman ranks for Retaliation of Shadows! Journeyman bonus gained: When you attack or cast a spell, there is now a 10% chance that it will trigger a shadow version that is 25% as potent as the original. (Personal attack or spell use. Group spells and rituals are not impacted.)

Exquisite Shell had only reached Beginner seven, but every little piece of protection was very welcome. Joe joined the formation, getting in position just as crossbow bolts flew from... apparently *everywhere* around them. A bolt passed in front of him, behind him, to his left, and to his right. Joe was about to take cover and find a way to strike back when the voice of their Drill Instructor rang out once more. "If you were hit by a bolt, you are not in the correct space. You're out of formation, and you will *rectify* that!"

"Dude, look at all that blood coming out of my arm! Sick!" the Dwarf two spaces to the left of Joe called out, grinning as he looked at his injured limb. "That's got to have some *serious* armor penetration!"

"That's right, and don't you forget it!" the Drill Instructor confirmed curtly. "Also, *shaddup*! Get in groups of four; that's one less than the total number of digits on your hand unless you cut something off between the barracks and here! Move!"

The Dwarves moved so fast that they left small whirlwinds of dust behind. By the time Joe looked around, everyone had partnered up. Well, all but one small group. They were looking at him questioningly, then staring pleadingly at the Drill Instructor. One of them, the one with the most magnificent mustache, shouted at the Drill Instructor with a gravelly voice, "Look at this guy! He can't keep up! You're gonna give him the opportunity to drag us down? What happened to the high standards that used to be required for joining the Legion?"

A bearded Dwarf in the same group spat to the side. "I'm so *happy* they are getting the chance for inclusion, but humans just don't have the same physical abilities as the rest of us! We are going to end up carrying its gear, having to support it on ruck marches, and what about fighting *monsters*? Forget about it!"

"Oh, I didn't realize that *you* were the one making the rules now!" the Drill Instructor shouted back, leveling a crossbow at the bearded Dwarf. "You must be on the *Officer's* track, or hoping to get on it? *Those* are the people making the rules, after all."

There was a collective inhale at the implied threat, and not a single Dwarf made another sound as Joe shamefacedly joined the party of three. The Drill Instructor grinned evilly and motioned for everyone to follow him. "You all know the rules. Try not to die during training. It sets you back a day, which means you lose all the reputation you would have gained for being an upstanding member of the Legion! You get paid every night at lights out. If you aren't there, I'm keeping that rep for myself! I'll drink an ale in your honor, then be back in the morning to work you twice as hard!"

"Pick your role in your new party, and get friendly! This is who you will be with until the end of training! If *you* fail, *they* fail. Remember, the only way out of the Legion is reaching *neutral* with the Dwarven Council!" At those words, Joe perked up and hurriedly looked at his reputation score with the Dwarven factions.

Current reputation:
Dwarven Legionnaires: -1000, Cautious.
Dwarven Council: -1000, Cautious.

"What the...?" Then Joe remembered that his deity bonus did not work with the Dwarves, because they also used reputation as currency. Before he started cursing this Zone again, he shouted at the Drill Instructor. "How much are we getting paid?"

Strangely enough, *surprise* was the main expression on the faces of the Dwarves around him. The magnificently mustachioed member of his party blinked, then snorted at him. "Who *cares*? The only thing that you can do with all that money is get out of training, out of the *Legion*! Who the abyss would want to have *that* kind of opportunity?"

"Success is its own reward!"

There was a roar of approval at these words, words that Joe would later learn was the mantra of the Oligarchy as a whole. He decided that he would just have to wait for the pay to hit his account that night so he could see for himself what he was earning. The Drill Instructor fired his crossbow at various trainees until order was restored, then continued with his explanation of what they would be doing. "Today, we are going to clear out a monster nest: Stone Lizards! Whatever group kills the most of them wins a week of characteristic training materials or a weapon upgrade; whoever kills one of them in the most impressive fashion gets an armor upgrade!"

"Weapons and armor!"

"Yeah!"

"Celestials, I hope it is really heavy! If I could just find a two hundred pound helmet-"

"Shaddup, the armor is mine! You don't have to worry about if it will-"

Every discussion in the area devolved into a massive fist fight. Strangely enough, anyone in a team did not attack each other, instead working to defend and take down the others with impressive efficiency. Joe looked around, waiting for the Drill Instructor to step in, sighing when he finally realized that the Dwarf in charge of their training had joined in the brawl.

Eventually, they calmed down and got into a marching formation, being led to a cave system and warned not to come out before killing at least two monsters for each member of the party. Joe took a moment to check the different roles that he could choose in the party, surprised to see that they were selectable, rather than based on class or levels. "Attacker, Vanguard, Scout, Support. I'm pretty well set up to be a support; any of you have an issue with me taking that?"

The other three just laughed and walked into the caves, making Joe question what they knew that he didn't. He shrugged and selected 'Support', then looked at the information that was available for their party. After closing his eyes and attempting to calm himself, he followed the three Dwarves on his team—all of them had chosen 'Attacker'.

"Can I at least get your names?" Joe asked as he ran to catch up to his stout team. He stood head and shoulders above even the tallest of them, but their speed was still higher than his, and he was having trouble forcing his way through the thick, energy-rich air of this plane. "All I see in my party interface is 'D1, D2, D3'. Do you guys really not have names?"

Joe was outright ignored at first. Then he grinned as he realized that he knew exactly how to handle people like this. He was prior service, and they were still trainees. He had tricks they would never see coming. "After all, if no one knows what to call you, you can't win the rewards, or be in charge."

There was a long pause, and the Dwarves came to an abrupt halt. The bearded Dwarf stepped forward and stomped the floor, leaving a deep indent. "I'm Broski. I'm the team leader."

"Eat feces, Broski! I'm Dudette, *I'm* in charge around here!" The intensely mustachioed Dwarf snarled at the first that spoke. Joe blinked at the realization that facial hair might be the only way to differentiate male and female in this zone... for him, at least. As far as the human could tell, there were no other differences. Their heads were all bald, and the armor that was worn constantly meant that there was no other clear way to-

Wham.

Dudette was punched into the stone wall by the final mustachioed Dwarf. "*I'm* Dudette, and *I'm* the party leader!"

Joe watched the fight play out over the next few minutes as the cave entrance they had chosen was painted with fresh flecks of blood, wondering yet again if he had made a terrible, terrible decision.

CHAPTER SIX

Joe cast Lay on Hands on Broski, wincing at the sound of the Dwarf's facial bones realigning and mending themselves. A glance at the party interface revealed that the three hundred points of damage he had just repaired had not even gotten the Dwarf *close* to his maximum health. The Dwarves had a crazy high constitution, and a rough estimate—by how much he had just healed up—placed Broski around two thousand health. If these Dwarves were the low-level ones, he would not want to fight a high-level version.

"It's settled then, *ri~ight*? We all had the chance, and proved our merit," Dudette smugly informed the others with a toss of her majestic mustache. Then she lifted a fist, getting a wince from the other mustached Dwarf. "*I* am Dudette, she is *Diane*. That's what you get for being so *weak*, Diane! People are gonna haveta *think* to remember your name! Last, that's Broski, the party leader."

"My name is Joe. Nice to officially meet you all," Joe chimed in, getting an eye roll from Dudette for his trouble. "We have monsters to kill, right? Anyone know anything about these, or are we all finding out together?"

"Stone Lizards, *support* Bro," Broski snorted and grimaced at the others. "Can you believe this guy? Can't even remember what we are going to be fighting. I thought humans were supposed to be brainiacs like those grass-fed Elves. So glad we get to learn that was a lie all along."

"Good one, Broski!" Diane high-fived the 'party leader', and the three Dwarves started walking deeper into the tunnel without another word. Joe was very uncertain how they were moving in sync like that, but he assumed they would just tell him to 'get on their level' if he asked.

The small party continued advancing along the tunnel, and to Joe's surprise, they soon emerged in a huge open plain. As soon as they were out of the tunnel, the Dwarves turned around and looked up. Behind them was a massive cliff face with strange nests built along the side. Dudette grabbed a rock and threw it at one of the nests, hitting it spot-on and getting a loud squawk in reply. Broski suddenly had a double-sided war axe in his hands, which he swung forward at nothing that Joe could see.

At the apex of his swing, Broski's war axe slammed into a translucent, two-headed lizard with wings. "Whoa, I actually *got* it!"

"Cool!" Dudette started swinging her oversized hammers at the air, but she didn't manage to hit anything, much to her disappointment. Joe was fairly certain that she thought that the air was supposed to be filled with monsters.

"That's wild, Broski; finish it off!" Diane ordered Broski as the lizard fell to the ground with a hiss.

"Yo, *I'm* the party leader, *I* say when I finish it off!" The male Dwarf waited a long moment, then cut the lizard in half. "Look at that; each half still has a head!"

Joe stared at the strange lizard that was definitely dead, looked at the Dwarves, then looked up at the cliff face. "I really hate to have to ask this, but I thought we were killing *Stone* Lizards? These seem to be more like… air lizards?"

A blast of wind hit Diane as she turned to yell at Joe, cutting off the ring finger on her left hand and spinning her in place. Broski snarled at Joe, "What are you doing, distracting us in the middle of a fight like that? Are you *damaged*, bro? These are Stone Lizards, because the best way to kill 'em is to hit them with rocks! Or we can get them *onto* the rock and cut them down! Why would you want to call them *Air* Lizards? Those ones are practically *made* of rock! You don't want to hit Stone Lizards with an air spell; they're pretty much immune to it!"

"Stupid human, not even understanding basic combat inter-actions. Every monster is strong in one area and weak in another! Stone Lizards are weak *on*—or when hit with—*stone*." Dudette paused in her admonishment as her hammer hit the left head of another lizard that was flying at her. "Wow! I got one! I guess... thanks for the chance to teach you something, support bro?"

The other head of the lizard bit at her, creating a cavitation bubble that blasted her hammer in the other direction as it came at the head. Sharp blades of wind formed, cutting deeply into her forearm armor, but the sharp currents failed to pene-trate. Seeing this, Joe realized that if the bite had landed, it might have deposited that air bubble directly into the arm; then likely would have blown it straight off. He double-checked his Exquisite Shell with a gulp and tried to spot any lizards that were flitting around them.

He knew they were nearby only because they sounded just like hummingbirds, emitting a low-pitched droning noise that put bumblebees to shame. They were just too fast for him to lock onto, certainly too fast to hit them with a directed spell. That meant there was only one thing for Joe to do; focus on his role in combat. He ducked down, scooped up the finger that had been torn off Diane, then grabbed her hand, aligned the finger against her protest, and cast Mend.

Her finger reattached without issue, and her health shot upward as her blood was replenished. Diane looked at her hand, gave it a test squeeze, then grunted and got back to the fight. Joe tried to think of what to do next. He was a support, but he should have spells that would work against these monsters. For instance, his Acid Spray was technically an earth spell? Or… was it a water spell? Either way, it was not *air*, so it should be at least *somewhat* effective against them.

All three of the Dwarves were facing the cliff directly, but the droning lizards were circling them at high speeds. Joe tried to equip his staff, but for some reason, it did not appear in his hand when he called it from his Codpiece of Holding. He thought it might have something to do with being in combat, though that had never been an issue before. He gave up and simply focused on casting Acid Spray up in an arc behind them.

Damage dealt: 106 (130—33 magic resist + 10% title bonus)

A cacophony of trilling shrieks tore through the air as the swarm of winged lizards dove through the green liquid and started to melt. Joe had never managed to regain his ability to channel spells, else he would have been pumping the air full of acid for the next few seconds.

Three things happened in quick succession after that: first, the lizards became much more visible, since their inner bodies were exposed. Apparently, only their scales allowed them to keep their camouflage working. Second, the Dwarves got very excited and started swinging at the lizards far more accurately. Thirdly, all of the lizards that had been hit by the acid tried to attack Joe at the same time.

Joe dove to the side, dodging out of the way of the first few air streams that were shot toward him, and confusing the Dwarves. Broski was at his side in an instant, pulling him upright. "Human bro, why are you getting out of the way? How are you going to train up your constitution if you aren't taking hits?"

"I can't take hits like you can!" Joe had finally lost his temper. These Dwarves were way too ridiculous! "I only have-"

He paused as he inspected his current health pool. "Holy guacamole, I have nine hundred and eight health?"

"Oh, wow." Broski pulled his hand off of Joe, concerned that he might accidentally damage the fragile human, "You're not kidding, man. You could only take like… three or four hits *total* from these little beasties before your whole body collapses!"

"Joe, bro," Dudette called as she walked over with her left arm swinging from her right hand, "Can you put my arm back on? I saw you work with Diane; can you do arms too?"

"You called me by my actual name…?" Joe stared at the open wound gushing blood where her arm should be, then jumped into action. While the other two Dwarves focused on smacking the lizards out of the air like irritating flies, Joe coaxed the flesh and bone of Diane's shoulder and arm together into a unified whole once more.

It turned out that a lizard had managed to land on her, then both heads had bitten in two opposite places at the same time, cleanly blowing the limb off. Joe had to pump a thousand points of healing into her, but soon she was using both of her hammers once more. A few minutes after that, they were surrounded by a dozen dead lizards. Joe looked at the notifications he had gained at the end of combat.

For focusing on your chosen role during combat, you get a perfect 1/4 split of experience! As your party has three members who have contested a role, they split the remaining experience!

*Experience gained: 600 (50 * 12 'Stone' Lizards)*

Skill increase: Mend (Student 9).

Broski looked at the others with a huge grin. "I know we could go back, but that's already half as many as the whole platoon got yesterday before everyone died! Why did they wait till today to put us in parties? This rocks! Why don't we go fight another nest?"

"Yeah, Broski!" Dudette called with a fist pump.

Diane sidled up to the bearded Dwarf and leaned on him. "Best party leader ever!"

Joe shuddered lightly as the three bald Dwarves that he could only distinguish via their facial hair flirted in deep bass tones. "I'm not sure how to react to all this. Should I-"

"Joe… *bro.*" Diane smiled at him uncomfortably, letting her arm drop away from Broski. "I don't know how to tell you this, but... you aren't our type. Maybe if you put on, I don't know, eighty pounds of muscle and start using a real weapon, instead of..."

She wiggled her fingers mysteriously to mimic spell casting, and Dudette joined in to finish the thought, "Beyond that, none of us feel very, um, *tingly*, around you 'cause of, you know..."

Waving at her face, Dudette shrugged and kept going when Joe gazed at her uncomprehendingly, "I'm sure that you will find someone who is into the total hairless look, but you won't find a deviant like that in *this* party."

Joe smiled and nodded, declining to speak any further. Confusion was one thing; accidental insults because he was voicing his thoughts was another. They spent the rest of the day clearing out three more large nests, then went back to their barracks. Joe had gained another eighteen hundred experience, and—strange rebuttals and cultural differences aside—was rather pleased with how the day had gone over all.

They dumped the corpses of the lizards into the collection bin, getting a raised eyebrow from the Drill Instructor. "You killed all of these? That's... well, looks like we have a new group record. Take these tokens to the Requisition Hall; you'll get a bonus of characteristic training materials."

"We set a record!" Broski fist bumped Diane, and the group started walking toward a small building that Joe had not yet seen. "Human bro, you ready for the chance to train your characteristics for the day?"

"I already maxed out my strength and constitution training for the day, but I can do any of the others!" Joe was eager to see how they did their training, and what sort of bonus they would be getting.

"I wanted the weapon reward." Diane grumbled in a deep bass tone, trying to snuggle in close to Broski again.

"How do you max out your... *ooh*." Dudette nodded at Joe with a knowing grin. "You mean what you can train in a day *without* materials. Do we have a surprise for you, bro. I think you are going to like the Legion a *lot*."

They entered the building, which contained only one grim-looking Dwarf behind a bar. After showing their tokens, the Dwarf counted them carefully and pushed out four large mugs. The thick liquid inside of the mugs was suspiciously familiar, and Broski's next words confirmed it.

"With the right stuff, you can double your gains in a day, bro. Let's hit the gym!" Broski clinked mugs with the others. "Joe, welcome to the way... of *whey*! Protein shakes, then squats! Bottoms up, dudes and dudettes!"

CHAPTER SEVEN

"Everyone, *wake up!*" In an instant, everyone was standing at attention at the ends of their beds. Their Drill Instructor walked along the rows, inspecting each person in turn. He stopped next to Joe, then turned and shouted at the Dwarf directly across from the human. "I'm early, but that's no excuse for looking so slovenly! Why are you disappointing our glorious Legion by letting your armor remain damaged? If I come back tomorrow and it is still in such a shoddy state, I'm going to make you go into combat wearing only a loincloth!"

"Sounds like a party, Drill Instructor!" The Dwarf was expecting to get punched in the face for his cheeky attitude, but instead the Drill Instructor let everyone catch a slight grin on his face. The collective clenching which the expression induced in everyone could have created a diamond under the right circumstances.

"You aren't much, but this is *not* the absolute worst cohort we have ever had in training! Listen up! You have all been here almost a month, killing monsters for the glory of the Dwarven Oligarchy!" Joe's eyes widened, and his hands started to tremble at the words coming from the bearded Dwarf's lips.

"A… *month?*" Joe could not believe what he was hearing. It felt like he had only been here a day! He went to open his character sheet but froze as the Drill Instructor started bellowing again.

"Today, we are going to do something extra-special! Our unit has been selected to lead a raid on a minor fort! Everyone who participates in the *successful* capturing of a minor fort gains two hundred and fifty reputation with the Dwarven Council!" The Drill Instructor scanned the room with a wide smile. "I know none of you are sick of seeing my ugly mug, but I am sick of seeing yours! Start getting that reputation, and buy your way into the Legion proper!"

"*Elf Death!*" The Dwarves and Joe shouted in unison. Joe shook himself abruptly; why… *why* was he just *going along* with everything? He had so much that he needed to-

Skill increase: Mental Manipulation Resistance (Beginner 0). You have broken through the training compulsion of the Dwarven Legion! Wow, look at that! Even when something is to your benefit, you find a way to mess it up!

Joe went pale as he finally broke through the light compulsion that had been placed on him as soon as he'd joined the Dwarves. He looked back on his choices over this last month, grimacing at what he had done. He… had devolved into a total… *Bro.* Yet, as far as he could tell, the only negative was the loss of time and how much he cringed when he thought about how he had been acting. Joe tried to help himself feel better by reminding himself that, as far as he was concerned, looking back at your past and shuddering at your actions was the best sign of personal growth.

He had made incredible gains with his statistics, but still, he looked at his characteristics in confusion. Shouldn't he have gotten… *more* if he were here almost a full month? A month of training should have given him a hundred or more total points, and he had gained less than a third of that.

Name: Joe 'Tatum's Chosen Legend' Class: Reductionist

Profession I: Arcanologist (Max)
Profession II: Ritualistic Alchemist (1/20)
Profession III: None
Character Level: 22 Exp: 274,676 Exp to next level: 1,324
Rituarchitect Level: 10 Exp: 45,000 Exp debt: 14,714
Reductionist Level: 0 Exp: 0 Exp to next level: 1,000
Hit Points: 1,573/1,573
Mana: 1,571.54/2,152 (581 reserved. 10% of maximum from both
Exquisite Shell and Retaliation of Shadows. 7% from Neutrality Aura.)
Mana regen: 44.54/sec
Stamina: 1,337/1,337
Stamina regen: 6.36/sec

Characteristic: Raw Score

Strength: 89 -> 129
Dexterity: 104 -> 129
Constitution: 85 -> 125
Intelligence: 138
Wisdom: 118
Dark Charisma: 80
Perception: 113
Luck: 59 -> 60
Karmic Luck: -1

Joe started carefully reading through all of the notifications that he had received—and not bothered to check—over the last few weeks.

Constitution has reached the third threshold! Bonus calculating... this is a characteristic that is not class relevant and has been increased through daily training. Calculation complete! Every point of constitution gained after reaching the third threshold will grant you an additional five points of health!

Strength has reached the third threshold! Bonus calculating... this is a characteristic that is not class relevant and has been increased through daily training. Calculation complete: 5% of your maximum stamina (rounded down) will be applied to your total health pool!

Perception has reached the third threshold! Bonus calculating... calculation complete! Cooldown reduction has been increased by 5%!

Current Cooldown Reduction: 15%!

"What is going on? I got past three thresholds and I didn't even *notice*? Not a single increase in mental characteristics? What have I been *doing*?" Joe's mumbling unfortunately summoned the ire of his Drill Instructor, who grabbed him by the head and chucked him toward the doorway. The Dwarf had realized early on that punching or shooting at the human caused an attack to come back at him. However, throwing did not seem to trigger the retaliatory strike. It had been a good lesson for both of them.

"All of you, get moving! We are going to be marching past a newbie cohort, so show them what *proper* training looks like!" The Drill Instructor followed them as they hustled outside and pulled out their shiniest weapons or gave their armor an extra buff to make it especially reflective.

There was no light beyond torches in their sconces at various intervals, as it was not even four in the morning. They started marching, following a route they had not taken before. The reasoning was explained soon enough, as they passed a group of extremely confused-looking Dwarves: a newly respawned cohort. Their Drill Instructor was shouting at them and firing bolts through their lines. It brought memories back to everyone in Joe's platoon, and they would have chuckled fondly if they had not been trying to show how very impressive they were.

"Today, you are all going to keep killing monsters for the glory of the Legion! Just like you have all week! I want you... *stand at attention*! Your senior brothers and sisters of the Legion are coming through!" They got close enough to hear what was being said, and the sloppy formation went rigid as Joe's cohort passed by. They passed the newbies, and the formation returned to normal, but then Joe heard a strange scene play out. "*Disgusting* showing! I'm ashamed to be in charge of turds like you. Now, all of you, I want you to make it up to me by getting *twice* as many kills as yesterday! I want you all to look at this human and feel bad about yourselves! He got *three* times as many Flame Lizards as any *one* of you."

Joe risked a glance back, and his heart leapt. The unknown Drill Instructor was standing in front of a familiar figure. "You! *Jaxon*, is it? Killing is good, but you need to learn discipline and how to follow orders! Starting today, *no disemboweling*! Clean kills *only*, you got that?"

"*Craw*... but *Drill Instructor-*" Jaxon's petulant words drifted on the wind, but after that, they were too far away for Joe to catch anything else. He started to laugh; Jaxon hadn't changed a bit... except he was apparently making sad dinosaur noises instead of normal human ones when he was upset.

The formation continued to march. An hour slowly passed, then two, and the Drill Instructor called out softly. "Company... *halt*!"

After getting everyone to face him, the Dwarf looked around with a troubled expression. "After today, there is a chance that we won't see some of you for a long time. Wherever we go, whatever we do, know that we will always be brothers and sisters in arms. Today is going to be a life-changing experience for some of you, and for those that come out unscathed, know that this is something that you will not have to go through again. Company... *charge*!"

The Drill Instructor's words were a potent, heady mix designed just for this group. A small fort came into view in the distance, and the platoon charged at the main gate directly. Something about the situation struck Joe as *wrong*, but he had no idea why. Attacking the main gate? No, that was something these battle maniacs would definitely do. They were alone? See above: battle maniacs. No, something the Drill Instructor had said...

"Won't have to go through this again? But attacking forts is the way we get the most...?" Joe's feet pounded the ground even as his mind whirled into action for the first time in weeks. "Something is wrong… it's a trap!"

Joe tried to stop, but he was carried along by the remainder of his platoon even as he shouted at them to turn around. They reached the main gate and blew through it without any resistance. When the last of them, the Drill Instructor, had come through the gate as well, a heavy portcullis slammed closed behind them. Somehow, their trainer had not come into the area fully, instead remaining just outside of the open area the rest found themselves in. Laughter rose from all around them, including from the Drill Instructor. He shouted one last phrase, sending the platoon into an outright panic.

"Welcome to the Officer Selection course!"

CHAPTER EIGHT

Before the platoon could get too wild, another voice rang out and made them stop what they were doing. For some, that included attacking the wall, while others were digging, and a few were even attempting to send themselves to respawn. "All of you will immediately halt, get into formation, and prepare for selection! Some of you *will* become Officers today, and there is not one pyrite-blasted thing you can do about it!"

So much whining came from the group that the Dwarf speaking to them actually covered his ears. "I know, I *know*! None of you want to crack the seal on the unused space between your ears; that is why you don't have a *choice*! Or is it…"

The clearly high-ranking Dwarf came into their range of vision, and Joe glimpsed a smile playing around his lips before returning to stoic grimness. "Perhaps you are just not up to the task? All right; in that case, if you think you are too weak and pathetic to become an Officer, and you'll give this opportunity to someone else without a fight, I'll open the gates right now! Any takers?"

No one moved, and Joe would have applauded the Dwarf

if he thought he could get away with it. The Dwarves around him seem to be having an existential crisis, staring at the ground, their hands, or each other as their ideals clashed. On one hand, there was *no way* they wanted to become an Officer! On the other… a female Dwarf piped up, "Officer bro, I'm not weak! You can send these other flawed specimens home; I'm at peak performance! They don't deserve the chance!"

"D*udette*-!" another Dwarf called at her in shock.

Before he could finish his outburst, a full dozen of the other mustachioed Dwarves spoke up in unison. "What do you want?"

Joe shook his head when he realized that every single squad had at least one member named 'Dudette'. The Officer spoke up calmly, rolling right over all the shouting troops. "First test is attention to detail. Drop as flat as you can get."

"*Oof!*" Joe knocked the wind out of himself with how quickly he slammed his body to the cobblestones below. An instant later, half of the platoon had *something* knock into them hard enough to send them flying toward the outer wall of the fort.

"Well, that's half of them disqualified." Joe probably only heard the mutter because his perception had increased above the one hundred point threshold. "You think I should send in the war golems? Not yet? Stone spikes in their head? Alright. Let's see how fast they can get up with all their gear on."

The voice of the commanding Officer erupted once more, "*Stand-*"

Joe was on his feet in an instant, as the rest of the words escaped the bearded mouth "-*up!*"

An instant later, a metal-tipped stone spike erupted from the ground where his head had been. Looking around, Joe gulped at the sight of corpses pinned to the ground everywhere around him. The second voice coming from *somewhere* came once more, "Pretty decent reaction speed on these ones, and we're down to ten now. Check the dexterity on that one after this. Do the skill test; doesn't matter how well they can follow orders if they can't *do* anything."

"Good. For those of you still here, it's time to figure out if you are worth anything to the Legion's Officer Corps. We don't need Officers that can *only* fight. Crafting, building, leading, strategizing... these are all important factors!" The Officer spoke out an instant after the other voice had finished, leaving Joe wondering just who it was that could order this clearly decorated Officer around. "Gather around me now. It's time for... the test!"

Joe scanned the group, finding that he recognized none of the surviving Dwarves. He thought back to his party and shrugged lightly. He'd had fun with them, but clearly something had been very wrong with the training environment. If he got out of there and spent time around more highly-specialized professionals, Joe wasn't going to be upset if he didn't already know the people he was training with; he liked meeting new people. The Officer started walking down the line, holding up a slate.

The powerful Dwarf would touch the slate to each forehead and mumble a few words. Joe could hear him clearly, as the Dwarf was not trying to hide what he was doing. "Leadership at the Expert level... locked until level thirty. No crafting; strategizing at Beginner ranks, starting at twenty-five... combat is the only way back for you. *Disqualified!*"

Just like that, the Dwarf he was testing was tossed toward the entrance of the small fort, and the Officer moved down the line. "Weapon smithing at the high Expert ranks, locked till twenty-three? Not bad... oh, a weapon-specific profession unlocked at twenty-five? Welcome to Candidacy!"

The Dwarf he was speaking to went pale, then was tossed by an unseen force deeper into the fort. The Officer continued down the line, "Disqualified... abyss, *absolutely* disqualified... disqualified, you're in, in... huh. A human?"

"Yes, sir." Joe saluted casually, knowing that the Officer was used to casual or blatant disregard for the rules from the troops.

At least he was not expected to slam his forehead into the person testing him.

"Well… this affinity slate isn't going to work on you, now is it?" The Officer put away his testing device and pulled out a pad of paper and a quill with a grimace. "That shows us the skills and talents that can be regained over time if one of our people comes back to us. Sometimes it's just too far away to bother trying to regain it. Most of the time, in fact. How about you? Leadership skills? Crafting? What have you got that would make you a good Officer Candidate?"

"I've been learning how to create buildings, and-"

"How cute, *humans* making buildings." The Dwarf snorted and struck a line through his paper. "Anything else? Don't you *want* to be an Officer? You seem like the type that would enjoy… I don't know, just sitting in a dark room and *thinking* for a few days straight?"

Joe opened and closed his mouth, trying to speak a couple of times, but not knowing exactly what to say. It was a *bizarrely* effective insult. "My base class is a Ritualist. I have taken up ritual-specific smithing, alchemy, enchantment, matrix creation, and my first specialization was as a Rituarchitect. I can bring up any building, provided I have the blueprints and materials, or bring *down* any building, given enough time. My second specialization was directly approved by my deity, and I am a champion of that same deity. I also have healing spells at a decent skill level."

"You're a *ritualist*, you say?" The Officer paused, looking into the distance.

That same small voice reached Joe's ears very faintly. "He might be after the Grand Ritual Hall. Boot him."

"Well, sorry to say, I just don't think you offer-"

Joe cut the Officer off before he could get another word out, "One of the things that I built in the previous Zone was a Grand Ritual Hall. Artifact rank. It has the ability to upgrade to Mythical, provided I can meet the criteria to make that happen.

Go ahead and let your boss know that I have no interest in stealing secrets from your Ritual Hall."

Silence filled the air between them. Joe knew that the Officer was hoping for direction, and the other person involved was doing their very best to ascertain if Joe could hear them when he talked. Joe watched the silence turn slightly darker, and remembered that he had something in his ring that might work to sway opinion in his favor. Luckily he had none of the strange performance issues that had been occurring recently; the Dwarven automaton, 'The King that Might have Been', appeared in a heap on the ground.

The Officer stroked his beard and nodded consideringly as he stared at the damaged device. In the next moment, the automaton vanished, and a light gasp came across whatever communication channel was open. "Fine. Welcome, *Candidate.*"

"Thank you, sir." Joe nodded and peered deeper into the Fort. "What's next?"

"OCS." The Dwarf grinned at Joe's blank stare. "What, you don't know what Officer Candidacy Selection is? If you thought being a Legionnaire was difficult… well, you've got an interesting time coming at you."

Joe felt a *thump*, and found himself flying through the air. It felt like he had been kicked in the behind by a giant, but he did not know where the attack had originated from. He hoped that somehow, somewhere, whoever had just done that to him had gotten a shadowy slap to the face. He landed flat on the ground, his chin bouncing twice on the cobblestones, and found himself staring at a pair of boots.

He lifted his eyes only to be greeted by a red, twirling mustache. "Looks like you are going to be the last recruit? Good. You're making me nervous, listening in on my conversations and messing with my people. Let's use that to make the *Elves* nervous; what do you think?"

There was no time to answer, as she turned and started shouting in the direction Joe had flown in. "This should be plenty, gotta leave room for others. Well, what do you think it takes to become an Officer?"

The lady Dwarf scanned the others' faces and nodded. "I'm glad no one answered. If you had, it would mean that our secrets are getting out into the world! Then we would have needed to determine if you were a spy, or just *talking* to spies! Ha!"

Each of the other Dwarves joined in on the laughter, but her face firmed up as soon as they started. "I am General Mayhem, and I can tell you what it takes right now. Quest, issued!"

Quest gained: Ranker. You have been given the chance to become an Officer of the Magisteel Legion! An Officer has full citizen rights, and privileges befitting their station. To succeed, you must demonstrate not only your willingness, but your ability, *to benefit Dwarvenkind. Your starting rank will be determined by your accomplishments when you return to your superior Officer to complete this Quest. Rewards are as follows:*

Lieutenant: You have benefited a Company-sized contingent. Your reward is a rank, and lots more work to come.

Captain: You have benefited a Battalion-sized contingent. In addition to your rank, you will gain 1000 reputation with the Dwarven Council.

Major: You have benefited a Regiment-sized (2-3 battalions) contingent. In addition to your rank, you will gain 2000 reputation with the Dwarven Council and a small homestead.

Colonel: You have benefited a Brigade-sized (6+ Regiments) contingent. In addition to your rank, you will gain 3000 reputation with the Dwarven Council, a small homestead, and a large plot of land to do with as you will.

General: You have benefited the Legion as a whole. In addition to your rank, you will gain 4000 reputation with the Dwarven Council, a small homestead, a command of your own, and a large plot of land to do with as you will.

Noble (Major General): You have completed a task, or created something that benefited the Dwarven Oligarchy as a whole. In addition to your rank, you will gain 5000 reputation with the Dwarven Council, a small homestead, a command of your own, immunity from past crimes, and a large plot of land to do with as you will.

Higher ranks of nobility are theoretically possible.

Failure: fail to create benefits that would gain you a Lieutenant ranking within six months. Penalty: demotion to the Legion as a private, and a gag order on all Officer requirements.

"I'm not sure if you are getting a clear picture of what this *means*." General Mayhem shouted in their faces as they stared at the reward list hungrily. "You do *whatever it takes* to get the highest rank you possibly can. If you go crazy, if you make everyone in this entire world hate you... but you benefit all of Dwarvenkind? Instant nobility. Forgiveness for what you needed to do to get there. I will tell you now, I will tell you clearly, and then you will never hear it again..."

"We expect you to make *any* sacrifices you need to make, so long as we win this war against the Elves!"

CHAPTER NINE

Silence reigned in the area as General Mayhem scrutinized them, wondering if her blunt explanation would be taken the way that it *normally* was. She slumped and closed her eyes as it began.

"Free pass to steal stuff!"

"Woo!"

"They're gonna be *so* sorry they ever treated me-"

General Mayhem shouted them down in an instant. "Hold it! Forgiveness only means *after* the fact! You get caught doing things that hurt our people, you still become a wanted person! I'm telling you that the ends will only justify the means *if* you do enough! I started as a General, and I single handedly planned, mapped, and executed the takeover of two major forts and all the minor forts associated with them! You think you can do better than *me*?"

"But you just said-" A random Dudette revealed her confusion to the group, allowing the General to have a target for her ire.

"That we expect *you* to make sacrifices! Not to settle personal vendettas, not to use your Candidacy as a tool against your own people. Whenever you turn in the quest, or reach the end of the quest time limit, everything you do will be assessed. You might do enough early on to end the quest early, but you can always refuse and try for higher!" Mayhem scowled at the stunned lot of Dwarves, her mustache quivering as she held in her fury. "If you do a whole lot, but what you do was straight evil, and wasn't enough to bypass the standard structure and reach the nobility? Do you really think we won't court-martial you?"

"Land? Space to build up my own base of operations... how *I* want it? That's what I wanted from the start..." Joe wiped his bald head, glad that she was taking this time to clarify right away. They were far too many atrocities that he could unleash upon their enemies if he knew there wouldn't be negative consequences for him. Actually... according to what General Mayhem had just told them, he could *still* create widespread devastation, so long as no Dwarf... Joe raised his hand.

"What are you, a child?" General Mayhem waved a hand at Joe. "If you have something you want to know, now is the time to ask. Just speak."

"What if we do something absolutely terrible, I mean really, *really* terrible, more *evil*, actually... but only to the Elves?" Joe's question made the General smile.

"War crimes? Sounds like something that gets you promoted. Just make sure you never let the Elves capture you for any reason, but that same logic applied as soon as you joined *us*." Mayhem turned to address the group as a whole. "Listen up. As a Candidate, you basically get to do whatever you want. You want to requisition goods? Do it. You need someone to teach you something? They *will*. The Legion will cover all the reputation losses during your Candidacy. Just remember, at the end of this Quest limit, if you are found to have been taking things just to take them... you better hope that you reach nobility."

She let that announcement sink into their thick skulls, then turned and started walking away. "Are there any questions on this? No? Everyone follow me. There is one last thing to do."

The entire company followed after her, slightly nervous after what they had just been told. They were going to need to balance acquiring power with covering their own rears, but there were a few of them who were already planning on going all-in. Joe was among them. There was no point in striving for anything less than nobility. If he only had six months to reach the highest heights, he would do it. If he couldn't do it, he would simply need to start at the bottom and work his way up again.

It would be annoying, but at least he would have done everything in his power, and would have no regrets. Joe refused to allow himself to hold back; as much as he truly wanted to just tinker with his own fun things, there was something thrilling about having a spelled-out goal. Something so clear that he could practically see the end in sight already.

"You have passed all of our tests to enter as a Candidate, but you still need one more thing." Mayhem led them to the center of the fort, and at the exact center of the fortress, a larger-than-life statue awaited them. It was so colossal that the head of the Dwarf it depicted brushed against the ceiling. "Every fort has a final Guardian; for Dwarves, it is always standardized and modular. For *Elves*…"

All the Dwarves in the room spat on the ground, and Mayhem continued, "It is a plant. Their Guardian is always a cross between a tree and a carnivorous flower, a pain in the rear to kill every single time we have to do it. Everyone thinks it might actually be a weed-hybrid, since it is just *that* hard to get rid of. But… for us, our Guardian has always been the bravest of all Dwarves, the one who went first."

Each Dwarf slammed a hand against their chest and shouted in unison. "*Core Digger*, swing strong, dig deep, and bring us home!"

Joe got caught up in the emotion that poured from every Dwarf around him. Some of them had shouted with pride in their voice, some with sadness. It was a ritual he did not understand, and as a Ritualist, he did not like that. Luckily for him, before he could open his mouth, General Mayhem spoke.

"Cory Dugger, the Core Digger! Guardian of the Dwarven race, first and last of his name! Before you stands the newest cohort seeking Candidacy! If any of them hold treachery in their heart, *pick* them out so that we may remove the cornerstone of insurrection!"

Joe winced as he glanced at the massive pickaxe being held casually by the… he wanted to say 'statue', but it was moving. This was clearly a golem or automaton. Steam hissed from each of its joints, and the Guardian began to shift. It crouched down until its face loomed only half a dozen feet above them all, and the gems it had for eyes swept across the entire room. Those same eyes acted as flood lights, so it was very clear when the construct was looking at one of them.

It had paused for a moment when inspecting Joe, but the human faced the Guardian without flinching. It stood and jerkily nodded. "Candidates. Added. To. Whitelist."

The booming, mechanical voice made everyone except for General Mayhem wince. She allowed a half-smile to bloom on her face, then turned to face the newly-minted Candidates. "Congratulations. You now have six months to work yourselves to the bone and prove yourselves to the Oligarchy. Thanks to the magic of 'whitelisting', no Dwarven Guardian will attack you unless you strike first. Now, final thoughts? Make sure to ask if you need anything. Step forward when I call your names; you are going to be assigned to a mentor who will be your national liaison."

Quest updated: Ranker. You have been fully accepted as a Candidate! Title Gained: Candidate.

Candidate: for the next six months, the Dwarven Oligarchy will hold off judgement upon your actions. Reputation gain and reputation loss have both been halted. At the end of this six-month period, all of your actions will be judged by General Courts-Martial. This title will be upgraded upon completion of the quest 'Ranker'.

Caution: you have too many titles! Which title will you replace in order to take this Mandatory title?

Joe looked at the list available to him, and got rid of the first title he had ever gained, 'Try Me with Trials'. If he could take anything he wanted, there was no need to be charismatic about it. He stopped fiddling with his stats and jerked his head to attention when General Mayhem called his name. "Joe! You will be assigned to Major General Havoc."

Muttering broke out around him. "*Havoc?* As in-"

"She can't be serious, right? What did he do to deserve going to *that*-"

General Mayhem's voice raised above all other noises. "As a class focusing on... magic, we needed to have an expert on board to keep an eye on you. Joe... I should say sorry about this, but I'm not actually upset. A human in the Legion is cause for concern, and your people will need to work harder than anyone else to prove themselves."

"Seriously?" Joe got his question out just before he was whisked away from the fort in a wash of mana. If he had been paying attention previously, he would have noticed the same thing happening to each person that had been assigned previously. When his surroundings stopped swimming, he found himself sitting at a desk across from a Dwarf.

Joe glanced around the room, completely uncertain how to handle the situation he found himself in. The trappings of the military were nowhere to be seen, not a single award was in sight, and the Dwarf across from him was the most disheveled representative of the race he had ever encountered.

The person he assumed to be Major General Havoc was staring at him with cold eyes, wearing a near-modern lab coat. His beard was singed and burned, shorter than any beard that Joe had ever seen a Dwarf sporting before. This was also the first person with not only a beard, but hair on his head. It had clearly not been cared for, and what remained was disheveled and steel grey.

Major General Havoc was smoking a fat cigar, and took a

deep pull from it as he studied the human in turn. He glanced at a pile of scrap metal next to the table, the broken automaton that Joe had offered to get into the Officer's track. Showing a wild smile underneath his thick protective goggles and clearly still-broken nose, the Dwarf asked a question that instantly made Joe like him one-hundred percent more.

"Who'd ya tick off to get assigned to *me*?"

CHAPTER TEN

"I don't want to think of this as a punishment." Joe grinned at the steampunk mad scientist Dwarf. "I see our meeting as a glorious chance to prove myself. I think they knew exactly what they were doing; you don't look like the kind of person who is going to be telling me 'no' very much."

"That's just it, ya spooky bastard. I won't *stop* you, but I'm not gonna *help* you much either." Havoc scrutinized Joe for a long moment, the intensity of his gaze the only reason that Joe could tell his eyes were open at all behind the mirrored lenses. "Abyss... I can see it in your eyes. You're going to be trying for nobility, aren't you?"

"Seems like the appropriate plan of action." Joe smirked at his assigned mentor. "In fact, I already have a plan to-"

"Look, human. I got nobility on my first try. Do you know what I had to do for that?" Havoc took another deep pull of his cigar and let the smoke slowly release from his nose. "I got access to one of the largest assets from a bygone age, a building that allowed me to use forbidden magic at a steep discount. I took the entire six months I was allocated, releasing the results of my research there at the absolute end of the time limit. I made it impossible for anything to grow in a huge swath of land for just shy of a decade, then launched a large-scale offensive the likes of which hasn't been seen since."

"That's how I got the *lowest* Noble title: Major General." Joe paled as he realized that someone had already done what he was planning. Havoc kept going when Joe remained silent. "I took four major forts and thirty-six minor forts in one fell swoop, making it impossible for the Elves to take it back. Or... so we thought. You think *you* can do something like that?"

"You cast the Ritual of the Lonely Tree, and they found a way *around* it?" Joe inquired curiously when it seemed that Havoc was done speaking. "Did it reach the final stage, or did it get interrupted somehow?"

His query was met with silence; a silence that stretched long enough that Joe started to become very uncomfortable. Havoc's fingers were twitching as though he were trying to decide if he was going to reach for a weapon or call for assistance right away. Finally, he made a decision and simply spoke.

"No... I was not able to cast the ritual. How... no, obviously you have some knowledge that they think... I'm starting to see why they sent you to me, human. No. We did not cast that ritual; we couldn't make it work. Not without beggaring the Oligarchy. We cast the area spell 'Salt the Earth' and released my personal creations to wipe out all life within hundreds of miles. They had been designed based on the intended function of that ritual you mentioned. I don't mind telling you this... sure, it used to be a national secret, but not so much any longer."

"Because they found a way around it?" Joe inferred, getting a nod in reply. "How do you counter-spell something that creates a physical object? Doesn't that force a huge amount of salt into the ground? What personal creations did you use, and is that something that I can get access to?"

Havoc was sitting forward now, his grin widening as he found that Joe was someone he could have an actual conversation with. "They made a new type of plant, one that *thrives* on salt. In fact, it drains all the salt from the area and makes a 'fruit' with it. Turns out, all we did was get a three-year respite, then gave them an easy way to stock up on spices and ways to preserve their foodstuffs. Abyss, since they are Elves and the salt becomes plant-based, they can make the 'fruit' collect itself. After they harvest enough of the fruits, the ground is able to support normal vegetation again."

"Well, that... *really* destroys my original plan." Joe pulled out a chair without invitation and sat down. "I figured that if I had access to your Grand Ritual Hall, I would be able to put that ritual together and easily step into nobility. I get a discount on rituals, and six months should have been enough time for me to pull it off."

Havoc chuckled at Joe, then offered him a cigar. Joe declined, instead grabbing a mug and summoning this coffee elemental, Mate. A moment later, a steaming cup of espresso was flowing down Joe's throat. Noting the piercing look that Havoc was giving him, Joe asked Mate to prepare a second cup. They sat in the stillness and relaxed, but eventually, the Major General was the one to break the silence. "It's not a *terrible* plan. There are a few flaws, but the ritual itself directly kills the plants in the area, right? The area spell we used only made it so that new things couldn't grow. That's a pretty significant difference. You set that off near their capital and their most powerful guardian is wiped out. Main issue is going to be surviving putting it out. My research tells me that ritual takes over a week to reach completion."

"Mind going over one or three of the flaws in my plan? I'd love to find a better way, or maybe you even have some schemes you could share?" Joe wryly grinned at the Dwarf. Havoc nodded and started writing on a paper, creating bullet points and a flowchart. Joe flinched at the sight. "A world and a plane away from humanity, and I still can't get away from PowerPoint..."

"The premise is good." Havoc flipped the page over so that Joe could see it. "Here's what I see as the major flaws: You are looking at an upper Master, maybe lower Grandmaster, ritual. I don't know what your skill level is right now, but are you actually confident in casting that level of *anything*? Next, as I mentioned, the resource cost alone is what stopped us from being able to use this last time. How do you think *you* could combat that? There aren't enough things that you could grab from us to make it happen. Let alone the Core you would need to power it. Finally, you claim that you could use the Grand Ritual Hall—the existence of which is a national secret that I would *love* to know how you learned about—but you haven't shown me any indication that you can control a Legendary building like that."

"*Legendary?*" Joe breathed the word with delight. "I was only able to make a modular Artifact-ranked."

"Should not have said that... maybe I should just wipe his mind and be done with-" Havoc was chastising himself, but paused and looked up with great interest. "Wait. You *made* an Artifact Ritual Hall? No. Skip that. Give me view access to your status."

"You understand that I can hear you when we are sitting right across from each other?" Joe looked at the other man with dead eyes, but Havoc didn't flinch from the stare. "Isn't giving access to someone else a *very* bad idea?"

"Just do it," Havoc grumped, unwilling to concede the point. "I need to know what you can do, in order to help you as best as I can. Also, I don't care if you can hear me. If I decide that your mind needs to go, there's nothing you could do about it. We're in my seat of power. I could take out the entire Legion from here if I only needed to protect myself."

Joe winced at the realization that he really had no choice but to follow orders. Again. He still *hated* that feeling. "I thought you weren't going to stop me, but also had no plans to help me?"

"Then I found out that you weren't a random muscle-for-brains that got dumped in here as punishment. You haven't called me 'Officer Bro' a single time, or sent yourself to respawn by trying to slam your head into mine." Havoc snarled as he thought of the last Legionnaires that he had needed to work with. "Do you want my help, or no? I have no idea how long I'll want to give it to you, so you should take the *opportunity* to *improve*."

Instead of answering verbally, Joe swiftly shared his status sheet, and Havoc started leafing through it. "Interesting... your cover was a cleric? Abyss, you are the champion of a deity. Don't use that for anything, or you're gonna tick me *right* off. Let's see... lots of health or healing aspects to your build. Very little in the way of attack spells, and you're practically useless in physical combat. Ah... *there* it is."

"Ritualist, Rituarchitect, and this one, Reductionist. I know what the first and second ones are; can you give me a breakdown on the third? These are very impressive skill levels in the Ritualist tree... you even got a path advancement that made it into multiple passives?" Havoc regarded Joe again and nodded approvingly for the first time. "We can work with this. I think I know a few ways to get you what you'll need to wipe out Elves efficiently. Now, tell me about that Reductionist class so I don't need to read your notifications for the next three days."

"It's..." Joe hesitated, unsure where to start. "Thing is, I got that class right before I came here. I haven't actually had a chance to test it out at all, and I have almost no information on it. What I know about the class is that it changed how I will be working with materials going forward, but even that was pretty hard to understand without any practical data or experience."

"That's fine; let's go give it a test run right now. What do you need?" Havoc stood and marched them out of the room, down an empty hallway, stairs, and eventually directed them into an open warehouse area. Not a single time did Joe see another person, or anything that might represent a personal item, art, or pictures. "Come on. *Speak*, human! Do you need ink? Something to break down? How do you do things? Burn them? Rot them?"

"Well-" Joe suddenly realized that he didn't actually know

what he was supposed to do to make his class abilities function. He pulled open his notifications and found the class description, hoping that it could give him a better understanding of the next steps. "There was something that came up when I got the class; let me..."

You now have the ability to process all materials down to basic components. All raw materials, processed materials, and items are able to be 'reduced'. You are able to reduce all materials by using mana alone. There is a ritual now engraved upon your being, a ritual that only requires the empowerment of mana to function.

Any sensory abilities now also inform you of the value of anything that can be reduced, as well as the amount of material you will attain by reducing it.

You can use the reduced material in any form of crafting, as a replacement for all components, ingredients, or other required material.

"According to this, I should just be able to directly touch something, focus on it, maybe even hear it if it is magical, and it will tell me what it is worth?" Joe tried to access his storage so that he could pull out a log, but nothing came. He frowned and tried with another item that he knew he had. Nothing. Before he could start to panic, Havoc handed him a ball of unprocessed ore.

"Looks like you are having performance issues. Please stop grabbing at your crotch. Try this; it's just iron, and it doesn't matter if it's destroyed or not." Havoc waved at Joe to hurry up and get the process started. The Reductionist touched the ball, then let his mind slip into the feel of an Intrusive Scan, feeling his mana dip for a flash; too little to see before regenerating the spent resource.

Item: Iron Ore
Reduction value: 10 Common aspects, 43 Trash aspects.
Reduction cost: 5 mana per second.

Then Joe's mana just kind of... swirled out of him; and he could see an intricate ritual light up across his body. He went from sporting clear, unblemished skin, to the most tattooed person he had ever seen in his life, all in the span of a moment. "Hope that's not permanent... a whole career in the military didn't convince me to get a tattoo; certainly didn't mean to get one accidentally. I wasn't even drinking!"

The ball of iron ore took five full seconds to completely reduce, and Joe was left with... nothing. No aspects, whatever those were, and thankfully no tattoos, either. He pulled up his status screen and found nothing to indicate that the aspects had been stored. There was nothing on the ground, nothing on him. As his last option, Joe checked his notifications and had to hold himself back from growling.

53 aspects lost! You do not have any external storage devices that can contain aspects, and your bound storage device is full! Either create some space in your bound storage device, or have external devices ready to store aspects!

"What sort of external devices can I *use?*" Joe whispered darkly at the system, which refused to answer him. "What do you mean my storage device is *full?* I was able to put an entire warehouse in there, and I never heard a single complaint about lack of space!"

"Hold up a moment..." Havoc looked at Joe askance, his lips pulling his face and wretched beard into a scowl. "What kind of storage device do you have that can hold an entire warehouse?"

"A full one, apparently." Joe shook his head at the thought and tried to carefully explain the fewest details that Havoc needed to know about his exile. "When I left Midgard, I was able to take anything with me that I could carry. I admit, I have been having some trouble accessing it since I got here, but I figured that had more to do with the Zone than the device... Havoc? What... why are you shaking your head like that?"

"Let me guess... you can't get any *individual* item out? Even if you know for a fact that it is there?" Havoc took a few steps away, making sure to stand well behind Joe. "How much space was it supposed to have? Don't give me that look; I have no interest in stealing from you. How much space?"

"Thirty cubic meters." Joe tried again to pull out a weapon, or herb, *anything*. "You're right; I can't get anything out."

"That's what I thought. Thirty meters, huh? That's massive for a storage device, but certainly not enough to contain an entire warehouse." Havoc grinned and shook his head. "Not without... well, you'll see. Try to take out *everything* at once, and make sure to be moving backward when you do it. I'd recommend jumping backward, actually, after seeing your jump skill. I want to know the story behind *that* when we have some more time."

Joe crouched down, wanting to get this over with, both so that he knew what was going on, and in order to alleviate his nervousness. He jumped backward, ordering the device to eject everything from the spatial codpiece at the same time and drop it on the ground.

Boom.

A massive brick appeared in the air in front of Joe, the sheer mass of it slamming it to the ground and shaking the tiled floor where they stood, even breaking it in a few places, if the sounds were anything to go by. Havoc took a step forward and eyeballed the condensed matter.

"Wouldn't you say that looks to be about, oh, three point one-oh-seven meters on each side? Thirty cubic meters on the dot. Yup. Destruction by compression." Havoc's words barely reached Joe, who was staring at the cube in horror. The human reached out a hand, hesitating to touch it; hoping that this was just a bad dream. "It's not *all* bad. You must have a very high-quality spatial device, or else it would have just exploded and crushed you with the brick. Maybe taken out a small town with the backlash of all that mana being released. At least this way you get to keep the container... but this is just a block of broken things, at this point."

CHAPTER ELEVEN

"At least *some* of this needs to be salvageable... right?" Joe slapped his hand on the cube that stood roughly twice as tall as he was, and activated his... it was Intrusive Scan, but not, at the same time. He decided to think of it as 'Ritual of Reduction'. In a flash, his mana had washed over his cube and returned with a base value.

Item: Hyper-compressed cube. Note: most items compressed within this cube are raw resources. Anything not a raw resource was destroyed, dropping its aspect value greatly, and increasing 'Damaged' aspects. Several Cores are trapped within, as energy cannot be destroyed.
Reduction value: Unknown.
Reduction cost: estimated at 125 mana per second.
Viable bound storage device detected.

There was a lot of information to unpack in those few simple sentences. "What in the...? One hundred and twenty-five mana per *second*? Why is it so much more than before? Why didn't my ring count as a valid storage device?"

Determined: valid query about ability. Mana cost is determined by the *rarest aspect contained in the object to be reduced. Each aspect above Common rarity adds a multiplier of '5' mana per second. Common = 5. Uncommon = 5*5. Rare = 5*5*5. Ritualist class bonus to Ritual of Reductions' cost has <u>already</u> been applied. Increase class level to drop cost further.*

Bound storage devices must be soul-bound to be valid as aspect storage. The energy of raw aspects is especially volatile and deadly if used incorrectly. Soul-bound devices can only be accessed by the bound user or a skilled thief.

"Learning any *fun* things, human? Care to *share*?" Though Havoc's words were caustic, he had affixed Joe with a hungry stare. "Let's tell each other information all the time, so that one of us does not need to put the other in a lab for testing or dissection. Lots and *lots*... of testing."

"Calm down... Sir," Joe muttered and held up his shaky hands while digesting the information he was learning. He looked at the cube and paled. In a sudden panic, he grabbed his hand and sent his mind into the storage ring on his finger. "Oh, thank the celestials above, it's still there."

Never had he been so glad to *forget* to do something. Joe still had his cauldron in his ring, along with various blueprints and a few other miscellaneous items, like his weapon-equipable Taglock. If he had lost all of that, specifically the cauldron, there was a good chance that a shadowy organization of Alchemists was going to try to melt chunks off of him until they were satisfied that he no longer had the Cauldron in his possession. Noticing that Havoc was about to start pulling out his own beard hair, Joe explained what he had just realized, and Havoc nodded consideringly.

"Hold on." The Dwarf stopped Joe from attempting to reduce the cube. "How about we try out your ability on a few different things before you tackle that gigantic beast? What happens if you can't *finish* reducing something? Does it all fall apart, or can you keep going after you regain your mana? Sure would be a shame to lose all those... aspects."

"Good plan." The two of them grinned at each other, each

feeling surprisingly comfortable with one another. Joe was wondering if perhaps he should have been hanging out with other magical-classed people; perhaps his obsession with growth and development of his skills in magic were not so strange after all. Maybe it was his desire to do everything alone, or in secret, that was the actual hindrance.

Havoc started bringing out various items; so many, in fact, that Joe started to hesitate at taking them. The Dwarf noticed his discomfort and laughed. "You think *this* is a lot? You could technically requisition every single thing that I have, everything that I own, and you are daunted by a few scraps?"

"I think I could *try* to take it all. Something tells me I wouldn't be able to actually *do* it." Joe watched a smug expression appear across the Dwarf's features for a moment, then took a deep breath and attempted to adjust his mindset. "That's right, I have the ability to 'requisition' stuff. I know it, logically, and I have been planning to use it. It still feels… strange. It's like getting a massive student loan that you might not have to pay off if you get perfect grades your entire college career, but you would need to pay double interest on if you got a single 'B' in a course."

Havoc waved away Joe's concerns and shook his head, handing over a simple dagger. "Just shut up and start small."

Item: Iron Dagger.
Reduction value: 8 Common aspects, 19 Trash aspects.
Reduction cost: 5 mana per second.
Viable bound storage device detected.

Joe let his mana pour out of him, and his body lit up with the intricate tattoos that signified his Ritual of Reduction. One… three… five seconds passed, and the dagger simply vanished as though he had stored it in a spatial device. In a way, that was exactly what had happened.

Aspects captured: 7 Common aspects, 11 Damaged aspects, 19 Trash aspects.

"Hold up, I didn't get all of the aspects?" Joe's bald brow furrowed as he opened his logs and attempted to find exactly what had happened. He read over the process carefully, and his lips pressed into a hard line.

Iron Dagger suffused! Capturing aspects… bound storage device is not specifically designed for capturing aspects. 10% of Common aspects have been damaged, lowering rarity! Common aspects converted into Damaged aspects.

"Let me guess; by the look on your face, something went wrong. My bet would be that you do not have a storage device that is designed for these 'aspect' things, and so you lost 'em all?" Havoc scratched at his beard and tried to think of a solution. "We can do some research, but I've never heard of aspects before, so I have no idea how we can put something together to hold them."

"Me neither." Joe sighed and waved at the other things in the area. "Perhaps when I level my class up, it will give us more information? Let's do the next test."

They used another iron dagger, as similar to the first as possible. This time, Joe supplied Mana for only four seconds and then abruptly cut off the power supply. The dagger shuddered and cracked, falling apart completely when Joe applied just a little bit of pressure to either end.

Aspects captured: 5 Common aspects, 15 Damaged Aspects, 40 Trash aspects.
Iron Dagger destroyed!

Joe attempted to convert the remainder of the dagger, but only got Trash aspects. He looked over at Havoc and winced. "Good call on holding off on the cube. The rest got turned into trash."

"I thought that might be the case. If you take out the essential parts of something, the Rarity is going to drop. Abyss, if you take a Legendary sword and snap it in half, you might only have two chunks of a *Rare* sword because the Magical Matrix on it has been damaged so badly." Havoc had Joe continue testing on rarer things, culminating in a Unique-ranked breastplate.

"Six hundred and twenty-five mana a second." Joe gulped as he looked at the armor. "If it took five full seconds to reduce a dagger, how long will this take? I can only hold out for two and a half seconds. Are you sure we should do this? The armor is definitely going to break, and I am not going to be able to capture all of the aspects…"

"Did I tell you to hesitate? Or did I give you a task to complete?" Havoc waved a hand imperiously at Joe. "Get after it."

Joe started pouring his mana into the ritual, and the breastplate began to shine. One second passed, two… and Havoc slammed a bottle into Joe's mouth. The human was so shocked that he almost failed to continue, but he gulped the liquid down and watched as his mana was restored. It stayed at full for another five seconds before starting to drop slightly, and the breastplate vanished at the end of ten full seconds from the beginning of the process. "Havoc! What *was* that?"

"Rare-rank Mana Philter. Hard to come by, very expensive. Using those like bathwater will *really* make the court-martial stand up and take notice. Mainly because I think we have a *single* Dwarven alchemist in the entire Oligarchy?" Havoc ignored Joe's sputtering and demanded, "Well? A breakdown, please!"

"That's… I… over six thousand total mana used." Joe deflated and started going over the details. Havoc listened greedily, writing Joe's words out on a pad of paper. "I gained one hundred and eleven Unique aspects, eighty-two Rare, two hundred ten Uncommon, and a bunch of the lower ones."

"Good. Now, any class experience gained?" Havoc smiled knowingly as Joe checked and found a big fat zero waiting for him. "Now, what do you think you need to do to get experience?"

"Since reducing things does not give experience by itself, I can only assume that I will get experience when I make things with the aspects." Joe was almost bowled over by Havoc clapping a hand on his back.

"Good! Oh, if you got that wrong, I was going to punish you so badly. Now, how do you make items out of aspects?"

"I have... let's just start testing, alright?" Joe pulled paper and ink from his ring and started to draw a circle. The paper took the ink, but as soon as the circle was complete, the entire thing burst into flames. "*Ow!*"

"You aren't hurt," Havoc scoffed as Joe dropped the flaming paper. "You were just surprised. I know you are wearing a shield of some kind. What was that all about? Why didn't that work? You're so bad at coloring that the deity of artistry cursed you or something?"

Joe pulled up his notifications again, already sick of needing to open them so frequently.

Attempt at creating a ritual circle detected. Warning: all crafting can only be completed via aspect usage!

"I can only use aspects?" Joe slapped at the screen, only to have his hand go right through it. "How! *How* do I use them?"

Checking... no skill trainer available. Aspect crafting tutorial is available for purchase! Cost: 5,000 reputation with a deity of your choice. Reputation loss must leave you at neutral or above!

Joe stared at the black-hearted fee listed. "Kind of pigeonholing me here, aren't you? This seems like a blatant attempt to force me to regain favor with Tatum."

There was no response, though Havoc looked at Joe a little strangely. Joe shook his head. "I just got the opportunity to get a tutorial on crafting with aspects. What do you think? Is that usually worth doing?"

Havoc's eyes practically bulged out of his goggles. "Never, *never* turn down a system-generated tutorial. You cannot get a better, cleaner, more direct tutorial or method of training *anywhere*. It practically offers to make you the subject matter expert for the entire Zone!"

"Guess... I'll buy it then." Joe accepted the cost and

watched as various numbers dropped precipitously from his status screen.

Aspect crafting tutorial purchased! Would you like to take the tutorial now?

Joe didn't hesitate to accept. He was practically useless without his ability to even make a simple ritual diagram, let alone draw a circle. "Yes."

CHAPTER TWELVE

The world around Joe faded into a dense fog immediately. He wasn't entirely certain if he had been moved from his position, or if he were in the same spot but completely zoned out. Joe was standing in a world of mist, but the condensation began to visibly coalesce in front of his amazed eyes. Joe flinched as the shifting world began speaking to him in a powerful voice. Every word from this unknown being burned itself into his brain, making it nearly impossible to forget.

Crafting with aspects is the process of seeing beyond what is, to what could be. By using energy directly and following the pattern created with alchemy, blacksmithing, or a myriad of other crafting styles, you are able to minimize and standardize the requirements for every part of the crafting process. Let us review the different standard materials.

A weak dark grey flame appeared and was introduced at the same time.

Aspect of Trash. This is the most basic form of aspects, but also the most widely used. Every item, consumable, or anything else crafted... makes use of aspects of Trash. It is the most basic aspect and is more useful than you may ever comprehend.

Three more wispy flames appeared in front of Joe, a light grey, white, and silver. The voice continued speaking.

In order, these are Damaged, Common, and Uncommon aspects. For the majority of all crafting, these are the aspects that are going to be the most frequently used. We'll begin with a simple example of using aspects in crafting. Let's make a Beginner-ranked ritual diagram.

In order to make a Beginner-ranked ritual, two ritual circles are needed. Let's work together to create a ritual using aspects!

Joe rolled his eyes at the condescending tutorial. However, he had played enough games that he knew that he should follow along closely. He couldn't count the number of times that he had assumed he would understand how to do something, then tried to do it without the tutorial's help—and failed miserably— in other games he'd played throughout his life.

A Novice-ranked ritual circle can be created using either Trash or Damaged aspects. Of course, there will be a slight efficiency difference between the two. Damaged aspects will increase the potency by a minute amount, but using Trash will be more cost-effective over time. The second circle, the Beginner-rank circle, requires—at a minimum—Common-ranked aspects. In order to use these aspects to draw your circle, you must use your mana to shift an aspect into an inscribing utensil. Try this now!

Joe reached out for the Trash aspect, but his fingers went right through it. As the aspect went over his hand, it *burned* him right through his shield; the weak aspect shaving off fifty points of his health in an instant.

Please make sure to use caution! Injury from base energies leads to true damage!

"Great. Once again, I am working with volatile energy that will likely end up exploding in my face or working so differently that I accidentally kill a bunch of people." Joe tried again; this time, instead of directly touching the aspect, he allowed a little bit of mana to escape his fingers and swirl around the dark grey wispy flame. That seemed to work, so he bent his mind to the task of shaping the small flame into a stick, then into a fountain pen.

Great visualization technique! You have made a basic, trash-quality aspect fountain pen! Using more potent aspects will require more specific and detailed input, since aspects tend to become a little grumpy if they have to go into something that they see as a lesser vessel!

Now that you have a basic writing utensil, try drawing out a Novice-ranked circle!

Joe made a simple ritual diagram on the ground, the most basic that he could think of: a perfect circle. As he drew on the foggy ground, a wispy grey meter appeared in his heads-up display. As the circle grew, the meter dropped rapidly. He completed the diagram, and it shone a beautiful light grey to signify completion.

That was a heady feeling, a strange dopamine hit that made Joe strangely happy. Something about seeing results immediately upon finishing a project, even a small one like this, was oddly pleasurable. He had a feeling that he was going to enjoy working as a Reductionist.

Great! As you can see, when you are using aspects to craft, you will automatically use stored aspects. For the purposes of this tutorial, you will have unlimited resources, but nothing that you make in here will be available outside of the training area. Please remember that you will not be able to re-access this tutorial upon completion!

"Well, there go my plans of perfecting all of my rituals." Joe sighed pseudo-glumly. It was hard to actually be unhappy when he was learning a new skill that would affect everything that he did from this point forward.

Now that you have created a Novice circle, try creating a Beginner-ranked ritual circle using this same writing utensil!

Joe started working on the second circle without any hesitation, knowing that it would likely not work. That was okay; it was important to follow along with the instructions so that he would at least learn the consequences. But he was not expecting the deep pain as his 'pen' exploded, taking his hand and his arm up to the elbow along with it in one deadly, white fireball.

The Reductionist went spinning across the foggy area, blood flying in an arc in the opposite direction. Joe landed heavily, stunned from the impact and how violent the reaction had been. He went to cast Mend on himself, but the damage vanished and his body returned to normal before he could use the spell. "From now on, maybe I won't listen to *every* instruction that it gives me."

As you can see, there is a furious reaction when a higher-order aspect is used through a lower aspect crafting implement. Remember, in order to create a Beginner-ranked Circle, you need—at a minimum—Common-ranked aspects. You can use higher order aspects to create lower-ranked circles, but it is a waste of resources! Try creating a Common-ranked writing utensil now!

Joe reached out to the wispy flame that was a pure white, once more allowing his mana to swirl around it and pull it into the shape of a fountain pen. Just before grabbing it, he had a premonition of danger and ducked away from it.

It was a good thing he did, as the explosion it created was almost twice as potent as the one from the Trash-aspect pen. The flames hissed in the air, lashing out with flares and bursts, until all the captured aspects had been released.

Looks like someone forgot that they needed to make a more impressive writing utensil! Hopefully this serves as a warning going forward!

"I don't know why this tutorial is so vindictive, but I guess I should have expected it, based on previous interactions with the system." Joe scoffed as he tried to think of the 'writing implement' that he would attempt to make next. He had a feeling that every single one of them would need to be different, each more impressive than the last, which meant he did not want to start with an exceedingly *fancy* pen, he just wanted something *slightly* more intricate. Joe would save the peacock feather quills for the Unique or higher ones down the line.

This time, as he used his mana to form the pen, Joe visualized embossing Tatum's symbol on the side as a pure-white grip. He reached out hesitantly and gripped the pen, waiting to see if it would explode in his face. Nothing yet. He reached down and started drawing out the second Circle, composing a simple diagram and a complete ritual. This time, as he wrote out the diagram, not only did his Common-ranked aspects resource bar drop, the Damaged and Trash resource bars dropped as well.

Excellent choice of writing utensils! As you can see, when you are crafting at a higher rank, all aspects below that rank are also used to stabilize and enhance the higher-rarity aspects. By crafting more carefully, increasing your skill level as a Reductionist, or as a crafter of the type you are attempting to emulate, you will reduce your overall resource draw.

Let's move on to learning to craft in different disciplines that you have started upon! Please choose one of the disciplines that you would like a happy tutorial for! Options: Alchemy, Blacksmithing, Enchanting.

"I need at least to know how to make the main crafting implements for all three of them, so let's just go in order." Joe selected alchemy, and the tutorial began immediately. He needed to use a cauldron that the system provided, and what looked like a giant stirring spoon that he was required to make out of aspects. It was a strange spoon, because beyond having a scoop, it also had a lid on it. That allowed him to stir, collect, and contain the aspects as he made a potion. "This makes me rethink drinking actual potions... if I can make them out of simple Trash aspects, what am I putting in my body?

Pondering the fact that he could convert human waste into viable potions was fairly disgusting, and he resolved to use Draughts—made from Common aspects—at the minimum from now on. There was one additional component to consider with Alchemy, and that was controlling the temperature of the cauldron. At this level of potion making, it was fairly straightforward. Still, he knew that there was going to be plenty that he could learn from alchemical skill trainers.

From there, he moved on to blacksmithing, which required him to make an ingot hammer out of aspects, then use a normal anvil to craft the strange energy into a solid material. Slamming a hammer down on energy was a new experience, and one that he looked forward to repeating in the future.

Enchanting was a pleasant surprise, because he found that he could use the same inscription tool that he created when drawing ritual diagrams. After he had absorbed the four crafting disciplines that he knew currently, Joe thought the tutorial was going to complete itself. Instead, it threw a curveball into the entire system.

Great work! Now that you have created various materials and consumables, let's try making a Rare-ranked... anything! When going from Uncommon to Rare, an additional component is needed! Energy!

"Isn't *all* of this energy?" Joe muttered to himself. Luckily, the system clarified for him in the next few lines of text.

One way to think of the difference of crafting Rare-ranked objects and above is to assume that it is an 'endothermic reaction'! Not only do you need the same components as you did before, you also need an energy source that allows you to force the components to react in a new way! Only, instead of adding heat, you are adding power directly from: a Core!

Joe decided to go with what he was most familiar with and began making a Student-ranked ritual diagram. To save on time, he crafted his inscription tool in a similar manner to his Common aspect writing implement, but turned the top half of it into an eagle feather, making a fancy—but not too fancy—quill. It worked, and he started sketching the fourth circle of the ritual diagram immediately. This time, not only did he start seeing a decrease in his resource bars, but an additional empty, energetic blue bar appeared. Joe didn't think too much of it until he tried to draw the circle and nothing happened.

Please bind the Core to the aspect section in the crafting tab of your status sheet. For the purposes of the demonstration, you have been granted a Core that you can bind immediately!

A shining, round Core appeared in Joe's hand, and he had an idea. Using his Ritual of Reduction, he attempted to reduce the Core directly.

Item: Core (Rare).
Energy value: 5,192/5,192
Reduction cost: Cannot break energy down further!

Seeing no other option, Joe followed the directions and found the Core tab, added the Core, and tried drawing once more. The resource bars went down, the circle was drawn, and the ritual diagram was completed. Joe inspected the energy resource bar, wondering how much of that core he had spent.

Energy value: 4,751/5,192

"So, I spent about four hundred and forty-one points of energy from the core." Joe mused, looking at the bars and trying to get a feel for how the conversion worked. "How…?"

You have completed the tutorial! Another tutorial may become available at a later date, based upon your usage and accomplishments. Try new things and increase your class to unlock further instructions!

With no more warning than that, the foggy world around Joe vanished, and he found himself back in the room with Major General Havoc. The Dwarf took a long draw of a thick cigar and stared Joe down. "Well? Are you going to take a tutorial or not?"

"Already done." That answered one question for Joe; he had not moved from his spot in the world.

The goggles covering Havoc's eyes gleamed. "An instant download of information? That's a very good tutorial, indeed… as expected of the system. So… you learned new things?"

"Show me."

CHAPTER THIRTEEN

One of the greatest benefits of having his Legendary codpiece was that Joe could bring things out of it to any part of his body whenever he wanted. It was time to show Havoc what he had learned, and Joe knew better than to hold back. With a thought and a handful of mana, Joe grasped forward and called forth an aspect of Trash.

The dark grey wispy fire appeared and was immediately surrounded by his light blue mana. Joe didn't bother to put much effort into the design, making a simple stylus. After it was formed, the aspect solidified into an actual physical object, though it was practically weightless. He was about to create a simple Novice-ranked Circle, but thought better of it. Perhaps it would be better to see how many aspects he had first? Calling up his crafting tab, Joe was pleasantly surprised to see what had been stored.

Aspects gathered
Trash: 1,001
Damaged: 712
Common: 238

Uncommon: 210
Rare: 80
Special: 0
Unique: 51
Artifact: 0
Legendary: 0
Mythical: 0

Core energy: None bound

Feeling better about the sheer amount of aspects that he could access, at least for Novice-ranked things, Joe drew out a simple circle and let it sit on the ground. Major General Havoc watched with great interest and tried to figure out what exactly the circle was supposed to be doing. Joe let him study it for a long moment, but before the Dwarf was forced to ask, Joe activated the ritual and stepped back.

The circle lit up, glowing a deep red light, slowly shifting to blue and back again. Havok waited for an explanation, but Joe was watching the circle happily. "This is very nice, sure... but just tell me. What does it do?"

Reductionist Class experience gained: 1!

"It makes pretty lights. This thing is the equivalent to a cantrip, only *technically* a Novice ritual, and they really don't do much. Also, it looks like I figured out how to gain experience. I need to use the aspects that I collect by making something out of them," Joe answered easily, a huge smile on his face. With every bit of acquired information, the more and the faster he could grow. "I'm just happy because I didn't have to add any other components than aspects. I used to have to break out silver, small carbon filaments, and very thin glass for this ritual, so I never bothered to make it. Essentially, I've made a magical version of a glass light bulb."

"You mean a Nixie tube?" Havoc ventured after a moment, trying to translate Joe's explanation into terms that he understood.

"You have light bulbs?" Joe gaped at the Dwarf, who seemed affronted at the surprise in the human's voice.

Havoc harrumphed and glared at Joe through his thick mirrored goggles. "Our technology has been at *your* level of modern for literally thousands of years. There's not much you *can't* do when you have magic and science. The things our magitech can do would make you fear for your sanity. Anyway, what's the *point* of this light? Why did you make it?"

"I made it to show that I *could* make it," Joe explained after a moment of contemplation. It made sense that their technology was more advanced than he was used to; they did have various golems and other technological wonders. It was just hard to rectify people who used crossbows and hammers in combat with people who were technological savants. That, and the only people he had met were... Legion. "I also explored how to work with enchanting, alchemy, and blacksmithing. I should-"

Joe paused, horror on his face. "I forgot to figure out how to make buildings! Son of the *abyss*! I... wait, no. That is just rituals. I'm okay."

"Calm down, human. Was there something in that coffee you drank?" Havoc muttered disparagingly. "Or is this just a normal human thing? Questioning yourself out of nowhere and panicking for no apparent reason? You talk aloud frequently."

"Yes, that is a very human thing." Joe nodded seriously. Havoc winced at the thought of an entire *race* having anxiety for no good reason. "I learned that I can break down pretty much anything into aspects, and use that energy directly in the crafting of other materials, goods... basically *anything*, as long as I have access to the needed ranks of the discipline."

Havoc took a short pull from his cigar, which was burning down to a small nub at this point. "I could see a few uses for this. Let's talk this out. You have six months to complete your quest for Officer Candidacy. It sounds like you want your big goal to be wiping out a few Elven forts, but if I may make a suggestion... there are a few other things we could really use as a Dwarven Oligarchy. No one ever said that you had to do one big thing; if you did a bunch of small things that added up over time… things that help the nation…"

"I can reach nobility by doing small things?" Joe didn't buy it. The quest clearly stated… actually, no it didn't. It hadn't said that only one thing counted; it simply let him know that everything would be tallied. All of the positives, all of the negatives. If his net positive was enough to help the entire race of Dwarves, that was how he would gain nobility. "I see. What did you have in mind, Havoc?"

"You remember that mana potion that I gave you? I mentioned that we have only one Alchemist for our entire people?" Havoc waited for Joe's nod. "The reason behind that is that alchemy is a specialty of the Elves. People who are good at it are seen with suspicion, unless they are *so* good that they can produce enough to help everyone. Actually, let me amend my previous statement. When I say we only have one Alchemist, I mean only one who will practice publicly."

"You want me to… what? Make alchemical goods? I can't do it; I only have access to making ritual specific potions and whatnot." Joe was going to go on, but Havoc raised a hand to slow him down.

"Your class; not your current one, your previous one, the builder. Rituarchitect. I have read about that in our records. That used to be something that was a fairly common class, but it died out. Not sure why. You can create buildings and such, yes?" Joe responded in the affirmative to Havoc's question, so the Dwarf hurried to finish his train of thought. "Our Alchemist is working in a Common Alchemist workshop. If you could benefit him enough, make his production go through the roof, what he does from that point on might count as you creating a benefit for us. What do you think? Worth a shot?"

"I'm on board." Joe contemplated one of his other quests that was still in progress, where he needed to make a new workshop for Jake the Alchemist. He could practice and refine the workshop he created and outfitted with the Dwarven Alchemist as a practice run. "Do you have any blueprints for alchemy shops? I can get started right away!"

Havoc stared Joe down, long enough that Joe started to get uncomfortable. "You realize that we are masters at creating buildings and architecture, correct? Have you considered that if we had the blueprints to an alchemy workshop that was better than what we have currently, we would have already built it? No, of course not. Fact of the matter is, it takes an Alchemist of a higher level working *in conjunction* with an architect in order to create a building that is specific to them. Our guy is not there yet, and it will be years until he is. Unless, of course, he is able to work in a better workshop. Then he would progress faster..."

Joe caught on to what Havoc was getting at. "That would *also* help my case."

"Exactly. Here's the hard part. You want to get a better place, you gotta *steal* it. If you can get into a major fort occupied by Elves, they're almost guaranteed to have an Uncommon alchemist workshop. At minimum. If you can get into one deeper in their territory, you are looking at Rare, or something better. If you get into their capital? There are rumors of a *Legendary* alchemist's workshop." Havoc caught the flash of greed that crossed Joe's face, and he approved of it. "What you need to do is sneak into a fort and see how they are laid out. It's chaos every single time, since they just throw up buildings willy-nilly. Nothing like us; we *plan* our cities. Still, at least you would get a glimpse of what the building would look like."

"Can we make that happen?" Joe had to swallow his excitement. Perhaps it was because he had been with the Legionnaires for so long, but it took a hard question by Havoc to bring him back to reality.

"Are you *ready* to go into a fort?" Havoc looked at the dark cloak that Joe was wrapped in, the giant Cube that contained all of his compressed and destroyed materials within it, and the human's weaponless hands. "Looks to me like you would get splattered across the ground if an Elf *looked* at you funny; and I gotta warn you, they are pretty funny lookin'. How about we get you outfitted and ready for combat before sending you to your death for no particular reason? What do you need?"

Joe barely needed to think about it. "In terms of weapons and armor... I have a cloak and a codpiece. Hard stop. My Cores are somewhere in that Cube, so I am going to be stuck using rituals that are under Rare quality. I need a weapon, as well as clothes or armor, and aspects. Any chance that you have access to lots of gear or weapons that you don't need? Maybe a little-used workshop I can reduce for aspects?"

Havoc looked at Joe, and a slow smile started spreading across his bearded face. Joe didn't particularly enjoy the look of it, but before he could run for the hills, Havoc grasped his arm in a vice-like grip and started walking. "I can do you one better. Have you ever been in a Dwarven landfill before?"

CHAPTER FOURTEEN

Major General Havoc absolutely *abused* the ability to transfer between major forts. Every time someone tried to call him out on it, he would just point at Joe and mutter 'Candidate rights'. Every time they needed to walk from one area to another, the Dwarf would loudly talk about the area, as if he was trying to prepare Joe for a mission. Not a single person dared to actually stop them, which was what Joe assumed the point was. Act confident, like you belong there, and people look the other way. "Over here is the Fields of Blood; it was one of my first conquests. The scars are still healing, *hee...*"

"See that?" Havoc pointed at a pillar of smoke in the distance. "Minor fort that got hit by a meteor recently. Pointy-ear mass-murdering *beasts*."

Joe decided against pointing out that he had proudly just pointed out the 'Fields of Blood'. A place didn't earn a name like that casually.

"Over there is the rest and relaxation area. The light one contains the Caves of Solitude, one of the best places to try out new things without interruption." On one of their last stops, Havoc waved at two mountains that appeared tiny due to the sheer distance. "The dark one is Gramma's Shoe, the most active volcano on all the planes. Practically an eruption every week. It's so dangerous to be nearby that it's almost the only place in this Zone that hasn't been a battleground. Even though we can see it, that's a three-day forced march from here. I point these out so that this next transfer means even more to you."

"On to the Capital." One last flash of light, and Havoc pointed to the mountains again. "See that? Now they're only about a full day's march from here. That should give you a clue to how vast our territory is, as well as how much uninterrupted supply lines between forts means to our people."

There was one final surprise on the trip, right as they were finishing their journey. Somebody zipped past the two of them so quickly that Joe could only make out a blur. A panicked voice trailed after them, "*Oh-abyss-someone-help!*"

Joe stared after the afterimage that was already vanishing into the distance, before turning to Havoc, "What was *that?* Should we go and help whoever that was? Was there an attack?"

"Yeah... don't worry about her." Havoc shook his head and looked at the ground. "There's no help for her. One of you humans decided to focus way too hard on one single skill, specializing over and over again in the same thing without getting the characteristics required to properly use it."

"What... um. Any idea what she did?" Joe couldn't help but feel sympathy for the poor lady; he too had done things that he should not have been able to do. He rubbed his hand over his bald head as he reminisced.

Havoc started to chuckle, which seemed fairly out of character for him. "I know *exactly* what she did. She specialized in 'power walking'. Apparently, that was a form of getting healthy back in your world, and she was addicted to what she called 'mall walking'. Anyway... she was working as a courier, back on Midgard, and specialized three times in movement-type classes. She put everything she had into dexterity and constitution, then hopped on the Bifrost. She's been here ever since, steadily increasing her body stats. Unfortunately for her… her perception is somewhere in the first tier still. Once she starts moving, she can't see where she is going, and moves in pretty much a straight line until she runs into something. Screams the whole time. Pretty funny, actually."

"That's horrible! Can't you-" Joe was going to say more, but Havoc cut him off. The human looked around, noticing the utterly massive city they were in. They had to be up on a mountain; the view gave that away. They were in the fortress area, nearly at the summit itself. For some reason, Havoc grabbed him and *ran* away from the fort, and Joe's view dissolved into streaks as they travelled downhill. When they finally stopped, they had crossed several districts and a huge park, almost reaching the outer wall. "What was *that* all about?"

"Either the restraining order or the warrant was going to start messing with me if we hadn't hurried."

"The *what?*" Joe opened his mouth to press for more information, but Havoc shook his head.

"Enough now. Game face on; we're here. Now, once you go in there, you're going to have to make your way to a door if you want to get out. Here is the security code, which you'll need in order to open the door from the inside. Watch out; such a huge area filled with gear, even busted, tends to draw scavengers. Doesn't matter if they're animals, monsters, or people. I recommend finding a door, then working until you get what you need." Havoc waved toward a garbage can that was on the side of the street. "Well? What are you waiting for? *Everyone* puts every failure into the landfill. There are almost certainly going to be things in there you can break down, all the way to the Mythical tier! You just need to find them."

"You want me to get *into* the garbage can?" Joe could not quite get past that fact. "Then just… what? Root around for a while?"

"Basically… yes." Havoc pulled the lid of the garbage can off, and it expanded wide enough for Joe to fit through sideways, if he wanted. "Take a week. Fill up on aspects."

"But I need weapons! Armor! Supplies?" Joe took a step back from the crazy Dwarf. Nothing that he said was swaying the Dwarf in the slightest.

"*Fill. Up.* Consider it a very, *very* important test." Havoc chuckled darkly and gestured at the opening. "You can requisition anything you need... but you won't know what *exists* unless someone tells you about it. Do this my way, survive a week down there at a minimum, and I will get you a weapon that fits your class and abilities. I'll even get you someone that can teach you to use it properly."

Joe tried to protest, so Havoc simply raised his voice to talk over him. "Here's a hint: the doors are spaced one hundred feet apart, and every ten feet vertically. The walls will have measurements on them. If you can clean enough of the muck off, you will be able to find your way pretty easily."

Quest offered: The Treasure of Trash. Havoc wants you to go into a landfill within the Dwarven capital. If you survive a week, he will get you a weapon specific to your class. He is definitely *not trying to use you to solve the massive garbage issue the Dwarven people have been concerned about for a decade or so. Rewards: new weapon, minimum Rare rank. Failure: upon death within one week, no additional assistance will be offered from Havoc besides the minimum he is required to provide.*

"Seriously, man?" Joe was about to argue, but the quest acceptance button suddenly gained a ten-second timer. The human plodded forward, grumbling the entire way, then pulled himself up onto the edge of the trash can and glared at Havoc. "You had better put together some *amazing* intel for me."

The human slid forward and started dropping. The tube was either magically slick, or just... Joe decided to think of it as magically slick. It was *not* slimy. He heaved for breath; the air was absolutely *ripe*. "Don't look at the wall you're sliding on. Don't do it, Joe. *Ugh*...! I looked."

Debuff added: Legionnaires' disease. You can expect a cough, shortness of breath, high fever, muscle pains, and headaches!

Joe landed heavily, plopping directly on some shards of metal that dug into his skin, only stopping once they hit bone.

Damage taken: 40 (fall damage halved due to Jumplomancer skills!)

"Ugh..." Joe groaned as he yanked the shards out of himself. *"Mend.* When did I turn my shell off?"

Please note that teleportation between fortresses deactivates any passive Buffs or spells which are not permanent enchantments! This is to ensure that reinforcements to fortresses must include healers and others that can add buffs.

Debuffs added! As there are multiple, they have been broken down into easy categories for explanation!

Bacterial diseases include:
· salmonellosis
· shigellosis
· staphylococcus
· tetanus
Viral diseases include:
· gastroenteritis
Parasitic diseases include:
· hookworm
· threadworm
· roundworm

"*All* buffs are deactivated? Abyss!" Joe stopped reading and activated Neutrality Aura as fast as he could. The stench lessened instantly, but he was still getting a lungful of filth with every breath. A few seconds of coughing later, his head stopped swimming long enough that he could read his messages again.

Calculating... as each of these were rapidly introduced and have not had any time to set in, Neutrality Aura has resolved each issue. Please note: you are in a toxic environment. Neutrality Aura, subcomponent 'gas exchange', is lowering the damage you are taking over time.

Debuff added: Toxic... everything. All air, ground, and liquids in the area are toxic. -10 health per second. Neutrality Aura is regenerating Health at 30 health per second. Damage is cancelled out, but please note that you are currently in a downdraft of fresh air.

Joe stared at all of the information that had appeared in the last few seconds, his hands literally shaking with rage at being tossed down here by the 'mentor' he had been assigned. Joe was at least starting to understand why being assigned to him was considered a punishment. He had thought it was because Havoc didn't like people, but it turns out it was because the madman was just ready to abuse anyone in his command under the guise of an 'experiment'. The fortress that had been empty, except for the two of them, should have tipped him off; but there was nothing Joe could do at this point except try to power on.

"I would already be dead without this skill… at least I won't have to drink anything down here. Hooray for passive hydration… that's… pulling water from the area around me. Ew." Joe closed his eyes and powered up his Exquisite Shell, absolutely ready to not take any more damage from stepping or falling on something. He peered around the absolutely dark area, as happy as ever with his passive Darkvision. He was standing in a… the mountain the Capital was built on must have been hollowed out; that was the only reason he could come up with to explain the immense cavern.

He glanced up and could see the ceiling of the space. Joe had fallen maybe fifty feet total after exiting that tube, and he wondered how high—full?—the landfill actually was. After walking over to the wall and sitting next to it, he allowed his aura to begin dissolving the thick, crusty slime that was coating the stone walls. He wasn't overly concerned about getting dirty; his shell kept new things from sticking to him, and his aura was constantly cleaning him. It took about four minutes to finish, but a large section of the wall was now clean. He easily found the markings that Havoc had mentioned, and tried to make sense of them.

+4189, -22.

Joe eyeballed the distance between his position and the 'door' he had fallen through, which was roughly one foot above the marking. No, it was likely *exactly* one foot above. "There's over four *thousand* feet of filth in here?"

He tried to look across the room but could not see the other side. Whether it was because it was too dark, or just too far away, Joe couldn't tell. He did know that it was an utter behemoth of a space, and there were probably literally hundreds of square miles of space in the cavern. Joe knew that he had been at the extreme outer edge when he had dropped down here... did that mean this space went under the entire city?

"How... how in celestials' sake am I supposed to find *anything* in here?" Joe closed his eyes and flopped backward onto the soggy floor. He laid there for a moment, contemplating making a trash angel, when his ears started to ring with very soft sounds. "Great, now I have tinnitus?"

...Seventy-six Rare...

...Eight thousand Trash...

"I'm hearing numbers? Am I going crazy? My debuff list was empty when I last...?" Joe abruptly sat upright, and the sound stopped. He closed his eyes and leaned his head toward the floor again, and the sound started up very faintly. "*All* sensory abilities give information on aspect count! That means I'm either getting the info from Hidden Sense or Magical Synesthesia. Either way..."

"Sounds like..." Joe's eyes popped open, all of the angst and desperation gone in an instant as a plan started to take form. "I have a way to find whatever is waiting for me."

CHAPTER FIFTEEN

Joe started toward the sound, which vanished as soon as he opened his eyes. "Huh… seems like there's just too much sensory overload. Can't focus on it."

Eyes tightly closed, he tried to pinpoint the sound, then opened his eyes and followed the direction it had come from as he picked his way through the garbage. He repeated this process until the sound of 'something Rare' was coming from directly below him, then waited for the gunk beneath his feet to be atomized by his Neutrality Aura. Once the film of filth had been removed, he reached down and let his mana pulse out.

Item: Bag of Trash
Reduction value: 86 Trash aspects.
Reduction cost: .2 mana per second.

"Oh. Neat. So, each rarity level *down* also drops the cost by a fifth?" The bag vanished in a flash, as did all the garbage it contained. That was a stroke of good fortune; he had been worried that only the bag would be absorbed. Food scraps, cans, broken glass; he went through all of them. Listening for the sound again, Joe found that it was closer than ever before, but still a good distance down. This process continued for several layers, and he kept needing to restart whenever the pile became unstable and collapsed in around him.

Eventually, he needed to allow himself to get buried. As Joe continued to struggle downward at an incline, he trusted his shields to keep him safe from any sharp objects, as well as getting crushed. Surrounded by the refuse, he was able to keep his eyes constantly closed as well; following his auditory skills soon led him to what had been calling out to him.

Item: Failed Shield of Hatred (Rare)
Reduction value: 76 Rare aspects, 90 Uncommon aspects, 388 Common aspects, 453 Damaged aspects, 645 Trash aspects.
Reduction cost: 125 mana per second.

Joe didn't hesitate, allowing his mana to swallow the shield whole. Six seconds passed, and in an instant, nothing was left behind. He checked the gained aspects and grumbled. "Lost about ten percent of all the good ones."

Quest gained: Failed Shield of Hatred. After trying and failing to make a lowly Unique Shield, Grandmaster Blacksmith Iron McPoundy found that what he had created was too durable to easily destroy. Hating his failure, he threw it in the garbage. He has been terrified that someone would discover this catastrophic experiment and leverage it against his reputation. Let him know that it is gone forever. Reward: Reputation, variable. Failure: None.

"That's... unexpected." Joe opened his eyes and contemplated the surrounding filth with a new perspective. "If I can complete quests like this, simply by turning them in... this place really *is* a goldmine for me."

However, Joe was now faced with a new fact. He was upside down, and probably at least a dozen feet below the surface. "Didn't think that one through... gonna be a lot harder to go up than down."

If only there was a way to get rid of all the trash without

having to *reduce* all the garbage directly... Joe slapped at his head, only the garbage and shield stopping himself from braining himself. "I *literally* have a spell designed to destroy trash. *Acid Spray!*"

The liquid sloshed out from his palm and ate its way down, though a fair amount rebounded and splashed off his shell. He *was* buried, after all. Trying to use the spell as carefully as possible, Joe soon became the cause of a huge garbage sinkhole. Use after use, fifteen minutes of near-continuous casting, and his hand finally met open air. He wiggled forward and pulled himself onto the edge of the ravine he had created. "Boom. Success."

Hiss

Joe paused and turned to look at the sound. "Please just be a rat or something."

It *was* something; he'd had that part right. Joe's eyes were locked on an utterly *massive* two-headed raccoon, and it was clearly displeased that it had been disturbed. With foam draining from its mouths, the beast launched itself at him and used his shelled body to form a crater in the soft garbage pile. "Dark Lightning Strike!"

The soft sound of his spell striking was offset by the massive explosion that followed in the next instant. Joe was driven deeper into the garbage with the bloated corpse of the raccoon shielding him from a fireball that had sprung into existence.

Damage dealt: 110 (90 Dark element damage resisted by Rotting Rabid Raccoon)

Damage dealt: 3,000 (Environmental)

Damage taken. 50 (50% Dark element resistance)

Damage taken. 1,200 (Environmental, crushing)

Experience gained: 28

"Ugh... how hard did that hit me?" He pushed at the raccoon, but it wasn't budging. He started washing it with acid and was surprised when a message appeared.

Exquisite Shell: 1,096/2,346

"Been a while since I've seen you, shield damage indicator... or maybe I've just been avoiding you? Certainly not a fan of hand-to-hand fighting." Joe scanned the combat logs and realized why there had been an explosion. His use of Acid Spray had caused a buildup of hydrogen gases. Combining that with the methane natural to the area and lightning... well. Big boom. "I'm surprised it wasn't worse, actually. Why didn't this whole place go up like a bottle rocket?"

There was no new information forthcoming, so Joe resolved to do his own research later. He was certain that it had to be a magically induced reason; maybe there were containment fields or something? As he pushed through the raccoon, he noted that the garbage wasn't even on fire. Definitely some magical trickery going on. Joe emerged from the raccoon like a parasite tearing through the lining of a stomach, a fairly decent analogy for this area.

He was going to leave right away to avoid fighting anything else that might have been alerted to his presence by the explosion, but something within the monster called to him. His eyes drifted up to the space right where the two heads connected, and he lightly sprayed it down. As the flesh melted away, a shining Core was revealed. No, twin Cores! He grabbed them eagerly but almost dropped them in disgust.

Trash-grade monster Cores found! Would you like to convert this into experience points? Current worth: 89 experience points.

"Of course they're Trash grade." Joe had to swallow back his emotions as the indignation of being here washed over him again. "At least it's *something*. Bind core for crafting?"

Trash-grade monster Core bound. 89 energy points available for usage while crafting!

"A *one-to-one* conversion?" Joe had to pause and remember that he only needed to use Cores in the creation of Rare or above... things. Crafts? That would work. "Everyone needs to use Cores when they are making stuff. This is normal."

Joe sat on his furry new rug and frowned at the literal mountain of trash, with flecks of treasure hidden within. "It's going to take *forever* to sort through all this stuff. I have to stay here a week, and... what am I doing?"

He half-stood, then realized this spot was actually as good as any other for thinking. "I'm a *Ritualist*. I don't need to swim through trash or keep spamming spells over and over mindlessly! I can, and need to, *automate* this!"

Joe even had a perfect spell to use. With a flick of his wrist for showmanship, he pulled out a ritual paper and started converting Acid Spray into a ritual diagram. An hour of intense concentration, two, and he had a model that he was pretty certain would work as intended. It was slapped together and poorly done, which reduced the potency of the ritual back to Novice rank, even though his spell was in the Apprentice rank, but even that was within his plans. He took a few moments to draw out the ritual using aspects on the paper, and soon, it glowed a wispy dark grey.

"Totally a waste to use this for such a weak ritual," Joe sighed as he prepared to activate it. He paused, stood, and got into position like he was about to throw a frisbee. As soon as he had poured mana and the second Trash Core's power into the diagram, he whipped the paper away. It didn't go terribly far, but it was far enough that he was only caught in the outer edge of the spray it created.

Ritual of Sprinkling Acid (Novice) created! This ritual creates a fine mist of Weak Acid that will eat away at its surroundings for up to four hours! Can only remove Common or below ranked items. Make a stronger version to get rid of more stuff in one go! Range: 15-foot radius. Time remaining: 3:59:46.

The ritual did its job perfectly; after only a few minutes, Joe could neither see the ritual nor the acid from his re-seated position. He had planned on following after it rather quickly, but a dense cloud of smoke had started to rise out of the pit the acid was creating. As a test, he threw some fruit peels into it. There was a deep hiss, and the smoke started melting the rotting foodstuff. "Acidic smoke, got it. No reason to breathe *that* in."

An hour after he'd started the ritual, the ground began to

shift. Joe judged that the garbage had been reduced at about a foot per minute, and what was around the pit of empty space had finally destabilized. The varying sections of the landfill came into stark relief as garbage the next section over remained in place. He should have been expecting that the area was magically sectioned off; the area that had shifted was one hundred feet *exactly*. That must have been why the explosion he'd caused hadn't gone too far; there were internal safeguards in place.

Once the garbage had fallen by ten feet, the sections opened and allowed the nearby waste to slump down and fill the unused space. Once everything had settled, Joe closed his eyes and slid down into the deep crater that remained. No resonance at all; nothing hidden or magical. That meant that only Common or below rarity items remained, as far as his magical senses could detect. That was okay with him; he was only on the edge of the city limits. It was time to move deeper.

"Can't just stay here 'cause it's safe and the most comfortable area. I need to get out there and get the absolute *most* out of this trip. After all..." Joe turned his eyes to the center of the landfill, and a plan began to form. If he wanted the *best* trash, he needed to get under the most valuable shops and creation centers. If he wanted to leave as close to the end of the week as possible, he needed to start moving while muttering to himself.

"Staying in your comfort zone means that you lack dedication to improve. A lack of dedication is an insult to those who believe in you."

CHAPTER SIXTEEN

"Cone of Cold!" Joe directed the freezing blast at the two-headed vole that had burrowed out of the trash and jumped at him. He had been attempting to stay away from fire or electrical-based attacks, since he was hoping to avoid blowing himself up again. The vole took the final attack and fell, so Joe walked over to its body and stomped heavily at the base of its necks, breaking the frozen portion open and retrieving a single Trash Core.

He had learned something interesting after fighting a few of these: if he followed their tunnels back to their nest, there was *almost* always at least an Uncommon item stashed nearby. Of course, if they were not near enough to their nest, Joe would just be wasting time searching for it. It was a good reminder that monsters were supposed to have treasure, and natural monsters tended to hoard it instead of carrying it on them. Though he struggled to keep it in his mind, Joe needed to remember to play by game logic before anything else.

Skill increase: Cone of Cold (Beginner V).

Joe had been traveling toward the center of the landfill for the last day, and monster attacks were becoming more and more frequent. He had defeated several raccoons, skunks, and voles now, but he was expecting to see stronger creatures soon. He had been making good time and figured that, within a few hours, he would be directly under the main portion of the city.

Boom.

He looked to the side as a house-sized ball of trash dropped from the ceiling and slammed into the landfill. Just after the enormous sound of the impact, something roared a challenge, and a section of the landfill went up in flames, a fire that reached all the way to the top of the chamber and illuminated the ceiling. It was strange to see a dark sky filled with open pipes, but he was becoming more used to it.

Another thing Joe had found was that whatever the shielding was between sections, it only contained items for a little while, though fire was confined until it was suffocated. He could cast spells between the different sections, and there seemed to be no limit for how far anything other than fire could travel in a straight line.

The downside to the bellowed challenge and plume of fire was that he was pretty sure that it would be the most profitable destination. There was an adage that the most dangerous things tended to give the highest rewards. If that wasn't the most dangerous thing in this entire junkyard, Joe didn't know where to look for it. A nearby sound dragged him out of his thoughts, and he cast a Cone of Cold without looking. "These voles are starting to bother me."

"*Brooo…*" a deep voice groaned at him. Joe flinched to the side and almost fell over at the unexpected voice. His eyes shot to the area he had fired his spell, and he found a bearded Dwarf covered in a rime of frost.

"I'm so sorry! I didn't know anyone else could survive in here…" Joe rushed over to help the Dwarf, but as he got closer, he began noticing that large chunks of its body were missing. "You… aren't alive, are you? Intrusive Scan."

Name: Zombified Dwarf.

That was all Joe needed to see. He re-cast Cone of Cold,

which set off the new bonus to Retaliation of Shadows for the first time. A shadowy version of himself appeared just as he began casting and followed his motions exactly. The regular spell, and the secondary spell hit at the same time.

Damage dealt: 112 (168 cold damage resisted). Zombified Dwarf is Brittle!

"It's dead; of course it's resistant to the cold." Joe sighed as he tried to decide what spell to use next. On the positive side, being brittle had made the zombie very slow, since its body was frozen stiff. That gave him a few extra moments to decide how he should handle the situation. If a Dwarf as a zombie was anything like a living Dwarf, it had a massive amount of health that he would need to whittle down. Cone of Cold was simply not going to do it, not when the vast majority of the damage dealt was flat-out ignored. "What was that… sixty percent cold resistance?"

He started going through his spell list, searching for anything that he could use to destroy the creature without potentially blowing himself up. He briefly considered using Acid Spray, but he had a test that he wanted to run after the Dwarf was defeated. Looking up, he oriented himself by inspecting the pipes that were just barely visible on the ceiling. He had discovered earlier that a pipe would be open at the exact center of each section in the landfill.

Damage taken: 1,400!

Exquisite Shell: 946/2,346

Though his body did not take any damage directly, Joe went sailing away from the massive haymaker that he had just taken to the face. He was moving so fast that one of the section barriers blocked his movement, and he stopped as painfully as if he had hit a wall. Two hundred more points of damage came off his shield, and the zombie was already almost on him by the time he got back to his feet. "Enough of *that*!"

He stepped through the barrier and cast Dark Lightning Strike on the zombie, happy that he no longer needed to drop the spell on his own head to use it. The lightning hit, followed by the expected methane explosion. It was nowhere near as violent as the original mix of hydrogen and methane had been, but it still cooked the Zombie Dwarf for eight hundred damage. The blast also sent the Dwarf flying... directly at Joe.

Joe *jumped* back, but he needn't have worried. The undead hit the barrier and crumpled just as he had done, sliding down to the ground where Joe blasted with a Cone of Cold, and again, until he saw that the brittle status had come into effect again. "Just die again, abyss it!"

"Corify! Dark Lightning Strike! Cone of Cold!" Joe sent spell after spell at the Dwarf until it finally *stayed* down. He stood over the corpse, panting for breath and waiting for his Mana to regenerate. It didn't take long. Joe reached out and attempted to reduce the zombie's corpse. He wasn't certain if it was going to work at first, but then mana blasted out of him and drained him dry over the next three seconds. Neutrality Aura went down, as did his Exquisite Shell. The body didn't fully disappear, but it did break apart into large chunks after his Mana had faltered. A few notifications appeared, as well as a quest alert that made him cringe.

Experience gained: 1,215.

You have gained a Special aspect: Zombified!
New aspect crafting tutorial available: 'Special' Aspects.

Quest alert: Dead and Dumped (Unique). Someone in the city above has been shirking their duties in proper disposal of corpses and has been tossing them into the landfill instead. It is unknown how long this has been going on for, but the restless dead have become a serious threat in the under-ground. Find a way to destroy all of them and stop more from being dumped. Reward: variable. Failure: a potential Dwarven Zombie outbreak right in the capital city of the Dwarves. This will give a huge advantage to the Elven nation.

"That's just... great." Joe looked eagerly at the new tutorial, only pausing for a moment to see the cost. "Five hundred reputation with Tatum? Is this because the system is *giving* me knowledge, instead of me seeking it out myself?"

Reputation increase: Tatum +50.

"That's clear enough." Joe shrugged and took the offer anyway, pausing only to reactivate Neutrality Aura when he had enough Mana. The debuffs he had accumulated in the last few seconds started to vanish, and another notification appeared.

Thanks for your purchase! Current reputation with Tatum: 3,542 (Friend).

Starting tutorial now!

Once more, Joe found himself in a misty world, but this time, a *green* flame coalesced in front of him. He waited for more instruction before trying anything or reaching out for it. The system seemed to approve of that and launched into an explanation as soon as he settled in to wait.

Special aspects are just that! Special! They are a… flavor of magic that has been added to something, which can be found in certain types of crafting material. They are often—but not always—found in Unique items. Special aspects can change the function of a craft, just like adding modifiers in normal crafting. As an example, consider the effects of adding alchemic or enchanted components to a ritual.

You can have access to up to five different Special aspects no matter how many containers you have for them. If you want a sixth, you must release or use one of the others. Just as with normal aspects, you will need to create a crafting tool specific for the Special aspect in order to use it! For the purposes of the demonstration, you will have enough aspects, a workstation, and the knowledge of how to create a simple dagger. Do so now!

Joe decided to get started right away and attempted to make a hammer out of the green aspect that has been given to him, which appeared to be a copy of the 'Zombified' aspect he had just gained. No matter what he did, though, he was not able to shape the aspect into a hammer. The tutorial came through when he was just about to give up.

As you can see, a Special aspect by itself does not work. You will need to combine the aspect with whatever rarity of aspect you want to use it with! Try again!

Rolling his eyes, Joe pulled together Uncommon aspects, as well as the zombified aspect, eventually managing to form an ingot hammer that shone a sickly silver-green. Using the aspects to craft the hammer went smoothly, even without guiding the process as carefully as he normally did. A new design formed on the striking plane of the hammer, a stylized Dwarven face. Joe got to work immediately, forming a dagger with uncharacteristic ease: surely an effect of the tutorial he was in.

When he finished crafting the weapon, the hammer he was using shattered and its shards vanished. Joe lifted up the newly-made dagger, letting out a low whistle as he read over its abilities.

Zombified Stiletto (Uncommon Special). A dagger designed specifically for killing Dwarves, this blade hungers for the flesh and blood of what it once was. Effect: Adds 50-80 piercing damage on strike. +20% damage when attacking a Dwarf. 5% chance to raise a slain Dwarf as a zombified thrall. 1% chance to raise a slain Dwarf as an uncontrolled zombie. Note: This weapon is highly illegal within areas controlled by the Dwarven Oligarchy.

Tutorial complete!

Joe was once more standing in the landfill, his hands empty, but his mind full of plans for the future.

CHAPTER SEVENTEEN

"Almost a full week now." Joe stood atop a section of the landfill that was especially tall, looking between the various 'mountain peaks' that he had visited over the last few days. Seven redesigned rituals had been placed on the peaks: Acid Spray rituals at the Beginner ranks. The main reason he had needed to redesign the rituals wasn't for more potent acid, but so that he could include a time delay in their construction. They would still only be able to damage items at Common rarity or below, hopefully leaving him with a treasure trove at the bottom of the pits after they finished digging for him.

"If everything goes as planned, I have five minutes until they all start up at the same time…" Joe attempted to shake the oversized metal bin he had placed the final acid ritual on, making sure it was firmly in place, then took a running start and jumped from the mountain of rubbish as hard as he could. Thanks to the less than firm footing, he wasn't moving fast enough to cause the barriers to activate, but with his increased strength, he was able to get a solid distance away from the ritual itself.

He slammed into the ground with the force of a man who

had leapt off a mountain of trash as hard as he could and approached terminal velocity. Joe chuckled at the inane thought as he struggled to dig his way out of the mushy crater. "Did I get a concussion on the way down or something?"

A gentle rain started, and panic flashed across Joe's face. "The area of effect is higher than I calculated!"

Damage taken: 55 (Acid rain is dealing 55 damage per second.)

The liquid was draining off his shell, but Joe had to *hustle* to get out of range. Not only was he concerned about his shell's durability, but the ground was already beginning to sink. If he got trapped in a sinking zone, he would soon need to start worrying about the acidic gases as well as everything else. A broken cry arose in the distance, increasing in volume as more and more voices joined in. The rabid animals and zombies caught in the acid were furious about the sudden yet unrelenting gradual damage to which they were being subjected. Joe gulped and moved faster.

Eventually, he surpassed the edge of the acid and looked back. A flare of flame lit up the underground, and he hastily guesstimated the actual effect of the series of acid spray rituals as they misted over the edges of the 'peaks' he had placed them on. "Maybe... a thousand feet in diameter? That's a *lot* more than I thought I would get."

To be fair, he had crafted the ritual to release the liquid as forcefully as possible, using intentionally weaker acid for a greater range. Even so, he was pleased to see everything work out so well. The garbage was reduced at about two feet per minute, and he had *hours* remaining-

A thunderous roar and splashing drew Joe's attention to one of the 'mountains' he had selected. He could just barely make out the rotting forms of a huge group of zombies that had attacked the thing damaging them. They tore the ritual apart, and it appeared as though the ritual had discharged all at once, dousing the zombies in everything it was supposed to release over time. Joe waited for the experience to roll in, but... nothing. "That's odd... I've gained experience for fringe kills in the past? Why not these? Did they not die?"

Hello there, youngster! Thank you kindly for your inquiry. I regret to inform you that the experience from residual damage has been... nerfed? Yes, that. We recently implemented a system that allows intent *to carry weight in experience gain. There were some people planning to break a Zone in half so they could 'claim the kill' for everyone and everything on that Zone. Your ritual was not intended as anti-personnel; it just so happened that it* did *hurt things. None of that sweet, sweet experience for you. Please note that if you create whatever this was again for the express intent to kill things, the costs to do so will be* vastly *higher.*

My apologies for any inconvenience and for the interruption to your day, but I am here to maintain the balance and must fulfill my role.
~A.

"Who are... wait, I see the sign off, but I didn't know there were any active admins. Are you from the game company?" Joe waited for a long few seconds, but there was no reply to his questions or concerns. It seemed that message had been a pre-recorded response in anticipation of someone becoming grumpy about not getting experience for something they had done in the past, rather than an actual person currently watching him and giving him answers. "So you just irrevocably nerf my class and walk away? This is unacceptable! You are going to require different resources for the same effect?"

Joe lodged an official complaint right away. He was *not* going to let this stand.

With nothing else to do for the moment, Joe sat on the garbage and waited. At the end of his rituals, the area of garbage that was being doused in acid should have dropped by about five hundred feet? Not terrible for a Beginner-ranked ritual. With nothing else to do while he waited, Joe decided to burrow into the trash and activate Essence Cycle. He had not gained a single bonus characteristic since he had come down here, and Joe was feeling like he had been slacking.

He was not prepared for the overwhelming dark-aligned mana that was flooding the place. Normally, when Joe activated this ability, he was immediately aware of large surges of dark mana, but they were interspersed with all sorts of other colors. In fact, it usually tended to look a bit like a kaleidoscope, which was fun and always interesting to stare at. Here... darkness. All encompassing, saturated darkness. Then the darkness filled with numbers. Joe sat for an unknown amount of time, contemplating the darkness and data before finally managing to voice his thoughts.

"But *why*? Why is it so *dense* here, compared to anywhere else? Is it the garbage? The fact that things are rotting, that things are breaking down here? Is the garbage itself releasing dark mana?" Essence Cycle was broken as a notification shocked Joe into coming back to himself.

Skill increase: Essence Cycle has reached Beginner 0! You have spent time actually using this skill in varying environments, attempting to understand the why. *It matters.*

Tier increase bonus: You are now able to activate Essence Cycle without dropping into a meditative state. This allows you to follow mana emanations to their source, as well as moving between active and inactive states without an outside influence.

Characteristic points gained: +5 perception! Sometimes it is not necessary to make great leaps of logic, or to bend your mind to a strenuous task. Sometimes it is just important to look at the heart of a matter and see *it.*

Joe immediately reactivated the skill and peered around. Now, instead of just a dense cloud around him, he was able to see that the darkness was striated. The refuse was indeed releasing mana and pushing it into the air. He stood and picked his way to the densest nearby cloud. As he stepped into it, he checked his characteristic sheet to see if anything had changed. He smiled as he noticed the difference immediately, then choked on the air and stepped out quickly.

Column of Choking (methane, carbon dioxide, heavy metal toxicity).

-30 health per second. Neutrality Aura is balancing the damage. Caution! No oxygen; gas exchange cannot function! Suffocation imminent.

"What in the abyss…?" Joe dropped his gaze to the ground, then cast Acid Spray on it. He started burrowing down, turning on Essence Cycle every thirty seconds or so. "What in here is so toxic that it is pumping out nastiness like this? I'm gonna find you."

As he sank closer, the numbers in the column shifted. The aspect count increased as he dug lower, and finally, ten feet down, he uncovered a huge barrel that was rusted to the extreme; almost to the point of falling apart. He *almost* cast Acid Spray again, but something told him to take a look at it more closely instead of destroying it the easy way. Bracing himself, he eased forward and checked it directly.

Item: Barrel of Slag
Reduction value: 131 Unique aspects, 200 Rare aspects, 280 Uncommon aspects, 310 Common aspects, 543 Damaged aspects, 1,023 Trash aspects.
Reduction cost: 625 mana per second.

"That's handy." Calculating the size of the barrel, Joe figured that he would not be able to get everything on the first try… unless… *maybe* he could, if he was willing to take some damage. He deactivated his Exquisite Shell and Retribution of Shadows. When his mana was back to full from releasing those, Joe took one last deep breath of clean air and deactivated Neutrality Aura. He held his breath as long as he could, which was *just* long enough to refill his mana to the limit. He activated his Ritual of Reduction, and the barrel was covered in his dark blue mana.

One second… two… at four, the barrel showed no hint of falling apart, and Joe's mana bottomed out. The pain hit his head like a Dwarven Warhammer, and he gasped. Big mistake. A whole host of debuffs scrolled across his vision, but he only had eyes for the barrel itself. Was it going to fall apart, now that he had weakened it?

Three more seconds passed, and all that happened was a large amount of rust falling to the ground. Perhaps... it had been in such poor condition already that his mana didn't do much to it? Joe watched anxiously as his mana refilled and his health dropped at almost inverse proportions. He was forced to cast Mend on himself twice, and his health was still down to almost a quarter when he finally reached full capacity.

Once more, he allowed his mana to flow out of him and into the barrel of slag. This time, it was fully reduced to aspects. He literally breathed easier after that, as the barrel was no longer releasing toxins. As soon as he had recovered enough mana, Joe quickly reactivated Neutrality Aura and sat down. His spell got to work on all of the bacteria, parasites, and damage that he had brought into himself by breathing in such foul air.

For a long while, Joe simply sat and rested, waiting for the opportunity to go out and damage himself for personal gain again. Then he heard a sound like rushing water. "What's going on? There can't be a waterfall in here, can there?"

The ground beneath him shifted, and Joe realized what was happening: his rituals had dug far enough down that the surrounding piles were becoming destabilized. Joe scrambled up out of the hole he had put himself in and tried to run out of the area that was being impacted. Unfortunately, he had truly underestimated the far-reaching effects of his ritual.

He tumbled backward, barely managing to get his Exquisite Shell in place before he was buried under the landslide of his own creation.

CHAPTER EIGHTEEN

Havoc paused from tinkering with his new super weapon, a mana-magnetic meteor mitigator. He tapped one large finger against his lab table, wondering what was bothering him. "Those Elves have been using meteors as their main weapon for the past six months; this needs to be my main focus. If I can use their *blasted* spells against them, we won't have to worry about them taking out large contingents of our troops. Oh?"

He was getting a notification? Someone had completed a quest he had sent them on? *How?* No one *ever* completed his quests, since practically everyone was entirely incompetent. Havoc lifted the corner of his mouth, allowing an open gap. A tiny rocket attached to his cigar on the table fired up, launching his main vice into his mouth at the same time as lighting the cigar itself.

"Huh. The scavenger-classed human actually pulled it off?" The Major General grumbled deep in his chest. He had been certain that particular Candidate would kick the bucket on the first day. In fact, he was *so* sure that he hadn't bothered to do any of the work he had promised the lad. No matter; Havoc was a resourceful Dwarf. "He might be worth something, after all. At least he's not here demanding payment yet. Let's go see some old friends."

Havoc started walking, leaving behind the temporary lab that he had set up in the capital city, a personal estate that he kept for the rare occasions when he was allowed to come back. With every step he took, other Dwarves dove out of the way, scrambling to avoid garnering his attention. Weak-willed, the *lot* of them. He was the last person still living to achieve nobility during his time in the Legion, which just went to show how far their race had descended into passivity. At this very moment, the Elves were likely planning to storm one of their forts, and his own people couldn't look him in the eye!

"Have you all no *shame?*" Havoc snarled, causing the people that had stepped aside to flee to safer areas. His hand twitched and dropped toward his pocket, and he barely stopped himself from activating his 'personal safety' device. No... *no*, that was what had gotten him banished to that empty laboratory on the border. The council had warned him: any more collateral damage, 'accidental' or not, and he would lose his funding.

"Hypocritical wastes of *space* don't deserve to... no... deep breaths, Havoc," he reminded himself, letting go of the orb that had mysteriously appeared in his hand. As far as he could remember, he hadn't intentionally pulled out *the device*. "Old McPoundy should have everything I need for this. Easy-peasy, Elf-neck squeezy."

Hurling himself through the crowds at breakneck speed, he soon arrived at the forge closest to the castle: the smithy of Grandmaster Iron McPoundy. Havoc wasted no time with pleasantries, kicking the door off the hinges instead of taking the time to twist the intricate metal doorknob. If there was only one thing that Havoc could complain about when it came to foremost Smith in the nation, it would be that he spent far too much time on making things 'pretty'. *Functionality* was king.

However, he had *plenty* more than just a single thing to gripe about. The Dwarf had an entire *list* of grievances when it came to the metal-shaper. The main one, the big one, was that the

Grandmaster always tried to play up an air of mystery and untouchableness. Havoc peered around the room, observing dozens of weapons appearing in the hands of the Smiths that had been training when he entered. Currently, the room was entirely silent.

"Hanger-ons!" Havoc bellowed to the room full of people that had only become more nervous when they realized who had entered the workshop. "Where is my little brother? *McPoundy*! You have five seconds to get out here before I start breaking things! I don't care how far in 'seclusion' you are; I don't care one *whit* about giving you 'face', or any of this other garbage that you have been picking up from hearing Elves talk! First thing I break is your anvil; next thing is your trainees! We're in the Capital! They'll revive tomorrow, but how much time will you need to spend training them back to-"

"Hold on a *moment*, will ya? Murderous degenerate..." Havoc crashed into a wall as a metal-shod boot tried and failed to cave in his sternum. A bearded Dwarf built like a short defensive wall strode heavily toward Havoc, even as the latter calmly stepped forward out of the crumbling mortar he had been embedded in. "What did I warn you about the *last* time I saw ye, *Hank*? Why do you always barge in here, insult me, insult my employees?"

"Hello, little bro. I go by 'Havoc' these days." The mad-scientist Dwarf cracked a wide smile, and smoke released from his mouth, even though there was no cigar on his lips. "I need a favor from ya. Need a custom weapon; I got a magic-type *human* mentee assigned to *me*, if you would believe it. Joined the Legion not long back, currently in Officer selection."

"How is that *my* problem?" The burly Dwarf demanded, stalking closer and closer toward Havoc until the shorter Dwarf needed to back away to be able to see his face. The smith was clearly trying to edge the scientist out of the forge.

"Hey. Let me say it again, McPoundy. He's been assigned to *me*." Havoc let a little smile show when his brother's face contorted. "That's right, someone wants him to *fail*. Someone took an actual, *promising* Candidate, and gave them to *me*. I'll tell you right now... the human passed my first quest."

"Hortatory." McPoundy sighed as his arms dropped from a defensive position in front of his chest. "It always comes back to that. You come in here, a man that I'm sick of seeing, extort me, and depend on my voluntary compliance. You listen here... just because someone can complete one of your inane quests doesn't mean they are someone deserving of *my* work. If you want me to make something for them, Candidate or not, I'll be judging them for myself. I will hear nothing else about it. I'll give them a fair chance, and you will leave. Now."

"Happily." Havoc turned on his heel and stormed out of his brother's forge, trying not to show his true, seething rage. This meeting, in fact, had been one of the most cheerful reunions with one of his previous contemporaries. The fact that he was not outright attacked was likely due to their relation more than anything else. Certainly more than respect for Havoc's position or threat level. "Now who to see..."

"Human's weapon is taken care of... I need to find him trainers, put together a squad that he can't boss around... scratch that. I think he is going to need to be a lone agent like I am. We'll call him a consultant." Havoc browsed the various shop fronts and work areas. "Armor? Yes... who do I know that can stitch together some good Mage gear? Potions? Components should be taken care of... Cores?"

"Hocus-pocus always takes so much effort." Havoc muttered as he went from shop to shop, acquiring things in Joe's name, shamelessly using his Candidacy instead of paying for services. By the end of the day, Havoc had created a full suite of options for Joe, ranging from high-end teachers that could start in a few weeks, to gear that would be perfect for supplementing his abilities and playing to his strengths.

"Heh." Havoc chuckled as he looked at the total reputation bill for the services. "Never say I don't do right by the people assigned by me. Least not the ones that prove themselves. Where is that human, anyway? I can't imagine that he stayed in the dump longer than he needed to. I'm betting he hunkered down near an exit and got out as soon as the quest completed."

Hours passed, and eventually the Dwarf went to bed. Nothing. No sign of the human. Rather than becoming impressed, Havoc was faintly disgruntled. "There's no chance that being down there is actually *useful* to him, right? Or maybe he just got trapped in the garbage? Well... then he should show up sometime soon; the debuffs down there are enough to kill a Major, and getting buried is a death sentence."

Havoc arose the next morning and waited longer, becoming increasingly impatient, until the human finally appeared. Still, it had been over a day since the quest was complete, and the Dwarf wanted answers. Trying to remain calm, he adjusted his goggles and gave Joe a stare-down. "You're late."

"Hmm?" Joe unenthusiastically replied. The Dwarf observed the man, noting the extreme fatigue apparent on his face. Havoc knew that going into the landfill created long-lasting debuffs if you lived long enough to face them, but he could tell with a sniff that this human didn't even have '*Stinky I*' on him. "I have... just so much to talk to you about."

"Hold up." Havoc's notification was flashing at him like a strobe light, indicating that he was going to start getting punished if he did not pay out the quest rewards immediately. "Before you say anything else, I'm going to let you know that you passed my quest. I have a whole bunch of things for you to look over, and we have figured out some directions that we can go. Just had to let you know before the world started chucking lightning bolts at me."

"Has... that happened to you before?" Joe glanced at the Dwarf sidelong.

"Hasn't happened in the last couple a' months." Havoc shrugged, calming down now that the system knew that he would be fulfilling his oaths. "What took you so long to get back here?"

"Horde of Dwarven zombies down there." Joe's statement was casual, but it made Havoc freeze in concern. "Got a quest to clean them out; couldn't manage to finish it before I died. Still, that's not what got me in the end."

Havoc took a long draw on his cigar to hide his shaking fingers. He couldn't offer a quest to take out the zombies down there; *no one* really could. There was no reward that could match the danger. The landfill was pretty much death for anyone who entered it. Frankly Joe should never have been able to survive that quest. There was a reason that Havoc was going all-out on making sure he fulfilled his promises; he didn't want to end up as the 'boss' of an instant dungeon beneath the city. "So… what eventually gotcha? You really like to leave big pauses when you speak. Are you sure you aren't an actor or something?"

"Hubris." Joe answered grimly, ignoring the slight taunt. "I kept making one mistake after another. I knew that there was a big baddie down there, but I got way too involved in collecting aspects. At one point, I dropped a bunch of acid on the garbage, got pulled into the collapse, and I thought it was over. Nope! As soon as I dug my way out, I found an absolute treasure trove of things to break down. I kept going, going, going. Dropping my shields so I would have just a *little* more power, taking chances that I really shouldn't have, but I was gaining so *much*."

Havoc waved for him to continue, and Joe launched back into his story. "I found an Artifact down there, Havoc. An *Artifact*. I was so excited that I went over and tried to check it out. Don't worry, I wasn't dumb enough to attempt to break it down without a lot more power to draw on. It gave me a warning I had never seen before: 'You can't reduce living things'. I thought it was just talking about… you know… how enchanted things are 'living'… but then it stood up."

"Hidden Guardian, Havoc." Joe's eyes were burning with a combination of indignation and excitement. "There's a malfunctioning Guardian down there, and it's a big one. I thought I was just walking over to break down a boulder that had somehow become an Artifact; turns out it was a fingertip. It was *not* happy that I had grabbed it. Apparently, that counted as me starting combat. I didn't even see it move, Havoc. I only know how it killed me because of my combat logs."

"How are you so happy about this?" Havoc wondered the question aloud.

"Hidden. Guardian." Joe's eyes were shining with a manic light. "I'm not telling you that it is the boss of a dungeon, I'm telling you that it is the name of a *quest*. If I can fix up the area around it and convince people to stop using that space as a landfill, I can reclaim that Guardian as a second protector of the capital. How does that sound?"

Havoc blew a cloud of smoke out of his nose, deliberating over the details and Logistics that would go into not only cleaning out the garbage and the monsters, but also convincing an entire city to stop putting their garbage in the place they had dumped it for generations. He decided to give Joe an honest answer.

"Hard."

CHAPTER NINETEEN

Joe didn't go over the majority of his experience with Havoc, but the details were certainly on his mind. He had learned a few interesting things while he'd been in the landfill, and while the hidden Guardian was certainly the *most* interesting, it certainly wasn't the only information he had found.

At one point, he had nearly died because he tried to rely on an old gaming trope he had heard about over and over. He cast 'Mend' on a zombie as it was coming at him, expecting that the healing of the spell would damage the undead creature. Unfortunately, he had forgotten that Mend was a *dark* spell. In practically no time flat, the zombie had gone from jogging at him to *sprinting* at him. He wouldn't be doing *that* again.

When he had managed to return to Havoc, Joe had been on his last legs. He wanted to hear the Dwarf out, but instead found a bed and slept for nearly twelve hours. The rewards will be there after he woke up, after all. Once he regained consciousness, he decided that he should take stock of the changes over the last week or so. First, he browsed through his spatial devices.

"Eighteen Trash-ranked Cores, some Unique garbage that I

need to break down; I have my ritual and spell books, ritual papers, and… that's about it. What about aspects? I feel like I made a good haul…"

Aspects gathered
Trash: 10,253
Damaged: 8,312
Common: 5,951
Uncommon: 2,983
Rare: 1,132
Special (Zombified): 323
Unique: 735
Artifact: 0
Legendary: 0
Mythical: 0

Core energy: 81/81 (Trash)

"I…" Joe stared at the numbers, "…*really* want to make this into a ritual that I can use on large chunks at a time."

Pulling out a small chunk of garbage, Joe tried to reduce it at the same time as studying the ritual on his body. He saw the glowing lines appear again, but they did not *mean* anything to him when he saw them. A couple more attempts, and he'd made no progress whatsoever. He rubbed his eyes, then paused as he had an idea. He activated Essence Cycle, then reduced the-

"*Wow.*"

The ritual within him lit up, shining lines radiating out from his spine until they reached his skin. It was… beautiful to the extreme, but also *incredibly* abstruse. The only thing that Joe could really compare the lines to would be a spatial device. There was no way that the sheer size of the ritual should have been contained within a fleshy body; it was within him, it *was* him. "Is this what a *class* looks like?"

It was not just the energy within him that was impacted.

With Essence Cycle, he could see that all of the floating energies in the air were being condensed, swirled, pulled to enter him. The energy that was taken in flowed along his skin, intermingled with his mana, and exited the ritual that was Joe, the Ritual of Reduction. The power flowed back out of him, and for the first time, Joe was able to see a physical object being reduced into aspects.

Caution! You are attempting to see into the inner workings of Sage-ranked spellwork! Calculating... intelligence threshold far too low!

Joe's eyes bulged, his mana backlashed, and his head exploded with a retort like a grenade detonating.

He ignored the message that appeared to him when he was in his respawn room. He had died twice in the last day, and Joe had a fleeting thought that he should be upset at this point. However, he could not manage to get into that frame of mind. He was too elated. *Ecstatic*, in fact. "I have a working model of a *Sage-ranked* ritual! It's... I'm barely *touching* the potential of this class!"

Beyond the direct excitement of having such an interesting class with a huge amount of growth potential, there was something about dying for new knowledge that was practically nostalgic. He was trying to think back to the last time he had been working on a spell model that had backfired so badly, it had actually managed to kill him, and he could not easily think of one. It did resurrect a different, unpleasant thought in his thankfully reconstituted head, however.

"Have I been getting... complacent?" Joe's brow furrowed. "When was the last time I was really pushing the boundaries of my magic? I know that I have been focused on my class, but... I'm so far away from even being able to *study* the depths of my own abilities that I died when I tried. What do I need to do? Just get my intelligence to that level? No... I need to get my skill to a point that I can use it. I need to have the intelligence to match... I'm... I'm so *excited*!"

Pulling open his status sheet, Joe instantly started wincing as he saw the downgrade in experience. "*Feces*... I lost three levels.

Name: Joe 'Tatum's Chosen Legend' Class: Reductionist
Profession I: Arcanologist (Max)
Profession II: Ritualistic Alchemist (1/20)
Profession III: None
Character Level: 19 Exp: 192,704 Exp to next level: 17,296
Rituarchitect Level: 10 Exp: 45,000 Exp debt: 14,714
Reductionist Level: 0 Exp: 176 Exp to next level: 824
Hit Points: 0/1,573 (Currently respawning)
Mana: 0/2,152 (Currently respawning)
Mana regen: 44.55/sec
Stamina: 0/1337
Stamina regen: 6.36/sec

Characteristic: Raw score

Strength: 129
Dexterity: 129
Constitution: 125
Intelligence: 138
Wisdom: 118
Dark Charisma: 80
Perception: 118
Luck: 60
Karmic Luck: 8

"I'm all the way back down to level nineteen... yeesh." Joe puttered around the room, messing around with various things. Then he noticed that one entire wall was filled with a flashing icon of an unopened letter. He tapped it and found hundreds of letters from his mother, his guild members, and his Coven. He paled as he went through them, concerned that things had gone wrong. After a short while, he had to wipe out his moist eyes.

His mother had written him a letter every single day, ever since he had been exiled. He sat and read through each one, then composed a reply that went over most of the things that he had been going through. His Guild had questions for him about the new Zone, which he offered answers to as much as he could. Finally, his coven had mostly technical questions that he was happy to resolve. It was always refreshing to see someone else's work and discover ways that he could help them improve or improve his own things, based on their creativity.

Before Joe knew it, the portal had opened and it was time to leave. Thanks to the large amount of time that he had been forced to spend in the room, Joe had gone through all of the emails. He promised himself that he would take time to regularly answer questions and emails in the future, but he needed to find a spot where he could access the mail portion of the game. He had thought that he would need to find an actual post office of some sort, but once again, the game came through in a way that he did not expect.

Feeling refreshed, re-centered, and ready to roll, Joe stepped out of the portal and came face-to-face with Havoc.

"Do you have *any* idea how bad it looks for me when my trainee's brain matter is splattered all over the room I gave him in my house?"

CHAPTER TWENTY

"What are we doing?" Joe finally broke down and asked the question. He was standing in an empty room with Havoc staring at him; the only thing that had moved in the last five minutes as they watched each other was a long line of smoke that lifted into the air above the Dwarf.

"*We* are doing nothing. *You* are about to impress me." Havoc's words were not a guarantee, nor were they a plea; they were a demand. "I let you go into one of the most highly restricted, most dangerous, and for you... potentially most profitable places under the protection of the Dwarven Oligarchy. You are about to show me that you did not waste your time huddling in a corner the whole time you were down there."

Joe made a 'what the abyss' motion with his hands. "I already told you that I went and did all sorts of things! I found a Guardian-"

"Oh look! I can turn lead into gold and fart rainbows!" Havoc rudely interrupted. "There, I *told* you! Now you are going to *believe* me, right?"

"Just..." Joe's arms dropped to his sides. "Fine. What do you want me to do?"

"Make me something new. At the minimum, I need you to make me something that we can use to conquer a minor fort."

"That's unreasonable!" Joe declared without a second thought. "We were going to do a whole bunch of little stuff to start with, weren't we? Infiltrations, an Uncommon alchemy house, a-"

"No, that was a lie to get you to go along with my plan to dump you in the garbage. I never expected that you'd pull through." Havoc didn't hold back at all, his voice rising as Joe gaped at him in shock. "Let me *explain* something to you. You, if you haven't noticed, are a human. You are trying to get nobility among the *Dwarves*. Whoever sent you to me had it out for you; they want you to fail. They *expect* you to fail. Do you actually think we can convince the upper echelon to make you a noble if we try to play it safe?"

"But… I thought everything was based on merit?"

"*Think*, for pyrite's sake! Do you think normal accomplishments will get you into the nobility? You'll get a rank, at best! Unless you manage to pull in a whole fecal load of accomplishments to offset the current nobles directly going against you from the start. Abyss, at this point you're going to need to capture a minor fort, just so that you don't get brought up on charges for all of the things that I am requisitioning on your behalf! That's why I gave you this task now."

"*What?*" Joe stared at the Dwarf, who gazed calmly back. Joe knew that someone had it out for him; that was the problem with some people who were given authority. Not many people were truly deserving of the authority that they had, and sometimes they would take whatever modicum of power they had and use it maliciously. That was unsurprising… and yet, he was not expecting that Havoc was going to be racking up a giant bill 'for him'.

Havoc coughed into his fist. "Right. Well. a little bit of background information. The forts are system devices. Even if they are reduced to rubble, in a day, they will be back to their most basic form. All of the upgrades and buildings that we make are gone if we break them in the attack, though we reclaim at least a portion of the resources if we take it. What I'm trying to say is that destroying them directly isn't an issue. Keep that in mind when you are planning an attack."

"I want…" Joe stopped himself and shook his head. He could only hope that Havoc had good reasons for doing what he was doing. "Fine. What should we be expecting in terms of resistance? I need to plan for that as well."

"Contrary to popular belief, the forts that are closest to our territory are *not* going to be the most well-defended." Havoc opened his palm, and a small projection appeared above his glove. "Because they change hands so frequently, all of the bonus fortifications and buildings get wiped out on a regular basis. The complacency that has set in within this generation has made things a little worse. These days, border forts are used almost exclusively to gain combat experience; the Oligarchy is barely even trying to take the forts. For… for abyss… when the Legion *does* take one, they are almost as surprised as the *enemy*!"

Joe took an involuntary step back; Havoc had been *roaring* by the end. His veins were bulging, his beard was quivering, and it was clear that this was a sore spot for the Dwarf. "So… what you are saying is that I should go all out; don't worry overmuch about the consequences of destroying a border fort? But buried in that is a hint that I should take more care when I am taking on more well-established things, if I want to be able to loot them or learn from them?"

"Looks like all of those weeks devoted to increasing your intelligence weren't *entirely* for show." Havoc huffed out his breath and waved around the empty basement workshop that they were standing in. "This place isn't reinforced, so try not to blow it up; but if you *do*, at least it is empty. Now, tell me what you need, and I'll make sure you have it. You only get one chance to impress me."

Joe considered for a while, comparing the options that he had available, and things that he had successfully accomplished in the past. Finally, he settled on a plan. "The main thing that I will need is something that can kill off the Guardian, which is a plant. Secondary to that is going to be finding a way to take out the defenders. They have lots of magical power, but not much in the way of health, correct?"

"More than you might think. Not as much as a Dwarf, certainly, but look at _you_. How long did it take you to go from big brain to balanced body?" Havoc made a chair appear, and he sat on it. Joe realized that he wasn't the only one in the room with a spatial device, but he had to hold back before he started asking questions about the size or rarity. Asking someone else for their secrets was the same as asking for their weaknesses, and he had the feeling that Havoc wouldn't share that information lightly.

"I need something like this." Joe pulled out a ritual paper, as well as a magically enhanced blueprint paper. "The first one will let me make rituals that can be used like spell scrolls. The second one will let me make buildings, or at least allow me to take blueprints and turn them into rituals that can be enacted anywhere. They are really hard to get, and really expensive back on Midgard. What is that going to look like here?"

Havoc examined the two different types of paper, felt them with his fingers, and assessed their quality. "Something like this is not an issue. I'll send the requisition order now."

Joe looked at the Dwarf askance, "When you say it's not an issue, do you mean that you are just going to tack it onto my bill? How easy would it be for a normal person—who can't just order people to get things for them—to get a hold of?"

"Do you _really_ need the entire nation to hold you in high esteem? Why not just let a small—very select—group of people think you are a good person?" Havoc chuckled evilly. It took Joe a moment to realize what the Dwarf was really saying, but then he ran his hands over his head in consternation.

"You mean it normally costs reputation with the Dwarven Council, don't you?" Joe had learned that a thousand reputation with any merchant organization could be exchanged for ten reputation with the Dwarven Council. It was always more profitable—and more difficult—to have a good reputation with higher ups. Similar to his experience in Midgard, where having high reputation with the ruling family had made it easier to gain reputation with all sorts of affiliated... anything. Working in the Legion gave him one hundred reputation a day, which meant he could gain one point of reputation each day with the Dwarven Council by literally fighting their war for them.

"If you wanted cheap magical things, you should have joined the Elves," Havoc chuckled darkly. "Good thing for us that you didn't; our histories show what actual Ritualists can do."

Joe looked up hopefully, wondering if he was about to get invited to the Grand Ritual Hall. Havoc ignored him and waved at the papers in Joe's hands. "Use those; the others will show up when possible."

"If we're going to be like that..." Joe decided to fully embrace the suck. Somehow, he understood at a deep level that his accomplishments for the most part would be going to pay back the cost of what he would be making. He was going to have to go all-out if he were going to achieve grand accomplishments that would overpower the *negatives* of getting there. "I also want powerful Cores, and blueprints for defensive installments. Siege equipment would be nice, but only if they are buildings. Get me anything that you think would be helpful, just like we agreed before I jumped into the landfill."

"He's starting to get it." Havoc's shoulders started shaking, and soon he was roaring with laughter. "He's finally starting to *get* it!"

The Dwarf watched on as Joe got back to work, waiting until the human was fully distracted before letting out a small fart. It shimmered away as rainbow smoke before dissipating entirely, while Havoc kept a close eye on the human to make sure he didn't notice.

CHAPTER TWENTY-ONE

"It's been three days, human," Havoc whispered into Joe's ear, the deep voice buzzing unpleasantly. That, combined with the surprise visit, caused Joe to slap out in shock. He missed by a wide margin, and Havoc waved at him to hurry. "Time to step up to the plate and grab the bull by the horns."

Joe frowned at the Dwarf with slight disgust. "Where did *that* come from?"

Havoc looked surprisingly proud about his terrible mixed metaphor. "I took a council-designed course on humanity. They only let a hundred people in, but it gave us a nice look at your world's previous technology and conversational ability. Stop trying to dodge the question. Either show me what you have and what you are working on, or get out."

"Fine, take a look. Chill." Joe produced his redesigned ritual diagram and handed it over. "I know this spell, 'Wither Plant', and I've reached Apprentice five with it. I managed to make a scroll, and converted that into a ritual. Thanks to the spell scrolls that you 'acquired' for me, I was able to join this with a draining spell, making a first generation 'Mana Wither' spell."

"*Why* did you do that?" Havoc tapped the diagram, making Joe wince. "What does it do?"

"Careful with that, please; it is the only prototype right now. As to *why*, you need some background information first." The Reductionist took the paper back and gently set it on the floor. "One of the difficulties of my rituals has always been the fact that I need to assign the targets *before* I activate the ritual. That is, I need some blood from everyone who wants to participate or will be *forced* to participate. Unfortunately, that is considered a component, meaning I can no longer use blood as a targeting method. Even trying to reduce my own blood only gives me common aspects. Nothing special. However…"

Joe tapped at the inner circle of the ritual, "I am still able to create a… let's call it an 'opt in', which is made with what is essentially my personal mana frequency. In short, I can directly build myself into the ritual. That allows me to activate it, direct it, turn on or off, and so forth. The draining element serves two functions. One: it is terribly and intentionally inefficient, as it drains mana impossibly fast from anyone that is participating in powering it. Two: I don't need to build in selected targets anymore. Anyone who uses mana within the bounds of the ritual are automatically considered to have 'opted-in' to powering the ritual. I thought that perhaps I could use this to empower other rituals or store energy, but…"

"Just doesn't work?" Havoc nodded knowingly even as Joe looked at him with hope. "If you constructed mana batteries, you might be able to use this idea to charge them, but ambient mana won't just get pulled in, am I right?"

Joe regarded Havoc with great interest. He had not been able to figure that detail out and had thought that perhaps it was an idea he would need to let go, but it sounded like something Havoc was familiar with. "No, I *can't* just use ambient mana. You're right. But if I cast a spell in the area, it starts to drain me as long as I am within the area of effect. Why won't it grab from the environment?"

"You only have basic Essence in the air; nature doesn't *generate* mana. It *collects* it. That's how you get mana-imbued objects. First thing you'd need to do is find a way to suck up what's in the air, then combine it together to make Quintessence. Still, that's not mana, but it might serve as a supplemental power source if your target is natural, or flowing through a body." Havoc rubbed his beard consideringly. "Things breaking down *do* generate mana, but only things that have been imbued with mana. Throwing away a banana peel and facilitating a breakdown will generate Essence, but not mana. Damaged gear, components, anything that is tossed away will release their stored mana as they decompose… you see what I'm getting at?"

"What's the difference between mana and this 'Essence'? Oh, you're thinking that I could use the mana released from the landfill to power rituals in the landfill?" Joe shrugged at that thought; it was something he had already planned on pursuing. "I would need an extremely powerful ritual to be able to impact something of that size. Or a significant number of smaller rituals. We'll put it on the back burner for now. Point is, I am pretty sure that when I activate this ritual, it will allow me to start withering all plants in range. Anyone or anything that starts releasing Mana will help to power the ritual once it gets going. My concern is that it does not differentiate between friend and foe."

"What you *should* be worried about is someone breaking it." Havoc rumbled as he eyed the paper that Joe was being so careful with. "I'm not just talking about this prototype. Elves are *excellent* spellbreakers. Got nothing better to do than look at strands of mana and figure out how to wiggle it. Plus, I got you those *incredibly* difficult-to-acquire scrolls so you could *learn* the spells, not so you could slap it into a one-time effect."

"Yes, we will need to protect the ritual. As for the ritual diagram, well…" Joe shrugged helplessly. "I could have learned the spell, but I have a chance of failing, and I would need to use it constantly to get it to this level again. Right now, I can use it at an Apprentice level in a ritual, and I might be able to improve it further in the future. Even so, I had to strip away all of the 'active casting' portions so that it didn't blow up in my face when I was converting it. It's rare that it happens, but better safe than sorry. Now the scroll isn't usable for learning to cast it, so is there any chance you can get me another Scroll of Mana Drain?"

"I just told you that scrolls are very difficult to come by… usually we can only get them if we take a major fort relatively intact. Think about how rare *that* is." Havoc decided that Joe had a good point, however, and let the issue go. "So *no*, as far as this is concerned, we do *not* have a duplicate of the scroll. How will this be useful against the Elves?"

"Basically, I set this up, it passively drains the mana from anyone in the area, and hopefully kills the Guardian by destroying the root system." Joe waved at the small model of a fort that Havoc had set up. "In terms of combat utility, as I said, it will drain the mana from the Elves as soon as they cast even a single spell, making them weaker over time and reducing their ability to regenerate their mana. This is perfect for an enclosed space like a fort; a place where we can set the bounds of the ritual without having to worry about our targets making a break for it or escaping. In addition, if they get drained far enough… it will start taking health from them if they try to cast anything. I can tell you from experience, that is *very* distracting."

"I like it. Perfect little surprise." Havoc waved at the little structures that Joe had set around the model, "Even if it will likely only work once. That should be enough to cover what we've done so far. What's the rest of this for?"

"Defensive structures." Joe's face scrunched up in frustration as he studied the figures. "I've been trying to figure out how to replicate your magitech cannons, but I'm running into issues with the power supply and enchantment, and… wait a second… why will it only work *once*?"

"Hmm… oh? You're using a magical attack, right? Any

Elves that survive will be able to parse that and create a counterspell. Big, magical effects only work once against them. Remember, they figured out a way to break what *I* hit them with, and we thought it would keep them away *forever*. Little ritual like this? A known draining spell? We'll be lucky if they don't break it while we are attacking." Havoc's eyes were drawn back to the defensive tower replica. "You said that you were having issues with power supply? Enchantments? Why are you having issues, and when did you have time to look at those enchantment formulae?"

"Basically, I need to study them for a long enough time to make my own versions. As for when I looked at those, a higher constitution means less need for sleep. Combine that with my coffee elemental-" Joe was going to say more, but Havoc cut him off.

"You don't need to do everything yourself, Candidate. If you can figure out how to construct the towers, we can have the enchantments ready to be placed on them. That's easy enough." He paused for a moment to chuckle at Joe's slightly open mouth. "Modularity is a big deal to Dwarves. Things blow up too often *not* to have easy replacements. As for the power supply… what's the issue there?"

Joe nodded in thanks. "That'll work for the enchantments. I appreciate it. As to the power supply, I can't figure out what you are doing with these. As far as I can tell, every time you fire, the cannons should have about a… I'm estimating a twenty percent chance of just… self-destructing? I have no idea what you are doing here to keep that from happening."

"Formations, arrays, and liquid cooling," Havoc replied dryly, getting an eye roll from Joe. "You are correct; they tend to blow up for… just… no reason whatsoever. In all honesty, the Cores that power everything eventually overload. The enchantments don't get damaged, and the towers themselves are not an issue; the actual trouble is the fact that we don't have stable power sources. We use Cores directly, and that means we are taking Quintessence and trying to use it as a mana source. The inefficiency of doing things like this means that, obviously, they overload themselves sometimes."

"The formations that we use are made to protect against this; they are the very reason for modularity. Essentially, we judge when a Core is about to overload and slingshot it a few hundred feet out—hopefully into the ranks of the Elves. In fact, that is partly why they are towers, not just defensive encampments, or things that we can move from place to place easily. Gotta be able to dump the danger. Hopefully on someone else."

Joe stared at Havoc long enough that the Dwarf started reaching for something in his pocket as a nervous tic. The Reductionist didn't really notice, simply struggling to find the words to ask the question that was forming in a non-disparaging way. "Why... in the absolute *abyss* would you use *Cores...* right... you can't convert them to batteries. Okay. I think I found a solution to this problem."

He immediately sprang into action, pulling out a ritual that the Dwarf had never seen before. Joe, *far* too used to working alone, started muttering to himself as if he were using a voice-to-text program. "I could create the ritual directly, using aspects. I'm still going to need to find something that can withstand the energy conversion. Maybe I should forge it myself as well? I wonder what that would look like... will the aspects just directly convert into matter as I am making something? It did in the tutorial... let's see. Havoc, here."

Joe pushed over his notes, "What sort of metal do I need to use in order to resist a meltdown with this kind of power requirement?"

If there was one thing that Havoc understood, it was material compositions. He swept a practiced eye over the equations and data summaries while his right hand left his pocket. "From what I am seeing, you could use regular iron with a core of silver, but that would only last so long as you did not want to use it fairly consistently. High Steel would be a better choice, but..."

Havoc chuckled at a thought before saying it aloud, "if you aren't making it yourself, and you are going to requisition it, I would highly recommend Ghost Silver with a High Steel core instead. You would be able to throw a Core in there up to the Artifact rank and keep it going pretty much permanently. What am I looking at?"

"It's a Ritual of Enchanting, mana-battery specific. I forget the proper name for it off the top of my head," Joe absentmindedly answered the Dwarf. "It allows me to directly enchant Cores and turn them into mana batteries. You know, so that I don't blow myself up when I am making a defensive building?"

"Hey. If we *could* do it, we *would* do it. I could make this, sans the ritual part, but it would take a ton of my time for each individual Core. Is it worth it? Can I really make a difference with just a few?" Havoc shrugged at the diagram carefully, clearly understanding almost all parts of it, but still disregarding it. "Clever workarounds are what we do best. We've also got metal to spare, one of the benefits of mining like we do. You want me to requisition enough metal for you to make this? Does it need to be shaped like this, able to move... hey, when this expands, is it a gyroscope?"

"It is." Joe was completely unsurprised that the Dwarf understood the intention of the metal frame. "It has to be able to enchant a Core from all sides. Also, yes, if you can get someone else to make that, I'll be able to focus on just completing my rituals. If we can delegate this, it would save me a lot of time. Actually... the metals you mentioned? I think I would need a higher blacksmithing level before I could even *heat* them properly."

"It'll take a week or two, but I'll get it done." Havoc lazily glanced to the side as an alarm sounded. His eyes sharpened as he recognized what the klaxon call was shrieking about. "Well, human... looks like you will get a chance to show off your fancy magical device. We just lost a fort. I'll make them hold off on the counterattack and claim the assault in your name. That means that the success is yours, but the failure would be as well. We don't have to worry about that, though, do we?"

"I... t-this is only a prototype! I've done no testing! If we just charge in-" Joe stuttered as Havoc started tapping at something only he could see. He gave Joe a thumbs-up and shut him down with a simple sentence.

"It's done; you have twelve hours to get this ritual up and running."

CHAPTER TWENTY-TWO

The Legion was on the move, and a frantic Joe was jogging along with them and trying to triple-check his diagrams at the same time. Not a single person gave his muttering a second thought; hundreds of Dwarves were marching in time, their heavily armored boots striking stone at a grating frequency. Wherever they went, they created an instant trail. Fields and underbrush were trampled into packed earth; green landscapes churned into mud.

Walking alongside the Legion were huge automatons that released huge bursts of steam with every few steps they took, likely thanks to the 'liquid cooling' Havoc had told Joe about. They were powerful and agile attackers and defenders, and seemed to have their own form of built-in intelligence. Based on their appearance and functions, Joe had a sneaking suspicion that they were based off the juggernauts and defenders of various places of power. For the first time, he started to understand how the Dwarves were able to fight back against the Elves, even though they did not have direct magical support. "Havoc, quick question for you. Why haven't I seen any places dedicated to deities? These look a lot like Juggernauts."

Joe was clearly referencing the metal behemoths, but even so, Havoc made him sweat a little bit before deciding to answer. "Suppose it doesn't hurt to let you know; I'm gonna be shouting about this when we get there, anyway. You have a brain in your head, so you'd figure this all out from context even if I tried to keep it from you. The Elves are a theocracy. There has been a large push to get rid of all the so-called 'minor gods' from this Zone, and we managed to make it happen for our people."

"What do you have against the deities?" Joe was surprised by the mentality. "I'm a Chosen of Tatum; the benefits have been really helpful, and he doesn't pretend to be anything other than a powerful faction leader."

"Success is its own reward," Havoc muttered bitterly, bristling at Joe's words. "Working for them is just a different type of warlock contract, isn't it? Getting power you haven't earned from a powerful entity, just not demons or cursed objects? I prefer our creations. No 'divine energy' powering our defenders and keeping us safe. Water and Cores go in, steam and Elf-death comes out. Much safer, in my opinion."

"Cores again? I thought that was just a mounted cannon issue." Joe shook his head. "How often do *these* go boom?"

"Not as often as you might think." Havoc waved at the closest one just as it was hidden behind a gout of steam. It made for an impressive sight as it stepped forward heavily. "At least, not outside of battle. We put in low-ranked Cores during travel so that there is a smaller chance of overload; then we switch them out with higher-ranked ones when we are ready for them to fight. They move around pretty good like this, but just *wait* until you see them zipping around at full power."

Joe was suitably impressed; he had already been complimenting their abilities in his mind, and this was only travel mode? Havoc broke his train of thought. "Let's go over this one more time. How close do you need to be to take out the Guardian?"

The Reductionist considered his ritual, trying to put together a comprehensive answer for his… mentor.

Ritual of Withering Mana (Apprentice). This ritual is designed to wither not only plants, but anything or anyone that actively uses magic within the area of effect. With enough outside power, this ritual becomes self-sustaining and will only end when mana is no longer supplied to it for a set amount of time.

Area of effect: 50-meter radius.

Mana input required for self-sustainment: 110 mana/second.

"The model shows that the basic forts' walls are at least twelve meters thick." Joe ran the numbers in his head as he explained. "Since these ones are not upgraded, from the interior wall to the other side of the fort—the total diameter—should be only about seventy-five meters. We need to get through the wall and at least halfway to the Guardian in order for this ritual to have the greatest effect. Otherwise, we are just going to be guessing and hoping that the Guardian is closer than the exact center."

"Walk me through that process again; how are we getting through the wall?" Havoc grinned as he lit up a cigar.

"I have a ritual that can tear down any building. Walls are considered buildings." Joe chortled along with Havoc at the thought. "I know that a ritual can only work once against Elves, or at least *you* think so, but I highly doubt that a more advanced fortification wouldn't have someone that could stop the ritual anyway. That's why I'm willing to throw this away against such a small target. Havoc… a lot of this is based on the assumption that they haven't sent any real powerhouses to the border, at least not in the amount of time that they've controlled this territory."

Havoc nodded along with Joe's answer. "Pretty standard practice; takes about a week for an area to get stabilized. If there *is* someone here that is outside the scope of what you can handle, I'll take over."

"You? You'll go directly into combat?" Joe stared at the Dwarf, who was practically a steampunk mad scientist, and shrugged at the toothy smile he got in reply. The man was pretty wild, but Joe had no indication of how powerful he actually could be. He seemed confident, and anyone who knew about him seemed to be slightly on edge, so Joe simply needed to trust that he could get the job done. "How long do we have until we lose all the Dwarves that were sent to respawn?"

"We'll burn that bridge when we cross it." Havoc smoothly moved on even as Joe's eyes twitched at the terrible metaphor. "Get ready to go."

The barrier wall surrounding the Fortress came into view in the distance. The glare coming off of the surface gave Joe pause; weren't the walls supposed to be... stone? Havoc cleared up the confusion in an instant. "Abyss, they're working fast. A hundred reputation says that they are gonna to be doing a big push for the major fort if they've already upgraded their walls to steel-coated stone."

"If it makes you feel better, when I raze a building, we get all of the building materials that went into it." Joe's eyes glittered as brightly as the sun-reflecting wall. "I wonder if we can exploit this? Can we just start getting a huge amount of materials by taking down a wall and having it rebuild within a day?"

Havoc took that happy dream from him immediately, "No, the fortress will only rebuild itself to the basic form if it changes hands. We'll not be able to strike a deal with the Elves to give a fortress back and forth between us. Certainly not for *stone*, which is what it reverts back to if we destroy it. Just focus on doing your job, and be greedy when it won't impact the mission!"

The Dwarf stepped forward and seemed to transform into a different person, reminding Joe that he was not just a crazy old coot in a top hat; he was also a powerful and authoritative Major General. "All troops, prepare for battle! Artificers, exchange automaton Cores from travel... to *combat*! Engineers, set up defensive encampments! Healers, get ready; this is the most rested you get to be all day long!"

The walls of the fortress came closer and closer. Havoc touched his throat and shouted, the words powerfully magnified. "Elven invader scum! You have one minute and five seconds to abandon this post. After that, not a single one of you will survive! The Lord of Slaughter marches against you!"

"Your mother wears a green hat, ya chowderhead!" was the only verbal response. A cloud of arrows took flight, followed closely by various glowing effects. The Legion barked a thundering '*Huoh*'. In an instant, Joe and all of his allies had gained a combat buff.

Anti-Elven Phalanx formation (Small). You are part of a group of at least three hundred people with a unified goal. -5% damage from projectiles. -5% damage from spells. 3% chance to pierce illusions.

"I like *that*," Joe muttered excitedly, his skin tingling from the protections that came into effect. "Is this a raid buff?"

"Nah." Havoc nudged him with his elbow, in the best mood that Joe had ever seen him. "*This* is a raid buff. Time's up, Elves! I am the *Lord of Slaughter*! Legion of Steel, on the order of Candidate Joe, take that fort!"

The Lord of Slaughter stands with you! -30% sensation of pain. 25% bonus damage dealt with melee weapons. 10% reduced damage taken from all sources.

"What... is *that*?" Joe gazed at the buff in awe as all sensation seemed to vanish, the tingling a distant memory. "Is that a spell? An item? How do you *do* that?"

"It's a title, and I'm a noble." Havoc casually pulled a small sphere out of his pocket. "By the way, looks like there *is* a bigshot here, or those Elves woulda messed themselves, not called out an insult. You're gonna have your work cut out for you. Get up to the wall; I'll keep them busy."

The Dwarf held up his hand containing the sphere, and a dense field of power left a shockwave in the air as it traveled upward. As it reached roughly a hundred feet above their heads, a ball of flaming light dropped out of the sky and twisted around... whatever it was that Havoc had just set up. Instead of landing in the center of their formations, the streak of light impacted hundreds of feet away on the open ground.

A mushroom cloud of dust, dirt, and fire crossed the distance between the epicenter and over to where they were standing in less than a second. The Dwarves didn't flinch, instead taking the cover provided to charge forward at the wall ahead. Havoc sneered up at the structure an instant before it was hidden by the debris, locking eyes with an Elf in particularly regal clothing.

"Pah. You always like to open with a meteor, *Francine*. At this point, it's practically boring. We'll fix that soon." Havoc's face was filled with dark joy as he stared at the shining Elf maiden standing in the air above the minor fort. "Can't believe they'd risk you out here, so something big must be about to go down. Still... can't wait to have you back on our side."

CHAPTER TWENTY-THREE

Havoc's battle with his Elven rival wasn't something that Joe could participate in, but frankly he didn't even know that it was happening at this moment. His entire focus was on the walls ahead of him, specifically the need to destroy them utterly. Joe had been on this Zone for almost a couple months now, and he felt like he had accomplished nothing of note.

Now he was running along with a river of shining metal and steam, while fire and dust tried to choke him. The Dwarves were chanting their war cries, the automatons were rumbling alongside them, shaking the ground with every step. Spells and arrows were impacting the ground around them with the force of artillery shells; the blasts made sense for the spells, but Joe could only assume that each individual arrow was heavily enchanted. "This is a *lightly* guarded fortress?"

A ballista bolt tore directly through an automaton, the well-placed projectile managing to damage and expose the internal Core to the open air. The light around the construction dimmed as the Core itself seemed to suck in everything around it. Joe pounded the ground with his feet, trying to get away from the blast zone. However, it seemed that the Dwarves were used to this occurrence. Instead of fleeing, two of the other automatons grabbed at their falling comrade. One stabilized the machine, while the other pulled out the Core mechanism and threw it like a fastball over the wall in front of them. The explosion it generated shook the air, but more importantly, it slowed down the attacks raining down on them for a few precious seconds.

"Shields *up*!" a squad leader called out. Smoothly, gracefully, every Dwarf that was carrying a shield lifted it at the same time. An artillery spell landed directly above them, detonating in the air to inflict the most amount of damage as an attempt to scatter the unit. The well-timed order caused the mana of the attack to be reflected, the powerful wind spell turned into a simple breeze by the dense and interconnected enchantments on the shields.

Joe marveled at the efficient movements the Dwarves were showcasing. Back on Midgard, if he had been able to get his guild to move like this, they would have been untouchable, even during the mass incursion by the other Noble Guilds. Another order rang out. "Let's knock on the door, Legion-style!"

Contrary to what the order actually stated, no one went near the gates of the small fort. Joe wasn't entirely certain if it was because they knew it would be more heavily trapped, or if everyone was truly focused on the fact that he was going to take down the wall. Or, perhaps, this was their standard tactic? The only reason Joe thought that might be the case was the fact that the automaton running alongside them shifted into a low configuration as they reached the metal-clad stone of the walls. Their fists came together, their arms and back locking into the form of a gigantic battering ram.

The feet of the automatons dug into the ground, providing a stabilizing platform. With a discharge of power, one of the newly-conjoined battering rams rocketed forward, retracting almost as quickly once it dug into the wall. A second attack landed at the same spot a moment later as another got into position.

Slam. Bang. Slam.

In just a few seconds, the two battering rams had hit the wall five times, six… and there was already a hole in the defense that was as deep as the length from Joe's knuckles to his elbows. They kept going, and to cover them, the Dwarves pulled out *grenades,* of all things. Joe shook that thought out of his head; they weren't grenades as he knew them. They were round, enchanted consumable items that would release all of their power in one burst to destroy themselves; all so the enemy could not use them against the Dwarves in return. Fire, force, electricity… there were even a few sleeping spells snuck in among the others. Were they back on Midgard, Joe would liken this to throwing fistfuls of gold at the enemy and hoping it held them back just a few seconds longer.

Mainly because the—he was just going to go ahead and call them grenades—were not actually effective weapons against the Elves. If they did do damage, it was only because the affected Elf was unprepared. Every single one of their enemies had some form of shield, shell, barrier… something that stopped the actual damage from getting through to them. The concussive force was merely throwing off their spells, their aim, and possibly pushing the lighter foes off the wall or away from an advantageous attacking position.

It did make Joe wonder what kind of enchanting force the Dwarves could muster. Enchantments, even single-use ones like this, were expensive and hard to create. He knew that much. In fact, he was almost positive that they would get a better weapon if they made a similar thing with alchemy, though Havoc had explicitly stated that there was apparently only one decent Alchemist in the entire Dwarven Oligarchy. Still, if they could make something that would get in the air, it would likely go right through whatever protections the Elves were using to shield themselves from the blasts. He jotted that down in his mental notebook, "I should actually keep that in mind."

Even with all the protective measures that they could put in place, the Dwarves were no match for an entrenched force. Spells were starting to come down thick and fast, flaming oil was being poured over the wall, and large stones were being dropped on them. One of the squad leaders grabbed Joe and shoved him forward as the left automaton was pancaked into the soft earth by a boulder four times larger than Joe. "Magic Bro! Get up there and break that wall, bro! We're all counting on you; we believe in you! You can do it!"

The Dwarves around him cheered as Joe raced forward and embraced the scant protection hugging the wall provided, trying to put as much of his body as possible into the freshly dug hole. A ritual diagram appeared in his hand, the prepared Ritual of Raze that he activated as soon as he could target the wall itself.

Class experience gained (Rituarchitect): 400.

Class experience gained (Reductionist): 200.

Joe sunk mana into the ritual, and the ritual Rings spread out from the points of activation and began moving along the wall. One of the ritual rings settled around Joe's feet, moving with him as he turned and ran back into the protection of a Dwarven phalanx that had coalesced for the express purpose of getting him out of the danger zone. He was hustled to the back lines, the entire time targeted heavily by the defenders. For every few feet that they moved, one or two Dwarves were taken down by the concentrated spells... all so that the ritual would go off without a hitch.

The human could only hope that their sacrifice had been worth it, and that they would be able to take over the fort and resurrect them here within the next few hours. Even though Joe could die and resurrect on his own, he knew for a fact that if he was killed while this ritual was in effect, it would stop working entirely. Until the wall was down, at least enough for them to get over it, Joe's only duty was to stay alive. This gave him some time to wonder why he had gained class experience in two different classes. Looking over the logs gave him plenty of information.

Ritual activated. Ritual falls within the purview of the Rituarchitect class. Calculating experience based on ritual tier and difficulty level of deployment. Ritual of Raze is a Student-ranked ritual for tearing down buildings. Difficulty assessed as 'Medium'. Active combat zone mitigated by defensive forces.

Ritual activated. Ritual has been created using the abilities of a Reductionist. Calculating experience based on crafting tier. Assessed as Student-ranked. Experience allocated: 200.

"I can't tell if it is a blessing or a curse that Reductionist does everything by multiples," Joe sighed as he tried to figure out the math behind his experience gained in the Reductionist class. "This should be easy to deduce. I know that when I made a Novice-ranked ritual, it gave me twenty-five experience. How do I extrapolate two hundred out of twenty-five? Novice times four? Nope, I would only be one hundred. Twenty-five to the fourth? That's... big no. Doubling? Twenty-five, fifty, one hundred, two hundred. That works *this* time, I guess I will have to make more things and see if it is correct *every* time."

+100 DE. Congratulations! Since you have found hidden information without going through a tutorial to learn it, a portion of the cost of the tutorial has been granted to your main deity as Divine Energy! Normally this is not a message you would see, but as you have a quest to gain Divine Energy for your deity, you have been granted access.

"Got experience as a Reductionist for making and activating the ritual, as a Rituarchitect for taking down the wall." Joe read the message and realized that he had not looked at his quest to help out Tatum in months. Still, there was only one actionable piece of information he could take away from it. "I think that notification proved that doubling was correct. Going in the notes!"

CHAPTER TWENTY-FOUR

The Dwarves had made a tactical retreat in preparation of charging, and the Elven defenders were frantically attempting to destroy whatever was obliterating their walls. Since the ritual diagram had literally been buried inside the very walls that it was destroying, they were having no luck disrupting the source. Every few minutes, another ten feet of wall was returned to its component state, forming neat stacks of stone and metal outside of the fortress so that the Elves couldn't even use the material as projectiles.

Ten minutes, half an hour, an hour later... and the call to charge went up. In just a few minutes, the ritual diagram would be exposed, and the Elves would likely destroy it immediately. A stream of silver-clad soldiers charged forward. As soon as they started moving, Joe swore he saw a Dwarf slap a fireball to the side with a Warhammer, once more making Joe wonder what sort of enchantments they had access to.

The human was in the center of the formation, yet even so, he stuck out like a sore thumb due to his height. Joe was at least a feet taller than even the tallest Dwarf, and that fact made him an easy target for Elven aggression. Every inch of ground he trod on was bombarded with concentrated arrows and spells filled with both mana and deadly intent.

With their enemy's fire focused on him—literally, in some cases—another platoon of Dwarves was able to flank the defenders that had lost the height advantage in every way that mattered. Bursts of light came from every Elf in their path as repeated melee strikes popped their shields like soap bubbles. By the time Joe reached the much-diminished wall, the initial path was clear. Joe felt overwhelming relief that this was going so well. "Stage one complete. Gotta get halfway-"

It was then that Joe noticed that the fortress was retreating into the distance. He, along with all the other Dwarves, were sprinting straight at it, but their target never seemed to get any closer. As soon as his conscious mind made that realization, he blinked and felt his eyes clear. Whatever had been overlaying his vision vanished, and he saw that roughly half of the Dwarves that had been running with him were now on the ground, 'running' as if they were in a dream. Their legs were twitching, but they were being trampled by the other members of the Legion that had not been caught by the illusion.

The interior of the Fortress was heavily trapped, showcased by the front ranks of Dwarves tumbling right through the 'ground' and into a spiked pit where they were torn apart by animated plants clearly controlled by Elven magic. One of the platoon leaders pulled out a small compact mirror and crushed it in his hand. He threw the resulting glass powder into the space where the Dwarves had fallen, and the pit became clearly visible. "Mental illusions *and* soft light illusions... watch your step! Make sure you know the ally next to you; the cheeky brats like to use personal glamour while we are watching the environment!"

Half of the Dwarves were punched in the face by their brethren, and were punched back in kind. Anyone who didn't bleed, but instead had stopped the fist with a magical barrier, was immediately beaten into the ground and sent to respawn. Every time, an Elven body was revealed as soon as their health hit zero. Joe was only spared this treatment reluctantly, when he reminded them that he was a human mage.

Every few steps forward set off another attack of some kind; whether it was getting shot at, spells flying toward them, glamoured assassins… but finally, they were almost to the inner walls of the keep. Joe motioned and shouted to the platoon leader to get his attention, "We're already closer than we need to be! Set up a defensive perimeter, and I'll activate the ritual immediately!"

The Dwarves cleared a space directly in front of Joe, and with a simple hip thrust, a huge stone disc slammed onto the ground out of his spatial codpiece. Joe placed a hand on the ritual he had laid out and allowed his mana to flow into it, activating a single glowing ring at a time. It exhausted his mana supply, but soon the ritual was spinning up. Joe had been concerned that he would not be able to catch enough Elves in the area actively casting spells, but he had underestimated the Elves' dedication to protecting their new fortress.

Class experience gained (Reductionist): 100.

The shields that were raised in order to protect him were deflecting fire, snakes of liquid darkness, and beams of light that often managed to go right through the shield and damage the Dwarf holding it. The ground around them began to writhe as the plants in their encirclement were targeted for spells such as Control Roots, Overgrowth, and Plant Detonation. The sapping aspect of the ritual came into full effect, latching onto anyone casting a spell and beginning to drain them. It wasn't powerful enough to take everything they had, but the draw was enough to deplete their mana regeneration capabilities. Most of the Elves didn't even notice… at least not fast enough to do anything about it.

The spells came thick and fast, boiling the air and sending Dwarf after Dwarf to respawn. Then, a strange shift occurred as the spells began to just… peter off. There was a strange lull in the battle as the Elves began to panic and the Dwarves began to chuckle expectantly. Joe looked down, checking the ground for any signs that the ritual was affecting the plant life in the area. Everything appeared to be normal until he swiped his hand across the grass.

The small green blades moved along with his hand, fluttering into the air and leaving a streak of dirt on the ground where he had touched. All of the weeds in the area had lost their root system, and someone had noticed Joe motion. "*Bro!* Dudes and Dudettes! Magic Bro Joe *did* it! *Cha~a~arge!*"

His new moniker was taken up as a war cry, which made Joe's teeth ache, but he wasn't about to tell three-hundred-pound Dwarves coated in two hundred pounds of metal armor and carrying eighty pound weapons to stop... much of anything, really. He was just going to go ahead and let the Legion call him whatever they wanted to; so long as it kept them smiling at him.

The Dwarves flowed around Joe as if he were a rock in the center of a river, realizing that the human's part had been played. He followed along, as there was nothing left for him to do here; the ritual was self-sustaining, and he *really* wanted to see the Guardian of this small fortress. The hard work was being done by his Dwarven comrades, and the only time he saw an Elf was when it was peeking down from a rooftop to send a deadly weapon or effect toward him... or laying on the ground, already sent to respawn.

A thunderous *crash* rang out as Havoc made his glorious return to the battlefield, destroying the portcullis and wooden gate at the front of the small fort with a single attack and a scream of frustration. "*She got away!* Abyss it, *Francine!* Legion! Slaughter *everyone;* tear this place down to the smallest stone! Leave only a single survivor so that they can spread the truth that their Commander happily abandons them when a *single* titled Noble arrives on the scene! They fear *one?* Wait until the Legion marches as a whole!"

Lord of Slaughter II has taken effect! The leader of the enemy troops in the area has abandoned their post. None can stand against you, and few will even try! All original effects increased by 5%. Elven morale has hit its lowest point. There's a 50% chance that your enemies will flee before you!

Joe allowed the Dwarves to go in first, as their physical stats and chances of survival were much higher than his own. He did not even have a proper weapon yet, since Havoc had said they would need to 'visit a friend of his' before they could find something 'just right'. Joe took a moment to check his status sheet, though he knew that not much had changed.

Name: Joe 'Tatum's Chosen Legend' Class: Reductionist
Profession I: Arcanologist (Max)
Profession II: Ritualistic Alchemist (1/20)
Profession III: None
Character Level: 19 Exp: 192,704 Exp to next level: 17,296
Rituarchitect Level: 10 Exp: 45,000 Exp debt: 9,600
Reductionist Level: 0 Exp: 476 Exp to next level: 524
Hit Points: 1,573/1,573
Mana: 1,336/2,152
Mana regen: 44.55/sec
Stamina: 898/1337
Stamina regen: 6.36/sec

Characteristic: Raw score

Strength: 129
Dexterity: 129
Constitution: 125
Intelligence: 138
Wisdom: 118
Dark Charisma: 80
Perception: 118
Luck: 60
Karmic Luck: 8

Joe was pulled from his introspection by a metal-clad hand grabbing his shoulder and spinning him around. He came face-to-face with Havoc; he had never seen the Dwarf have such a red face. He couldn't be sure, but Joe was almost positive that the Dwarf was close to weeping. However, he would never be able to tell behind those thick, reflective goggles the Dwarf wore at all times. Havoc was breathing heavily, gripping on to Joe so tightly that his Exquisite Shell was taking damage and starting to crack.

"If you ever… and I mean *ever*… run into Francine… you kill her, Joe. You do everything you can to kill her *immediately*." Havoc's voice was ragged as he shook his mentee. "You *remember* this, human. If by some terrible chance, those Elves win this war, and Francine is not back by my side… all you will find remaining of me or my research lab is a crater. I *will* be with her, one way or another."

Mandatory Quest gained!

CHAPTER TWENTY-FIVE

Quest gained: Living Revenge of the Fallen. Major General Havoc has issued a mandatory quest for you. He believes that the Elven Mage known as 'Elfreeda' is his lost 'Francine'. Although there is no way for him to prove this, there are characteristics that lead him to believe that slaying this Elf would bring 'Francine' back to the Dwarven Oligarchy. If you encounter the Elf 'Elfreeda' and do not make an attempt on her life, Havoc will have nothing to do with you from that point forward. Rewards: Maximum reputation gained with Havoc. Potential asset for the Dwarven Oligarchy. Failure: Havoc destroys himself and everything that he can take with him.

Joe felt a pounding headache coming on. "I *knew* that I should not have read that quest right now. I abyssal *knew* it, and did it anyway."

Havoc entered the fortress, practically dragging Joe along with him. The Dwarves that had entered beforehand seem to have run into a stalemate, not able to move forward, not able to retreat without being attacked. The Elves were hurling insults as barbed as their arrows, "Ay, it's getting pretty friggin' short out there."

"If you were wicked smart like we ah', you'd go hang out in your own place! We cannot live under the same sky!"

"Look at these chowdaheads; they don't know the immensity of heaven an' earth! Beat it in the amount of time it takes an incense stick to burn, or we're gonna bust ya down!"

"It'll take a *whole* lotta time to describe what I'm going to do to ya, but it's going to happen in an instant, shorty!"

Havoc's goggles reflected the sight in front of him, though Joe could have sworn that the reflection was on fire. "Get those automatons up here! I can't do everything for you, ya lazy metal-shelled layabouts! Are you going to let *walls* stop you?"

"Nah, Major General Bro!"

"I got this; I'm going to use my head!" One of the Dwarves bull-rushed the stone wall and slammed his helmeted head into the structure, leaving a surprisingly large dent but rendering the Dwarf insensible.

For his part, Joe stepped forward and coated the wall with a generous amount of acid. The next Dwarves that slammed themselves bodily into the wall tore out larger chunks, but Havoc's voice made them hold back from continuing. "For celestial's *sake*, at least use your *warhammers!*"

It was a war of attrition at this point; the Elves behind the barricade continued to shape stone and call upon their spells to refill anything that was damaged or destroyed. The Dwarves didn't mind, didn't slow, and cheerfully slammed the reforming wall to pieces. With Joe's ritual still draining the mana from anyone who cast a spell, the wall was being reformed slower... slower. By the time the automatons had arrived on scene, there was already a Dwarf-shaped opening ready and waiting.

The battering rams that the automaton had used to take chunks out of the outer wall had shifted configurations once more. Now they were using pickaxes placed on a gyroscopic circuit. Every hit simply caused another pick to swing up and over, and in mere minutes, the defenses were gone and the Dwarves rolled over the few remaining Elves before confronting the Guardian.

Joe wasn't sure what he should have been expecting, but the interior of the keep itself was filled with plant life, the walls were made of living wood, and the carpet was lush grass. In the center of the building stood a massive sunflower, a plant that the Dwarves all regarded with great hesitation. Joe heard one of the platoon leaders mutter, "Celestial feces, how did they get a Daisy Duke in here in under a day?"

"Isn't that a sunflower?" Joe felt that his question had merit, since it looked exactly how one would expect a sunflower to appear.

"Nah, bro." A mustachioed Dwarf slapped him roughly on the shoulder, getting a slap in return from Joe's shadow. It only made the Dwarf chuckle, which was why Joe kept the retaliatory effect on at all times. "Every fort has a different guardian; the Elves can't figure out how to standardize anything! Whenever we have the fortress, we make our guardian modular, and upgrade it. *They* use different plants every single time, even if they recapture the same fortress! That's a Daisy Duke. Just wait, you'll see."

The Dwarves were taking no chances; the front line pulled out metal rods that Joe had not yet seen in action, activating them all in sequence. Joe flinched backward as flames erupted from the tips of the metal rods, filling the space with an inferno. Enchanted rods as flamethrowers? Though the fire only reached roughly fifteen feet in whatever direction it was pointed, it was enough to ignite any of the plant life that it came in contact with.

The effects of Joe's ritual could also be seen. The initial wave of flames had caused most of the smaller smoldering plants, which had lost their roots, to lift up and flutter through the room, quickly creating a wildfire that spread rapidly. Elves that were hiding within the strange underbrush started to screech, giving away their position to the Legion, who took the initiative to send them to respawn.

As the sweeping fire reached the base of the Guardian, which Joe was *definitely* going to continue calling a sunflower, the top of the plant started to swivel. The flower, which had been facing the sky through the open ceiling, turned to face them. Instead of standard flower fluff, an actual face was glaring out at all of the Dwarves and Joe: golden cat eyes, bright teeth, and a roar generating enough wind force that a few Dwarves had to grab Joe to keep him from lifting off the ground.

"Abyss! It's *not* a Daisy Duke!" Havoc shouted at the others, "Get ready for a serious fight! They didn't use a flower here; they used a *weed*! It's a *Dandy Lion*!"

At that moment, Joe noticed a small top hat nestled away in the flower fluff, or mane, of the Guardian. "It's a weed? That would at least explain why it hasn't fallen over yet; weeds tend to have stronger root systems than standard plants. It *has* to be weakened, though!"

"All units, attack immediately!" The Legion rushed forward, at least fifty Dwarves with bladed weapons dashing to the base of the flower before it could launch a retaliatory strike. They cut its stalk at an angle, as though they were trying to fell a tree. The weed twisted and swiveled, slamming its maw down and crunching through the armor of a target like a hungry child chomping directly into an orange without peeling it. Damage was done to the soft flesh underneath, but the outer shell of armor stopped the vast majority of the bite.

Joe raised his hands and tried to cast a spell, only to feel a massive headache set in immediately. Confused, he looked at his mana and realized that it was completely drained. "*Ahh*! Abyss, that's right! I cast Acid Spray in the area of effect of the ritual!"

Before he could beat himself up too much about losing all his mana to his own ritual, Havoc noticed his plight and grabbed Joe by his robe; chucking him almost all the way back to the entrance of the room with a single toss. The human hit the ground heavily and rolled, his Exquisite Shell taking four hundred and forty-one points of terrain damage, even though half of it was mitigated by his Jumplomancer abilities.

At first, he thought that Havoc had tossed him away because he was useless, but then Joe saw small seed pods floating around the area where he had been standing, as well as hovering over the remaining members of the legion. Just as he noticed them, the room flashed white as each of the pods detonated with the force of a brick of C4. Even as far away as Joe was, he still took three hundred eighty-six points of damage to his shield.

Exquisite Shell: 1519/2346.

Joe wasn't concerned for his own health; he was almost certain that that blast was a last-ditch effort to take out as many Dwarves as possible, and he was positive that it had a significant effect on the Dwarves who were only protected by metal and personal constitution. He wasn't wrong; as his vision returned, Joe spotted twisted bodies laying all over the ground, even if most of them were still alive and kicking. The Dandy Lion was still alive as well, though it was slowly toppling to the side as its root system finally disintegrated to the point that it couldn't hold up the oversized Guardian.

Joe felt something *click* in his mind, and he realized that the ritual had ended due to lack of input. His mana came flowing back to him second by second, and he sprinted to the nearest Dwarf, who clearly had a collapsed lung. Blood-flecked spittle sprayed from the Dwarf's mouth every time she breathed out; her mustache was already matted and sticking to her skin. Even so, she managed to ask Joe questions as he started to treat her. "Is... *hack*... is that a rib poking into my breastplate? It got *cough* through the armor?"

"It did, but don't worry, you're going to be just fine. *Mend!*" The Dwarf managed to hold back a scream as Joe shoved her rib back into her chest, and his spell took the pain almost instantly.

"You better make sure to leave me a scar!" the Dwarf threatened him, not even slightly playing. Even with just a single treatment, she was already breathing and speaking easier. "No one is going to believe that one of my bones was hard enough to cut through Manasteel!"

"It had some help-"

The Dwarf cut him off instantly. "Yo, bro! This is an *accomplishment*; don't be trying to take that from me!"

"If you're well enough to mess around like this, you're going to be just fine." Joe left her there to recover, moving to the next, and treating the most serious cases he could find. He only glanced up from his work once, when cheering broke out near the downed Guardian. Havoc was standing near the enormous plant, and had gripped just below the base of the flower, where the stem was attached. In one powerful heave, he had torn the entire Lion's head off of the weed. The cheering reached a fever pitch and the bloodthirsty Dwarves started hacking up the rest of the Guardian.

Joe shook his head and kept moving among the injured.

"These Dwarves are insane."

CHAPTER TWENTY-SIX

The fort had been captured, the remaining Dwarves healed, and the fallen troops recovered. Standing and watching as the fort was slowly re-grown into a Dwarven-held area, Joe found that he was at something of a loss for what to do next. It seemed that everything in this Zone was geared toward large-scale conflict and group raids. He specialized as a crafter and was effective at single-target or small-party combat. The main questline here was pushing him into Zone-sized issues, and all the things that he had to do just to pay off some of the debt 'he' had accrued was pulling at him.

"I'm caught in the survival trap." Joe sat on the destroyed grass in the keep. The realization came only after he had finished healing as many Dwarves as he could reach before the remainder stabilized themselves or died. No one had seemed overly concerned at the thought of dying, which was a testament to the sheer amount of faith they had in the respawn system. They had been influencing him heavily, and it was only after seeing the brutality and lack of care for their own—or each others'—lives that he had been able to step back and ponder the situation.

"I keep skirting around this issue… it's just so much *easier* to let someone else make the choices." Joe's head was in his hands; luckily, the last of the Dwarven blood had already been erased by his Neutrality Aura. "I need the land I'd get from becoming a Noble, my *guild* needs it. I need to do quests to make this happen, but… this is just… *war*. I don't want to be in a war. I want a giant enclosed space where I can practice my magic. My military days are supposed to be behind me."

"Other people can activate the rituals, so why did I come out here and do it personally?" Joe thought about his circumstances for a short while and tried to face the facts. "It's because I don't feel that others can do the job as well as I can. So what? Am I all-powerful? I could always make a backup if they fail. I don't need to be doing this. I don't need to bull-rush ahead; I need to sit back and make a *plan* instead of just reacting to what comes my way."

"Joe!" Havoc startled the human out of his introspection and motioned toward the fallen Dandy Lion. "Can you do anything with this? Want it before it vanishes?"

Joe eyed the massive Guardian corpse with interest and nodded. "Well. There might be *some* benefit to coming out here."

As he made his way toward the pile of organic material that would become aspects, Joe's eyes flicked to the notifications about his skill increases.

Skill increase: Mend (Journeyman 0). Congratulations on reaching the Journeyman ranks! You've done so much of the healing! Twenty percent more of the healing, for sure! Bonus gained: Maximum Mend. Upon casting Mend, the target can gain bonus health for up to 30 seconds. Maximum health: 50% of maximum health from skill.

Skill increase: Retaliation of Shadows (Journeyman I).

Skill increase: Coalescence (Student V).

Skill increase: Exquisite Shell (Beginner IX)

Joe didn't want to acknowledge how nice those skill increases were. He wanted to maintain his resolution to work on his skills by adventuring and provide for the war effort at a distance. There would *always* be loot; war was synonymous with profit, but the fact of the matter was that he could've gotten the same crafting materials from ore that he could from refined gear. He sighed as he placed his hand on the Dandy Lion and let his mana surge.

Item: Guardian (Elven).
Reduction value: 134 Unique aspects, Special (Anima) 100, 122 Rare aspects, 683 Uncommon aspects, 1,884 Common aspects, 5,684 Damaged aspects, 6,166 Trash aspects.
Reduction cost: 625 mana per second.

After canceling all effects and getting back to full mana, Joe began the process of reducing the Guardian. He lit up with dark lines and had to resist the temptation to activate Essence Cycle. There was no need to blow his head off right now. One second passed, three… Joe sank to a knee just before the fourth second, and the rest of the Guardian rotted away into a pile of unusable mush. He looked over the aspects gained, smiling softly as his mana deprivation headache started to pass. "Got almost ninety-five percent of it!"

Aspects gathered
Trash: 9,491
Damaged: 8,771
Common: 6,341
Uncommon: 4,911
Rare: 1,134
Special: 100 (Zombified). 100 (Anima).
Unique: 326
Artifact: 0
Legendary: 0
Mythical: 0

"Oh? I got *all* the Special?" Joe stared at the Special Anima that he had just gained, but it didn't give him any hints as to why it hadn't depleted by going into standard storage. "Anima has something to do with being anima*ted*, right? As in 'living'?"

"Time for us to go!" Havoc's orders weren't just for Joe; they were for everyone that had joined in on the expedition. "This place is building up, so get out of the way! Your Officers are working on respawns. Make sure we don't miss even a single Dwarf! Look for your friends tomorrow; today, you need to set up a defensive perimeter!"

Joe was already walking away and had decided that he needed to hide from the world for a while. Havoc saw him going, but said nothing to stop him: the human was at least moving in the correct direction for safety. He also knew that seeing combat like this could change people, in ways large and small. The Dwarf mulled it over and decided to give the human some room, but also make sure he would come back. "Joe! When we get back to the city, I will distribute your quest rewards immediately. We'll also go over what you have earned from me, and from this mission."

Though he hesitated, Joe didn't turn back, simply thanking the Dwarf and continuing on his way. As he walked along the demolished path that the Legion had left in its wake, Joe decided that he needed to take a detour. He got off the beaten path and strolled into the forest within the fort's area of influence—which was slowly wilting away—simply to take in all the greenery and colors of the woods.

Meow!

A sharp sound reached his ears, and Joe's eyes slowly turned to spot the source. "Was that a cat? Why would there be a *cat* out here?"

He moved faster, knowing that a domestic animal wouldn't have a chance at survival if they met a monster. "Here, kitty kitty!"

Joe stopped himself from calling out again, knowing that he shouldn't be giving away his position like that. The meow came again, more frantically, along with hissing and the unmistakable sound of spells and combat. Joe burst through the last bit of foliage and ground to a halt. "What the-?"

A cave opening descended at a sharp angle into the ground, almost more of a hole in the forest than anything else. Standing at the edge of the—either hole or sharp-angled tunnel—were several broken and bloody Elves that were fighting a housecat. The Elves were shouting something, but their words were mostly unintelligible to him; only a few insults were in a language that he could understand.

"*Move*, foul thing! When the pheasant and the turkey fight each other, it's the hunter who benefits!" Joe was mostly certain that this insult was actually a plea, but it didn't matter to him. When he saw an arrow pin the cat to the ground, all he could see was red.

"Mend!" Joe's first target was the cat; then he released a Dark Lightning Strike, triggering his bonus. A second bolt came down on their heads, but both bounced off various mana barriers and *jumped* at the Elf that had shot the cat. His tackle took the Elf to the ground, but again did no damage through the shielding. Perceiving that an aggressor was in their midst, the Elves switched targets and bombarded Joe with their various attacks. Joe winced as he realized that he hadn't refreshed his shell before leaving on his own.

"Ow!"

"What was that?"

Exquisite Shell: 921/2346.

Skill increase: Dark Lightning Strike (Apprentice V).

Joe smiled as he tried to choke the Elf; his Retaliation of Shadows was slapping the Elves with each attack they sent his way. The smile vanished when he realized that he was in a bad position. If they could have used their most powerful attacks, he wouldn't have lasted very long at all; luckily, he was rolling around with one of their own. Joe would have been far more surprised if they *hadn't* hesitated, but it would have at least justi-fied the war in his mind.

He wanted so badly to see them as brutal attackers that

cared nothing for friend or foe alike. It would have been so *easy* to hate them if they were monsters through and through.

"Hold! Stop; we need to get Elvis and get out of here. Havoc is almost certainly still looking for survivors." A shining face dominated Joe's field of view, then a telekinetic hand wrapped around him and lifted him into the air. It wasn't attacking him, so the Elf didn't get slapped. Joe stared at the golden skin of the Elf keeping him in the air, activating Intrusive Scan.

Elfwyn Searinglight
Highest stat: Intelligence
Ongoing effect-

Slap.
Exquisite Shell: 683/2346.

Joe's head rocked back as a second mana-made hand was formed and hit him across the face. Elfwyn was staring at him with cold, dead eyes. "How *dare* ya look me in the face, ya friggin' worm? You're a thousand years too early to be lookin' at swan flesh. How did ya find us?"

Joe didn't bother to answer, his eyes searching out the cat that the Elves had been attacking. He sighed in relief when he saw that it was gone; hopefully it had escaped. The Elf hit him again, getting another slap in retaliation but ignoring it. "How did you *find* us? The illusion is in place; can you pierce illusions?"

Exquisite Shell: 410/2346.

"I'm just the advance party. You were right; the whole Legion is looking for anyone that escaped." Joe's dark chuckle riled up the Elves, and they started to panic. All of them except Elfwyn.

"Relax, he just lied. He's alone." Elfwyn's dismissal caused the others to calm down so fast that Joe realized she must have a spell that could detect lies. He started cursing in his mind, and prepared himself to head for respawn. "Let's take him captive, and we'll figure out what he's doing. Human, work with us, and you can switch over to the Elven side. The *winning* side. Ya *gotta* realize that's the truth, right?"

Mental Manipulation Resistance has rejected an attempt to enthrall you!

Joe went limp and read over the notification, apparently giving his eyes the correct 'glazed' look Elfwyn had been looking for. She set him down and started walking, and didn't stop when he began following her. Elfwyn motioned for silence, and the group stepped into the hole in the ground.

As he entered, Joe was reminded of the tunnel that he had once taken to get to the Dwarven training area, but this time, he was paying close attention to what was going on. They walked for a short while, until they came to a branching path. Joe's ears were ringing, and the noise got louder, the closer they came to the intersection. There was obviously something very hidden, or very enchanted, at that juncture. He only knew one thing for sure: he couldn't go in there.

The group paused, looking around nervously as Elfwyn stepped forward and mana started to flow from her into… something. She smiled at Joe and sweetly stated, "Accept the prompt, my pet."

Joe nodded slowly just before a notification appeared.

Elfwyn has started teleportating her party! Would you like to join her? Destination: Elven border fortress 'Daffodil' (minor). Yes / No.

Joe pressed 'no', just as every other Elf vanished in a stream of light that flashed down the tunnel like lightning. Or… "More like data that just entered a fiber optic cable."

He knew it wouldn't take them long to realize that he had not been enthralled, so Joe chased the sound he was hearing and frantically scraped at the rock and earth in his way. "Where is it, where *is* it?"

His hands reached hard stone, and he didn't even realize what he was touching until a notification appeared.

Would you like to capture this travel shrine for Occultatum? Currently, it is dedicated to: Madame Chan- _ERROR_.

Would you like to capture this travel shrine for Occultatum? Currently, it is dedicated to: Gaia. Caution: There is only one Deity with representation in this Zone. Capturing a shrine may have unintended consequences. Yes / No.

Joe mashed 'yes', and his mana began to flow out of him. A perfect circle that formed this section of the tunnel melted away from the stone, and an open book-shaped shrine formed in the center of the tunnel.

Zone Alert! A second Deity has found representation on Zone 2 (Svaltarheim / Alfenheim). Speak to 'Joe Candidate' or find a place of power devoted to Occultatum to join the faction!

You have gained 100-

You have lost 100-

Caution. Several hundred messages detected. Aggregating messages… you have gained 3,167 reputation with the Dwarven Council. Current reputation: 3,314. You have reached 'Friend' status with the Dwarven Council.

You have lost 5,000 reputation with the Elven Nation! Reputation rank 'Blood Feud'. Reputation rank cannot decrease further.

Joe stared at the messages in abject confusion. "What in the *abyss* did I just do?"

CHAPTER TWENTY-SEVEN

"Well, kid, you've gone and done it now." Havoc let out a sigh and a cloud of cigar smoke. They were back at what Joe had just learned was Havoc's family estate in the Capital city of the Dwarves. "You let the abyssal gods loose on the world. We were so *close* to forcing *Gaia* out of here, and then the war would have been our own, instead of a great game for the bored people looking down from Valhalla."

"And now people want to talk to me?" Joe guessed, going off the defeated air Havoc was exuding.

"Yes, people want to *meet* you," The Dwarf spat, kicking a chair so hard that it slammed into the wall and shattered. Extra impressive, since it was wrought iron. "I need to give you your rewards first, so come with me. Also. A letter came for you, and it's sealed with magic. So, here ya go, hurry up and read it."

Joe glanced at the letter, but seeing Havoc's interested leer, decided to open it later. This made Havoc's mood worse, but he kept his cool as they walked, taking some time to go over the changes in Joe's status. "You'll be happy to hear that all outstanding debts are paid. Taking back that fort was almost laughably easy, and since the raid had been authorized in your name, you got all the credit."

This made Joe remember that he would have received all the *blame* if he had failed, but Havoc powered onward. "That's most of what we had to talk about. You're all caught up. Adding an abyssal *god* to the mix changed this up as well, and paid off a chunk of *my* outstanding debts that had been made in your name as well. That's why you likely got a reduced increase if you gained reputation. Oh, double check: you should have gained fifteen thousand experience as well for your double share of the raid."

"That's why I lost five thousand reputation with the Elves but only gained roughly three thousand with the council? You *preemptively* spent it?" Joe made another connection. "Hold on, how much was that *worth*?"

"Reputation is worth whatever you can spend it on," Havoc replied evasively, quickly motioning at a massive forge they were walking toward. "Look, over there! That's where we're going right now. I have a set of gear on backorder at the enchanter's right now, but you need to go in person to get a weapon made."

"Why? Wait, no; stop trying-"

"Clothes can be worn by anyone, but the weapon used is an expression of the wielder," Havoc interjected loudly, drowning out Joe's arguments. "You need to go in there and leave a good impression on McPoundy. Just let him know you're there because I sent you."

"You're not coming in?" Joe quizzed with great surprise. "Why didn't you just *send* me here, then?"

"I'm only coming in if I *have* to come in." Havoc's words were a threat, and made the hair on Joe's arms stand on end, as though the world had just become static-charged. "Go on. Don't you dare accept the tripe he offers you."

Joe looked at Havoc, then the forge, and walked inside with a long-suffering sigh. He had *wanted* Havoc to help him, right? The building was exactly as he had expected it to be: loud, hot, and full of Dwarves that clearly *loved* forging. A smile appeared on his face. "This is what I always expected joining the Dwarves to be like.."

"Good day, human." A voice to the side called Joe's attention, and Joe turned to find a mustachioed Dwarf smiling professionally at him. "I fully understand that the call of this workshop is a siren song to those that wish to improve themselves and better what they can create. I am so sorry to need to be the one to inform you that only the most talented of *Dwarves* get to study under Grandmaster. While your interest is appreciated, if you want a closer look at what we can do, you need to go around and into the shop."

"Hello! So sorry for intruding, but I'm actually supposed to be here. I'm Candidate Joe." Joe nodded to her in a friendly manner, but only got a grunt in reply as she turned away and started hammering a red-hot ingot. "I need to find... a Mr. McPoundy? I have a-"

Exquisite Shell: 1,823/2,346.

"Stupid Bro!" A hammer bounced off Joe's head, and he whirled around, prepared to fight. Someone had just tried to assassinate him! He came face-to-face with a bearded Dwarf with wild eyes. "How *dare* you talk about the Grandmaster with such an irreverent tone! Did you walk in here hoping to prove yourself by making an enemy out of every true Dwarf-"

Joe punched the Dwarf in the face, hitting him with a Dark Lightning Strike at the same time. His enhanced strength stat, combined with the forced rigidness from the electricity coursing through him, sent the Dwarf flying back to land heavily against a standing anvil. Though Joe didn't want to do it, he needed to stoop to this Dwarf's level to prove his point. "How *dare* I? You sound like an Elf! How arrogant can you be, *bro?*"

"Enough." A tired voice carried through the room as the red-faced Dwarf stood and prepared to bull-rush Joe. "He's here for a quest, and *Major General* Havoc—his mentor—is standing outside just *waiting* for a reason to bust in here through the restraining order."

"Restraining...?" Joe looked back at the door. Havoc was

looming in the doorway, straining against a force that was blowing him back, no matter how hard he tried to push in. His eyes were bloodshot, and his face was shifting like someone caught in the wind during a freefall. Straining against the boundary, Havoc's hands grasped either side of the doorframe. Seeing that the fight had ended, Havoc snarled and took a step back, pulling out a cigar and looking away as if what happened inside didn't matter to him. The deep indents in the metal doorway said differently. Joe turned back to face the huge Dwarf that was speaking to him.

"I'm Grandmaster Iron McPoundy; hurry into my private forge. I'm working on a project, but you can't wait out here." McPoundy glared at Havoc and made a rude hand gesture. "That brat would find some excuse to come in and take some kind of petty revenge for the restraining order I got placed on him after his *last* visit!"

Joe walked through the small doorway that hung in the middle of the open space, and the wall sealed itself behind him. To the rest of the people in the forge, the doorway vanished entirely. Joe looked back and was surprised to see the general workshop as if he were looking through a window. "Is this a pocket dimension?"

"That it is." The Dwarf started swinging a hammer instantly, the force of each blow creating a shockwave of pressure and sparks. Joe's shield started deteriorating right away, and his eyes widened when he noted that the Dwarf showed no signs of stopping. "Impress me by surviving while I fix this enchanted sword."

"What's—*clang*—wrong—*clang*—with it?—*clang*." Joe shouted his words in between hammer blows, and to his credit, McPoundy gave him a concise answer.

"I already enchanted it, but I fumbled a few of the formulae, so I'm just trying to pound some kinks out." McPoundy was living up to his name, and Joe was about to ask more questions, when the *sword* spoke.

"I like feet."

Clang.

McPoundy only hit the sword faster. "Quiet, you!"

"Harder."

Clang.

"Ugh." McPoundy sighed in relief as the words stopped coming out of the sword. "Any enchanted item is at least a *little* alive, and they only get more so as they increase in rarity and age. Sometimes forging the enchantment out and starting again is the only way to remove the impurities."

You are receiving tutelage from a Grandmaster! Ritualistic Smithing and Enchanting (general) will increase at a high rate!

Joe's focus narrowed, his entire self immersed in watching the process as McPoundy worked. He activated Essence Cycle and observed as the Dwarf worked seamlessly with flame, liquid metal, and mana. Joe snapped out of his work-induced haze only when he ran out of mana and his Essence Cycle turned off. He healed himself, turned off other passives, let his mana refill, fixed his shell and jumped right back into Essence Cycle.

Eventually, McPoundy smiled at the sword, crushed a Core in his hand, and sprinkled the dust along the new lines of enchantment formulae he had carved into it. Joe saw the skill get activated and gained some small insight into how the dust was formed and used. McPoundy sighed happily and held up his sword. "There. Finished."

Skill increase: Ritualistic Forging (Beginner 0 -> Beginner VI)

Skill increase: Enchanting (general) (Novice IV -> Beginner 0). Congratulations on reaching the Beginner ranks! All Novice enchantments are 20% easier to create! All Beginner enchantments are 10% easier to create. There is a 5% chance of creating Apprentice-ranked enchantments.

Joe looked at the sword in astonishment. It had a glowing title, as McPoundy hadn't bothered to hide any of the information.

Sword of Hamstringing. (Pseudo-Artifact) This sword no longer likes feet; instead, it only likes chopping them off! 50% chance to cleanly cut off a foot when attempting to do so. Created by Grandmaster Iron McPoundy.

"Still, a failure." McPoundy sighed and threw the sword

toward a garbage chute. Joe screeched and jumped to intercept it, slamming into the blade, which went right through his re-weakened shell and cut into him before clattering to the floor. McPoundy turned on the human with death in his eyes, "Lad, you must be utterly brain damaged. Put that in the trash right this *instant!*"

"Grandmaster... *McPoundy.*" Joe healed himself and straightened up, pulling the sword upright until he was standing with it point-down against the stone floor. "I knew I had heard your name before. Please give me a chance to explain."

"Make a case for why I should help you any further than the minimum that Havoc blackmailed me into doing. Tell me why I should bother, now that you are planning on stealing and showing off a sword that I want *disposed* of. You have one sentence, or you're going out."

Joe collected his thoughts into a single, succinct statement. "I destroyed the Shield of Hate."

"That's..." McPoundy, who was already reaching for Joe's neck, paused, stopped, and took a step back. "How do you know about that? How did you... I made that back when I was a mere Master, and I've told *no one* about that... item. You destroyed it? *I* couldn't break it back then. How did you? Prove it."

Joe gazed down at the sword in his hand, and a smile swept across his face. "It would be my absolute *pleasure.*"

CHAPTER TWENTY-EIGHT

The sword finished vanishing into aspects and remnants, and Joe stared at his updated listing with flushed cheeks. He was panting from the heat and mana deprivation, but he was excited. This was the first time he had gained Artifact-ranked aspects!

Aspects gathered
Trash: 10,314
Damaged: 9,902
Common: 7,421
Uncommon: 5,222
Rare: 1,834
Special: 100 (Zombified). 100 (Anima).
Unique: 554
Artifact: 55
Legendary: 0
Mythical: 0

"It wasn't a true Artifact, but it had aspects of it," Joe muttered excitedly. His eyes flashed over the numbers, and his intelligence and wisdom tried to work together to intuit a pattern. No matter how he considered it, it seemed that each item produced different amounts in each aspect.

"What are you whispering about? Numbers of some kind? Were you weighing it or trying to balance the blade? You think an Artifact—or in this case, Pseudo-Artifact—happens by chance alone?" McPoundy snorted even as he secretly admired the ability to erase failures so easily. "Is it *surprising* that my creations are both works of art and also mathematically perfect in all ways?"

Skill gained: Smithing Lore (Beginner II). Your insight and tutelage under a Grandmaster have allowed you to develop a deeper understanding of smithing. There are depths to every craft that are difficult to dive into, but as this skill progresses, you will not just be hitting metal with a hammer; you will be forging. Bonus for reaching the Beginner rank: There is a 100% chance to automatically create a template for the next item you observe being made. (One-time use). You must have the permission of the smith you are watching in order to copy their craft.

That blew Joe away. All the other lore skills had given him passive bonuses to creating things, but this was the first time a lore skill had given him something active. Before Joe could say anything, McPoundy continued. "After seeing this, I suppose I believe you about the shield. I'll tell you now, if that shield somehow resurfaces, you'll have made an enemy for life. As a reward for your help and *silence*… I'll work with you to make a weapon you can use. Something just for you. I'll even let you stand at my side and keep gaining skill levels as I do the work. Yes, I can see you absorbing everything I say or do; you must have some *small* skill in smithing?"

"I'm a Beginner level five in Ritualistic Forging," Joe admitted freely. "While I like the ability to forge, I preferred having a limited skillset that I could level faster."

The Grandmaster winced at Joe's explanation, but not for the reasons Joe was expecting. "That's… I can barely remember the time when a smith under the Expert rank has been allowed to learn from me directly. We need to get you out of here before someone learns about this, gets jealous, and starts a clan war. I'm unsuitable as a master for you, but I can show you a few things as we get your gear together. Here is what your options *were* going to be…"

The Dwarf motioned Joe over to a table that had somehow been… elsewhere… until he wanted it, then had the human inspect the three items that were waiting.

Scythe of Rituals (Unique). This weapon was designed for a Ritualist that has focused on the path of hunting single opponents, and uses a specific ritual to weaken or destroy his enemies. There is space for ritual circles up to the Student rank on the blade, as well as a socket in the handle for Cores to power them. Damage: 2.31x slashing damage, where x = Strength.

Barbed Chain of Taglocks (Unique). This chain was designed for a Ritualist that has focused on applying multiple rituals to groups of enemies. Each barb can contain a ritual circle up to the Beginner rank and includes a wearable bandolier of socket containers for Cores. Damage: 1.83x piercing damage, where x = Dexterity.

Spyglass of Ritual Projection (Unique). This spyglass was designed for a Ritualist that refuses to close on his opponent. It can project an active single-target ritual up to the Journeyman ranks, and includes a 'decorative' handle that can hold Cores to power the ritual. Can be used up to Perception/50 (rounded down) times per day.

"These are all…" Joe was shocked by the Unique weapons in front of him. He almost didn't know what to say.

"Edgy?" McPoundy cut Joe off with a laugh before the human could make the mistake of complimenting how amazing they all were. "I know, I *know*. I made them intentionally insulting and gave them arbitrary limits. Practically trash, all of them. You can blame Havoc for forcing the issue, but it turns out, I actually like ya. So… what can we make for *you*? What would suit you properly and help you grow over time? What is a fitting weapon that you could use, a weapon that has the capability to grow your skill into the Sage ranks?"

Joe tried to shake the image of himself swinging a scythe around in a battlefield out of his head, ignoring the idea of binding a powerful enemy with a chain that sapped all their stats. Apparently these weapons were 'laughable', and he didn't even know *why*. "I... suppose I don't know. I've been a spellcaster my entire time in Eternium, and I have always acquired weapons only for whatever convenience they offered. What would you suggest?"

McPoundy thought for a long moment. "I suggest taking some time to think about it. Don't take something that has a limited use; I can't imagine you will have many chances to ask a Grandmaster to make you a custom weapon."

"What did you mean about having the capability to grow into the Sage ranks?" Joe forced himself to ask the question, though it made him feel foolish when the smith had mentioned it so casually.

"Hmm? Oh... well." The Dwarf grumbled softly as he tried to put his thoughts in order. "Right... again, I am used to working with powerful and *skilled* people. People that have a base of knowledge from experiencing life and working with people as they, too, learn. Listen, everything can *theoretically* reach the Sage ranks. But levels increase with use, practice, and *especially* innovative usage. Why do you think there are legends of a person slashing at the air and killing another person hundreds of feet away? A dimensional slash, if you will?"

Joe shrugged at the question. "I... assume that they would be at least a Grandmaster?"

"No matter how well you can swing a sword..." McPoundy put a hand on Joe's shoulder, "it would never cut someone outside of the blade's reach. Someone who can do something like that has fused their skills and spells in unique ways, and has made something that is their own. The path beyond mastery is almost *never* a single skill. In fact, single-skill Sagehood is the rarest of all paths to succeed upon. It could even be considered the most potent, since there is only a single aspect to study and perfect. The detriment… It will *never* be the most versatile. Put some thought into this choice. I will make something uniquely yours, and even refuse to make it for another, so that you have the best chance at reaching the summit of your chosen path."

With that, Joe was shown out of the forge with stars in his eyes and his head spinning with ideas. "Why couldn't *he* have been chosen as my mentor?"

"So sorry you couldn't get a *good* mentor." Havoc strode next to him, a glower indicating that he had taken offense. "Already told you, kid. It's because someone wants you to fail, and they want it *bad*."

"I still like *you*, Havoc. He was just so charis-" Joe reached out to pat the Dwarf's shoulder, but a razor-tipped spike extended from the Dwarf's shoulder as his hand neared it. Joe jerked his appendage back, barely able to stop himself from touching the poison-leaking spike. As his hand moved away, the spike also sank back into Havoc's clothing. "What was *that?*"

Havoc smirked. "You think I'm stupid enough to let a Ritual user *touch* me? You'll also find that any hair or bodily material that comes off me is instantly incinerated. Now, why do you like my little brother so much?"

"Brother? Wait, are you serious?"

The Dwarf waved behind them, "Yeah, McPoundy. My brother. What's the big deal? He hits metal, and his blades cut real nice. *Ooh.* So what?"

"He took some time to teach me directly." Joe struggled to express his thoughts in a cohesive manner. "Havoc, he's a *Grand-master*, and he's going to teach me while making me a custom weapon."

Havoc took a pull on his cigar, then waved it around as they walked. "So? I'm a Grandmaster thrice over, and you haven't asked me to teach you *jack*."

Joe almost tripped on his own feet as he jerked his head to stare at his suddenly-smug mentor. "Thrice… you have *three* skills at the Grandmaster ranks?"

"Enchanting, Sculpting, and the natural progression of the two: Golemancy." Havoc's mood seemed to turn for the better, though he was still sullen.

"Are you... is this an offer to teach me?" Joe offered the question hopefully, all thoughts of McPoundy having already fled to the darkest portions of his mind.

"I'll tell you a fact." Havoc pushed open the door to his manor. "Becoming my Apprentice is going to be harder than becoming a Noble, and I *refuse* to pass on anything to some random slob. Figure out a way to impress me while I'm stuck with you, and we'll talk some other time."

"What would impressing you look like?" Joe repeated the question twice, but Havoc simply ignored him and let the door swing shut as he vanished into the manor.

CHAPTER TWENTY-NINE

Joe was mentally drained after such an *interesting* day. He went to 'his' room and dropped onto the bed, abruptly launching himself off as the blanket gave a furious yowl and his Exquisite Shell flickered.

Exquisite Shell: 2345/2346.

Health: 1,504/1,574

There was a tiny **slap** as his shadow materialized and hit something, pulling Joe's attention to a small animal that was hissing at him. "A cat? Why is there a *cat* in here?"

His mind flashed back to the cat that the Elves had impaled. After peering closer, Joe determined the cat wasn't the one he had saved earlier. "What breed of cat are you... what I saw earlier was a Birman; you... I have no idea. Query?"

Query succeeded! What a waste of getting an answer from what is essentially a god-like figure, but sure. He's in a good mood today. This cat is an 'Abyssinian' breed. According to information publicly available to humans, it is one of the oldest known breeds and is recognizable by its distinctive features.

Skill increase: Query (Novice III). You can use this once a day. It is a powerful tool. Why are you not? -Tatum.

The message made Joe remember a few other powerful one-a-day skills he had, and he swallowed hard as he realized that he had gone this whole time without increasing his lore skills every day. He kept his eyes on the cat, then glimpsed the scratches on his arms. "How did you get through my shield?"

Combat log:

Joe startles Unknown.

Unknown counter-attacks and deals 1 physical damage, 69 true damage.

His eyebrow lifted, and he stepped away from the cat, which started to calm down. "True damage? Now I have to watch out for *true* damage? What in the world *are* you? Who let you in?"

The cat didn't speak—which was actually surprising in a magical world like this—and simply stared at him, as if telling him to figure it out on his own. Seeing that it wasn't coming after him beyond that first strike, Joe started dealing with other pressing matters. The first order of business was to boost his lore skill and get back to using his beneficial abilities. "Knowledge, Smithing Lore!"

Skill increase: Smithing Lore (Beginner III).

Information on materials and alloys flowed into his mind, stopping sharply after three seconds. Joe held his head as the influx and rapid mana usage created the expected headache. The cat observed all of this calmly, and Joe glared at it. "You know, a *dog* would care if someone were in pain."

Not getting a response, Joe decided that he needed to see someone friendly. "Mate, come on out!"

The coffee elemental bubbled into existence on his arm, steaming happily. Joe held out a hand, willing the shadops to… "An~n~nd I forgot that I can't make cups out of shadows anymore. It's been almost two months; why is that still my go-to?"

Joe searched through his ring and pulled out a small teacup, grimacing as he noted a large chip in it. "How did I break this?"

Everything was harder before coffee. Joe had Mate make a small but potent cup of espresso and took a long minute to savor it. He motioned at the cat with the broken cup. "Want some coffee, cat?"

Mate then noticed the cat as well. It bubbled and steamed, and the cat hissed. Mate hissed like a kettle, then vanished into Joe's sleeve once more. Joe stood and slowly backed away from the cat, "What are you, *really*? I don't trust anything that my coffee doesn't."

At that moment, the letter that Joe had gotten earlier in the day somehow 'fell out' of his ring. That had never happened before... and shouldn't have been *able* to happen. A spatial device was a sealed space. There had to be some shenanigans afoot. Trying to keep an eye on the cat, Joe opened the letter and read over the information, a frown growing on his face the entire time.

To whom it may concern,

As thanks for your self-sacrificial gesture of saving me, I have applied to have you honored by our royal family. What I did not expect was that you have proven yourself worthy of an audience from the Queen herself. Please prepare yourself, as she will be arriving shortly. I recommend having a feast prepared, and a place of honor for her Majesty to take her ease.

My deepest thanks are yours, for saving me from the thoughtless Elves that made an attempt on my life.

Your biggest fan, Cindy Clawford.

"The Queen?" Joe looked up at the cat, who was currently sitting in a regal pose on his bed. "You're a Queen? Of what? Cindy *Claw*... nope. *Nope*. What's going on?"

The cat released a light sigh and jumped off the bed toward him. Between one breath and another, the small animal shifted into a small person, roughly the size and height of a nine-year-old human. "We are Queen CleoCatra, and we will forgive this im*purr*tinence only because we saw you unseal the letter; we understand that you could not have expected our arrival. We suppose that one of the risks of being a hidden race… is that no one knows who or what we are. Joe, we are here at the behest of one of our subjects, a celebrity among us, to judge you for rewards."

"I *really* have no interest in-" Joe was cut off by a sharp gesture from the tiny woman, who looked very human, if you ignored that her ears were faintly furry and her hands extended claws when she was upset.

"It is not up to *you* if we decide to reward you or not," Cleo-Catra hissed at him. "You have saved one of our people, and now ask for no reward? You have met our people before, and they even assisted you to make an intelligent choice that impacts you today. Why do you dislike us so much that you would happily reduce our Karmic Luck to such a degree?"

"Wait, you know what Karmic Luck does?" Joe almost took a step forward, but a lazy slash from a clawed hand forced him back a step.

"There are *few* things we have no knowledge of. We took the day to follow you and study your struggles, and we have decided upon helping you in what you lack most. Therefore, we will take steps to rectify this weakness on your behalf." CleoCatra's eyes shone a deep blue and held a surprising depth of wisdom. "You may ask your questions."

"I…" Joe was surprised to find that he had numerous questions. "You said you were a *hidden* race? What does that mean? Also, are you speaking about yourself using the royal 'we', or is there a group of stray cats following me around?"

Reputation with Occutatum has increased by 500! Congratulations on finding a hidden race! Current reputation: 4,042. Reputation rank: Ally.

"I speak for my people as a whole." Cleo stated directly, if somewhat snippily. Joe decided not to call her people 'strays' again. "We refused to enter the war between sentient beings. We will not be a Unified, nor a Shattered, race. This has benefits, as well as certain… downsides; the main one being that *all* the others in the conflict see us as weak for our neutrality. We are not welcome in most populations, if they find my people among them. Hence, we are loath to leave our best forms and take on the appearance of others."

"Why did you refuse to enter the fight?" The question seemed to jump from his mouth on its own.

CleoCatra took it in stride, letting out a yawn that exposed too many sharp teeth for her to be mistaken as a human. "Too much effort. None of our people want to create or go to war. Why should we, when others willingly become our servants as soon as we appear?"

Joe nodded at this explanation, since it was well known that becoming a pet to another group meant that your progress would stop, for one reason or another. "If you don't mind me asking... what are your people called?"

"We..." CleoCatra posed proudly, "are the *Nyanderthals!*"

Keeping himself from laughing was a harder challenge than fighting the Zombie Dwarves in the landfill had been. Joe managed to only cough and wipe his watering eyes. "I... thank you for your offer of help. Oh, you mentioned that I had met your people before?"

"Once. You were looking for inspiration and found some of our people playing in their human forms. You joined in, and they offered you some chalk in thanks for your participation." CleoCatra saw that Joe didn't remember, but she didn't seem to mind. "You likely mistook them for children, if that helps."

"Not... no, not really. Sorry." Joe decided to get to the point he was most interested in. "You said that you found what I 'lack most' and were going to help me? What exactly did you mean by that?"

"Well, human that has been blessed by the gods from your first moment here..." CleoCatra's eyes flashed alarmingly. "We find that what you lack most is the ability to properly deal with, and learn from, *failure*. So, we have come here to save you by forcing the issue. You can thank us later."

CHAPTER THIRTY

"I mean..." Joe stared at the cat queen with total befuddlement. "Can we... not? I like not having extra failure to deal with. I'd like to go back to the point where I was saying 'no' to the reward, please?"

"You do not understand our decree. You think of it as a threat?" Cleo ignored him and pulled out documents from a storage device, handing them over and decisively stating, "No. We have decided that we are going to help you with these problems. These are an act of gratitude for rescuing our subject. As payment for our continuous services, we will require food and warm areas for sleeping, perhaps belly rubs if you have been extra good."

With that final assertion, she hopped back toward the bed, a cat once more. No matter what Joe stated, asked, or demanded, she refused to leave her cat form again. "I still have questions, you frustrating feline!"

"Why are you yelling at a cat?" Havoc appeared in the opening of Joe's door, and was watching the interaction with amusement. "They're domesticated monsters from another Zone. *Pets*. They don't speak."

"This *cat-*"

Hiss.

The noise made Joe realize that he was about to let the cat out of the bag, so to speak. "This cat… won't move off my bed!"

"Are you trying to go to sleep? What's the issue? Also, we have that meeting with the third Princess; you don't have time for bed." Havoc noticed the paper in Joe's hand, scooting closer instantly. He could tell that there was something magical going on here. "Was that your letter? What is it… a template?"

Joe looked at the paper that CleoCatra had thrust into his hands for the first time, noting that there was indeed a weapon template on it. However, no matter how he studied it, the details made no sense. "Yeah… I got this as a quest reward."

Havoc took the paper and looked it over, frowning and handing it back after a long moment. "Pah. Blacksmith stuff, there. You're gonna need to take it to McPoundy if you want to make heads or tails of it. I can tell you all about the enchantments it needs, of course, but they are all out of context. Why would this need to expand to such a degree that it requires spatial enchantments? Hmm. That aside, are you ready to go see the Princess?"

"Sure, how far away-"

"She's downstairs." Havoc looked at Joe and grumbled, "You look as good as a human can reasonably be expected to look, and at least you have no smell. At all. Not sure how you manage it, but it's nice. Most of your people smell like leftovers, cheese, and onions."

Joe ignored the jab and glanced down at his simple gear. He was dressed in a simple shirt, shoes, and pants; his codpiece underneath, and his Robe of Liquid Darkness over it all. As he didn't currently own different clothes, Havoc was correct in thinking that he looked as good as he currently could. He followed the stomping Dwarf down the hall and into the reception area.

Various guards surrounded a Dwarf with braided golden

hair and matching mustache, the first Dwarf Joe had encountered that had hair on her head. She looked over Joe in confusion, then turned to Havoc. "It's a... *male* of its species, is it not? How can they tell?"

"Mostly guesswork and bone structure, Princess Dawnesha Embertank." Havoc was clearly providing Joe with the Princess' name discreetly, which Joe appreciated. "He's alone here, as well; most other humans are in training or active Legion members. Those that didn't join the Elves, that is."

"Did you not *prepare* him for this meeting?" The Princess inspected Joe critically, noting that his eyebrow was starting to twitch. "He looks like a vagabond."

"For your *information-*"

Joe was cut off by Havoc smoothly. "Ah, he just returned from a meeting with Grandmaster McPoundy, and we had no time to find a tailor. Besides that, he has a misguided sense of honor, not wanting to requisition clothing as a Candidate."

"Did he not just come into a significant amount of reputation? He should have had plenty available for a rush order..." The Princess sighed and waved away that line of thought. "Human, do you need another human party member to feel more at ease here? I am looking to join your... faction... and bring my followers under its banner. What would ease that transition?"

"He has never requested human companionship, my Lady," Havoc joined in once more. "He is entirely focused on his craft, advancing himself, and progressing the Dwarven Oligarchy. A true believer of meritocracy."

"So it's just a *coincidence* that, until now, he's been poor *and* miserably lonely?" The Princess scoffed at her own comment. "I've heard what it is like to be under your thumb, Havoc. I want to hear it from him."

"Um." Joe wasn't sure how to reply to this fast-paced conversation.

"I will have you know," Havoc snarled, causing the guards in the room to tense up, "he's not alone here because of *me*.

Look: no hair, beard, or mustache. Completely hairless. He's alone because he's *hideous*."

"Please stop trying to stand up for me." Joe coughed violently to draw their attention back to himself. "Lady… Embertank, as far as I can tell, you are only here to join under my deity? I will certainly make this happen, but… why? Haven't your people been fighting to remove the influence of the deities from this Zone?"

She narrowed her eyes at Havoc, as if something had just been confirmed. "Only a certain *splinter group* has focused on that. The vast *majority* of us enjoyed the additional benefits and powers that those that had gone before could afford us. I'll tell you now, as a show of my commitment to this cause, I have already begun the construction of a Grand Temple in this city. In addition, I will ensure that at least ten more are completed in the nearest surrounding major forts. From there, depending on the followers and abilities granted, we will expand further."

Joe gulped at the thought of the amount of Divine Energy that would produce for Tatum on a daily basis. "You have ways to make them?"

"My people are known as the greatest stoneworkers, and some of the best are even Grandmaster Sculptors." Her glare only darkened at Havoc, who responded by lighting up a cigar. A tiny fan popped up out of it and blew the smoke into her face. Scowling, she ignored the pungent fog and continued speaking to Joe. "The first Grand Temple will be done within the day, though the others will take at least a week each, estimated to finish in under two months. The delay is due to travel time for building materials; I hope you understand."

"That… will certainly not be a problem. If you don't mind me asking," Joe struggled over how to phrase his next question. "If you can make all these shrines and temples, Grand ones even, why haven't you until now?"

The Princess nodded, as if expecting this line of inquiry. "It's fairly simple. There was no way to class change into a cleric or any other derivative of a holy class. Without the places of power being dedicated to someone, there was no way to *make* new classes or dedicate these places. That meant that there was no reason for the structures to exist; they would have just become strategic resources for the Elves if a fortress was overtaken."

"I see." Joe glanced around, realizing that everyone was watching him expectantly. "What is it that I can do for you... currently?"

With barely a moment's hesitation, Dawnesha kneeled down and bowed her head. "I humbly request to be made into the High Priestess of your deity for this Zone."

"So... very *humble* of you, indeed." Joe blinked a few times and released a great sigh. "Why?"

"I am the third Princess." Dawnesha remained in the same position, making Joe somewhat uncomfortable. "I cannot become the ruler, as that role is reserved for the first Princess. The second Princess has been charged with our military might. The position of third Princess has long been designated as a holy position, and I have been stymied my entire life. It has put an incredible pressure on our society, and my sisters are concerned that I will attempt to infringe on their... influence."

"That's why you would put so much into this effort. You're attempting to avoid a civil war... but I thought this was an Oligarchy? Beyond that, do you even know which deity I am the Champion of?" Joe already knew that he was going to try to make her the High Priestess. Having control and direct access to the entire theological aspect of a society was too good of a chance to pass up, and she was going to bring in just... *so much.*

"Occultatum," she answered easily, unstrained even though she had remained in the position for over a minute at this point. "I read the message, just like everyone else. As to the Oligarchy, I am a clan princess. Though our ways have changed over the millenia, the great houses have not given up all of their traditions."

"Are you aware of Occultatum's domain? The rewards and

detriments for joining with him?" Joe's questioning was half-hearted, and it showed.

"Does it matter?" She gazed up with her eyes shining, full of ambition. "Whatever it is, there *have* to be benefits. Anything is better than letting only the Elves have divine support. Imagine the Legion becoming supported by *clerics* again."

"The healing spells *are* pretty potent," Joe admitted easily, his final resistance shattered. "Okay. I'm sold. I'll ask; the worst he can do is say 'no'. Tatum, Dawnesha Embertank wants to join your faction. Pretty sure you've heard her offer, what do you think?"

Query has already been used today! Cooldown: 21:34.

"Oh."

"*O-oh?*" Dawnesha's eyes filled with fear when no notifications appeared. Her lips quivered, fearing the rejection she was sure Joe had just gotten. "Wh-why not?"

"It's not a 'no'," Joe assured her, causing her to take a deep breath of relief and pull on her mustache with anxiety. "We can try again tomorrow, in about twenty-one hours. I already used up my ability to… convert things today. With the… shrine. Yes."

"Oh… that makes sense." She stood and smiled weakly at him. "Then shall we meet at the Grand Temple on the morrow and hold a ceremony for the conversion of both at the same time?"

"That sounds… great." Joe nodded furiously. At the sight of her expressive and hopeful face, there was no way that Joe was about to tell her 'I can't make you into a priestess and fulfill your lifelong dream… because I already used my power today so I could ask about the breed of my new cat'.

CHAPTER THIRTY-ONE

Joe stared at the new clothes on his bed as he heaved for breath. Steam was coming off his skin, and he was currently regretting telling Havoc that his characteristic training had stagnated. The Dwarf's response had been a kindly smile and a curt 'walk to your room'. Then he had left, striding quickly out of Joe's field of view.

The human hadn't expected that as soon as he turned away from the Dwarf, a... *golem* of some kind would attach itself to his body. His limbs were bound to each other, and it was trying to force him into a fetal position. Joe had needed to use every ounce of physicality he had just to remain standing. Walking up the stairs and down the hall to his room had taken the entire training time required for the day—four hours and three minutes, thanks to his Artisan Body—and as soon as the golem sensed that he had gained his points... the constriction ended.

Characteristic training complete! Strength, Dexterity, and Constitution +2!

Skill increase: Artisan Body (Beginner II).

"Couldn't I have gotten that skill increase *during* training? Oh *yay*, I can get two points per day, and that little monster knows it." Try as he might, he couldn't find the golem after his training ended. All that remained was his moist human self that was steaming mad, as well as just plain steaming. "It's still on me, waiting until tomorrow, isn't it?"

"Meow." CleoCatra didn't seem to mind his suffering. A hiss announced her desire for food, but when the human set some in front of her, she sniffed it and walked to a different spot.

Joe ignored the cat and donned the tailor-fitted clothing that had been procured since the meeting yesterday, once again pleased with the self-cleaning function of his Neutrality Aura. The pure white monster-silk shirt and pants were... weird. Comfy, though. New shoes and socks completed the ensemble, with his usual black robe to top it all off. The new clothing increased charisma by ten percent when worn as a whole set, with no other benefits aside from not getting arrested for indecency, but they still made Joe feel strange. "Time to go and get a huge jump forward in bringing Tatum back."

The nice thing about a golem wrestling him for an hour was that his mind had been taken off the very *public* event that he was supposed to be performing at in just a short while. That was gone, so all he could do at this point was power on. Clean, trained, and rested, Joe started walking. "Mate, I'm gonna need a strong brew."

The coffee elemental swirled around and up his arm, and Joe searched for a coffee cup to put him in. Sadly, there wasn't one remaining in his ring, so Joe ended up drinking coffee from a bowl. While *he* was fine with this, it seemed to upset Mate a little, showcased by the overtly bitter flavor. The Reductionist studied the little brown bean-eyes that were staring at him pleadingly, and Joe knew that something had to be done. "I'll work on getting you a proper cup sometime soon, okay? There's a lot going on, Mate!"

Blub. Mate... agreed? Or perhaps Joe was simply ascribing emotions and thoughts to it, but at least the small elemental went back into his sleeve without an issue. Either way, Joe did not have enough time to deal with every single problem that cropped up. Wearing his black-over-white clothing, he made his way up the slopes and closer to the center of the city. The capital was situated so that every new District had a wall protecting the inner portion. At the very center was the keep, a single building that was meant as the last refuge of the Dwarven nation, which was large enough to hold all of them, if the need arose.

The next ring down contained the noble quarters, including the Royal Palace and council chambers. After that was the Religious District, which had been empty for so long that it had been converted into parks and green space. Joe was on his way there now, but he had to pass through the Living District, where he was currently, as well as the Tradesman District. It was going to be a slow trip, since he needed to hoof it on foot.

Mounts were not really a thing, since most people could run as fast as horses after they had reached a certain level of strength and dexterity. Using animals or automations had just never really come up. No one was going to sacrifice their training time for comfort, not when their entire worldview revolved around war.

The roads within the city were delineated pretty clearly. 'Messenger', 'high speed', 'jogging', and finally the last one, the 'walking' lane, which Joe entered. Since there were very few restrictions on spatial devices in this Zone, he didn't need to watch out for carts, wagons, or any other vehicles. However, he *did* need to watch out for the Dwarves moving at 'walking' speed.

"Slow Bro!" A bearded Dwarf that Joe could barely see laughed at him.

Another zipped past him, shouting, "Bald Bro! Get in the children's lane if you can't keep up!"

Frankly, Joe had not even noticed the children's lane, but even now that he had, he wasn't about to let go of his dignity so easily. He started running, letting mana flow to his feet as he switched over to skipping. That was when things got weird.

The Dwarves that had been zipping past him just a moment

ago seemed to pause as his speed reached theirs, and then Joe was flying past them. Seeing this as a challenge, the Dwarves abandoned the walking lane and began chasing after him, taking the jogging lane and sprinting as hard as they could. It appeared that the lanes were meant more as 'top speed' lanes, because most of the hairy people that were moving along the running lane were still going much faster than the sprinting Dwarves in the jogging lane.

"What is going *on* right now?" Joe was less concerned about the other people; instead his mind was entirely focused on analyzing what had changed. "There's no reason I should be this fast. I've been actively adding my jump to everything since I first found out that I could. I'm skipping and supplying mana... but I've done this practically...! Is it... oh!"

That was when Joe remembered his massive increases in his physical characteristics. "*Jump* is modified by strength and dexterity! This is *awesome*!"

Seeing as he was nowhere near the fastest person on the road, he had no good frame of reference for how fast he was going. Still, Joe approached the Religious District far sooner than he had expected. He had planned to ask directions from there, but a solitary building was visible in the green space between the defensive walls. Just as he was debating getting off the road, he saw that there was an exit onto a street that had clearly been created recently. *Jumping* over the other lanes of traffic, he landed on the fresh cobblestone and sprinted toward the Grand Temple.

Before long, he approached the large crowd, but they parted when they sighted the expected bald Human coming toward them; Princess Embertank had prepared them well for his arrival. Joe slowed down and attempted to appear grand and serious for the occasion, but he couldn't stop a huge grin from spreading his face. This was his ticket back into having a deity on his side again! The Princess was flushed, her mustache quivering with excitement and nervousness. She swallowed deeply, then curtsied lightly toward Joe. "Is everything ready?"

Joe checked his cooldown timer for Query, letting the last few seconds tick away before nodding. "Ready."

"Then let's go inside." She led the way into the Grand Temple, the huge doors swinging open with a simple gesture from her. The crowd followed behind them, strangely silent, at least for Dwarves. There were only a half-dozen belching tournaments, three farting competitions, two fist fights, and one count of drunken warbling.

The inside of the temple was strangely plain. Huge marble columns supported the ceiling, and everything was accented by alternating black and white colorations. Joe raised an eyebrow and gestured at the surroundings, and the princess knew what he meant immediately. "This is the standard, basic template for a Grand Temple. We add nothing, simply providing the raw materials and space for whatever deity is going to control it."

That made sense to him, so Joe questioned no further. They walked up to the blank slab of an altar together, and he turned to face the Princess. "Ready?"

"For literally my entire life," she replied with a fire burning in her eyes.

"Okay then." Joe took a deep breath and intentionally verbally activated Query. "Tatum, this Princess wants to be your High Priestess here. You in?"

Query successful! Tatum groans at your lack of proper ceremony, but has excitedly accepted.

New achievement: 'You join me, I make you OP.' You have converted your first follower on a new Zone, and they have become the High Priestess! Your reputation with Occultatum has increased by 1,000! New reputation Rank: Extended Family. You have gained 10,000 experience!

You have regained level 20! Cleric spell 'Planar Shift' is once more available for use!

"Abyss, I didn't even see that it had been blocked," Joe muttered, quickly coming back to the present as the princess was coated in a column of darkness. It wore off a moment later, and she graced at him with a bright smile under her fluffy mustache. The only physical change that he could see was that her eye color now shifted slowly between a deep blue and a mysterious black.

"I finally... *finally* will be able to fulfill my life goals. *Thank you, Joe*." Before she could get all teary-eyed, Joe nodded stiffly and smiled.

"Congratulations, princess." He put his hand on the altar and motioned for her to do the same. "Sorry, but this next part is gonna suck."

"Success is its own reward, and even if it is not perfect, I am just happy to advance," the newly-minted High Priestess stated boldly.

Would you like to capture this Grand Temple for Occultatum? Yes/ No.

"That's great, Princess. Just remember that." Joe accepted the prompt, and both winced as their bodies began leaking power.

CHAPTER THIRTY-TWO

The Princess Priestess had a surprisingly large pool of mana, which Joe realized was likely due to her lifestyle as a Noble since birth. Between political intrigue and her life's mission of becoming a priestess, she had likely focused all of her spare time on increasing her intelligence and wisdom.

Even still, the two of them alone did not have the power to convert the entire Grand Temple. As their power swirled out of them, other Dwarves stepped forward from the audience and lent their own energies. Soon, the entire structure had been converted. As an unexpected bonus, as soon as the temple was complete, the entire Pantheon that Joe had formed in the previous Zone became represented here.

One of the altars blazed with red fire, representing Tommulus, Greater Deity of Fire and Berserkers. One of the altars sprouted into a woman-shaped tree, as Spriggan, the Minor Deity of Nature and Fertility, took shape. Finally, an off-tune bugle blast heralded the arrival of Hansel, the Greater Deity of Bards, Teachers, and Political Assassins.

A stunned silence fell as hundreds of Dwarves saw the

choices that were suddenly before them. All sounds had ceased, beyond Joe and Princess Embertank's labored breathing.

"Wait a blasted minute… we wanted *one*, and *four* pop in! These deities are multiplying like cockroaches!" A typical Dwarven grumble eased the tension and made the group chuckle. Joe sat down and listened to the conversations around him as he skimmed through the notifications that had appeared.

You have earned a reward from the continuous quest: Reclamation of the lost.

Critical success! You have captured the only Grand Temple in the Dwarven territories, and your Pantheon currently has the majority of all Dwarven parishioners!

Buff applied: Faction Lead I. As you are the champion of the dominant faction in this Zone, you have been granted additional power to fulfill your duties! Total mana +1,000! This buff can increase in power. Please note that the current Zone is considered as two separate Zones until the war has been decided!

Joe groaned in pain as his body swelled up like an over-inflated balloon. For a long moment, it appeared as if he was having a body-wide allergic reaction. Then the new influx of mana found the proper channels within his body and seamlessly integrated. He glanced over at Princess Embertank—no, *High Priestess* Embertank—and knew that she was undergoing some changes as well. "Increased stats, or a direct addition to your power?"

"Stats." She groaned as she held her head. "And so *many* quests! I'm also back to level one."

"What? Why would that happen?" Joe scrambled to his feet just in case he needed to make a quick getaway. "I've never heard of that-"

"Oh, calm down. It was my choice." She stood on shaky legs as she held her head. "It's not like I lost all of my stats or anything, but I had to give up all of my previous class skills and abilities in order to become the High Priestess. It's going to take a lot of work to become powerful again, but at least I am not *really* starting from zero. I've never heard of a level one person

having over a hundred and fifty points in each of their characteristics."

"That's something, I suppose," Joe carefully stated, still
uncertain of what to do next.

"I also inherited the 'Paying a Great Debt' quest. I'm sure
you'll be happy to know that we should be able to finish that
quest off in about one-and-a-half to two weeks." The High
Priestess' assertion made Joe freeze once more, and he hurriedly
pulled up the quest.

*Paying a Great Debt. By choosing to remain faithful to your chosen deity,
you have agreed to take on their debt. Find a way to pay off
13,000,000 Divine Energy. Current DE generated:
1,536,750/13,000,000.*
Altar: 11
Shrine: 22
Temple(small): 1
Temple(mid-sized): 3
Temple(grand): 2
Champion defeated: 3
Followers: 310

Joe confirmed that he had only gained roughly eleven
percent of the total Divine Energy he needed, then looked at
the Dwarf for an explanation. She waved around the room, and
smiled brightly. "I have roughly a quarter of a million followers
that will be joining this pantheon over the next few weeks. After
they have all converted, since followers generate twenty-five DE
per day, we are looking at six and a quarter million DE per day.
Expect this quest to be completed likely earlier than I even
mentioned."

"So many…" Joe whispered in a shaky voice. "I had
expected it to be *years*."

"This will be me doing my duty, but you are always
welcome to grant me bonuses for a job well done." She winked
at him, her charming disposition slightly offset by the glorious

mustache she was sporting. "Now, if you don't mind, I have so very much work to do."

Joe nodded and walked away as she began to open the altars for conversion. The Dwarves that had been waiting passed along information they found, and soon there were four lines for each altar. Unsurprisingly, the longest line was for Tatum, and the shortest was for the Spriggan. There were not many Dwarves that wanted to empower nature when their opponents were followers of Gaia. Before he left, he swung by the altar just to double-check that there wasn't anything waiting for him.

Laying his hands on the altar, the Reductionist felt only a warm glow of happiness and acceptance. He had quite a while to go before he was able to get a new cleric ability or spell, since he had only just regained access to level twenty. Joe patted the book-shaped altar, looked around at the newly-made Juggernauts and small Tree Ents that would protect this place, and decided to leave.

He trekked along the pristine new road until he found his way back to the main street, and further into the Tradesman District. Entering the forge, Joe found most of the Dwarves staring at him with absolutely gloomy smiles pasted on their faces. A few started walking toward him, and one held out a hand. "Candidate! It would be a true joy for me to be able to teach you about seniority and-"

Grandmaster McPoundy's door popped into existence and the Dwarf himself stepped out. "Joe, it is good that you are here! Today, you choose the item that you receive as a Candidate, and our next encounter will only be in order for me to hand over that item after it is made. Get in here so that we can get this over with."

Joe heard what he was saying, but it sounded like a prepared speech, stilted and wrong. Before he said anything, he joined the Grandmaster in his small pocket dimension, then let his words fly. "What was that all about?"

McPoundy wiped his forehead with a cloth and frowned at Joe disdainfully. "Didn't I tell you that there would be blowback from allowing you access to this place? Those brats out there want to know if I am training you secretly, instead of them. They have worked—and paid—for the privilege. At this level, that can't be negated just because a Candidate has arrived."

"Hence the clear explanation of how many more times I would be able to come here without causing an issue." Even though Joe understood the logic, he was disappointed. He had been hoping that he would be able to train his ritualistic forging with the Grandmaster, perhaps becoming awesome at it. "I see."

"Well, I told you not to come back until you were ready for me to make you a weapon. What did you decide on?" The Dwarf got straight to the point, either not understanding or not caring that Joe was disappointed. Probably the latter. "Something like what I mentioned before, or did you-"

The Dwarf paused as the weapon template appeared in Joe's hands. He took it and started examining it, his own fingers beginning to tremble as he unfolded the paper over and over. He shook it once, and the paper transformed into a three-dimensional diagram of a complexity that reminded Joe of a step-by-step guide for making a nuclear missile from earth. "Where did you *get* this? This is…"

McPoundy ran his hands over the shimmering document. "You have no idea, do you?"

"Not a clue," Joe admitted cheerfully. "Didn't even know it unfolded; I thought it was a single page of paper."

The Grandmaster chuckled, high-pitched like the start of a panic attack. "You… hahaha… you're holding a Sage-ranked template, and you calmly hand it over, thinking it's just a neat piece of paper."

"Sage-ranked?" Joe nodded with purposefully calm interest, pretending that he wasn't screaming internally. "That means that this will become a… Mythical weapon?"

"It does, lad." McPoundy shook his head at the thought. "I know that you don't know what that means here, Joe. Let me be the one to broaden your horizons. Whenever you are crafting, you always have a chance of creating something of a higher tier. A Grandmaster trying to create a Sage item? That usually falls into about a one-in-four million chance. That's a point zero zero zero zero two five chance. Having a template? That brings it up to *one* percent. One in one hundred."

"In fact, the only way to step out of the Grandmaster ranks and into the Sage ranks is to craft a Sage item." McPoundy clapped Joe on the shoulder. "This is my ticket into the Sage ranks!"

Joe looked at the smith, then at the diagram, and extended a hand. The diagram vanished into his spatial ring, and McPoundy started sputtering and grasping at him, his strong hands bouncing off Joe's Exquisite Shell. "Human! What are you *doing*?"

"I'm now opening negotiations." Joe chose his words very carefully. "I'm not just going to *let* you have a Sage ranked diagram to use for free."

"It's a weapon I'm making for *you!*" McPoundy roared in exasperation, staring at Joe's ring hungrily.

"No, we *already* have a deal that you would make a weapon for me." Joe shook his head and waved at the table containing all of the 'trash' that the Grandmaster had previously made. "Frankly, any of those 'edgy' ones would be fine with me. What are you willing to do so that the path of a Sage can be held in your hands?"

"Human… you could squeeze blood from a stone, couldn't ya?" A long silence stretched between the two, until finally McPoundy started laughing. "Fine; what do you want?"

"*I* want to be able to make this," the diagram appeared again between the two, though Joe didn't break eye contact with the Grandmaster, "on my own. I want you to teach me."

CHAPTER THIRTY-THREE

McPoundy ran a hand through his beard, then tugged on the hair as he stared at the diagram that was just out of reach. "Yer asking a lot. More than ya think. To make this weapon, a single discipline isn't enough. Do you even know what it *is*? The weapon?"

"I don't." Joe beamed a brilliant smile at the Dwarf.

"It's weapon*sss* that were made by some Sage in the distant past, and the end result is specific to a base class of Ritualist. Note the stress I put on that. I didn't misspeak; this is a set of weapons that function as *one* weapon." The Grandmaster ran his finger over some of the words on the paper, and they were suddenly legible to Joe. "I don't know what they do, but *look*. This section requires enchanting. Here, to *use*, but not *build*, this section... you need to be able to make rituals at a high level. Again, to *use* these here, you need alchemy. Thank the celestials that you don't need it to make the original weapons. Seems like some after-creation add-on."

"So... to *build* them requires smithing and enchanting?" Joe winked at McPoundy, "The two areas where you are a Grandmaster?"

"Ah. Perhaps you *did* know what you were asking for." The Dwarf chuckled lightly as his chest puffed up proudly. "Not many people out there that can-"

"I need to assume that this design also involves Sage-ranked *enchantment*. I also must assume that would allow *you* to advance further. I'll take that into consideration, thank you." Joe's words seemed to make McPoundy physically ill. "As payment for having access to a Sage-ranked smithing item, I want you to teach me until I am at least a Master. As payment for the Sage-ranked enchantment, I want you to inform my 'handler' that I gave you this, and have it count toward my candidacy. Lastly, I want this item as my weapon, and for it to never be made it for someone else."

"Done." McPoundy held out a hand so cheerfully that Joe wanted to hold back and drive a harder bargain. Still... he didn't want to go back on his word. He reluctantly let the handshake happen, and the deal was struck. The Grandmaster chuckled, eying the paper. "Now, the first thing I would like to do is get started on this weapon. I'll tell you a quick trade secret: when a high-ranked diagram is made, there are almost always the lesser versions within it, if you know how to look."

With a mischievous grin, McPoundy took the weapon diagram and cheerfully started examining it. Joe was still uncertain as to *why* he was looking for a lesser version, and so he voiced the question. The Grandmaster stared at him in surprise. "Do you think Mythical ingredients suddenly just fall into your lap? Following the diagram as-is gives me a one percent chance of completing the weapon. If I start with lesser versions, I can build up experience and know what I am doing before I start wasting materials."

That made sense, and Joe did his best to follow along with all of the explanations that were pouring from the bearded mouth across the small table from him. Descriptions of alloys, tensile strength, torque ratios, how to determine if dragonfire was a requirement or a suggestion, and folding metal took center stage.

Skill increase: Smithing Lore (Apprentice 0). Congratulations on increasing the depths of your knowledge! Perception +5.

As soon as the informational barrier was breached, the words coming out of the Dwarf were strangely easier to understand. It took almost four entire hours, but McPoundy had extracted an Expert-ranked subset from the diagram and was beginning the process of making the weapon. "Look here; this section is all about taking manasteel and elongating it into wire. We'll take the wire and use it... here... no, later."

The Dwarf lectured the entire time he was working, and Joe absorbed the instruction with rapt attention. The wire was turned into cable, then wrapped into orbs. Three hours after the work began, McPoundy set six perfectly smooth orbs on the rickety table, which buckled under their weight before the legs snapped entirely. The flimsy pieces of wood fell to the ground and stayed there without the slightest bounce or rolling. "Well... prolly shoulda replaced that a long time ago. It's fine. Don't even know why it was in here, to be frank. Next, the enchantment. Let's get started."

Smithing Lore one-time use effect has been used! You have gained the design template for Ritual Orb (Expert). Expert ranked Smithing or Ritualistic Forging is recommended before attempting to create.

Joe almost kicked himself when he saw that he had used up his forgotten bonus, but he calmed down when he realized exactly how far away he was from being able to manage to make even *that*. Instead he listened closely to the Dwarf's wealth of knowledge about vectors and energy flows, the position of the moon, and the quiet voice in his heart that called for peace and tranquility. The words were mesmerizing, and Joe almost fell asleep many times. Only the fact that he *needed* to understand allowed him to keep his mind open and attentive.

Enchanting Lore reached Beginner nine just as McPoundy was finishing the explanation. As soon as he noticed it, Joe activated *Knowledge,* and the skill increased in rank.

Skill increase: Enchanting Lore (Apprentice 0). Congratulations on increasing the depths of your knowledge. Enchantments now require 5% fewer components to create!

Skill increase: Knowledge (Beginner III). Sometimes a boost to knowledge at the right time is more effective than using it consistently!

"-and that's the only time I'll ever speak of it." McPoundy wiped a tear from his eye and took a deep breath. "Thank you for not laughing; I knew that you were the right person to open up to. Please, though… just never bring it up."

"I'm… bring what up?" Joe locked his eyes on McPoundy, who smiled brightly and pounded him on the back.

"That's the spirit. Thankee, lad." The Grandmaster handed him the orbs, as well as two worked-leather cuffs. "Here you go, then; try them on."

Joe took the cuffs and examined them.

Control Cuff (Masterwork). These control cuffs allow the wearer to control the weapon 'Ritual Orbs'. They were created by Grandmaster Iron McPoundy, and are able to control Ritual Orbs up to the Master rank. They have no attack nor defensive value. Durability: 500/500.

"These are *really* durable for… leather?" Joe looked questioningly at the Dwarf to double check. McPoundy nodded, so Joe returned his attention to the orbs and tried to learn how to use them.

Ritual Orbs (Expert) (Masterwork). Can be controlled via Control Cuffs or option one, listed below. Each individual enchanted Ritual Orb can be directed separately if you can control them properly, or all of them can be directed as a unit. Each orb deals a base of 100 blunt damage. The orbs have additional properties as listed below.

Option 1) Enchanted Characteristics: Each Ritual Orb can be bound to a single Characteristic with an associated Enchanted Ritual Circle*. By binding the characteristic, the Orb will gain an increase in damage, and will shift the damage type it inflicts. If you can control them properly, they will also be controllable without a Control Cuff, based on the characteristic score.

Assigning a characteristic automatically grants the Orb the 'recall' ability, and it will return to you after five minutes if left behind, forgotten, or stolen. The assigned Characteristic will also empower Option 2.

Caution! After binding a Characteristic to a Ritual Orb, if the orb is destroyed, the bound Characteristic will be treated as if it is half its actual value until a new Orb has been bound.

Option 2) Alchemical Binding: A single spell, skill, or ability can be assigned to each Ritual Orb by using the associated Alchemical Ritual*. So long as the Orb has a Core or Mana Battery powering it, you will be able to use the spell at will, without draining your own mana, if you can control them properly.

Caution! While the skill/spell/ability is bound to the Ritual Orb, you will only be able to use it through the Ritual Orb! If the Orb does not have enough power, the spell/skill/ability will fail to activate.

Option 3) By focusing your ability to understand Magical Matrices into the Ritual Orb, you can assign the interior with a configuration. Each orb can be used to create a single reusable ritual pattern. If you can control them properly, you will be able to have each orb create a ritual circle. Current Ritual Orbs: 6. You will be able to create a ritual up to the Expert rank with the current configuration.

Caution! Opening the Ritual Orb to create a ritual increases the likelihood of damage from outside forces. Durability damage is doubled once the Ritual Orb is unfolded. Each ritual circle must have its own Mana Battery or Core to function properly.

"That's… a lot of cautions." Joe scanned over all the options in wonder. He tapped on the underlined words and was *delighted* to see a specific ritual appear. "But… a reusable ritual circle on demand? Spells assigned to the orbs? Damage changes? This is *perfect*."

"Hold on to your hammer, now." McPoundy held up a hand

to make Joe consider his next words. "Let me expand on some of that caution. If you bind a characteristic to an orb, remember how it says you will need to replace it if it's damaged or lost? If you decide to use this weapon, that means you can never *not* use it. I highly doubt there is a ritual of *unbinding* that lets you walk away from this thing. At least, not without paying a heavy cost. Another thing; these things are basically *screaming* at you that they will be incredibly difficult to learn to wield properly."

"I'm seeing..." Joe perused the information again, reading more carefully and with less excited eyes. "Oh. This section. 'If you can control them properly'. Is that what you're talking about?"

"Exactly that. That statement shows up in every single paragraph except the 'cautions'." Grandmaster McPoundy gazed admiringly at the orbs one last time, then turned his eyes back to the template. "I want to keep going on this, but I have other responsibilities. It is going to take months of research before I am ready to attempt a Master, Grandmaster, let alone *Sage* version of these weapons. You should take those and start getting some experience with using them."

CHAPTER THIRTY-FOUR

Joe left the forge while studiously ignoring the too-wide smiles on the faces of all the other apprentices that were trying to draw the Grandmaster's attention. He hurried back to Havoc, straining under the weight of the six silver orbs. He cheerfully grumbled, "These things are like... fifty pounds each. Do they do a point of blunt damage per pound or something?"

Had it not been for his newly enhanced strength, Joe would have been stumbling along at best, or needing a cart at worst. He felt like the protagonist of an infomercial as he said, "There *must* be a better way!"

All at once, he realized that his excitement had completely gotten the better of him. Joe stored the orbs in his Codpiece of Holding, then put his hands on his lower back and forced himself into a better standing position. His spine crackled like a glow-stick being activated, and for a long moment, he missed Jaxon. He continued walking... then paused once more and put on the Control Cuff. One orb came out, and Joe stared at it even as his pace slowed considerably.

"Float." Joe ordered the orb. It didn't move. How dare. "Spin. Something. Do something."

He continued on like that for a few minutes, yet nothing worked. It took a force of will for him to not chuck the orb at the ground, but he was almost to the point that he *wanted* to-

Wham. The orb launched from his hands and left a divot in the ground. Joe stared at the dent for a long moment. "I can't tell if it was listening to me, or if I slipped and dropped the stupid thing."

"Orb... float?" He tried to pick it up, but it was wedged in the earth pretty good. No good. He tried to think through what had changed, but the obvious difference was that he had *wanted* the orb to slam itself on the ground. "This is another thing that goes by mental visualization, isn't it? Okay, then... let's go full mystic on this thing."

Joe pictured the orb floating up and hovering at eye level, and *really* wanted it to happen. He strained, pushed, and pulled, but the orb didn't move. Calming himself, he took a deep breath, letting go of his grumpiness. He focused on the space right behind his nose and left the subconscious part of his mind —what he called the 'monkey brain', since it was always chattering. Joe focused on breathing while he allowed his higher-order reasoning try to comprehend why this wasn't working. Did these orbs run on *emotion*? That would be a bad match-up for him, and he knew it. Joe wasn't overrun by his emotions; he tried to be calm and logical whenever he could. Breathe in, breathe out. Good monkey brain. "Orb, move to eye level and remain there."

Skill gained: Battle Meditation (Passive breathing pattern) (Novice V). Battle Meditation is practically a requirement for combatants that use exotic weapons. This skill allows for rapid understanding of exotic weapons, increasing skill growth by $2n\%$; where n = skill level!

Joe read over the skill he had just gained with a massive grin on his face. He *really* needed to try out more of his real-world coping mechanisms. This exercise had already increased his skill gain for exotic weapons by *ten percent*. That was a massive increase for just starting out. He refocused his eyes, but didn't see the orb. He looked down with a frown, noting that it hadn't moved from its divot. "I'm starting to have serious concerns over the usability of this weapon. Wait… *wait*."

Looking at the cuff on his wrist, Joe focused his will and sent a trickle of mana to the cuff. Then he visualized the orb lifting of the ground and hovering in front of him. Nothing. "Drat! I thought that might do it-"

Just before he released the cuff, the orb *cracked* and lifted off the ground, hovering in front of him. Joe stared at the weapon suspiciously. "Were you… *stuck*? If that was the reason you weren't…"

He let go of the mana but continued to picture the orb staying where it was. It remained in place. Joe saw it at knee-height, swirling around him, and then balancing on the tip of his finger. It smoothly followed his mental images, and Joe groaned half in exasperation and half in delight over the ease of use. "The cuff lets me control it pretty easily, but I can also supply mana to move it harder or faster? For instance, if it gets stuck?"

Skill gained: Assisted Ritual Orb Usage (Exotic) (Upgradeable) (Novice VII). This skill dictates the ease of use for the weapon 'Ritual Orbs', as it is assisted by the armor 'Control Cuff'. This is determined to be an exotic weapon. This skill is upgradeable. When you no longer require the Control Cuff to manage the orbs, a portion of this skill's levels will be allocated to the newly upgraded skill. Each rank allows for skillful control of a single orb, with each additional orb making the orbs 50% more difficult to skillfully control.

"That's a *lot* of modifiers…" Joe looked more closely at the skill, and more information appeared as he stared at the only thing he didn't understand, the 'exotic' tag.

Exotic Weapons are powerful pieces of equipment that feature unique abilities. Please note that due to their singular benefits, only one Exotic Weapon may be equipped at any given time.

"Oh. Well, that's pretty straightforward. Let's try this out." Joe pulled out a second orb, tossing it into the air next to the first. "That's not harder to control? What was this skill going on about?"

"Boom. I got this in the bag." He made the orbs dance around each other, spin, tap lightly. Joe repeated the commands he had done the first time, knee-height, swirling around him-

Wump.

Joe's Exquisite Shell shimmered violently, and he was shoved a foot to the right as one orb hit his knee and the other thudded into the wall of a building. He grimaced at them in confusion as both spheres dropped to the ground and stayed there. "What happened? Did I poorly visualize what I needed to do there? No... they become erratic after leaving line of sight?"

"*Hey!*" Joe's head whipped to the side as a furious Dwarf appeared, her mustache quivering. "Who's slammin' things into my wall? Thank you for this *opportunity* to teach you the rules of hospitality and personal conduct, Bro!"

The Dwarf scowled at the divot and stated a number. A single point of Reputation with the Dwarven Council vanished from Joe's status sheet. The mustachioed Dwarf nodded at Joe and put a hand on his elbow. "Thank you for being so kind and understanding, as well as avoiding a larger fine by paying up right away, Bro. With this kind of reputation as payment? Feel free to play with your balls here anytime you like."

Joe sighed as the Dwarf went back inside, then moved to a small window where she peeked out at him hopefully. He had no intention of damaging her walls again, much to her dismay. He pulled out his orbs, one by one, until all six were in front of him. When he could see them up close, all six were fairly easy to control and use. However, as soon as he needed them to take individual action or move out of his visual range, they would scatter and practically *try* to cause property damage. He ordered them to stay right next to his body, then swirled them around and *stopped* them as hard as he could. Joe stepped away, and studied their positions.

One was right by the window, almost touching it. The Dwarf was gaping at it in shock, but luckily Joe had stopped all of them in time. The others? All over the place. One had even gone straight up. Only one of the orbs remained where he had thought it should be, and even that… he couldn't remember if this was the one that should be there.

"*Whoo*, boy. This is gonna take some doing." Joe called all the orbs to him and stored them in his codpiece for easy access. "I'd ask Havoc for some help training this skill, but I want to learn, not get tortured into figuring it out."

He started back toward Havoc's estate in order to get back to work, but as if thinking about Havoc had triggered something, the training golem stretched out over his limbs between steps and wrestled him to the ground. It took almost five minutes just to get back on his feet, and Joe resigned himself to a slow, painful journey back.

Even so, he was grinning like a maniac. He had a weapon that would grow with him for the rest of his life. It was difficult to use right now, but Joe had all the time in the world to train his skill. He couldn't *wait* to get started. To that end, even as he fought his limbs for movement, Joe pulled out two orbs and set them to spinning *just* at the edge of his vision.

"I'm gonna grind the *abyss* out of this skill."

CHAPTER THIRTY-FIVE

By the time Joe approached the Estate, he felt like a melted candle. In an effort to 'see' how hard it was to gain characteristic points with the golem restricting him, he had turned off Neutrality Aura. His fancy new clothes were *slick* with sweat, and he was stumbling with fatigue and dehydration.

A little over four hours at barely a walking pace down the 'child' portion of the road had brought him back, and Joe was ready to fall onto the ground and stay there. He grabbed the doorframe and heaved for breath. "How do people *train* at the higher levels?"

He swung open the door, and Havoc looked up at him. His face twisted in disgust, and he shouted at Joe, "Hey! Don't come in here like that; you're disgusting. You smell like *cheese*."

"I can always trust that Havoc will tell me the truth of the matter." Joe sighed as the door closed by itself, slamming hard enough that his shell shimmered and his shadow appeared to slap the door. He sat down, activated Neutrality Aura, and pulled up his notifications, then his status sheet.

Characteristic training complete! Strength, Dexterity, and Constitution +2!

Skill increase: Artisan Body (Beginner III).

Name: Joe 'Tatum's Chosen Legend' Class: Reductionist
Profession I: Arcanologist (Max)
Profession II: Ritualistic Alchemist (1/20)
Profession III: None
Character Level: 20 Exp: 217,704 Exp to next level: 13,296
Rituarchitect Level: 10 Exp: 45,000 Exp debt: 9,600
Reductionist Level: 0 Exp: 476 Exp to next level: 524
Hit Points: 1,642/1,642
Mana: 2,301/3,152
Mana regen: 44.99/sec
Stamina: 341/1,381
Stamina regen: 6.36/sec

Characteristic: Raw score

Strength: 133
Dexterity: 133
Constitution: 129
Intelligence: 138
Wisdom: 118
Dark Charisma: 80
Perception: 123
Luck: 60
Karmic Luck: 3

"Hmm. Solid gains, but I need to do something about my mental stats. They're stagnating *hard*." Joe regarded the Artisan Body, confused as to why it had gone up a second time in two training sessions. "Is it because I trained two body stats? Three? Or because I did three twice each time? I'm not complaining, but I'd love more information... no pop-up. Abyss. At least it dropped the training time for individual training time to... divide that by four, multiply by skill level... just over thirty nine minutes? Nice."

Joe glanced at the two orbs that he still had moving in front of him. He blinked, and by the time his eyes reopened, they were out of position again. He growled at them, but they didn't seem to mind. "No skill up for you, yet? I'll just keep trying new things until I find something that works."

"*Weapon training increases at double speed while in combat.*" Havoc's voice blared next to Joe's ear. He jerked his head away and looked around at the source of the sound. Somehow, the doorknob had grown a metallic mouth. "*If you want to increase your skill with weapons, go kill some Elves or something.*"

"Wouldn't regular monsters work?" Joe prodded the… doorknob. It didn't reply, making Joe wonder if Havoc was upset that he didn't jump on board with going off to kill some Elves. He stood up and tried to go in, but the door didn't budge. "Havoc? Let me in."

"*I'm working on replacing the entire house with golems. That'll teach McPoundy to put a restraining order on his brother while said brother is staying in the family estate. Go away for a while, wouldja? Maybe my little brother will let you stay in the forge for a while, or maybe you can go* kill some Elves!"

"Are you actually kicking me out right now because you're jealous that your brother made me a weapon?" The doorknob shifted into a dagger as Joe reached for it, and only the fact that his shell was active at all times kept him from slicing his palm open. "Havoc! You are *ridiculous*! Fine! I needed raw materials anyway, I'm gonna go train in the wilderness! By myself!"

"*I'll know if you die. You'll respawn at that fancy new temple that I didn't want to exist. Otherwise, don't come back till you've gained a level, have something important to talk about, or kill a hundred Elves! I got nothin' for ya right now,*" the doorknob ordered in Havoc's voice.

Quest alert: Go Away For a While! Havoc is worried that he might accidentally kill you if he sees you again over the next few days. He hasn't killed anything since the minor fort takeover, and he's getting the itch. Better go do other things. Level gained: 0/1. Elves killed: 0/100. Important information gained: 0/1. Rewards: 100 personal reputation with Havoc. +10 personal reputation per Elf killed. Failure: Havoc kills you on sight.

"What do you consider 'important'?" Joe yelled at the door, getting no answer even after waiting a short while. He inspected his character sheet and winced when he saw how far from the next level he was. "Wait… I can't go off fighting like this. Havoc, you were supposed to give me armor after my quest with you!"

Thunder boomed as soon as Joe finished his sentence, and he peered up at the clear sky in concern. That sounded similar to the time the instant dungeon had been about to form back on Midgard. The roof opened, and Havoc's voice blared at the sky, "Pipe down, you overexcited rock! Or is it *the Administrator* today? No clouds; I bet it *is*. Listen here, *Sunshine*, I did my duty. He just hasn't picked his gear up! Is that *my* fault? No!"

The roof slammed shut, and a mail slot appeared in the door. A small envelope popped through, with an address and shop name on it. Joe opened the envelope and found a receipt for pickup inside. He looked at the door, then the sky somewhat guiltily, turned, and started on his way toward the shop's address. "No rest today, it seems. Wouldn't want a break after four *hours* of being squeezed by a golem, after all. Abyssal Dwarf, shouting at the sky."

Joe grumbled the whole way to the shop, not even noticing how much attention he had gained in his exchange with Havoc. It had taken almost fifteen minutes for the city to get back to normal after the thunder and Havoc's announcement that had followed. He stopped in front of the address that was on the paper, in front of what *had* to be the shabbiest shop in the District. "Odds and Ends? That was a franchise?"

He pushed the door open, surprised to be greeted by an older human lady who looked similar to the ancient woman that ran the shop down on Midgard. "Hello there, young man! Welcome to the Odds and Ends; are you browsing, or do you have a goal in mind?"

"I'm here for a pickup." Joe held up the receipt, and it whisked out of his hand into hers. She read the paper and nodded serenely. Before she could say anything more, Joe had to ask, "By any chance, do you know the owner of the Odds and Ends on Midgard? You look very similar. I also didn't realize there would be human shop owners here."

She looked surprised for a moment, and then a smile washed over her face. "Just me, so far. Yes, I know her very well. She's *me*, after all. Well… sort of. You can call me Minya, and let's not get into the details too much. With enough reputation, you can own anything you want as a human, and the Bifrost has never held me back. I'm an Arcane Loot Lord, after all. As to this order… how well would you say you treat your enchanted gear?"

Joe met her level stare, and was pleased that he was able to use his knowledge of her from the previous Zone to get ahead in life here. Or, at least enough to avoid a serious blunder. "Well, it's alive, so if it's new, I treat it like I would a pet. Otherwise, if it's older equipment, I try to treat it like a full-grown person."

All of this was false; he had never treated his clothes as anything but clothes. Still, he resolved to *try* to do that going forward. Maybe if he met a 'Minya' in yet another Zone, she would be able to see if he was telling the truth. She clapped her hands a single time, and a wide smile appeared on her face. "Perfect! I was going to give you a warning, but it seems you had more than just a casual interaction with my… sister. She must have sold you something?"

"Repaired something!" Joe answered too fast, not *technically* lying. He didn't want to try to explain that he had accidentally destroyed all of his previous enchanted gear.

"Is that so…? Well, this was a *very* odd order from sweet little Havoc, but there aren't many cloth enchanters in the city. Or perhaps he thought you'd have an easier time with a human enchanter?" Minya looked at him sharply.

"Never even crossed my mind." Joe's brow furrowed as he tried to figure out what she was talking about. He didn't even really dislike the Elves; he just needed to destroy them utterly and in every conceivable way. "Can I see what Havoc ordered? I need to get out and do some training as soon as possible."

"Certainly." She pulled out several boxes with a bright smile on her face. "Two rings, shirt, pants, socks, belt, gloves, and a facemask. It was a very... *strange* order. I'm happy to let you know that I was able to get all the requested options on them. Also, for this set, both socks count as a single item when worn together."

"In what way was it strange?" Joe pulled the first box open and tried to look at what was inside, but Minya's words caused him to curse Havoc out.

"First off, everything is a bright white. I thought that you might not want to be as visible in the wilderness, but Havoc told me that you needed to stop being so dark and... a word that means eight-grader syndrome? I forget the original word he used, but I remember the explanation." She shook her head as Joe's face flushed a bright red. "Then I asked, 'why a facemask and not a hat'? Havoc insisted that the less often people could see your face, the better, so I assumed you were trying for a stealth build, but then we come back to the issue of it all being white...?"

Joe took a deep breath and resolved to attack Havoc the next time he saw the Dwarf. "It's... fine. I actually can't wear hats; I have a title that makes them burst into flames and destroys them. Can I look at the items real quick?"

She waved at him to go for it, so Joe opened the ring boxes first.

Illusion Breaker (Ring): adds a 20% chance every five seconds to break out of an illusion you are trapped in.
Exotic Ring (Ring): Adds 10% damage dealt when using an exotic weapon.

"He must have known that McPoundy wouldn't just let me use a regular weapon, then?" Joe nodded excitedly as he put the rings on. They fit perfectly. Excited for what *else* the Dwarf had ordered, he pulled open the first clothing box and stared at the blindingly white shirt, then each piece in order as his teeth started to grind together.

Henley shirt of the Silkpants Mage. (Set Item). This fine shirt is intended to be worn as a set with other items. It is a custom build for 'Joe the stupid Human that can't do his own shopping', and offers unique benefits when worn as a set. Please note: Only one *set bonus is active at a time.*
One set item (Worn by itself): Offers magic damage reduction (MR) of 20. Any spell that hits the wearer is reduced in damage by 20.
Two set items: Offers magic damage reduction (MR) of 20. There is a 5% chance every five seconds that an enemy looking at the wearer is blinded for three seconds if the wearer is bald.
Three set items: Offers magic damage reduction (MR) of 50. There is an 8% chance every five seconds that an enemy looking at the wearer is blinded for three seconds if the wearer is bald.
Four set items: Offers magic damage reduction (MR) of 50. There is an 8% chance every five seconds that an enemy looking at the wearer is blinded for three seconds if the wearer is bald. All equipped set items will automatically recover durability when supplied mana from the wearer.
Five set items: Offers magic damage reduction (MR) of 50. There is an 8% chance every five seconds that an enemy looking at the wearer is blinded for three seconds if the wearer is bald. All equipped set items will automatically recover durability when supplied mana from the wearer. Skill levels with spells increase 25% faster.
Six set items: Offers magic damage reduction (MR) of 50. There is an 8% chance every five seconds that an enemy looking at the wearer is blinded for three seconds if the wearer is bald. All equipped set items will automatically recover durability when supplied mana from the wearer. Skill levels with spells increase 25% faster. Spell stability increases by 10%. Charisma is 50% more effective with Dwarves.
Silk Pants of the Silkpants Mage. (Set Item). These fine pants are intended to be worn as a set with other items. It is a custom build for 'Joe the stupid Human that can't do his own shopping', and offers unique benefits when worn as a set.

Joe didn't bother to read the description again, as it was the same as the first piece. After the pants, he didn't even bother reading the flavor text on the clothes. He simply took them into the changing room and put them on. He tried to put on the mask, but it had a special requirement.

Silk Socks of the Silkpants Mage.

Silk Belt of the Silkpants Mage

Silk Gloves of the Silkpants Mage

Silk Facemask of the Silkpants Mage. This item must be the sixth piece of the Silkpants Mage set to be equipped.

"Seriously? That means that the reason my charisma will be more effective on Dwarves is they can't see my face?" Joe pictured striking Havoc with lightning just to feel a little better. "If these weren't so useful, I'd be furious, you annoying Dwarf."

He pulled on the reflective clothing with a chuckle, throwing his Robe of Liquid Darkness over it to hide the brightness as best as he could. Joe stepped out of the changing room, unable to miss Minya's wince as she looked him over. "Ouch. I think you might want to do your own shopping from now on."

"Yeah, I get it. Thanks for the gear." Joe started chuckling darkly as he left the shop, trying and failing to think of what he could do as revenge.

CHAPTER THIRTY-SIX

Joe stepped right back into the shop. His first steps outside had been interrupted by the braying laugh of a mustachioed Dwarf that 'helpfully' informed him that his current formal shoes 'ruined the gravitas of his outfit'. In other words, he looked outright ridiculous. "Any chance you have some shoes that either match the clothes or my robe? I have normal shoes on, but..."

He walked out a few minutes later wearing white running shoes. They enhanced his speed out of combat by ten percent, which was nice. He was pleased to find that his discount at the Odds and Ends on Midgard somehow translated to this Zone, and even Minya had been confused as to why she was giving it to him. They had cost only five reputation with the Dwarven Council, which was... high? Low? He was still having trouble determining the worth of reputation as currency.

"If ten reputation is worth a full rank with any merchant, then even with the discount the boots were five hundred...?" Joe tried to decide if he was getting ripped off, but he really had no idea. Then he sighed as another revelation struck him. "Coulda just requisitioned them."

He started skipping down the road, trying to remember where he needed to go in order to teleport to an area where he could fight things. After searching for far too long, he simply went to the wall and took note of the *massive* amount of Dwarves on guard duty. "Yeah... there's gotta be plenty of things to kill around here if they are being this attentive."

Joe walked out of the gate, getting a nasty shock when going under the portcullis. As soon as he passed that point, all of his active skills were turned off, and the enchantments on his gear faltered for a moment. He stumbled, coming to his senses to realize that over a dozen weapons were practically at his throat. One Dwarf grabbed him roughly and inspected his ears, then seemed to realize his Candidate title was active. The bearded Dwarf awkwardly patted Joe on the arm and grumbled, "Sorry, Bro. Standard nullification field at all points of entry. Can't be too safe when there are so many illusionists out there. Let me help you through here. Can I carry anything for you, Friend of the Council? Need anything for your travels? Camping gear? Snacks?"

That was when Joe realized that he was about to leave a population center and go into the wild with zero preparation. "I... actually, that would be very useful. I need travel supplies and any information that you think would be useful when monster hunting. My... *mentor* suggested that I needed to gain some experience in this area before continuing on. I had planned to come back into the city, I think, but... perhaps I could spend some time in seclusion."

"Oh!" The Dwarf grinned widely and walked Joe to a gate-house. "I'm so pleased to be of service! Come, come! Human Bro, I have exactly what you want, and you don't even know it! Here's a map; this spot here is a cave system called the 'Caves of Solitude'. It's directly adjacent to Gramma's Shoe, so you wanna make sure to stay on the path; but if you go there, I guarantee that no other Dwarves are gonna bother you. I can even give you a quest to hunt down some Air Spirits. Good reputation, you get to be alone, plenty of space to work out issues. Sound like a plan?"

"Yeah... by 'Air Spirits', you mean earth-using spirits... would that be earth elementals?" Joe quizzed for clarity.

"O' course!" The Dwarf shook his head as if Joe was being funny. "You had to have been in the Legion for a while if you're a Candidate, so you should at least understand what *monster names* mean. Gear is here, standard stockpile; and here's the quest. Reputation or requisition?"

Quest alert: Wait, This Air Is Mud! The Caves of Solitude, a common destination for the discerning Dwarf seeking a little rest, have recently been used by Air Spirits as a rest spot for themselves. This is unacceptable, as only Dwarves and their allies should have rest and relaxation. Destroy the Air Spirits when you find them. Reward: 1 reputation with the Legion per spirit laid to rest. Failure: none. Deposit: 10 Legion reputation. Defeat 10 spirits and your deposit will be refunded.

Joe swiped his hand forward and took in the small pile of travel gear. "Requisition for sure. Where are the spirits coming from, if this is a new thing?"

"Want that quest too, bro? Gotta put rep on the line for this one. Messes up the rewards otherwise," the Dwarf cheerfully stated. He blinked a few times, and a quest appeared in Joe's vision.

Quest alert: Air Spirits Suck. The Legion has been asked to find the source of the encroaching Air Spirits. Yet, since they can sink into the earth, the source of the incursion has been hard to track. Find the reason the spirits are invading this territory, and put a stop to it or report the issue. Reward: 1,000 reputation with the Legion. Failure: None. Deposit: 100 Legion reputation. At a minimum, report the reason to refund your deposit.

Joe whistled at the quest. "That's a big deposit... why?"

"Caves of *Solitude* are supposed to be sparsely populated, Bro." The Dwarf punched Joe's shoulder in a friendly manner, taking out fifteen health and reminding Joe that he needed to reactivate his protections. "Some big shots go there, and they were getting annoyed at all the people crawling over their vacation spot. The Air Spirits can't do anything to *them*, so..."

"Could they be the reason the spirits are there? They want more privacy?" Joe's brow furrowed as he thought about the quest.

"Wow! The quest was just completed!" The Dwarf gasped. "*Really?*"

"Course not, dumb Bro." The Dwarf chuckled at him, and Joe laughed after a moment as well. "Gotcha, though. Nah, that's already been looked into. Want the quest or no?"

Joe looked at his untouched Legion reputation. He was sitting at negative five hundred and seventy; all of his pay so far *still* hadn't brought him up to neutral. Finishing this quest would take care of that, and at worst, he was out ten day's worth of pay from his 'basic training'. "Yeah, I'll take it.'"

-100 reputation with the Dwarven Legion! Current reputation: -670 (Cautious).

"Good hunting, Candidate Bro..." The Dwarf watched as Joe started sparkling, flashed with a dark light, then all traces of sweat vanished. "Candidate mage Bro?"

"Yeah, and thanks for the information." Joe walked out of the city properly this time, studying the map he had... gained. It listed various areas around the city, and included the average level and type of monsters that he could expect to run into. "Holy guacamole, this map must be worth... don't think about it, Joe. Don't lose or damage the map."

The Caves of Solitude were apparently more popular than the guard had let on, as there was a clear path that led directly there. Yet, the road was distinctly marked as 'not safe' on the map for some reason. There were... Joe looked at the map more closely. "What in the abyss is a 'Hammer Beast'?"

He didn't need to wait very long to find out. A creature rolled along the path, at first glance appearing to be an oversized boulder. As it neared Joe, the ball unfurled into a... the best way Joe could describe it to himself was an 'armadillo turtle'. It was heavily armored over its entire body, yet had an especially thick shell around its torso that it could curl into. Just like every other monster native to this Zone, it had two heads as well. They extended on flexible necks, and while it stood still, it strangely reminded Joe of a snail as it looked at him.

A heavily armored, spike-covered, *fast* creature. "Ah. Hammer Beast. Hit it with a hammer, because blades are just going to bounce off."

Joe once more groaned at the Dwarven naming conventions, but he had to admit that it was an effective way to describe and share the weaknesses. The beast jumped lightly into the air, snapping into a ball, then rolled at Joe aggressively. As a ball, it reached the center of Joe's chest at the highest point, and he knew that he really didn't want to get hit by that thing. He had a simple solution to this issue, and grinned cheerfully as he jumped over the ball and landed on his feet with a chuckle.

He looked behind himself just in time to see the spiked ball coming back at him twice as fast as it had been just a moment ago, and his eyes went wide as it crushed him into the ground and tried to turn him into a waffle. Specifically *not* a pancake, what with all the holes it tried to drill into him.

Sneak attack successful: 917 damage taken. (Crushing/Piercing).
Exquisite Shell: 2,645/3,562.

"Ow. Seriously, almost a third of my shell in one go?" The ball continued past him, reaching the spot it had started from and popping out to see if Joe had been destroyed. Joe groaned and got to his feet, staring murder at the Hammer Beast. "Oh, look, you have an attack pattern I can exploit. I *appreciate* the *opportunity* to test my new weapon on you, *beast bro.*"

Joe chuckled at the absurdity of his words as he mentally lifted two of his new orbs into the air. Maybe his time with the Dwarves was affecting him more than he thought it had been.

CHAPTER THIRTY-SEVEN

The Hammer Beast wasn't giving Joe any time to prepare himself, but that was fine by him... at first. Joe was all sorts of excited to have some ball vs orb action, until he realized that the beast's ability to maneuver was far superior to his own. In fact, all the beast's physical characteristics topped his by a significant amount.

Joe dove out of the way *again* as the beast rolled past him, still getting clipped by a spike on the outer edge of its armored shell.

Exquisite Shell: 2,299/3,562.

"Abyss! That barely *touched* me!" Joe wasted no time in striking the beast with lightning, completely forgetting his new weapon in his haste to deal some damage. The spell hit just after his shadow dissipated, missing the beast entirely but at least catching it in the area of effect.

Damage dealt: 267 (AOE of Dark Lightning Strike and 41% damage return from Retaliation of Shadows.)

Joe remembered his orbs, and looked around to find them. They had fallen to the ground and were just... *sitting* there... so he tried to get them back in the air and attacking on his behalf. Just as they lifted off, he had to move again as the beast came rolling back at him once more. The orbs fell to the ground as soon as his mind was off of them, but at least Joe had managed to avoid the follow-up attack. The Hammer Beast skidded to a stop, unfurled, and got a bead on his new location once more. With a sound a buzz saw would have been jealous of, the beast shot toward the Reductionist again.

Joe *jumped*, this time past the original attacking position of the beast, and sent a Cone of Cold at the creature. He missed entirely as the beast stayed ahead of the attack and moved over thirty feet in the blink of an eye. He was hoping that the layer of frost left on the ground would make it harder to roll on, but had forgotten the Hammer Beast's spikes, which allowed it to power past the area without issue like it was wearing cleats. It came to a stop right about the same spot it had started from, but it unexpectedly stayed in that position for a longer time.

It took an Acid Spray and a hundred and thirty damage on its shell for the trouble, but it was also able to find Joe as soon as the stinging liquid started to eat away at it. It let out a screech from both heads, and Joe felt *something*... latch onto him?

You have been targeted!

"What does that even mean?" Joe didn't have the option to look deeper into the message, as the Hammer Beast started moving in an odd manner that it hadn't used before. It shot directly at him, as per usual, but when he got out of the way, it no longer came back in a straight line. Instead, the beast swerved to put itself directly on a collision course for him again. "Balls! Attack!"

Joe ordered the two orbs off the ground and sent them spiraling in for an attack. They hit the beast head on, actually slowing the buzz-saw movement slightly. There was a tremendous **crack** and the orbs went flying into the long grass surrounding the road that Joe was on. A small notification let him know that they had hit for fifty-eight blunt damage each thanks to his new ring and automatically applied bonus armor penetration, but Joe lost sight of them entirely. *"An~n~nd they're gone."*

As the beast came at him, Joe went for the tried-and-true ploy, jumping over it to get into a better position for attack. To his terror, the beast bounced off the ground at him, and only the power that Joe had put into the jump allowed him to avoid taking a spike directly to the face. The ball whizzed under him by a fraction of a foot as he watched with wide eyes in almost slow motion.

Joe pulled two more of his orbs out of his ring before he hit the ground, sending them at the curving-around figure of the Hammer Beast. He urged them onto their greatest speed, casting Dark Lightning Strike just as they landed on the beast. There was a tremendous **bang** as the three attacks hit as one, and the beast was dazed by the various pains it was feeling, so much so that it flopped out of position and landed roughly on the ground. It bounced a few times, slowly coming to its feet and trying to reorient itself on the human causing it such injury.

Damage dealt: 1,180 (140 blunt + 1,050 Dark) (Perfect critical hit!) Target is dazed for four seconds!

Joe was astonished at the damage values that he had just seen, but he barely wasted a moment in getting his orbs back into position for attack. Since his target wasn't moving much, he pulled out the last two orbs and added them into the next attack, now having four orbs out and moving together to strike the beast. He tried to cast a spell at the same time, but the orbs faltered. To get around the complication, he sent all four into the air above the beast and simply moved them only up and down. Then he only needed to focus on *'hit it'* as he used both his hands to achieve the somatic portion of casting Cone of Cold again, this time with a reasonable certainty of hitting.

The four orbs bounced off the hardened shell of the beast, and Joe was pleased for the first time that they dealt blunt damage instead of anything else. His icy spray erupted from in front of his hands, this time catching the beast without issue.

Damage dealt: 457 (232 blunt + 225 cold!) Target has been inflicted with 'Brittle'.

The dazed effect wore off just as the orbs came down once more, only three of them landing but still doing enough damage to finish off the Hammer Beast. Its shell broke as the blunt attack took advantage of the brittle effect to deal double damage to rigid objects. The orbs finished out the fight embedded in the shell in three perfectly round divots.

Joe was wheezing from the effort this fight had required, and he stumbled over to the corpse, kicking it once for catharsis before storing his orbs. He touched the body and used a burst of mana to scan it, then let his ingrained Ritual of Reduction take the creature. There was no Core left behind, and Joe would have smacked himself if he wasn't afraid that his Retaliation of Shadows might show up and do it as well. "I really need to get better at using Corify."

After the aftermath of the battle had been taken care of, Joe waded through the grass and started searching for his missing Ritual Orbs. It took almost ten minutes of searching, since they had been buried in the tall blades, and he resolved to assign a characteristic to them as soon as possible so that they would automatically recall in the future. "Oh, I wonder what that Hammer Beast was worth?"

Experience gained: 114

Skill increase: Assisted Ritual Orb Usage (Novice VIII).

"That's... not much." Joe looked at the skill increases with slight despair. "Then again... it was only a single monster. Just because it was hard for me to fight it doesn't mean that I should get extra rewards for it... I guess."

He continued down the road, more carefully this time. On the map, Hammer Beasts were written in as one of the weaker things that he could encounter in the area. It also said that most things tended to move in packs, so he was getting slightly nervous about his choice to set out on his own. As a Candidate, he was almost certain that he would have been able to order a team to come with him as backup. Still... Joe took in the sights of grass and stony ground with a smile on his face. It had been a while since he had adventured on his own. It was refreshing.

That is, it was refreshing, until he heard the sound of buzz saws closing in on his location. "One, two, *four?*"

Joe counted the incoming noises with pure nervousness. He looked around wildly, realizing with dismay that there was very little cover. The capital wasn't overly friendly to nature, as that was the Elven domain, so trees were sparse and twisted. He had been getting closer to the Caves of Solitude, and the ground had started to shift from grassy plains to foothills and somewhat mountainous territory. There were several large boulders scattered around, and one caught his eye. It was shaped more like a pillar than anything else, reaching about twelve feet off the ground and having sheer sides.

The Hammer beasts were closing in, now visible and only... maybe sixty feet out? They were surprisingly hard to see when they were moving through grass, but Joe didn't pay too much attention to that. He got to the side of the pillar and looked up. "It's a great defensive location, but how do I get *up* there?"

He looked up, and a smile appeared on his face as he remembered, "I need to stop thinking like a baseline human. I have skills and characteristics now!"

Just before the Hammer Beasts reached him, Joe *jumped*, putting his skill and strength to the test. He needn't have worried, as he launched up and onto the pillar with an ease that shocked him. "One hundred and thirty-three strength really makes that skill overpowered, huh?"

Joe looked down at the four Hammer Beasts that were attempting to waffle him, and his grin only got wider. Six orbs dropped out of his ring, and lightning crackled through the air at the beasts below. "I need to remember to position myself for combat better in the future. I'm a *spellcaster*. I'm not *supposed* to meet these things head on."

It only took six minutes to finish off the beasts, and Joe

jumped from the pillar with a cheerful smile on his face. Whistling, he cleaned up the battlefield and continued on his way to the Caves of Solitude. He tossed a single Uncommon Core that was glowing brightly into the air, once, twice, then stored it away with a grin.

"I remembered to use Corify this time."

CHAPTER THIRTY-EIGHT

"Why am I not surprised?" Joe shook his head wryly when he reached the caves. A bustling market dominated the foot of a sheer cliff that rose high into the sky, with large banners announcing the 'best in getting away' supplies. He walked past dozens of vendors offering food pills that would allow him not to eat for three days, people selling dehydrated water, and all sorts of things that, frankly... Joe had no idea if they were real or not. Magic made fact out of a myriad of things that used to be false.

It was a massive outpost, but clearly poorly defended. Not a single defensive wall in sight, and the buildings were barely above Trash-rank, if his experience building structures was anything to go by. Joe could see why the 'Air Spirits' were such an issue here; there was likely very little that these people could do against them if the monsters were as powerful as they sounded. He inspected the people more closely as he went past, and revised that thought. They were all at least a *little* battle hardened; there was no way they could be otherwise if serving in the Legion was mandatory, as he had been led to believe.

"Don't go up there!" a bearded Dwarf shouted in Joe's face,

causing the human to flinch back and nearly topple over. "They're blamin' the spirits for all the deaths, but they aren't naturally aggressive! There's *Elves* in the ground, I tell ya! Let me help you; *listen* to me, bro!"

A few of the vendors swiftly surrounded the *exceedingly* filthy Dwarf and started marching him out of the area, offering soothing words and comforting thoughts, all while the bearded Dwarf was shouting that people needed to listen to him. Joe began to feel uneasy and decided that, even though it was starting to get late in the day, he should begin his climb.

Since he already had everything that he needed to survive for a solid week or so, Joe powered right past the 'Solitude Market' and onto a path that wound up the cliff face. The hike lasted about an hour, though there were some Dwarves zipping past him from time to time, making it obvious that higher stats would mean a faster ascent. Every time he thought he had found a cave, it turned out to be a divot with a smooth stone wall closing it off. Joe was starting to think that the caves were actually a myth, and the open air was what the Dwarves were after.

"It would make sense," he grumbled as he found yet *another* switchback. "Hammer beast? Hit it with a Hammer. Air Spirit means earth elemental; it would make a perverse sense if the 'caves' were an open air campground."

Just past the switchback, a large opening in the rock face loomed ahead. He stared at the opening accusingly, wondering if this world was intentionally messing with him. Joe looked around to see if he was being watched or followed, but there was no sign of anyone. The Dwarves he had seen earlier were long gone, and the sun was starting to dip below the horizon. "Sleeping in a cave, here we go."

He braved the opening and took a few cautious steps inside. Just past the mouth of the cave, the space opened up into a large room that had clearly been worked by someone. The walls were too smooth to be natural, and the ventilation was vastly superior to what he had been expecting. One thing especially stood out: a sign with a dial below it.

Set duration of solitude.

Joe thought it over and decided that three days should be enough. He turned the dial and instantly heard a grinding of stone. Looking back at the entrance, he found that a smooth wall was sliding to block the entrance, and his eyes shone as he realized that all the 'not-a-caves' that he had seen before were actually just occupied caves closer to the ground! He had simply been unlucky, in that he had been too slow to get an easy-access area. Once the door finished closing, a small slot flipped open next to the dial, with another small sign.

Core rates for formation.
Trash: 10 hour expansion.
Damaged: 50 hour expansion.
Common: 100-200 hour expansion.

While he wasn't exactly sure what that meant, he wasn't too worried about using up a Trash-ranked Core for testing purposes. He put a small, dull Core into the slot, and it fell down a chute. A moment later, the room started to *grow*. Joe watched in wonder as the cave that had been maybe four hundred square feet expanded in size until it was at least two thousand square feet of open space. "Well, I like *that*. I wonder what the difference is between rituals, enchantments, and formations?"

He sat down on a large pillow that he pulled from the camping supplies, and tried to decide what to do next. "I need to start raising my ritual skill levels up to a respectable level. That means I need to work on my crafting skills, which will also increase my class level. What I really need to do is find ways to work on *all* of them as much as I can."

Joe examined his Ritual Orbs, and thought again about how they seemed to require every part of what he could currently do as a Ritualist: Enchanting, Forging, Alchemy, Circles, and Matrices. "I suppose I could try to work on those skills...? Maybe start guiding my orbs where I want them to be? Oh... I can... yeah. How am I supposed to do any of this, though? I don't have any specialized tools."

He was stumped. While he did have aspects, he had no way of making anything other than ritual circles with the gear that he had with him. "At the most basic level, I need fire and an anvil. That would let me control the cauldron, as well as use an aspect hammer to forge tools. Ugh. I need to make tools, so I can make the tools that I have to use to craft the tools I actually need. I have some kind of an affinity to fire thanks to Hansel, but... no fire spells."

"Okay, I think I was woefully unprepared for this trip." Joe stood and walked over to the dial, trying to figure out how to get the door open. However, nothing he did could make the time go down, and he accidentally twisted it and moved the dial to *four* days! "That... wasn't what I wanted to do."

Sitting back down, he started going over his spells and skills, hoping for an epiphany. On that note, he also remembered to use *Knowledge*, which brought Alchemical Lore to Beginner six, and the Knowledge skill itself up to Beginner four. "It's funny, I have so much *theoretical* knowledge right now, but no way to implement it."

"Maybe I could summon something that has a fiery body, and use it as the basis for a small forge?" Joe wondered aloud as he considered the Planar Shift spell that he had yet to try out. "It's doubtful that I could get it right on the first try, but I have this book... is it worth a try? Who am I kidding? Of course it is! Worst that happens is I blow myself up, but at least that would get me out of the cave."

"To do this normally, I need all of *these?*" Joe ran a finger down all the various components on the book, and shuddered at the thought of having to figure out how to acquire them while trapped in a cave. "Tatum... this is a divine skill, right? Is there any way you could... update this so I can actually use it?"

There was no reply, but Joe felt the book *shift* under his hands. When he looked again, the recipes had been translated into 'Aspect Requirements'. "*Yes*! You rock, Tatum. Hope you get free soon, deity bro… I can't believe those words just left my mouth."

He completely forgot to look at the quest to see how it was progressing, so excited was Joe to try out a Planar Shift. "This looks like what I need… Extraplanar Forge Entities. Looks like the basic Novice version is a Coal Demon… not a huge fan of summoning evil things. Let's see… Beginner is a Flame Imp, still evil. Apprentice is a Slag Elemental? Seems like a *neutral* creature at least. Let's go with that."

The preparations seemed slightly odd, as he didn't need to lay anything out. The Reductionist just needed to form an Inscription tool out of Uncommon Aspects and start drawing out the modified ritual diagram that worked as the summoning target. Before he began, he looked over his aspects to make sure he would have everything he needed.

Aspects gathered
Trash: 11,314
Damaged: 10,431
Common: 8,850
Uncommon: 6,789
Rare: 1,909
Special: 100 (Zombified). 100 (Anima).
Unique: 570
Artifact: 112
Legendary: 0
Mythical: 0

He bound a Common Core to the beautiful silver quill that formed, and started drawing. An hour passed, and Joe felt pleased with the brilliant silver circle that formed the largest outer ring. He checked his aspects again, and his smile faltered as he realized that he had used nearly twenty percent more Uncommon aspects than he should have. There was nothing he could do about it, so he simply started working on the inner diagrams. They were easier to create, both the innermost dark-

and-light gray and second bright white ring taking a combined total of thirty-eight minutes to finish.

Aspects gathered
Trash: 10,879
Damaged: 10,383
Common: 8,760
Uncommon: 6,789
Rare: 1,909
Special: 100 (Zombified). 100 (Anima).
Unique: 570
Artifact: 112
Legendary: 0
Mythical: 0

Core energy: 1,755.5/1,958 (Common)

Once more, he read through the aspects. This time, there was a wastage ranging from fifteen to thirty percent. "Enough of *that*, what in the abyss is going on here? I know I didn't make that many mistakes. Even the Core lost thirty percent more than the recipe says it should!"

A new tutorial has become available: Proper Aspect Storage Containment Creation! Would you like to experience this tutorial? Cost: 3,000 reputation with a deity of your choice!

"Sorry, Tatum. Hope this doesn't hurt our relationship in the long term." Joe slapped 'yes', and was instantly submerged in a world of fog.

Reputation with Occultatum: -3,000. Current reputation: 2,042. Current Reputation Rank: Friendly.

Joe chuckled nervously when nothing appeared right away. "I really hope this was worth it."

CHAPTER THIRTY-NINE

Words made of wispy Trash aspects appeared in the air, narrated by the same calm tone as every other tutorial that had played. Joe sighed in relief, turning his attention fully to the training.

Welcome to the Proper Aspect Storage Containment Creation Tutorial! This section is designed to demonstrate the proper creation of Aspect-specific storage devices.

While it is possible to use any bound storage device to store aspects, there are many negatives that come with using non-specific storage. The most obvious and glaring of these issues is the loss of aspects during transfer. Whether it is during initial storage or practical usage, aspects are lost in the inefficient process.

Let's begin with the creation of an 'Aspect Jar'. An aspect jar is exactly what it sounds like: a jar-shaped receptacle designed to hold a single type of aspect. Contrary to its name, the jar is not actually hollow. In front of you is a finished jar, a recipe to create the jar, and all the materials needed to craft the jar! Start by inspecting the finished product, and do your best to create the jar on your own by following instructions.

Joe looked at the glass container, picked it up, and tried to find anything special about it. It looked like a growler, a jug used to hold about forty ounces of liquid. There was a small opening at the top, but the opening was only a small indent into the solid... glass? Crystal? It was hard to tell for certain. "Jar-shaped something or other. Got it."

He read the recipe next, took note of the materials, then the recipe again. "Glass, diamond dust, magna... um... System? I can't make this. This is clearly a crafting thing, and I can only craft using aspects. Wait... does that mean there are other paths to getting access to aspect usage?"

There was a long wait as the text hovered in the air. Joe wasn't certain that anything was going to change. With no other options available, he took the time and tried to make the item by following the recipe, but each time he put even two things together... they would break into multiple pieces and a warning message would appear telling him that he could only craft with aspects. "This is *clearly* not working."

Tutorial upgraded for free*. Welcome to the Proper Aspect-Created Aspect Storage Containment Creation and Usage tutorial!

"Long name, amazing results." He laughed in relief, but his eyes caught on something as the words vanished faster than they ever had before. "Wait a *second*, what's that asterisk-"

The end result is the same, but the recipe has changed! Now, instead of a varied list of goods that is fairly inexpensive, everything costs aspects and Cores! Congratulations!

"Woo." Joe cheered along with the tutorial just so it didn't turn mean. It appeared that his questions weren't getting answered.

Every aspect needs its own jar. You'll be happy to note, any aspect jar can be made out of any ranked Core! Each rank of Core has a storage capacity maximum and minimum, and creating a larger storage device requires aspects! Here are the Ranks and min/max!
Trash: 1-100
Damaged: 101-999
Common: 1,000-2,000
Uncommon: 2,001-3,999

Rare: 4,000-6,000
Special: 6,001-7,999
Unique: 8,000-10,000
Artifact: 10,001-14,999
Legendary: 15,000-20,000
Mythical: 20,001-?

"That was... convoluted..." Joe tried to read through it a second time, but the words were vanishing already.

You seem to be someone who learns by doing! Let's try making a Trash-ranked aspect jar! Take the Trash-ranked Core provided, and follow the instructions on the recipe!

Joe took a long, calming breath and skimmed the recipe. "Oh. That's not so bad."

The process was similar to enchanting, but less detail-oriented. It reminded him of something else that he had already done in the past, but for the life of him, he couldn't remember what it was. He needed to flood the Core with a specific aspect, then hold the Core with his mana in the final shape of the aspect jar. It went surprisingly smoothly... too smoothly. Joe was suspicious.

Item created: Natural Trash Aspect Jar! This jar has a maximum capacity of 100 Trash aspects, and as such required 10 Trash aspects to create, 14 were used.

Great job, trainee! You created a Trash Aspect Jar! __ERROR__

"Oh, come on. I don't want to lose *more* hair." Joe stared the error message down, but luckily the only thing that happened was a continuation of the tutorial.

As you can see, 10% of the maximum storage is required in order to create an aspect jar. Since you created the Aspect Jar without using the proper method, there was a 40% wastage! Oh, no! Let's look at the next part of the tutorial, and see if we can fix that issue!

"Deep breaths... this is a prerecorded tutorial." Joe looked down at the new jar in his hands. It was *shiny*. There was a light gray tinge to the natural blue of the reshaped Core, giving the entire thing the look of a flame trapped in crystal. He really felt that he could have just sat and stared at this all day. Luckily, the tutorial had a voice associated with it, or he would have missed out on the opening lines.

When storing or using the aspects within the jar, a proper Aspect Array is required. Let's go over how to make the most basic of Aspect Arrays: the Field Array! This is useful for times when you need to reduce something into aspects in the field, or when you just cannot be bothered to take it to a proper reduction site!

Take a look at the sketch, and try to form a three-dimensional version of the design around this Trash-ranked left boot! Once you have managed to form the array, place your jar next to the array and extend a line of mana to the indent of the jar!

More instructions will follow!

If the earlier section had been surprisingly easy, this section was *riotously* difficult. Joe had plenty of control over the mana when it was in his body, but it constantly wanted to steam away when he was extending it more than an *inch* past his skin. He ran out of mana over and over again, only getting better due to slamming his face against the issue constantly. He was sure that the tutorial helped, or he certainly wouldn't have learned how to make the Field Array in the amount of time that he did. Then, he got it. It *clicked* into place.

Spell learned: Field Array. (Max). This spell only has a single rank. By casting this around a target and linking it to an aspect jar, the target can be reduced with a maximum of 5% loss, +1% per rarity level of target aspect! Fixed cost: 100 mana. Can be maintained indefinitely. User cannot move more than five feet from the array, or it will break and need to be re-made.

Skill increase: Mana Manipulation (Student V).

"Wow." Joe stared at a message he hadn't seen in *far* too long. "I suppose that makes sense... manipulation of mana outside of the body *was* really difficult."

Congratulations on learning the Field Array! Let's try it out: reduce the boot and guide the aspects that try to escape into the array, draining them into the jar!

A flash of mana later, the boot was gone. Light grey wispy

fire illuminated the array, and all of it was pulled into the jar. He wanted to check it out, but the next section was already starting.

Great work! As a note: recreating the array with more permanent and aspect-absorbent material will allow you to minimize losses when reducing items or creating new ones!

Now let's use the array to create a second Trash aspect jar! Using the array, surround the Core, link the Trash aspect jar, and place your hands in the 'hands here' aspect-influx zone. It has been highlighted this time, so make sure to memorize the pattern for future use! Then, guide the aspects along the mana tubules and convert the Core and aspects into the pattern required for an aspect jar.

It went quickly, just as it had before, and once more, there was a notification of a 'Natural Aspect Jar' being created, an error, and a congratulatory message from the system. Then, it seemed that the tutorial was complete.

Don't forget that you can use more potent Cores to create larger jars! You can also vary the size of the Field Array to surround larger or smaller objects as needed! New information is now always available; in your crafting section, pull up 'Aspect Jar' information to refresh your understanding of your storage needs!

Then Joe was back in the cave, staring down at a completed Planar Shift ritual. He blinked a few times and blearily scanned the enclosed space. Just like every time before, it seemed that no time had passed at all. He couldn't be *certain* of that, as there was nothing in the cave to show time, but he *felt* that it was correct. "I... okay, I think that entire thing was telling me that what I really need to do is create a permanent building where I do my crafting. I need a potent array if I ever want to work with Mythical aspects, otherwise the loss is gonna be... just... huge."

Wisdom +1!

Joe gasped in pleasure. "A *mental* stat increase! *Ooh!*"

CHAPTER FORTY

Joe was dazed by the shift away from the misty tutorial world and back into his expanded cave. It took a few moments to reorient himself, so he reviewed his notifications. Nothing pressing or overly important demanded his attention, so he turned his eyes back to the summoning circles that were prepared and laid out in front of him. "That was a serious diversion, but at least I have a better understanding of what I need to be doing."

"As for this summoning circle... If I'm missing anything, I can't think of what it might be. Let's use the Planar Shift." *Something* was calling for attention in the back of his mind, a warning that he just couldn't put into words, but... he couldn't think of anything he was forgetting. Joe slammed his hand onto the circle and released a thousand mana into it before he could talk himself out of doing so. The outer circle lit up, then the inner, and finally the last one shifted from grey to black in an instant; the entire interior was saturated with the inky color, as if he had used the 'bucket fill' function in a paint program.

The black space seemed to *drop*, as if it had cut a deep hole into the earth that was trying to pull everything into it. He stared at the summoning spot for a long minute, nearly getting knocked back as a wave of heat blasted out and up. Instead of abating, the sweltering heat only climbed higher and higher, reaching a climax as a creature pulled itself into view. "Fire! Hot! Enclosed room! *That's* what I was forgetting!"

Reductionist class experience gained: 100.

Slag elemental. The entity was hard to describe, as it had no features. Even Joe's coffee elemental had tiny coffee beans for eyes, but *this*? There was only a strange pile of multiple goopy metals and impurities that bubbled and frothed, exuding *heat* the entire time. It was like… a metal slime. Joe reached out with his thoughts and his words, not entirely sure what would be the best way to open a line of communication. "Can you understand me?"

There was a returned feeling of agreement—and slight hostility—as well as an angry emote that the being was *cold*. It demanded heat as payment for continuing to remain on this plane, but… getting access to heat was why Joe had summoned this thing in the first place. He needed high temperatures *from* this thing. "Slag… pile. What I need is for you to heat things for me. Metals especially, but other implements as well. What can I do to make that happen? To make a deal between us?"

Mana.

The concept, as well as instructions, struck him like a hammer ringing a gong. Joe needed to link to it and let his mana feed the beast. All Joe needed to do was agree to the terms of the deal. If he cut off the flow of mana, the elemental would return home. If Joe turned hostile… he was threatened with becoming nothing more than a handful of impurities on the surface of the elemental. Joe had no problem with that, as he needed to work, not fight. In agreement with each other, the human instantly flushed red as mana started to drain out of him in a strange and unpleasant way. It felt as though his internal energy was being converted to fire before leaving his body, and he did *not* enjoy the process.

Link to Slag Elemental successful! Mana investment: 300, +30 per second. -4 health per second.

Skill increase: Planar Shift (Student 1). You did everything right, and even bonded the summon to your will on the first try! Critical success!

Caution! Although you do have a perfect fire affinity, as this is your first time using fire-type mana, you may experience some unpleasant side effects.

"That's an understatement." Joe wiped his nose, his sleeve coming away bloody before his Neutrality Aura scrubbed away all traces that it had ever been there. Joe watched the floor nervously as the summoning circles lifted and surrounded himself and the elemental, binding the creature to his will at the same time as putting the details of their bargain into play. At this point, if he had made a small error in the creation of the circles, the binding would fail and the creature might become hostile to him. Yet, his fears went unrealized as the elemental started following his orders right away. It moved into the exact center of the room and shifted its malleable form to focus and maximize the heat directly above itself.

"Right. The first thing I want to do is bind a characteristic to one of my Ritual Orbs, so let's make a..." Joe checked the data of the orbs, and shifted the direction of his thoughts. "Nevermind! That's an *enchanted* ritual circle. Which I could have done without a Slag Elemental. Or *instead* of summoning it. I... let's pretend this wasn't an accident and bind a spell. Potion making time!"

Without further ado, Joe dropped his cauldron out of his ring and on top of the elemental, which started sending him excited emotions. It rubbed against the metal of the cauldron, but it couldn't leave a mark, no matter what it did. The heat started to rise rapidly, but to its apparent surprise, the elemental couldn't heat it up even a single degree. Joe could, and did, by controlling the cauldron to absorb the heat in specific patterns. Feelings of amazement came from the elemental, and Joe grinned cockily.

"To create an alchemical ritual, I need alchemical reagents.

INFLAME

Potions. To make potions, I need to use this cauldron and the required aspects. Let's see here…" Joe opened the information on one of his Ritual Orbs and wrote down the recipe needed for making a binding potion. "Okay… I need to make a potion at the same rank as the spell if I want to use it at full power. Or I can make weaker potions and use the spell as a weaker version of itself, like I did when I made that ritual for spraying acid. My skill level for alchemy is at… Beginner three. Do I have any spells that I could use at that rank?"

Joe perused his skills and spells, finding two spells that would be a good fit for his first attempts. Both Cone of Cold and Corify were perfectly situated in the Beginner ranks, and the thought of automatically using them as on-hit effects was just… *exciting*. "Right… to make a Beginner-ranked potion, a Draught, I need to use…"

He glanced at his crafting sheet to double check, "Common aspects are the highest that would need to be in there. That should be pretty straightforward, since I have lots of those."

Joe formed an oversized spatula-bucket thing using Common aspects, nearly instantly holding a bright white… implement. He was sure it had a proper name, but, oh well. The aspects flowed down the tool, and he used his knowledge of alchemy to coat the cauldron in specific places. The aspects reacted to the cauldron exactly as he would expect standard components to do: burning, sizzling, becoming aromatic. It was odd, because he was working with aspects of Trash, Damaged aspects, and finally Common aspects; but it smelled like frying rosemary and garlic.

He followed the recipe exactly, and over the next forty-five minutes, the aspects began to congeal. Joe's attention to the heat didn't waver, and as the newly-formed liquid condensed, he began removing the heat entirely. One second, two… and the liquid flashed white. Joe scooped it up and poured it into a large bowl, eyeballing it carefully. "I have enough here for two portions, easy."

Reductionist class experience gained: 100 (50 x2).
Skill increase: Ritualistic Alchemy (Beginner IV).
Profession experience gained: 101 (Ritualistic Alchemist).

"Nice! Now to draw out the alchemical rituals." Joe pulled the cauldron into his ring, against the complaints of the Slag Elemental, and started sketching the ritual diagram that was displayed in the information panel of his orbs. "Two circles for a Beginner-ranked ritual, already have my inscriber…"

Joe muttered to himself for the next hour as he drew out first one entire ritual, then a second one. He checked them over carefully, finding no issues. They were perfect copies; both of each other, as well as the original diagram. "Let's *do* this!"

An orb went into each one, though he only poured the potion on the first, as well as placing a Common Core on the edge. With an outpouring of mana, the first ritual circles lit up. The pressure mounted, and Joe stared at it for almost a moment too long. Luckily, there was a built-in prompt.

Cast the spell you want to assign to the orb directly onto the orb!

"Corify goes first." Joe held out a hand and cast the spell on the first orb. He blinked as the knowledge of how to cast the spell vanished from his mind. It was a sickening, invasive feeling to have the thoughts scrubbed out of his head so completely.

Spell successfully assigned! Use a Ritual of Unbinding or break the Ritual Orb to regain personal usage of the spell! Remember to add a Core or Mana Battery to the orb so that it can cast the spell!

Joe held up the newly spell-assigned orb, noting that a small, glowing blue square had been etched into it. "Okay, that's super cool. Totally forgot about making mana batteries, though. Maybe I should hold off on assigning Cone of Cold…? Nah."

Repeating the process of ritual activation with a side of alchemy, he assigned the spell to the second orb. This time, a white swirl of wind and snowflakes was etched into the orb, and once again, the spell was removed from his mind. Joe admired the orbs in his hands, already plotting out the next steps.

"I need to assign characteristics to these, but first, I really need to figure out the battery situation." Joe sat on his sleeping bag for the next while, writing down the next steps he needed to take to make the weapons more powerful. He leaned back against the wall with a satisfied sigh, storing his notebook away. "Now to-"

Just then, the entire room *shrank*. The Slag Elemental was scooted *closer*; so close that it burned off Joe's left eyebrow before he could turn his head away. The human screeched as his skin began to blister. "Slag! Get as far away as possible!"

The Elemental did its best to comply, roiling to the far wall and squishing itself against it. Though it left a trail of molten rock on the ground, the heat directly impacting the Reductionist lowered enough that Joe wasn't literally dying by the second. Joe reactivated all of his protections and shielding, which he had taken off to ensure he had plenty of power for the rituals, and looked over to thank the elemental for following the orders so quickly. They were now in a four hundred square foot rock cave, and if it had hesitated any longer, Joe might have melted just like the wall was.

"Wait..." Joe squinted at the stone wall behind the elemental. "Rock shouldn't melt away as completely as whatever *that* is..."

Carefully making his summon move in time with him so that he didn't get scorched again, Joe went over to inspect the space where it had been standing. There was a small hole in the rock, about six inches behind where the wall 'ended'. It was especially visible because a strange, soft light was shining through. As Joe had Darkvision, he hadn't bothered to light any torches. That worked out well for him, because just as he peered through the hole, a hulking earth elemental, an 'Air Spirit', walked past... closely followed by what were clearly Elven summoners.

"Abyss. That crazy Dwarf at the base of the cliff was right." Joe watched as the Elf moved along, catching the exact position where they faded out of existence. "Oh, look. A fast travel point. No wonder the Dwarves could never figure out how the non-hostile 'Air Spirits' were attacking Dwarves in the caves."

Quest update: Air Spirits Suck. You found the reason the spirits are invading this territory! Either report your findings, or continue questing to put a stop to the issue on your own.

Quest update: Go Away For a While! Level gained: 0/1. Elves killed: 0/100. Important information gained: 1/1.

CHAPTER FORTY-ONE

The Reductionist now had a dilemma. Should he go and report his discovery right away… or should he enter the tunnel system and try to learn more information? There were pros and cons to each of the options. Namely, if he left the cave, the door would open and light would shine through and into the tunnels. The Elves might be given a chance to close this off.

But, if Joe was fast enough, he might be able to get an entire battalion of Dwarves back here. He would need to get out at night, and… he looked at the dial that still showed a 'four'. If the room shrinking back down was any indication, he was stuck in here for at least three and a half more days, unless he went out through the tunnel. Joe sat and watched the hole for another few minutes, but he didn't see any more Elves. That was unsurprising. He guessed it was… early. *Very* early. If the sun was going down—cut off by the mountain—around four in the afternoon the previous day, then it made sense that most rational people would be asleep.

"If I'm going to go… it needs to be now." Joe motioned for Salgathor—his new name for the Slag Elemental—to hurry over and start melting the wall. While he waited for an opening large enough to fit through, he cracked open his two Ritual Orbs and placed Common ranked Cores in them.

Ritual Orb of Corify. Charge remaining: 1,112/1,112. Cost per hit: 65. Cooldown: 4 Seconds.

Ritual Orb of Cone of Cold. Charge remaining: 1,545/1,545. Cost per hit: 195. Cooldown: 24 Seconds.

"That's… expensive." Joe winced at the hefty cost associated with using the now on-hit effects. "Cone of Cold can only be used eight times before it drains the Core?"

Slagathor finished melting into the tunnel and squeezed through. Joe gave the path enough time to cool down, then *jumped* through and started walking down the unlit corridor. The elemental started rolling alongside him, and Joe wavered between letting it guard the area, or just going it alone. "Hey… I've decided that I'm gonna need my mana, so I need you to go. If I call out into your plane another time, is there a way that we can work together again?"

Feelings of acceptance came back to him, so Joe cut the flow of mana between them. Since the terms of his side of the bargain were no longer being met, the elemental instantly vanished, like a soap bubble popping. Now down a protector, the human rushed over to the spot where he had seen the Elf vanish. He felt around, listening to his Hidden Sense, until he found the spot where he could take control of the point. He didn't activate it just yet, instead opting to use its function.

The point was set to 'open travel', likely due to capturing Dwarves and carting around massive creatures made of rock. A message appeared, asking if he wanted to travel to 'point Qfzt1554'.

"Don't mind if I do." Joe stepped through just as he blinked, and found that he was *sweating* right though his Neutrality Aura. A low red light filled the area, and the *heat*…! Quickly searching for a place to hide and figure out his next move, Joe spotted something that boggled his mind. Two things, actually.

He was clearly inside an active volcano. That was a pretty

big deal. It explained both the light and the heat. Frankly, ever since someone had mentioned a volcano a few days previous, he was almost certain that he would eventually go into one. The second chunk of news was a bit more alarming: he could see an entire fort within the cavern. If this was the volcano he thought it was, Gramma's Shoe, then it meant that there was an Elven outpost practically right *next* to the Dwarven capital city!

"*How?* How could this go undetected?" Joe breathed the words softly, not trusting that he could keep quiet enough at even a low speaking volume. His mind was buzzing with possibilities, but the main thought spinning around was that the Elven race were masters of illusion magic. Joe had only heard one thing about the most active volcano in the entire Zone, namely that it was so dangerous that no one should ever go there. Had that always been a lie, or had something changed?

"They must have this place layered in illusions so thick that you can *swim* through them!" Joe's eyes were so wide that it felt like they were about to fall out. He was glad that he had come here; there was no chance that they could have found this place if the Elves had shut down the fast travel points. He was frazzled, unable to even think about how he could alert the Dwarves or stop this…

"Wait." Joe peered at the fort in the distance. "Wait, wait, wait. That many illusions…? There *has* to be a permanent structure supporting something that powerful. I can do something about *that*."

The entire area was a series of lava flows that had hardened, and drifting ash had settled in thick drifts. There were plenty of niches where Joe could go to hide and get off the main path. As long as he avoided any actual lava… or was it magma? He was technically underground, so he felt that it would be magma, but it *was* on the surface… "What am I doing?"

Illusion Breaker (Ring) has come into effect!
Illusion broken through: Fae Beckoning.

"So there *are* defenses, even in here." Joe realized that he was standing up and staring at the lava in the distance, so he tossed himself back to the ground and started trying to blend in. His bright white clothing and reflective head wasn't helping him, so Joe did the only reasonable thing he could do: he turned off Neutrality Aura and rolled around in the volcanic ash that was covering everything. Sweat started to run down his body right away, and he began to *itch* terribly. "Whoo, boy. I've gotten really spoiled from being clean at all times."

Joe started to creep along a low patch, sliding forward using only his elbows and knees to maintain the lowest profile possible. The wall of the fort wasn't too terribly far away, maybe a tenth of a kilometer? The fort itself was roughly a kilometer from the stone wall in all directions, but the travel point was luckily far closer. His path couldn't be straight, as that would stand out to anyone that happened to be on guard. An hour into his snail-paced scuttling, he started hearing voices and the heavy grinding of stone that signified Earth Elementals in the distance.

"How could they think that a *Dwarf* saw through the grand illusion? I refuse to put those mongrels in my eyes!" A high-pitched, arrogant voice echoed over the empty space. "Even if they *had* broken through into the tunnels, there's no way they could have come through here. They'd have been caught staring at the shifting patterns of the lava on the ceiling by now!"

"The Lady Elfreeda is gnashing her teeth over this failure, *Journeyman*." Another voice cut off the first. "We *should* have closed the way to the caves a week ago. We have plenty of test subjects, and the illusions have proven to be perfect. The only reason they stayed open is the rank *lethargy* of the 'Helper' she found. Who forgets to close the abyssal *door* when we are this close to a successful strike at the heart of the short ones?"

"I still say that the Dwarf in that cave must have incinerated itself. The entire room was practically melted, as was the opening and path in a straight line. The wall to escape was still closed, and the Dwarves have no idea how to use any travel system other than the option provided by the fortresses; that Dwarf is long dead," the first voice petulantly complained.

"Still, *her* orders aren't something we can ignore."

There was more to the conversation, but they had been moving fast enough that Joe had needed to strain his ears just to hear everything that he had. His progress had come to a complete stop; he wasn't sure if the earth elementals would be able to detect him if he was moving and causing vibrations. Eventually, Joe had no choice but to start crawling again and hope the thick coating of ash prevented the elementals from detecting him. He was close enough to the unmanned wall at this point that he doubted anyone would expect him to be here, but if they were searching carefully... they would eventually find him.

Issue resolved!

The human had to grab his mouth and throat to prevent a scream from spilling out when the random fanfare and bugles started playing in his head.

Your complaint about the new 'intent' system factoring into kills has been resolved in your favor! After extensive review, it was shown that the deadly rituals you use instead of commonplace effects are more similar to a trapmaker or rogue's ability to use environmental effects. No longer will you need to worry about variation rituals; just clean or murder, all in one, to your heart's content!

While future actions—or wide-scale devastation released upon a Zone—may result in a different outcome or secondary analysis, you will be rewarded for finding and reporting this issue upon completing any future quest.

So long as the reward meets the certain criteria, it will be applied multiple times. For instance, a quest rewarding you with a thousand experience may also give you a thousand class experience!

Breathing heavily, he dismissed the notification as quickly as possible. There was nothing he could do with that information right now, but it still gave him a small thrill to see something resolve in his favor when it came to the system. Looking up at the wall he was practically huddled against, Joe raised himself to a crouching position and shifted around until he was fairly certain that no one would see him.

The gate was a solid distance away, and he hadn't seen a single Elf walking the walls. That may have changed since they had gone on alert, but he was going to have to chance it at some point. Now was as good a time as any. Eyeing the wall, he got into the proper position and *jumped*. He blew out nearly a hundred mana in an attempt to make a smooth landing, but he ended up only reaching a third of the way up the forty foot wall.

He fell and landed in an ignoble pile, kicking up a cloud of ash with his impact. "Well... plan B. Been wanting to try this for a while, so why not now?"

Joe pulled a single Ritual Orb out of his ring, and tossed it into the air. Up, up... he stopped it about five feet under the height he had reached last time, which was marked by a streak of black soot. "Okay, keep the orb in that spot, land on it, and jump again. Don't think, just *do*!"

Air rushed past his face, and he kept his eyes locked on the orb as he sailed up. His right foot landed on the orb, which started to drop almost instantly, but he managed to kick off it hard enough to get another third up toward the top of the wall. Another orb was summoned under his foot, and he kicked off that as well. Over the wall he went, rolling to be as flat as possible. Just as he arced over the peak of the barrier, he managed to lock his eyes on the orbs before they hit the ground and were buried in ash. In a moment, both orbs sailed up to his hand and into his ring.

Skill increase: Aerial Acrobatics (Beginner III).

"Haven't seen *you* in a while," Joe whispered at the notification with a massive grin on his face. That had been a *rush*. He glanced around the battlements to ensure there wasn't a patrol coming, then turned his gaze down into the unexpectedly massive interior of the fortress. "Oh, celestial feces. This is a *major* fort, isn't it?"

CHAPTER FORTY-TWO

The fort below was filled with a variety of 'buildings' Joe had never seen before. Only the wall that he was crouching on seemed to be made by hand, while everything else within the confines seemed to be some variant of a plant. Even so, the general layout fit with what he had been expecting to see.

"That must be sleeping quarters, that *has* to be a dining facility, and that…" Joe's eyes locked on a building that radiated a literal rainbow, which shot up and shifted into an aurora that couldn't be seen from outside the walls. "That's gonna be the illusion generation area. Oh, look. It's right next to the Guardian. What a shock; the most important thing is in the most protected area."

There were also *hundreds* of Elves milling about. There was no chance that Joe was going to be able to sneak through, and trying would end with him being caught and thrown into a prison. There was really only one option, but the chances of it succeeding were… slim. He reactivated Neutrality Aura and waited until his clothes were clean and sparkling again. Checking that his mask was in place, he stood up and calmly walked to the first set of stairs he could find, drifting down them in a careful yet grand fashion.

Then he just… strolled into the open area. He didn't look around, having already plotted out where he needed to go thanks to his previous vantage. No one said anything at first, but by the time he had passed the second building, he was starting to gather stares and hear whispers.

"Just don't talk to anyone…" Joe reminded himself, hoping that keeping his mouth shut—combined with his mask and confident manner—would stop anyone from realizing that he was not supposed to be there. Maybe Havoc *had* taught him something, after all. When he was over halfway to his destination, a young-looking Elf blocked his path. "So close."

"Yo, who ah' ya?" The Bostonian accent was extra thick with this one, and if Dwarven traits were at all similar, that meant that this Elf was fairly low-leveled, or at least low-ranked. Joe said nothing, simply continuing on in a straight line. Just before he would have run into the Elf, the long-eared androgynous male got out of Joe's way.

Small conversations rose all around them. "Hey, he gave Tony zero face there."

"Whoa, look at that big shot, he must be some kinda wise-guys or somethin'."

"Quiet down; that must be the Helper that the Lady called in. No one *normal* is gonna ignore *Tony*."

The Elf that Joe almost ran into, Tony, looked as though he was about to start a fight until the last comment rang out. Then he seemed to deflate slightly and called after Joe, who was still moving at a sedate pace. "Hey, youze the *Helper*? I got a bone ta pick with you."

Joe ignored the Elf and kept going, sealing in their minds that he was someone they shouldn't mess with. Still, he couldn't bear the pressure of their stares, and only went another block or so before turning into a storefront. He didn't go inside, merely pretending to peruse the items in the… window equivalent. It was some kind of translucent leaf, he was almost certain. He waited there for only a minute, then continued toward the illusion-generating area.

He almost made it, too.

The flashing building was in sight. Unsurprisingly, it was shaped like a tree and surrounded by strange, half-built structures. Half-*grown* or half-built? Frankly, this entire place was alien to him, to the point where he was questioning basic concepts. The architecture alone... Joe shook his head, clearing his thoughts just as an alarm bell went off. He flinched as a huge voice roared into some kind of enhancement system, "Intruder alert! There's a human in a black robe, wearing white clothes and a mask! Find him, and *capture* him! Do *not*, under *any* circumstances, allow that human to go to respawn! The capture field is being activated as quickly as possible!"

Joe calmly turned into the first completed building he could find, opening the door and closing it gently behind him. He pulled out the Ritual Orb that had Cone of Cold assigned to it, gripping the weapon tightly to help ease his nerves, as well as to better prepare himself. Another orb popped into his left hand, and he tried to run through any combat spells that might be useful. Before he could get far, he heard musical voices arguing, slightly further within the building.

The human pushed himself up against the wall, slowly approaching the room full of people that were clearly arguing. The door was open, and he could hear that they were debating over whether to join the search for the intruder or not. Not wasting any time, Joe peeked his head around the corner and cast Dark Lightning Strike at the loudest voices, wincing as he saw that the room was *full* of Elves sitting around a table.

As the lightning struck, Joe tossed The Ritual Orb of Cone of Cold in as well, hitting an Elf in the head as his back arched in pain from the shock of dark energy. Cone of Cold washed over the room, and not a single one of the... six Elves managed to escape the icy clutches of the spell.

Experience gained: 1,105

Quest update: Go Away For a While! Level gained: 0/1. Elves killed: 6/100. Important information gained: 1/1.

Just the Dark lightning Strike alone had killed the Elf it had hit directly, the splash damage and Cone of Cold had finished off the others in the next instant. Joe looked around the room in surprise; that had been *way* too easy. "They... oh. They didn't have any protections up. Why would they? They're in a 'safe' area. Solid reminder to me; shield up at all times. Now... what were they doing?"

Something on the table was calling to Joe, an oversized briefcase that was practically *singing* to his senses. He reached out and picked it up, undid the latch... and someone banged on the door he had come in through. Joe slammed his hips forward and pulled the briefcase into his codpiece just as a voice screeched through the door. "Honorable *Shapers*! I am so sorry to intrude upon your discussion. There's an intruder, and we've been sent to evacuate you until they have been found!"

Joe thought that this might be a good time to book it, so he frantically hurried through the small building. There were no extra doors, but there was a waxy leaf-window at the back. He grabbed at it, but the leaf demonstrated surprising toughness. He kicked it instead, and thankfully, his foot went through. Joe was able to tear a way out after that, but resolved to carry a knife or *something* the next time he left the protections of the Dwarven domain.

Now that he was behind the building, away from the streets, he found that he was also almost directly adjacent to the Illusion building. It was... really, the entire thing was a work of art. The building was almost the same size as the exterior of the Mage's college back on Midgard, but this structure was shaped like a massive pine tree. Every 'pine needle' acted as a relay for the light that was generated in the 'trunk' of the tree, flashing colors of varying intensity that added to the rainbow that spread along the ceiling.

He had no idea if the building itself was generating the illusion, or if it was just the shell acting as protection for the magic being worked within it. Either way, Joe was fairly certain that destroying one should get the other as well. He walked to the edge of the building and peeked around... to find the streets swarming with Elves. He could hear them from here:

"Humph!"

"How dare a toad look at swan flesh?"

"This intruder is a thousand years too early!"

Joe felt sick to his stomach at the sheer cliché arrogance that was being tossed around. "I really need to get outta this place. *So* glad I chose the Dwarves."

He *jumped* through the open space between buildings, front-flipping as he did his best to move as rapidly as possible. Joe got closer and closer to the strobing building, and was finally close enough to run a hand over the strange wood, no... crystal? It was a crystal grown to look like wood and pine needles, practically a christmas tree, but *why*?

Without a single sound, a ritual paper appeared in his hand, and he slapped it against the side of the building; a Ritual of Raze, ready to go. He hesitated, almost activating it right away, but that would give away his position immediately. Should he try to hide in the foliage? His hand brushed against a needle, and his shield took penetrating damage in an instant. Going up was not going to be viable, so that meant he needed to go inside if he wanted to activate his ritual in a semi-safe location. Since there were no windows that he could see in this building, the entrance was the only point of ingress.

Joe slunk around the wall, the bright colors flashing from the walls actually helping him as he went. He thought it would highlight him, but all it really did was keep Elves from looking directly at him and his reflective head. He had the door in sight when he heard someone call out, "Get two guards on the Prismatic Evergreen! I want *no* mistakes while the Lady is here!"

Giving up all pretenses of stealth, Joe dashed to the door, fearing that he would hear shouts of alarm. He reached for the handle, instead falling directly through the 'door'. "Of course the door was an illusion. Abyssal *Elves*."

The building he found himself in appeared to be a massive, open cone that twisted as high as a redwood on earth. The wall opposite him was so distant that it would have been hidden by shadow, had the light in the area been less *intense*. Either the space was an illusion, or the building was bigger on the inside. Spatial magic, again? He really shouldn't have been surprised, as this was *clearly* a powerful and rare building.

Joe's main concern at the moment was the cadre of Elves in the center of the room, a football field's distance away from him. Again, their distance had to be attributed to either an illusion or space-bending. Music, soft and entrancing, was flowing through the room, expanding outward from the Elves that were dancing in the central area. The rapid, pulsing strobe light of various colors was completely out of time with the music, but somehow the two interfaced and seemed to be whispering secrets of magic and forbidden lore to Joe. If he would just look *closer*, if he would just follow the light to… Joe blinked as a notification appeared.

Illusion Breaker's effect successful! You have been caught in 'Fae Beckoning' for four minutes and five seconds.

Joe was standing in a corner of the building with his nose pressed into the smooth surface of the wall. He stepped back and looked around; somehow, he hadn't been noticed during all of that. A glance revealed no enemies near him, just small growths of crystal slabs with shaped crystal ornaments displayed on them. Oh. A random dais as well; just to be consistent with the fantasy setting, he was sure. Beams of light reached from the pulsing glow in the ceiling, filtering down to each of the shaped crystals.

They had a look to them that Joe was familiar with, and if he was correct, it meant the crystals were stabilizing mechanisms for whatever spell was being continuously cast from this place. "I bet those are important for the continued successful camouflage of this place. Right, well, enough of that!"

He pulled out the Ritual of Raze that he had decided against using outside and stuck it in the corner. "If I get trapped here, I need to make sure that the Dwarves can figure this out. *Activate*."

A ring of light expanded from the pre-charged ritual, moving to surround the building and commence destroying it. A secondary ring appeared under Joe, indicating that that ritual was still active. Joe turned his eyes on the patterns etched throughout the walls as cries of alarm rang out. "I need to do more. I need to *fully* sabotage this place."

CHAPTER FORTY-THREE

Joe sprinted to one of the many strange objects that were scattered through the room on the crystal slabs and small plinths, skidding to a halt and slapping his hands on the perfectly triangular crystal. A flash of mana seeped out of him, and information appeared in his mind.

Item: Illusion Prism Focus.
Reduction value: 99 Rare aspects, 129 Uncommon aspects, 910 Common aspects, 7,991 Trash aspects.
Reduction cost: 125 mana per second.

"Yes please, and thank *you*. I wonder if it has no damaged aspects because it's in a perfect crystalline form? I really need to learn more about my abilities and what each aspect does." Joe let his mana seep into it for one second, two, then intentionally let go. He didn't want to fully destroy these, since that would be *noticed*. If he could weaken a bunch of them, then even if he were killed and his ritual was stopped, Joe would be able to feel secure in the knowledge that the illusions would break at some point. He hurried to the next one, then crossed the room after heavily damaging it. On the tenth, his reduction went too long and accidentally fully destroyed the prism.

The room strobed red as the beam of light that had been attached to the prism recoiled up into the mass of pulsating illumination. The lights that were attached to the other prisms thickened slightly, the surviving crystals needing to handle slightly more energy. Joe heard an Elf shout, "I don't care *what* the orders were, if this goes down, we're *all* abyssed! Just try not to kill him until it's ready!"

"Oh, I don't like the sound of that." Joe rushed over to the next plinth, destroying the prism entirely. Then the next. They were going down, but the effort was hard and draining. The light was pulsing harder, and the beams were growing thicker with each crystal destroyed, but it wasn't enough yet.

Capture field activated!

"What does that mean?" Joe's answer was a burst of mana shooting into the corner where he had activated the ritual. In the next instant, the ritual ring under his feet vanished. The ritual had been deactivated, at the least, in an instant. "Oh snap-"

In the next moment, he was flying across the room, a mana-made hand having slapped him harder than a train could have. Joe impacted a plinth at speed, his Exquisite Shell fracturing into nothing as blood splattered from his mouth. Joe's fuzzy thoughts reminded him that this was a good indication that his internal organs were damaged.

Damage taken: 4,308
Exquisite Shell: 0/3,586
Health: 920/1,642

"A *human*? Of course it was a human; a Dwarf would have been too obvious." The voice reaching Joe's ears was sharp and hateful. There was very little trace of an accent or strange dialect, making Joe nervous about the rank or power level of this particular individual. He turned his head and watched her as she walked toward him. "I am Lady Elfreeda, known as the Lady of Light, and *you-*"

A Dark Lightning Strike bounced off her, dealing no damage but managing to interrupt her train of thought. Elfreeda stared at the human in astonishment, and Joe let out a wet chuckle. "Mandatory quest. Need to try to kill you whenever I see you."

"A follower of *Havoc*. I should have known it from the start." Lady Elfreeda actually took a step away from Joe, for whatever reason. "Was this your great plan, human? An unguarded ritual? Breaking a few toys and diminishing the stability of the grand illusion an insignificant amount? What are you, a child? Let me explain to you what happens now. You go onto a small island surrounded by magma, unable to escape and tell anyone of the impending attack. Daily, you will be... *pressed* for information. Information that I know you'll have, as a follower of that *animal*."

Joe tried to use Dark Lightning strike on her again, but the spell failed. She smirked at him, "You think I can't lock down magic in my area once I've seen you use it? You poor, simple-"

A stream of acid sloshed over her, doing nothing but making her flinch. Anger colored her features as much as the strobing light did. "Enough of this. Take him, and we'll see how long he can last-"

As soon as she started giving orders, Joe reached up to the prism on the plinth that he had slammed into, reducing it and activating Essence Cycle at the same time. He stared at his uplifted arms and the ritual engraved upon them... and his head exploded, showering the area in gore.

Lady Elfreeda stared at the bloody mess left behind for a long moment, then shook her head and sighed. "Fool. All you did was save me a trip."

She was about to go find the island that he had been placed upon and begin the interrogation herself, but the sound of a crystal shattering drew her attention. One of the plinths she had been standing near had gotten a full dose of Joe's acid, as well as being greatly weakened beforehand. Another shattered on its own, the beam coming from the ceiling too intense for it to handle. A few more broke over the next few seconds, and the Lady paled as she whirled into action, attempting to stabilize the spell on her own. "Chain reaction of destruction? Follower of Havoc indeed. Get someone out to him, and get the Shapers growing new foci, *now!*"

―――――

Joe didn't open his eyes to the respawn room like he had expected. Instead, he found himself on a large rock surrounded by molten... Joe still hadn't decided for sure if it were magma or lava, no matter what the Elf had said. He checked his notifications, trying to learn where he had gone wrong.

You have been caught in a capture field! All major forts have the option of respawning a small number of the enemies killed into a 'jail' area instead of allowing them to actually die. Escape, be released, or be rescued if you want to get away!

Joe stood, almost gagging when he realized that his entire body *hurt*. Checking his health, he saw that it was only at one hundred, and an attempt to heal himself only resulted in a loss of mana. "Looks like I can still cast spells, at least. I didn't lose experience... so they must be paying the cost of my death instead of me? That must be one of the faults of something like this."

He limped around the rock, searching for anything he could use to help himself. The surface which had not actively melted was only about five feet in diameter, and the entire area was surrounded by a light illusion, creating a shifting wall that completely blocked his vision. He could be right next to more land, or surrounded by lava for hundreds of feet. There was no way to know without testing. Not giving himself a second option, he *jumped* as hard as he could, going higher and higher… then blinked, finding himself on the island once again. "Can't go through the illusion, then? Or… did I even jump? That makes things difficult."

Joe sat down and tried to think of a plan, but found that he could only groan and close his eyes. He was exhausted. He wanted a nap… he could plot his escape later. It would be better to just wait until—he jolted himself into motion as he realized that something was impacting his way of thinking. "That's not good. That illusion was *insidious*. I need to do *something* at all times, or I'm gonna give up."

There was only one thing that he could think to do while stuck on a rock with nothing else on it. He needed tools, and to prepare himself. *When* he escaped, Joe fully planned to be ready. "So… what should I make? Should I… can I reduce magma? I give up; it's magma. I can't exactly touch it, but maybe…"

Joe activated Field Array, the lines of mana arching out and dipping into the magma. He let his hand get close to the lava, but jerked it away with a hiss. An idea sparked to life as he activated Exquisite Shell, and he put his hand directly into the molten stuff.

-4 damage per second. (Bonus resistance to elemental effects.)

Joe flooded the small patch of magma with mana, finding that it was all rated as 'Common'. With the array active, he started reducing the boiling earth; content to just pull in aspects until his mana ran out. The magma poured back into position as it was reduced, slower than water, but it was so hot that it was fully liquid. Joe checked his aspects after the third time his mana ran out, seeing only one thing that he hadn't expected.

Special Aspect, Molten: 400.

"Molten?" Joe looked for more information, but just like with the other aspects, it seemed he was destined to use them to learn of their effects. "I want more of this… should I make a special aspect jar?"

After looking at his inventory, Joe found only a single Uncommon Core, four regular Common ones, one Synthetic Common Core, and a small sack of Damaged versions. "Let's see... I have over eleven thousand Trash aspects. No real point in making a great container for them, since they're... literally trash. Common is really the only type where it starts to matter, so how about we start with that? Common aspect jar, here we come."

Using the Field Array that he still had active, Joe pushed the first Common Core into it and began the process of creating an aspect jar. It only took a few seconds and the low cost of two hundred and thirty Common aspects, and he was holding:

Natural Common Aspect Jar: 0/1,820 Common aspects. This jar can be used to store and retrieve Common aspects. As it is a naturally formed aspect jar, it will collect Common aspects from its surroundings over time. Current rate of collection: 3 Common aspects per hour.

Reductionist class experience gained: 50

"Wait." Joe stared at the information. "*Wait.* This means I can create self-generating aspects? How many per hour would a Mythical Core generate? How would I even get one, though? Wait. Let's say I get a Mythical Core, *somehow.* Then I get the bare *minimum* of aspects I would need, because I certainly wouldn't waste that on Common... bare minimum would be two thousand. There would be a lot that goes right down the drain because I don't currently have a Mythical aspect jar..."

Joe grabbed his head with both hands. "I miss having *spreadsheets*! I never thought I'd say that. Initial investment, bare minimum, probably three thousand Mythical aspects. However... let's say I get just one extra aspect per hour per rarity level. The maximum would be... ten per hour? Two-forty per day, twenty-four hundred in ten days. Investment returned in two weeks, then a long-term supply after that. Still... I can't imagine the effort that would need to go into getting a Core like that. Let alone how many Mythical things I would need to reduce? Best I even have right now is *Artifact*, but there's no way I have enough to convert this Core into a Jar. Not a good one, at least. Unique, it is; let's try that with my best Core."

Joe set the Uncommon Core into the Field Array, then

began pouring out every last Unique aspect he had into it. One hundred, two, two-fifty, two-*ninety*... and the Jar was complete.

Natural Unique Aspect (Uncommon) Jar: 0/2,150 Unique aspects. This jar can be used to store and retrieve Unique aspects. As it is a naturally formed aspect jar, it will collect Unique aspects from its surroundings over time. Current rate of collection: 4 Unique aspects per hour.

Reductionist class experience gained: 100.

Aspects gathered
Trash: 11,967
Damaged: 11,421
Common: 9,636
Uncommon: 6,789
Rare: 1,909
Special: 100 (Zombified). 100 (Anima). 400 (Molten).
Unique: 280
Artifact: 112
Legendary: 0
Mythical: 0

Core energy: 1,755.5/1,958 (Common)

Joe stared at the jar in his hand that had just given him hundreds of experience, trying to figure out how he could make fifty more of them. He needed Cores. *Lots* of Cores. Pondering the data, he nodded; he was going to raid a storehouse when he got back to the city.

"I was right, at least with this one. Looks like only one additional per hour. Four per hour means almost exactly three days until I have a return on aspects." Joe looked at his other Cores greedily, "Hello my little *investments*. I can't wait to—*ow!*"

Health: 64/1,652

Joe yanked his hand *out* of the magma it had been submerged in, hissing as he cast Mend on himself. His health topped out at one hundred, and Joe glared at the molten rock that his... hand had been... *submerged in.*

"Mate. Hey, Mate, I need someone to talk to here. I think I may have thought of an escape plan." All he needed to do now was wait for his mana to return to full, and he was going to make a break for it. Mate bubbled up onto his arm and gurgled cheerfully; clearly, it agreed that diving into the magma was a good idea.

CHAPTER FORTY-FOUR

"A coffee elemental? Adorable." Joe whipped around at the unexpected voice, finding that he was suddenly not alone on the tiny island. The chubbiest Elf Joe had ever seen was standing there with him, a half-mask hiding his features. "*Ayy*, how fun. Let's start the process, shall we, brudda?"

Two more Elves were suddenly clamping thick manacles onto Joe's arms, and he hadn't even seen them approaching. The chubby Elf stepped close and touched both manacles, a spark of mana jumping into them. Right away, Joe felt his control over his mana falter and fade. The Elf kept speaking as if he were unaware of Joe's shock and outrage. "I can't believe them bigwigs would just send youze out here without applying prisoner cuffs. What a strange oversight."

Joe clamped his mouth shut, worried that if he started speaking, he would never be able to stop. Something about this guy... Joe just wanted to *trust* him. Then there was the fact that these Elves were appearing out of nothing. He had no idea what sort of illusion he was trapped in, and there was the chance that *nothing* here was real.

The chubby Elf got right in Joe's face. "So, let's start by

doing this here the polite way, yeah? Show me some face here, an' take off your gear. Rings, armor, anything like that. Then change inta this prisoner garb, yeah?"

The compulsion to do as he was asked struck Joe, but he tamped it down as hard as he could. This Elf must have an utterly insane charisma characteristic.

"No? You *don't* wanna be my friend?" There was a momentary pause, and the Elf let out what sounded like a truly saddened sigh. "You know how long it takes to get *every* item off someone? I don't know whether to laugh or cry over here!"

Seeing the stricken expression on the Elven face, Joe couldn't manage to keep his mouth closed anymore. "Why do you even need me to take the gear off?"

"Hey, look at us, building bonds of trust and stuff!" The Elf crowed, giving Joe a hearty slap on the arm. "You musta always been an upstanding member of society if you've never realized that someone can't take gear off you without permission."

Joe shook his head slightly, hating himself for speaking further. He couldn't *not* speak; and he was trying everything he could think of to keep his mouth shut. Words still forced themselves out through his gritted teeth, even as he snarled at himself to *stop*. "I... don't... understand. I lost a robe to a creature once, and I've seen tons of gear get destroyed."

"C'mon, round-ear, do I look like a boss monster with a rare skill? You think gear-breaking skills won't do damage to *you*, too? How many times wouldja pop back onto the island here before I managed ta' bust even just those shiny shoes you got on?" The Elf shook his head. "Howzabout just taking 'em off, yeah?"

"Bite me."

Skill increase: Mental Manipulation Resistance (Beginner I)

"I..." This was clearly not the answer the Elf had been expecting, and he didn't know how to handle the rejection. "I assume that was an insult, but it's a new one for me. Let's play it that way, then, yeah? Try and bust his armor till our resident thief gets here, boys."

Joe's arms were forced behind him until he felt like they

were about to break, then the back of his head was grabbed and he was slammed face-first into the ground.

Damage: 40 terrain.

"Come on, now; I know he was being rude an' all, but he's not even wearing a basic *hat*." The chubby Elf sighed in frustration at the antics of his helpers. "I was being serious, bust his *gear*. Oh, the mask. I see."

The Elf got a grunt of acknowledgement from the thugs, and a spray of acid covered Joe's front.

You have been caught in a capture field! All major forts have the option of respawning a small number of the enemies killed in a 'jail' area instead of allowing them to actually die. Escape, be released, or be rescued if you want to get away!

After a long moment of darkness, Joe was back on the island. He looked at his wrists, but the manacles were still there. The Elf shrugged at him, "See? Barely any damage to the gear; you just can't survive long enough for us to make the spell count. Hurts though, don't it? Ha! Hurts *donut*? You hungry, human? Oh, you don't need to worry about the shackles. Those are bound to me, not you. We won't hurt them."

Another blast of acid hit Joe.

You have been caught in-

Joe slapped the message out of his field of vision, trying to orient himself before his captors could get a hold of him again. No luck. There simply wasn't enough room on this tiny island to make any kind of headway. This time, they didn't bother getting close, simply giving him an acid shower from a distance. Each time the corrosive liquid bit into him, Joe didn't even have time to scream before the message reappeared.

You have been caught in-
You have been caught in-
You have been caught in-

"Hold on, hold on. So *enthusiastic!*" The chubby Elf laughed warmly, making Joe smile for a moment before he came back to himself. "See, human? It just takes so much pain and effort to do it that way. Why don't you just let us work with you here, huh? All we *really* want is information. Tell you what... my name is Eli; can I ask the favor of getting your name?"

Joe bit his tongue as hard as he could, instantly making it swell and bleed. Just in time. "Mahnamtheo."

"You're... Theo? Hello, Theo. I'm so glad we're getting ta know each othah betta'." Eli's accent was slipping more heavily, showcasing his excitement. Joe saw something shimmering, probably an outpouring of mana. It gently washed over him, and Joe felt *pulled* toward the Elf. "Theo, let's be good friends, eh? Let's just talk for a minute here. How'd you get here? Who sent you? Who knows where you are?"

Joe tried to answer everything, but his tongue hurt for some reason, and it was making his words unclear. Eli seemed disappointed, and that made Joe panic slightly. Eli was trying to help him understand what position he was in, and Joe wasn't able to answer! "Theo... why did you bite yourself, man? Now you need ta-"

You have been caught in-

Another respawn, but the bite of acid had been a wakeup call. Eli tried to captivate him again, but Joe simply refused to look at him. Every time he was called 'Theo', Joe drove the idea that he was a captive being interrogated deeper into his mind. Eventually, Eli sighed and brokenheartedly informed him, "Well, our resident thief is here. I guess we'll need to continue this conversation after we take everything away from you. Let's get to work, huh?"

A hand appeared over Joe's shoulder, holding up a Core. Eli took it and grunted. "Eh, pretty basic bauble, but experience is experience, right?"

The Core dimmed, and Eli tossed it to the side. "Keep it comin'; we don't have all day. Theo, this can all end if ya just take the gear off. We just need to make sure you're not protected from our work here, or have something dangerous ta spring on us."

Joe's head whipped around, trying to find the thief. If he could *see* the thief, there was a chance that every attempted theft would fail from that point onward. That was pretty much all he knew about the rogue classes, but he vowed to brush up on his studies if he ever got the chance. In the meantime, items were dropping in front of Joe like a shower, with Eli catching anything shiny and holding it in front of Joe as soon as it appeared. "Who carries this much copper around? *Why?* Why are you taking them out one at a time? Oh… didn't realize that was one of the restrictions, my bad."

That was all the confirmation that Joe needed to understand that the illusion he was trapped in could impact most of his senses. Unless the pain he was feeling was part of it, at least it was only light and sound? He took a deep sniff, but the air was filled with sulphur and ash. He couldn't use his senses to get out of this, he needed to find something clever… or he was going to lose everything and be trapped here until the war was over. Who knew when that would be?

"Ay, look at that! You got his shoes!" Joe's new shoes were caught by Eli and directly thrown into the magma. Joe looked at his feet that hadn't come off the ground. He had no *idea* how the gear had been removed. "That'll slow ya down; the rocks around here are pretty sharp, hey, Theo? Ya know, I won't break it if you just—*what the*—?"

There was a flash, some screaming, and what sounded like a small explosion. Eli glared at Joe, his previous levity nowhere to be seen. "I suppose I should have expected there to be a golem *somewhere* in the gear carried by a student of Havoc. I bet you don't even know what that thing could do to you, do you? If he wanted, he could have that thing wearing your skin while you slink around thinking you're an original."

"What does that even mean?" Joe slammed his mouth closed, but too late. Eli's eyes crinkled in pleasure; it seemed that he needed Joe to speak for his skills to work on him.

"Let's not worry about that. Just tell me, how many golems did you have on you?" Eli's words elicited an instant reply, and Joe could have screamed in frustration as he gave a concise answer.

"There aren't any more."

Eli nodded and grasped Joe's shoulder. "I *believe* you, Theo. Thank you for telling me. Ooh! Check out these glasses!"

Joe's Spectacles of the Scholar had landed in Eli's hands, and after a bored glance, the Elf smashed them and chucked them into the magma. "Ya know, Theo, eventually we're gonna get to something you really *do* care about. When that happens? This is gonna really start hurting. Hey, while we're talking, how did you find us?"

"I accidentally blasted a hole in-" Joe realized what was happening, and shook his head hard enough that it hurt.

"Oh... that's *so* great to hear." Eli's smile was far more natural now, as he realized that Joe just needed to be contained and they wouldn't need to worry that the Dwarves would be coming for them. "I think we can have a more relaxed conversation now. Oh, that looks fun."

Eli grabbed something that was flashing indigo out of the air, pulling it in close to inspect it. In under half a second, he and another voice were screaming as the light spread out and trapped them both in a pillar of purple flame.

Caution! Direct contact with aspects has dangerous consequences! Pulling aspects into the open air without proper preparation will result in the at fault party interacting with the aspect to become immolated!

Current aspect removed: Unique aspect x27.

Quest update: Go Away For a While! Level gained: 0/1. Elves killed: 8/100. Important information gained: 1/1.

Joe winced as his friend Eli burned. He remembered exactly how bad that had hurt when he had touched the *Trash* aspect, and... his eyes widened as his mana came back under his control. Eli must have perished. Joe was as free as he could reasonably be for the next while; at least until Eli was respawned in the major fort.

The human turned and dove into the magma, barely getting his Exquisite Shell in place before he slipped beneath the surface of the liquid earth.

CHAPTER FORTY-FIVE

The magma was *thick*, at least thicker than water, which made it harder to swim through. The density helped with the issue of sinking, allowing Joe to remain at a fairly level depth. He didn't dare to go above the surface; not only would the Elves be looking for him, but there was a chance that he would touch the barrier and get tossed back onto one of the islands.

He was keeping a sharp eye on his Exquisite Shell, but he thought that it was lowering at a reasonable level. Joe's strength was at one hundred and thirty-three, and there was practically no comparison to a human fresh off Earth. He clawed through the magma with the same force that a high-end front-loader would use to scoop a hole in the earth. Needless to say, he was moving *fast*. Far faster than he had ever expected he would be able to manage.

Then something *caught* him. Not a monster, more like a convection current. All of a sudden he was in a downward suction of magma, dropping a dozen feet in an instant. It hit just before Joe had planned to surface for air, so he had to work hard not to panic. Then he recalled that he had a spell that could help in situations like this. He cast Neutrality Aura in the next moment.

The tightness in his chest didn't vanish, but his darkening vision fixed itself. Joe was glad not to pass out while boiling rock pressed in on him from all sides, but now he had another issue: he had not a single clue where he was. The flowing danger zone had tossed him around to the point where he wasn't even sure which way was up, and he was running out of time. Joe pulled himself out of the current fairly easily now that he was expecting it, breaking from the undertow in an instant with a solid pull and kick, but...

Exquisite Shell: 1,836/3,586. You are taking 25 heat damage per second!

"It's only been a full minute since I started?" Joe wasn't foolish enough to speak the words aloud; he wasn't going to let his breath escape that easily. He kept swimming as hard as he could, paddling for another thirty seconds before he ran into something solid.

Exquisite Shell: 961/3,586. You are taking 25 heat damage per second!

Joe was going to attempt to climb up the solid rock, but his forward momentum had been arrested. Since he had come to a stop and didn't continue moving for a moment, the undercurrent grabbed him and sucked him deeper into the magma. Joe scrabbled for purchase on the stone, but his grip caused the superheated stone to *squish* instead of stopping him. The current sucked him into a volcanic vent, and suddenly, Joe was moving even faster than when he had been when swimming at full speed.

He was in freefall.

Joe's vision cleared up, revealing a massive, empty room that was only solid due to being mostly a mix of obsidian and a metallic substance. He landed in a pool of magma that was slowly increasing in height. Apparently, this cavern had only recently been melted into, as it was neither filled, nor even close to it. Still—Joe watched the magma get higher—it wouldn't stay empty for too much longer.

He swam through the magma pool, moving so fast that he left a wake behind. Joe pulled himself out of the pool, amazed that his Exquisite Shell had managed to keep him alive until this moment. Checking the remaining strength of his protection, he blanched and hurried to get to a 'safe' spot. Just as he got to the top of a small hill, his shell broke, and Joe felt the full heat of the room.

Health: 80/1,642

You are taking 20 damage per second!

"Mend!" Joe frantically slapped his chest, sending his health rocketing upward, as well as healing dozens of internal stress fractures and wounds. That much damage per second just by standing in the hot air really showcased how effective his shell had been at saving him. "Lay on Hands!"

With those two spells, his health rose by a full five hundred points. This gave him a comfortable amount to work with, so he cancelled Neutrality Aura to maximize his mana. He started choking in moments; clearly, the air was utterly tainted with harsh chemicals and fumes. Joe slapped on his Exquisite Shell, followed by his aura once more, taking a breath and waiting in place only long enough to gather enough mana to heal himself up the rest of the way.

Skill increase: Mend (Journeyman I).

Skill increase: Lay on Hands (Student I). Sometimes it pays to almost die and bring yourself back from the brink!

Skill increase: Exquisite Shell (Student II). Even lobsters boil in their shells, yet you just dove right on in and made it through. Impressive.

Skill increase: Neutrality Aura (Student I).

Title Gained: …Student of Defense. When focusing most of your efforts on surviving, you have found that you are better at it than expected. Increases a single defensive skill or spell effect by 10%. Once chosen, the effect cannot be transferred.

You have gained a broken title! You currently have the maximum number of titles. You can either replace one with this new title, or apply this title to another! You have five minutes to decide before this title is dismissed.

Joe looked at his titles quickly, a smile lighting up his face even though his circumstances were dire. Gaining titles was *rare*. He couldn't think of the last time he had gained a title out in the wild, based purely on his own effort over time. He scanned the list, dismissing them one by one. Joe didn't want to weaken an effective title, and didn't want to empower one that wouldn't be sticking around if he got something better. There was really only one choice, and he made it while laughing.

Are you certain that you want to apply '…Student of Defense' to 'Baldy II'? 'Baldy II' is a curse, and adding onto it may make it harder to remove if a cure is found. Yes / No.

"Yes. It's a part of me now, practically a calling card. I'm the hairless human mage that's going to take down the Elves, and I *like* it." Joe got ready to adjust the wording of the title, but the notifications shifted before he could get to it. The change and new wording startled him greatly as a strange choice was offered.

Hidden requirement met! You have accepted a cursed title and made it a part of who you are. You have proven that you are not willing to become a victim to circumstances, and you have earned a reward from CAL. Title has changed into a permanent effect: Boon and Bane.

Boon and Bane: choose a spell or skill to empower by 10%. Remain permanently bald. Cannot wear hats, but no longer lose your stealth ability in direct sunlight. Or, you can dismiss both the positive and negative effects and regrow your lost hair.

Joe looked at the options and ran a hand over his bald head. He had really come to enjoy his current look, and he didn't think that he was going to let it go now. "I'll take it. Empower… Retaliation of Shadows."

Boon and Bane applied!

Skill updated: Retaliation of Shadows (Journeyman I). 45.1% damage returned when attacked, with a maximum return of: 451 dark damage.

"Neat." Joe looked at his titles, and saw something that he

hadn't seen in a long time: an empty slot. "Guess I gotta do some awe inspiring things to get a new title."

He had considered boosting Exquisite Shell, but ten percent just wasn't enough to really help at this stage. Joe was getting his shell broken constantly by the potent enemies he was running up against, and he needed more ways to hurt *them*. Neutrality Aura had been a close second, but again, he needed something that was a bit more of an *active* defense. With that out of the way, he turned to the problem at hand; he was trapped underground in a room that was slowly filling with lava. Magma. Whatever.

"First thing to get out of the way..." Joe sent a pulse of mana into the manacles he was still wearing, and in just a moment, the Uncommon-ranked cuffs crumbled into rubble that he didn't even bother to sift through. "That would have been an issue if they had respawned Eli before I got those off."

Next, immediate survival was the priority. Joe needed to either block the flowing lava, or get himself out of there. Well... *both*, really, but he didn't know if tunneling out would just let more lava in. Joe hadn't had this issue since he had been searching for diamonds back when he'd tried minecraft. Now, he was planning on using the same tactics to deal with the problem. "I need to put a block in front of that flow so that the hole is plugged. How to *do* that is the question."

Joe opened his system notes and looked over the rituals that he had previously worked with. "This... the mana-sapping one; that doesn't *need* to be mana, does it? It could easily be invoked as energy. Heat is energy. Kinda. Okay. I can convert this to a heat-sapping ritual, but what is that heat going to do? If I just *collect* it, I'll melt the ritual and likely my face. I need to *repurpose* it. I can send it... down, if I pull that part from that ritual here, but there again, I run into the issue of breaking the ritual."

He pondered over the issue as the entire, massive cavern floor raised another six inches thanks to the magma. "What if I modify the Gravedigger's Requiem to move *horizontally* instead of vertically? Disperse the effect, then have it 'dig' through a wall using the heat instead of vibration? Do I have that kind of time?"

Eyeing the rising lava, Joe gulped. "I might not have the time… but I can't think of anything else that I could do instead. Time to do or die."

He really hoped he could do it. If this failed, he was going to die within range of the major fort again. Joe was *not* looking forward to another escape attempt.

CHAPTER FORTY-SIX

The first issue that Joe ran into was reworking the ritual itself. Just because he had an idea, didn't mean that he could flawlessly put it into practice. The ritual he finally came up with was only at the Beginner rank, because it *had* to be. After being robbed blind, Joe was down to a single Synthetic Common Core, and he had only found *that* after desperately searching through his ring.

Only being able to use a two-ring ritual limited his options greatly, and it also forced him to tear out *anything* that wasn't going to be producing the effect he needed. That meant limiters, variables that kept Joe safe, and most of all... control. This ritual had been boiled down to two effects: drain heat, and condense heat in a specified direction. If something went wrong, there was a good chance that Joe was going to either freeze or flash-boil just after activation.

Those risks meant that he needed to eliminate all of the physical impediments to success as quickly and thoroughly as possible. The place where he drew the ritual needed to be perfectly flat, and as similar of a substance as possible. First, he cast Acid Spray onto the obsidian, but that did nothing except make that area dangerous to sit on. The obsidian didn't react at all... which made sense. Kind of. It was *magical* acid, and it worked on armor and metals... so why not this?

Instead, he set up a Field Array and reduced the glass-like stone in a set pattern, making a perfect square with the sharpest edges he had ever seen on anything. Joe took out a paper and set it lightly on the edge of the square; half of it lay flat, the other half slid down the small incline and burst into flame. "That'll work."

Next up was inscribing the actual ritual circle, and here, Joe finally hesitated. There were only two functions, but he *did* have some special aspects. He decided to prepare the circles with the aspects, both to test them and hopefully give the ritual the *oomph* that it needed. Placing his hand back into the Field Array after adding the 'Molten' aspects—no jar yet—he created a pure white Common inscription tool, which swirled a reddish brown as the new aspect was added.

Then he made a dark grey Damaged tool, which only became darker as he poured in 'Zombified' aspects. Gear prepared and ready, Joe began the process of actually forming the ritual circle; starting with the inner circle, the 'drain heat' portion. On this one, he used the Zombified inscriber and rapidly drew out the circle. Luckily, he was drawing with aspects, not ink, as ink would have spread across the perfectly smooth surface no matter what he did to prevent it.

The outer ring, designed to send the heat directionally away as a cylinder, was composed with the Molten aspects. Joe set the Synthetic Core in the center of the ritual and started inputting mana. It didn't take much; one person was more than enough to power such a 'weak' ritual. His part done, the Reductionist stood back and watched as the strangely glowing ritual began performing its function. The room was filling faster now, *much* faster, and he realized that the magma must have eaten away a large chunk of the wall. If this didn't work, there wouldn't be a second chance.

Reductionist class experience gained: 50

Joe barely noticed the grey shadow expanding from the central ritual circle out of the corner of his eye, and he only dodged away from it out of base instinct. It wasn't attacking him, per se, but everywhere it touched took on a 'preserved' look. The stone itself lost its shine, and Joe started running out of room on the small island that his hill had become. There was another not too far away, so he *jumped* across the open space and quickly turned to watch what was happening.

Grey light reached ruddy heat, and a *hiss* sounded loud enough through the cavern that Joe was worried a cave-in might occur. Where the light touched, hardened stone was left behind. Still, it was up against magma on one side. The flash-frozen composite shattered, sending shards of super-sharp obsidian and hardened metals scattering through the area. Joe twirled in place, dropping to the ground and trying to shelter in the lee of the hill he was on. Constant elemental effects had created a deathtrap that he was uncertain he could withstand; flying flechettes and deep freeze in one spot, bubbling magma in the other.

At least he knew that he could survive in the magma for a few minutes, but the ritual? Joe wasn't sure, and it was still expanding. Though… slower? There was only so much heat it could take in at any given time, Joe supposed. Another interesting phenomena was happening as well: a cool breeze was being generated from the ritual area, but the superheated air in the rest of the cavern was naturally trying to rectify the balance. He was nearly blown off his small hill as wind started surging in the cavern in the form of small tornados.

Then the second portion of the ritual seemed to reach a threshold. Joe had expected the heat to be distributed in a nice, constant stream. Instead, it rose to critical mass and sent a beam of heat against the far wall as what could only be described as a barrel-width cylinder of plasma. Thunder rang through the enclosed space, so loud that his Exquisite Shell took damage, and his Neutrality Aura had to work on repairing his ears.

Joe's head was rocked against the hill, dazing him. He

thought it was over, but instead, the cold zone began expanding faster so that it could provide enough heat for the second stage of the ritual to activate again. More shards of stone, metal, and quartz flew into the air, hissing as they cut into the magma or pinging as they ricocheted off the solid surfaces. The wind began to pick up again, and he covered his ears when he realized that this was exactly what had happened just before the plasma beam had last fired.

Zzzap-Booom!

The concentrated heat of thousands of gallons of magma struck the wall after racing along the molten tunnel it had carved previously. Joe settled in to wait for the next repetition, but was instead *yanked* off his hill as the pressurized contents of the room were blasted into the new tunnel that had breached into open air.

His body slammed into the sides of the tunnel as he was dragged along. He, gasses, and magma were whipping along the hole, and the human was sent careening into the open air at hundreds of miles per hour. Joe broke the sound barrier, which was the only thing allowing him to survive the small volcanic eruption he'd just caused. He leveled out into an arc, managing to look back to watch the volcano. The inane thought of 'it really does look like a shoe' crossed his mind.

He wasn't entirely certain how fast he was moving, but his eyes locked on a disturbance just in time to see a line of plasma tear through the debris. His parabolic descent dropped him below it, yet even so, the heat dispersed into the area would have cooked him if his shield hadn't been resistant to elemental effects. After all the commotion, his Exquisite Shell was dangerously close to breaking yet again.

The ground was coming up *fast*, and Joe's enhanced perception allowed him to see the shocked looks from all the Dwarves he was sailing over. He only had one thought before he hit the ground and was sent to respawn.

"Made it."

Luck +2. You've made some wild choices. I love it.

You have died! Calculating… you have lost 31,200 experience!

Joe opened his eyes and was met with a clean white room and a beanbag chair. "Never thought I'd be happy just to get sent to my respawn room. Now… let's take a look at the damage. Status."

Name: Joe 'Tatum's Chosen Legend' Class: Reductionist
Profession I: Arcanologist (Max)
Profession II: Ritualistic Alchemist (1/20)
Profession III: None
Character Level: 18 Exp: 188,179 Exp to next level: 1,821
Rituarchitect Level: 10 Exp: 45,000 Exp debt: 9,600
Reductionist Level: 0 Exp: 876 Exp to next level: 124
Hit Points: 0/1,642
Mana: 0/3,173
Mana regen: 45.37/sec
Stamina: 0/1,381
Stamina regen: 6.39/sec

Characteristic: Raw score

Strength: 133
Dexterity: 133
Constitution: 129
Intelligence: 138
Wisdom: 119
Dark Charisma: 80
Perception: 123
Luck: 62
Karmic Luck: -4

Joe almost gagged as he saw that he had been tossed down to level eighteen. "That hurts, Eterium. I feel like I should get a break? That was a pretty wild escapade… wait, I got a luck boost there at the end. Fair enough."

At that point, the only thing he wanted to do was take a

nap. He had been awake for… he didn't rightly know how long, actually. Did his tiny deaths count as sleep? Did it help his mental state at all? Certainly didn't feel like it. He hit the bean bag chair and was unconscious in moments.

He awoke to a portal humming cheerfully right next to him, and Joe scrambled to his feet. There was an invasion coming, and he needed to warn the Dwarves that the enemy was basically hiding behind the curtains in their living room.

CHAPTER FORTY-SEVEN

Joe stepped out of the portal and directly into the new Grand Temple in the Dwarven capital. He went over and hugged the altar to Tatum, having a sudden realization that without Tatum, he would have been trapped on that small island until the Elves chose to let him go. There were very few times when he really thought about it, but he owed his start as a Ritualist to Tatum, and every success since then stemmed from that point in time.

"If being stuck away is anything for you like my time in that volcano was for me, I need to hurry up and get you free," Joe sighed as he slapped the altar good-naturedly. His ears twitched, and he looked over to see that someone was singing a bawdy tune near the altar to Hansel. He tried not to laugh, hoping that the deity preferred the not-family-friendly tune over what he had been stuck hearing on Midgard.

Remembering that he actually had an important, time-sensitive mission, Joe got to his feet and started hustling toward the door. He didn't know who to tell except for Havoc, and he was pretty sure that the Dwarf would be able to open the doors that he needed in order to mount a major offensive. In fact, he was almost certain that the Major General would mobilize more than even the Council would, given the chance.

"Joe." The human in question paused as the feminine rasp reached his ears. Calling a Dwarven voice 'feminine' was a misnomer, as it was deeper than all but the deepest of human male voices, but it was still... he met High Priestess Dawnesha's gaze as she walked toward him, her blonde mustache fluttering gently in the breeze her movement created. "Occultatum tells me that I need to speak with you. That you have found much, even more than you know."

That brought him to a screeching halt, all plans of leaving the area put on indefinite hold. "Tatum sent you?"

"Not exactly something that I'd lie about," the High Priestess stated haughtily. "'You're moving too fast, and you need to prepare yourself with what you have gained. You have much *hidden* within'. Those were his words, sent to me during a group session just now."

When a literal deity told you to take stock of the situation, it behooved you to listen. Joe's bald forehead furrowed as he pondered what had changed for him recently. "Dawnesha, I'm going to use you as a sounding board."

"As you need, Champion." Her answer startled Joe; it was far from the arrogance that she had displayed during their first meeting, or even at the start of this conversation.

"In the last few days, I've learned that I can create potent effects with more than just the base materials I have access to... I can empower them beyond the scope of their original purpose by adding in additional... I suppose '*intent*' is the word for it? They are still aspects, but their purpose is singular, and not quite as clinically correct as I wished them to be. They seem to mutate what I create. Those are the biggest changes, and only time will tell what all I can do with them. What I can create... what I can change. Time for experimentation that I don't have right now."

Dawnesha said nothing, only closing her eyes in silent contemplation. It was then that Joe remembered that she was the third princess of the Dwarven Oligarchy. "Oh, and I found a major fort hidden in Gramma's Shoe. There's a massive invasion that has been hidden behind an illusion, and now that I've escaped, I can't imagine that the war will slow down so I can run some quality tests."

"They're *where?*" At this, the Dwarves' eyes snapped open, filled with *fury*, not the concern that he had been expecting. "You're certain? You are. They *dare* to desecrate our memorial to Gramm'mama! *Dwarves!*"

Her last word rang through the temple, capturing the attention of everyone present. "We move to war! The Elves have invaded and have stepped into Gramma's Shoe! Their trespass has inflamed her ankle, perhaps even being the reason she erupts so violently! This *atrocity* will be repaid with what, in more peaceful times, would be *war crimes!* Alert your closest Legion, and upon the words and authority of Candidate Joe, backed by my own as Princess... I hereby mobilize the Dwarven Oligarchy!"

The room exploded into noise, shouting back a singular phrase that Joe hadn't been expecting them to cheer:

"*War Crimes!*"

It was an... odd choice for a rousing battle cry, but Joe could get behind it. Mostly. Slightly uneasily. Probably wouldn't be his first choice when going forward. Not exactly a slogan you could put on a shirt and wear in public.

Dark Charisma +10! Your words have incited violence on an unprecedented scale! Better hope you're not wrong! If they can't find someone to fight, they'll turn on you in an instant.

"Well, that's foreshadowing if I've ever seen it," Joe grumpily acknowledged the message. "I need to assume that the illusion is still active, and that it will turn away the Legion if we get close. I need to start making contingency plans."

"Joe," Dawnesha's voice halted him once more, "I didn't understand all of your talk on 'aspects', but... I don't think that was exactly what Occultatum was talking about. I cannot be certain, I think that there was a subtext of a *thing*. Not a revelation."

"That." Joe paused and thought for a moment, unable to come up with anything she could be speaking about. "I don't know. Perhaps I need to work on my Ritual Orbs?"

She shrugged helplessly. "Anything I know, you also know at this point. Occultatum is an enigma wrapped in a mystery, and his words can be difficult to parse."

Joe thanked her, then paused as he saw something on her robe. A sigil. Specifically the sigil of Tatum, that gave favor when gaining experience. Then he realized that he had never equipped it after getting a new outfit... back on Midgard. Screaming internally, he opened his menu and activated it, and the silver book appeared on his chest. Dawnesha smiled at that, calling after Joe as he left, "May knowledge find you, wherever you may hide."

"I don't know what that means!" he called back, hurrying to get to the door. The human rushed along the streets of the capital, somehow feeling... slower. He frowned down at his bare feet, only protected thanks to a shimmering shell, and realized that he had once again had an enchanted item destroyed only a short while after gaining it. Perhaps an awkward trip to the Odds and Ends was in order in the near future?

Dwarves were zipping past him on the roads, but Joe didn't allow his mind to wander. He needed to get to Havoc and let him know what was going on. After skidding to a halt in front of the estate, he pounded on the door and waited for the inevitable retribution from the golems composing the door. As he expected, a spike drove out of the door, aimed directly at his face. An orb slammed into it, breaking off the weakened metal and causing the door to whimper like a kicked dog. "Wait... do golems feel pain?"

Havoc slammed the door open and glared at Joe. A cloud of cigar smoke billowed out with the sudden change in air pressure, and the Dwarf's bloodshot eyes dug into Joe. "No. They are made to make sad noises like that so that some moron will sympathize with them long enough for the golem to get another attack in. You have one chance… *what?*"

"Quest complete?" Joe nervously told the Dwarf, who looked to the side and off into the distance. He recognized that stare. "Wait, do you have access to a status screen… nevermind. Stupid question."

"No stupid questions." Havoc thoughtfully absorbed whatever information he was reading, then turned his attention back to the human. "Only stupid people asking them. What is the information you found? You didn't kill Elves, and you *lost* levels like a moron, so it can't be those."

Joe wasted no time in explaining. "I found a major fort hidden in Gramma's Shoe. There's a massive illusion set up to protect them from discovery, and they are planning a full-scale invasion."

"Is that all?" Havoc shrugged and closed the door a small amount. "I already got the notification. The Legion is mobilizing. I don't need to do anything about that. Good job, I suppose. You can come back in. Rewards… yeah… I guess I can allot you some experience or something."

This wasn't the insane Dwarf that Joe had been counting on finding when he got back. Tired short guy tinkering with toys wasn't enough. Joe needed *Major General* Havoc, the Lord of Slaughter. His eyes brightened as he realized that he had the perfect catalyst, "Havoc. There's more."

"What is it, Joe? I'm almost done replacing the tile with mimics, and-"

"The fort is controlled by Lady of Light Elfreeda. That's the one you call Francine, right?" Joe stared at the Dwarf, who froze. "She's the one maintaining the illusion. I damaged a bunch of the stabilizers, so I'm sure she has her hands full keeping that building together. She'll *be* there."

"Building…?" That wasn't what Joe had been expecting the Dwarf to focus on. "This building… was it crystal? Lots of light in it? Looked like a pine tree, but shiny?"

"Yes."

Havoc's eyes started to glow, and he lifted a shaking hand to his lips, taking a deep pull from his cigar. "She abyssal did it, huh? We were led to believe that those plans were entirely theoretical. The misinformation to our spies… they must know every. Single. *One* of them. I'm sure they're dead by now."

"What plans? Havoc, what are you talking about?" Joe felt like he was only hearing a single person talking on a phone. He was missing too much information. "They know your spies?"

"It's an Artifact. It's called the 'Prismatic Evergreen', and if they really built it… it represents a *significant* investment from the Elven Theocracy." Havoc started to laugh maniacally; his hands were shaking in excitement. "*So* significant that there's no way she can run and leave it undefended. Francine… I'm coming to murder you so that we can finally be together again!"

CHAPTER FORTY-EIGHT

Havoc was shockingly lavish with the quest rewards. Joe stared at the small pile of Cores that glowed so brightly that his eyes were taking damage. Even so, he couldn't look away. "One Unique, five Rare, ten Uncommon…"

He took a deep gulp, unsure about the other item that he had been given. Joe picked up the metal pass and turned it over in his hands. "One permanent access pass to enter and leave the landfill at will. I guess I was given an exit pass the last time?"

At least he wouldn't need to drop down the garbage tubes again. Joe remembered all too clearly what it was like landing on broken glass and seeing the *sheet* of debuffs appear. Doors were nice. You could just go in them, or out of them. Very few surprises. Joe stared at the Unique Core and steeled himself against using it right away. It was a *powerful* Core, worth nine thousand, five hundred and fifty-eight experience, if he wanted to waste it by absorbing the power.

"Ten percent of its capacity… add on another ten percent of *that* to account for any wastage… a minimum of a thousand and fifty-one Unique aspects. That's enough to build… create… I can't even imagine." Joe sighed and inspected the others. Two of the Rare Cores were potent ones worth above five thousand experience, while the other three were in the four thousand range. "Assume roughly five hundred aspects each to use these. I could do Common or below, but what's the point? I need Rare or better."

"I should set up a powerful mana battery ritual, though. I've only got the 'overmorrow' before the troops are mustered, whatever that means. The best way to support the assault is going to be by making sure my side doesn't blow itself up." Joe pulled out his notes on the ritual and started reviewing what he needed to do. "First off, I need to increase the efficiency of this diagram. I did a decent job when I first got going with this, but my lore skills have all increased fairly... *knowledge*! Architectural Lore!"

His mana drained away, and Joe grimaced as Architectural Lore reached Beginner two. He needed to set a timer or something; that skill *needed* to be used. "My understanding is higher than it used to be, and the components needed are different. I need to translate it over."

Joe lay on his bed, poring over the formulae to differentiate what was a good idea, and what was a necessary detail. "I can pull this component, but this needs another decimal..."

Three hours later, he had pulled apart the data and condensed it down into a sleeker design. The next step was putting it back together and ensuring that it ran with the same power and efficiency. What he needed was not something that could be run on higher power Cores, but something he could mass produce without going insane or broke. It took a few more hours, but then Joe was ready to test the new design.

Congratulations! Your dedication to perfecting your craft has resulted in a successful revamped ritual, lowering the requirements to create it without sacrificing the potency!

Ritual efficiency increased! Ritual of Enchanting (Mana Battery) (Expert) has been converted to Ritual of Enchanting (Mana Battery) (Journeyman).

Skill increase: Ritual Magic (Expert IV).

Skill increase: Ritual Circles (Expert IV).
Skill increase: Magical Matrices (Apprentice V).

"Oh." Joe stared at the notifications, suddenly overcome by a deep-rooted need to improve *everything* he could possibly get his hands on. "Sometime soon, I am going to sit my happy rear down and run experiments for a *year*."

That wasn't today, sadly. Today, he needed to make this ritual and determine what all was needed in terms of aspects. The ritual itself would be embedded within metal, the best that he could replicate at his current rank, but for that... "Time to go see McPoundy."

He stopped himself before he could rush out the door. "No... need to make sure everything works correctly first. I can use this. Step one: make a low-powered mana battery. Step two: convince McPoundy to help me, at least if I can get in contact with him. Make a battery, use it and my position as a Candidate to make him help me, mass produce new, non-damaging power sources for the Legion. Step three? No idea, but step four is profit."

Joe reached into himself and began pulling mana out and shaping it into the strings that represented the Field Array. The size increased until it covered the entire area he would need for the ritual, settling into place after he strained for a few long minutes. Then his inscription tool was in his hand, a light blue which calmed his nerves. Journeyman aspects weren't a thing, which was just *lovely*. That position was used for 'Special' aspects, meaning he was able to use Rare aspects for the outer ring... he hoped. He wasn't entirely certain. It might mean he needed to use Expert aspects, and that would suck. "That's what tests are for!"

He started drawing out the outermost ring, holding his breath as he completed it with Rare aspects. There was no reaction, which was unsurprising, as he hadn't applied mana yet. Even so, if it had been done wrong... it might have exploded. Joe had died a *lot* during his time in this Zone, and he wasn't eager to replicate the experience. The next ring went faster, the two rings costing a total of sixty-two Rare aspects. "Not terrible... please don't explode?"

He swapped out his inscription tool, and the next three rings went *fast*. The moment of truth was upon him. Joe placed a Core in the center of the ritual, another to the side to activate it, and let his mana flow into the rings. "I have a fifty-eight percent bonus to spell stability, and I can easily make Expert ranked circles and below. Gotta believe in myself!"

The circle started up, and Joe relaxed as the familiar feeling of losing all his mana progressed. The ghostly circles lifted and started to swirl around the Core, an Uncommon one that should only take a short while to turn into a battery. The mana drain halted as the ritual became fully powered, actually giving Joe pause. "That was... I shouldn't have been able to do that so easily."

He opened his status, checking on his mana level. What he saw made him scream in excitement.

Current Mana: 402/6,347

"*Tatum*! Tatum's free!" Joe practically slapped the menu over to his unread notifications. There was a quest complete! It had to be!

Quest complete: Paying a Great Debt. Your rights to casual interactions and bonuses from and with Ocultatum have been restored. Stop breaking things. Consider this a warning. Rewards: Ocultatum has been returned to his proper position in the pantheon. Exp gained: 10.

"Ten... *ten* experience gained?" Joe stared at the notification uncomprehendingly. "That's it? I-"

The system would like to remind you that the main reward was the reason for the penalty. King Henry is currently alive on Midgard.

"Oh look, something I will never question again." Joe nervously turned off the notifications and waited for the ritual to finish. He recalled that he now had a *ton* of mana to play with, so he let go of his protections and re-activated them. "That puts me at... over ten thousand effective health."

Health: 1,642/1,642

Exquisite Shell: 8,822/8,822

"I forgot how much I like having absolutely unfair gobs of mana to toss at things." He sighed happily. Just then, the ritual process completed, and Joe reached out to catch the newly-made mana battery. As he stored it away, motion caught his eye. He turned to stare at CleoCatra, who was perched imperiously on his nightstand; her paw nudged a large chipped mug of cold coffee that had been sitting there for... who knew how long.

"Cat... what are you doing?" Joe watched as the cat slid the cup closer to the edge. "Why are you doing that?"

He knew cats liked to knock things over, but this was an intelligent race. "I haven't even seen you in *days*; leave the coffee alone. Oh, *abyss*. I haven't seen you in days... I was supposed to feed you."

The cat hissed at him, slapping the mug to the floor. Joe groaned and stood up to clean the mess as the cat flashed away and out of the room. "Hey! You can't just-"

Joe's gaze landed on the spreading coffee, fixating on a singular point just as the liquid coated the outermost ring of the ritual circles. He couldn't even remember what happened after that, simply blinking blurrily as dust rained down on his blood-soaked face.

Health: 736/1,642

Exquisite Shell: 0/8,822

You are severely concussed! -42 intelligence until effect is healed!

Charisma has reached a new threshold! Current Charisma is: 100.

Skill gained: Message (Novice I). You are now able to talk to anyone on your friend list, anywhere within line of sight! Cost: 1 mana per word. Cooldown: none.

"Stupid. *Cat*. Stupid *system*, probably telling me that I look better injured than I do normally." Joe slapped himself with a Lay on Hands, healing himself up and removing the debuff. He looked to the side, finding himself in a house where a Dwarven couple were frozen in the act of eating their dinner. "Hi there. I'm a... Candidate. Send the bill to the Legion."

They nodded, and Joe stepped out of the hole he had

created… only to fall two stories to the ground. Though he landed on his feet, it *hurt*. "Maybe I'm still concussed?"

"Is that message skill actually useful? Maybe in a party…? At higher levels, what then?" A thought crossed Joe's mind. "Wait a moment… the cat told me that she was going to help me fail. Did she mean she was going to point out my mistakes? Was this an attack or a learning opportunity? The Elf destroyed my ritual so easily… so did Cleo. I need to find a way to shield my rituals from getting damaged? Is that the lesson to be learned?"

"Either way, I think I'm becoming more of a dog person." He pondered on that as his Neutrality Aura cleaned the blood and dust from his clothes. Joe shook himself out of the fugue and started toward McPoundy's, thinking about the mana battery he needed to replicate, and one other, very important lesson.

"Don't forget to feed the cat."

CHAPTER FORTY-NINE

As pristine as ever, the human walked into the forge and smiled at all of the Dwarves that were eyeing him with ill intent even while smiling back at him. One of the bearded males walked forward, fairly beaming with hospitality. "Welcome back, Joe! I have been looking forward to the opportunity of explaining the importance of patience during personal growth. Just as the rest of us have worked hard to be able to study at this place, I am certain that learning to flex your patience muscle will-"

"Step aside," Joe ordered frostily, even as his Dwarven-society-demanded happy smile stayed in place. "I am invoking the right of Candidacy to hire Grandmaster McPoundy."

There was a collective inhalation of breath, and the angry undertones turned to pure glee as the people in the room started to laugh. The Dwarf that had stepped forward smiled happily, "I am sorry to inform you that you have just lost all chance at a high rank. You see, without being able to impact at least three major forts with the work you demand from a Grandmaster, there is no chance that the reputation you earn will ever balance against the cost you incur."

Joe's expression soured; that was information he hadn't been given in advance. "I'll-"

The Grandmaster stepped out of his private forge with flames in his eyes. Literally. It seemed as if he had a spell of some sort that allowed him to superheat things by staring at them. "Who *dares* invoke Candidacy on *me*? I'll make sure you're busted down to private! You... Joe."

The Dwarf sighed and gestured for Joe to join him, much to the 'hidden' pleasure of the Dwarves in the forge. Joe stepped into the pocket of dilated space and closed the door behind him. McPoundy was already shaking his head, "Someone got you real good. There's no way this won't go on your record, *Candidate*. What do you need?"

Joe had never heard such displeasure in this Dwarf's tone. It seemed he really didn't like getting ordered around. The human pulled out his new mana battery and handed it over. "I can make these, all the way up to Expert Cores as the base, and automate the process. Takes a couple hours per battery. I even made a spare leaflet that I can hand over to you so that you can start getting enchanters to perfect the design and start making them, though that will take a lot longer than how I do it."

McPoundy took the battery and inspected it, grunting a question at him after a long moment. "Why the abyss did you bother wasting all your time doing other things? If you would have started these when you became a Candidate, we'd already be upgrading the entire automaton corps. You make a reusable Core enchanter for each fort, just *one each*, and you'll max out your Candidacy card. Abyssal fool."

Joe felt his heart sink at those words. Had everything been a waste...? No. "If I knew that when we got started, I wouldn't have found the invasion point at Gramma's Shoe. I wouldn't-"

"I don't care about your harrowing adventures. *Results* are the only thing that matters in a Meritocracy." McPoundy was clearly in a bad mood. "What do you need from me? I just spent the morning getting orders from the council, and I've been delegating those all day so I could do what I *need* to do."

The Reductionist didn't hesitate. "I need to get more of these made. That means I need to make permanent rings, and I also recently found that I need to start doing a better job of protecting the rituals I make. I need advice, training, and plans for making my rituals safe from interference."

"No."

"Then I'm going to need... no? What do you mean 'no'?" Joe's words sputtered to a stop as the smith shook his head. McPoundy put his hand on Joe's shoulder, and started guiding him toward the exit.

"I have orders directly from the council. The edicts of the rulers of the nation supersede the *request* of a Candidate." McPoundy stopped and hesitated, seeming to come to a decision. "I can offer you the services of a Journeyman; they will make for an excellent trainer at this stage of forging. I, however, am of far too great of use to the kingdom right now."

"But... the Cores? Upgrading the Legion?" Joe sputtered, unable to process what was happening. Wasn't this Candidate thing supposed to be an immutable law or something? "We had a deal that you would train me up till I was a Master!"

"I *will* train you, I can't right *now*. As to the batteries, how long will it take to make one of these engravers? How long to engrave? How many can be done in the next few days, when the nation marches to war?" McPoundy's voice was a hammer slamming down on Joe's attempts to make rapid progress. "How will they recharge once they have lost their mana? That will take a specialized support unit, unless you have an option. Who will train *them*; how long will *that* take?"

Reading Joe's crestfallen expression, McPoundy relented slightly. "It's a good idea, but you are offering a long-term solution. We need something that can impact the war in only a few days. Let me introduce you to-"

"No..." Joe shook his head before McPoundy could offer one of his subordinates. "You're right, this is too slow. There are a few things I can prepare to help with the war effort itself; I just need materials. On that note-"

"Most supplies, especially Cores, have a mandate on them right now. You couldn't afford to go against that, and it has nothing to do with the value of the items." McPoundy hesitated again. "Look, if you need *stuff*, you need to get the supplies yourself. Now, you already used your Candidacy on me. Your account has a mark on it, and I did nothing for you. So, after this battle, when you need something, come here and ask for me. We will call this 'requisition' a... raincheck."

Joe could only nod and leave the spatial space of the private forge. He walked past the wall of smiling faces; the Dwarves were thrilled to see him be tossed out less than five minutes after entering. The human didn't mind; his thoughts were whirling, and he was clutching at straws. "What can I do in the *short* term for this? I'm almost certain that I'm going to need to figure out a ritual that I can use, but... what? I have some foreknowledge of the area we will be attacking, and know a bit about the people that are there. Perhaps I could draw a map?"

He shook his head at that; the map wouldn't be useful. The whole place was a giant empty cavern. Secret entrances? Zero knowledge. Joe didn't know anything more than the fort's layout. There might not even be an exterior entrance. Tunnel systems? See information on secret entrances. "Oh! Maybe I could set up a tunnel *digger*?"

With all the aimless thinking, as well as his rapid walking in a single direction, Joe was closing in on the gates to the city. He decided to get an outside perspective and approached a musta-chioed Dwarven guard, asking her about the idea of making a tunnel digger. The reply was something he should have been expecting. She laughed in his face, "You think twiddling your fingers is going to make you better at tunnel construction than the *Dwarven Oligarchy*? Even the Boring Corporation got their ideas from the Dwarves!"

"You knew President Musk?" Joe gave her an intense stare; the vanishing of the President had sparked a massive conspiracy theory throughout the entire Zone of Midgard. No one could ever find the man, and *many* had looked, not all with good intentions.

"Who?" The Dwarf seemed confused, which made Joe groan in frustration. "What's a president? Like a guild leader or something?"

"But you knew about the Boring-"

"Are you trying to distract my soldier, *human*?" A new Dwarf broke into the conversation, making Joe flinch. He had lost all track of his surroundings. "You, get back to work. You, human, stop interfering with our patrols, or I'll hold you accountable for any crimes that occur on this route."

Joe said nothing further, but he was happy to learn that the President might still be around, allied or at least *known* to the Dwarves. He'd always liked the guy, with his inventions that had all been about bettering mankind. Joe stepped under the portcullis and got a nasty shock once again, as the enchantments he crossed forcefully deactivated all his active effects. "Gah!"

A guard ran at him, weapons out. "Halt, under suspicion of-! Oh. You again. Didn't we talk about this? I... hmmm. Might not have. It's a crime to come through here with active effects unless you're under orders. Do it again, and I'll have to fine you. It costs Core energy every time the disenchantment effect is activated. Not something we can use frivolously, especially right now."

"Oh. Got it. We've met?" Joe looked at the bearded, armored Dwarf, and realized that he could never pick this guy out of a crowd. "Were you the guard that sold me the map to the Caves of Solitude?"

"Might have been. Might not have been." The guard shrugged evasively. "You all look the same to me. The hairlessness, single eyebrow, and white clothes are fairly eye-catching, I guess. Is that a popular look among your people?"

"No." Joe's deadpan answer made the guard chuckle. "Do you have a lot of infiltrators? This see a lot of use?"

"Not so much; not this deep into our territory, at least. Still, when you can't see the enemy most of the time, it's a great idea to keep an effect like this active." Something the guard said set off a lightbulb in Joe's head.

"Can't... *see* them? They can go invisible?" Joe tried to clarify what he was hearing.

"Well, only the really powerful pointy-ears go fully invisible. Most of the time, it's just really great camouflage, glamour, or illusions that kinda just make you... look away." The guard waved at the swooping lines that Joe had walked over. "An enchantment like this is really the only way to see through them. Other methods are too expensive, or too... hmm... 'Elven morality' for us to feel good using them."

"Need to break illusion, invisibility, not be morally corrupt, and cost-effective enough..." Joe's eyes lit up, and he started digging through his spatial ring. "Please be in here and not in the giant block of broken stuff...! Got it! Yes!"

The Reductionist pulled open his practically untouched copy of the *Grimoire of Annihilation*. Dark miasma drifted from the table of contents as he searched for something he only half remembered. "Ritual of the Insomniac Stalker, no... Ritual of the Lonely Tree? Nah, too scorched-earthy, and Havoc already said no. Here it is! *Ritual of Argus*. Five willing creatures including yourself, an eye spawns on the back of your head. Each creature included in the rituals has dark vision, cannot be ambushed, and can see... yes! Invisible things!"

Joe looked up to see the Dwarf looking at the clearly *dark* book with serious concern. Right. Rituals were frowned upon in most places, and this *particular* book had been designed with a 'this is probably evil' vibe to it on purpose. The human smiled and moved past the guard into the open countryside, thinking exclusively about the ritual. "Sure,the main components *were* the organs of my own race, and some other... shady things... but I can bypass all that with aspects! Okay, let's see... the main target of this ritual will also be able to mystically observe anyone attempting to see the target through mystic means. This lasts for seven days, or until dispelled by the caster."

"If I get this on the leaders of the assault, we'll be able to weed out any infiltrators before we leave. What materials do I need in order to make this happen?" He sat down next to the road and started translating the required goods into aspects and Core energy. "Looks like this is an Expert-ranked ritual... I'll need Unique aspects. I need Cores first, though."

Joe knew exactly where to go for that. He hurried down the road, running with a destination in mind. After a few minutes, he screeched to a halt. "No, wait. Havoc already gave me Cores that would be perfect for the ritual. Let's just go back and..."

The unforgettable buzzsaw sound of a Hammer Beast closing in on him made Joe curse and start sprinting toward his high-ground rock. It wasn't *too* far away, but by the time he spotted the large pillar of stone rising next to the road... there were almost a dozen Hammer beasts that he was needing to constantly dodge. Even so, Joe smiled, because all he could see as the spikey death balls hurtled at him was the small pile of Cores that he was going to turn them into.

His Ritual Orbs emerged and *cracked* into one of the attacking two-headed beasts at the same moment that he finally got into a good position to take down the beasts with minimal risk. His smile faltered, and he slammed his fist into the stone below him. "That is the *last* time I take a walk to get my thoughts in order! Dark room or a long shower from now on!"

CHAPTER FIFTY

Joe jumped off the column of stone, exhausted from having to constantly direct his ritual orbs into the patterns that he wanted. It was good training for future battle, and he had been able to safely destroy a full score of the Hammer Beasts, but it was frustrating that he needed to constantly visualize every aspect of the attack that he wanted to use. Even with a spell, he was able to visualize the spell form and put it out into the world; he did not need to maintain the shape in his mind after the initial usage.

"Although, now that I think about it, *would* that be useful?" Joe muttered to himself as he went from beast to beast, collecting their Core if they had one, and otherwise reducing the creature for aspects. "I already know that mana manipulation has leveled up a few times because I was working on controlling threads of mana outside of my body... is this an aspect of spellcasting that I have ignored?"

A few tests casting Acid Spray at the rocks in the area showed him that no, he had *not* been using spells incorrectly. "At least... I suppose it shows that only doing it a few times is not enough to change anything. Another thing to practice?"

Joe looked over his haul; three Uncommon Synthetic and

five Common Cores. Shaking his head ruefully, he chuckled and murmured to himself, "Something about having an ability tied to a Ritual Orb really makes it easy to remember to use it."

Experience earned: 2,370 (Hammer Beast x20)

Level up! Welcome back to level 19! Again!

"No light show or feelings of euphoria for getting back to this level?" He shrugged, although he was slightly saddened that he didn't get to experience that rush again. Just another reason to get to level twenty-two for the first time.

Battle Meditation (Novice VI).

Assisted Ritual Orb Usage (Beginner 0). Congratulations on reaching the Beginner ranks for this skill!

"Nice! That means that I can use two orbs skillfully, and another one fifty percent as easily, right?" Joe immediately pulled out a third orb and tossed it into the air alongside the other two. There was a remarkable difference in the ease of use, and he felt confident that he could control all three fairly easily in combat. As soon as he had collected all of the available loot, Joe turned and started running back toward the city. He needed aspects, *lots* of aspects, then even more aspects, and he needed them quickly. There was really only one place that he could go to make that happen, and luckily he had a permanent pass.

As he rushed toward the city to hop headfirst into the sewers, he felt like his body was on autopilot. Since his mind was free, he decided to open up his character sheet and see how things were going.

Name: Joe 'Tatum's Chosen Legend' Class: Reductionist
Profession I: Arcanologist (Max)
Profession II: Ritualistic Alchemist (1/20)
Profession III: None
Character Level: 19 Exp: 190,559 Exp to next level: 19,441
Rituarchitect Level: 10 Exp: 45,000 Exp debt: 9,590
Reductionist Level: 0 Exp: 936 Exp to next level: 64
Hit Points: 1,813/1,813
Mana: 6,662/6,662

Mana regen: 49.18/sec
Stamina: 1,491/1,491
Stamina regen: 6.45/sec

Characteristic: Raw score

Strength: 143
Dexterity: 143
Constitution: 139
Intelligence: 148
Wisdom: 129
Dark Charisma: 100
Perception: 132
Luck: 72
Karmic Luck: -1

Joe screeched to a halt as he saw the drastic shift on his character sheet. "That's not right. None of that is right. What happened to…? Everything jumped, everything jumped *way* too high! Tatum, is this something you did? Dude. I just got you back, don't mess with the system."

Activate Query?

"Yes, activate query, send a message to the admins, *anything* so that I do not get slapped with another penalty!" The Reductionist rubbed his bald head nervously. "I *just* got rid of that curse; I'm not going back to it! Every basic score went up a full ten points, and all of my experience went up an additional ten as well!"

Your concerns have been passed on! Occultatum sees your plight, and has elevated your error report! Expect a full audit shortly!

Joe winced the word 'audit', but waited patiently for an answer. Five minutes passed, ten, but nothing changed. He took a few hesitant steps, expecting that he would be whisked away as soon as he started moving. Still, nothing. Trying to put it out of his mind, he started running, feeling slow for some reason. "Right… lost my shoes."

He burst into the city, running past a confused guard, who had expected him to be gone for several days, before he ran into his first real issue. "Where is the entrance to the landfill? I came out of it… I think it was… no, I died in there. Never got out by walking."

He knew another way to get into the sewers, but there was only one way to do it *fast*. This time, however, he wasn't going to be jumping into the outskirts of the pile. No, he was going right for the expensive stuff. That meant that there would be a hard landing and monsters to contend with. That was fine. This time, he knew what he was getting into, and he had an oversized mana pool so that he could be his own backup. "Already have food packed, and I don't need water. Let's go."

With that, he raced toward the only high-end shop in the city that he knew would let him use their garbage chute: McPoundy's forge. Joe ran in, barely sparing a glance for the many exasperated stares he started to collect as soon as the door opened. "Pardon me; where do you all dump failures? Your access point into the landfill?"

"Center of the room," one of the Journeymen stated, getting 'cheerful' grins from his contemporaries. "What? What's he gonna do with that information? Get *more* training and cheat into a higher rank?"

Joe saw an opportunity and decided to run with it. "Hey, listen up, everyone. I know you don't really like the fact that I've been able to get special treatment. Let me make it up to you."

"I'll leave here like all other failures." He walked over to the chute and threw it open, getting a few laughs as he reeled back from the sudden wash of foulness that wafted out. He waved at them, double-checked his buffs, and jumped in headfirst. "Goodbye, cruel forge!"

The shouts of alarm that followed him in were more than enough to make up for the awkward entry.

"He's lost it!"

"Throw a rope in! That nutter bro is gonna get us all banned from the forge!"

"Stop him! McPoundy's gonna eat us for lunch if Candidate bro's death is traced back here!"

Joe chuckled the whole way down the slimy tube, his breath catching as he entered the open air above the landfill. The sight was magnificent, since he was approaching from far above and much nearer the center of the hollow mountain. "Oh, right; that's why Havoc dropped me at the edge. To get a soft landing."

The human was dropping directly toward a massive hillock of weapons and metals that had been deemed 'not good enough to distribute'. He twisted and got his feet under him, landing almost gently among the stalagmites of slag and shambles of rusting steel.

Exquisite Shell: 8,657/9,260

"Six hundred and three damage?" Joe looked at the treasure trove that he had literally fallen into, then back at the small dent in his protections. "Totally worth it."

A rope slapped into the side of his head, startling him. He looked up just in time to see it get cut in half as the protective shielding of the landfill recognized it as something attempting to 'climb up and out'. "Well, feces. Good thing I *wanted* to be here... nice of them to try, at least. First thing; set a perimeter."

He hadn't forgotten that the entire place was infested by zombie Dwarves stumbling around, and Joe didn't want to stay focused all the way up to getting munched on. Luckily, he had something perfectly suited for this sort of situation. "Quarantine area should almost guarantee me some peace and quiet."

Since the ritual was so simple and easy to set up, in less than twenty minutes, he was able to activate the two circles.

Class experience gained: 50 (Reductionist).

The soft sound of materials rotting was covered by a sudden rush of clawed feet skittering away from him, and Joe shuddered as he realized that he was hearing literally *thousands* of small things moving. Rodents? Perhaps, but what level did they need to be to survive in an area like this? "Well... at least I know they are all under level twenty-nine, or they'd be all over me right now."

"Oh… I'm at only fourteen experience from the first level as a Reductionist." Joe looked around, then at his status screen, then around again. "Alright. It can only help me to have a higher class level, right?"

He found a tower shield that was almost perfectly flat, and decided to use it as a base for an Apprentice-ranked Ritual of Acid Spray. That would let him get the level up in an instant, wouldn't take too long or cost too much, and would still be useful in getting through the muck that filled the area. Barring usefulness for unearthing high aspect-rarity goods, he could always toss it in a space beneath residential areas and use it to clear food and trash waste.

Ten minutes for the first circle, fifteen for the next, and twenty-five for the third. Almost an hour used, but hopefully not wasted. Joe lugged the shield to the edge of the area defined by the Quarantine Area, then swung it around in a wide arc, releasing it like a discus just after activating it. The shield flew like a frisbee, its weight ensuring that it was going slow enough not to activate the boundary shields.

A rain of acid fell from it as it travelled, but Joe wasn't following it. He was staring gleefully at the message waiting for him. A shock of silvery energy pulsed through him, not as potent as a character level increase, but still very welcome. His fatigue vanished in a haze of delight, and he sighed happily as he read the notification.

Class experience gained: 100.

You have reached Reductionist class level 1! Congratulations! Your understanding of reduction has increased. Bonus: you are now able to expend mana with a greater throughput so as to reduce within an area of effect. The area must be within an Aspect Array. (i.e. Field Array).

"Level one, just like that." Joe stretched his neck, rolling his head from side to side. "Sure, I need to figure out what that bonus means, but I have plenty of things to test it on."

CHAPTER FIFTY-ONE

Joe walked over to a stalagmite and extended his Field Array around the metal spire. He touched the metal and let his mana inform him of the requirements.

Item: Slag Pile.

Reduction value: 739 Rare aspects, 2,149 Uncommon aspects, 3,819 Common aspects, 7,381 Damaged aspects, 10,843 Trash aspects.

Reduction cost: 125 mana per second. Estimated reduction time required: 40 seconds.

"Oh? It gave me an approximate reduction time?" Joe was *extra* pleased about this small change. "That means there is an estimated cost of... five thousand mana. I can foot that bill. Let's see; just shy of eighteen hundred mana reserved by my buffs. Let's drop the shield... okay, that gives me enough to spare. Do I just... will it? Or *push* on the mana?"

He tried to push the mana, but it was even easier than that; a notification appeared as he attempted to reduce the slag.

Activate area of effect? Instant cost: 5,000* mana. Estimated reduction time required: 1.5 seconds. More or less mana may be required after initial investment. Yes / No.

The asterisk opened a sliding scale on the mana which

allowed him to play with the mana investment. When he added more, the reduction time increased. When he made a lower initial investment, the estimated time went higher. "I see. Pretty user friendly."

He put in the entire amount and started reducing. As soon as it started, he dropped to the ground and his eyes rolled up into the back of his head. It felt like his spine had been pulled out through his chest, but it only lasted for just over a second.

You are unconscious! Time remaining: 5… 4…

Waking with a gasp, Joe shot to his feet and looked around, making sure that he wasn't being attacked. Then the migraine hit. He groaned and sank back down to his knees, his normally mana-suffused body unable to bear the sudden and instant loss of his entire mana pool. Luckily, his mana was coming back steadily, and each second brought relief to his body, as if he had been starved and dehydrated, but now had a direct IV drip pouring saline into his system.

Luck +2!

When he was once more able to see through his bleary eyes, Joe inspected the remnants of the slag spike. The vast majority of it had disappeared, leaving behind a perfect slice at the base that appeared as polished as glass. He touched it, just to see how clean the reduction had been, and smiled when he felt almost no friction at all. "This could have interesting applications… no more dropping my mana pool like that, though."

He had expected that his mana channels—which had been widened—and the fact that his mana pool had been dispersed through his body, would help him deal with the rapid drain. Perhaps it had, actually. He hadn't lost any health, but if he'd had an enemy near him, the test would have ended in disaster. "Let's try over there next. This was a good source of material, but I need common stuff too, right?"

Joe walked to the edge of his active ritual, and started extending the Field Array. This time, he didn't have a set goal in mind; the Reductionist just wanted a *huge* area. His mana raced out of him, worming through the garbage and extending further than he had ever managed before. Just as the first mana tendril reached past the ten meter mark, the entire thing collapsed. "That's the limit, huh? At least for what I can't see clearly, and only for now."

Starting again, he made sure to guide the mana more carefully, and kept it tied to himself whenever it started to waver. Just as he approached the previous boundary, he stopped and set the mana in place. "Now, that's good, but how do I…?"

Uncertain how he would be able to reduce what was in the area, Joe paused and tried to think logically. "This… clearly this is all disparate garbage. A touch of mana isn't going to let me identify it. To reduce things in an area, I need to use the Field Array, so that has to tie into this process."

Joe placed his fingers on one of the mana strands and attempted to send a mana 'pulse' through it. The first did nothing, so he sent a second, this time trying to tie his mana into the array.

Item: Approximately 10 cubic meters of Common and below material. Reduction value: unknown. Total mass: 5,740 pounds of material. Reduction cost: 5 mana per second. Estimated reduction time required: 600 seconds.

"That's ten minutes of reducing." Joe tapped his fingers together as he thought. "*Or~r~r* a total mana cost of three thousand if I do it all at once? I can handle that. My mana regen won't even notice it. Okay… area of effect, and…!"

The pile of rubbish vanished, only a few small chunks hovering in the open air before falling to the ground. Joe bent over, clutching his chest as his body once again *lost* a huge pool of mana. "That's… so *unpleasant*! I need to figure out—oh! I can hook mana batteries to my Field Array! I don't need to do this directly; I can practically automate it!"

That led Joe down a rabbit hole, his excitement rooting him in one spot for almost ten minutes as he plotted out what would be needed to make an aspect generator function the way he wanted it to. "I'd need a large structure with a permanently-built Aspect Array, and it would need to be strong enough to function for a long period of time. I'd need huge jars that could store all the aspects being generated, Mana Batteries powerful enough to keep it running, and either a system or workforce that could keep them charged."

While his mind was running through various daydreams to determine what the building should be shaped like, a zombie wandered into the area in front of him, falling into the pit that had been dug out by the reduction.

Living creature detected in Field Array! This is not allowed! *The reduction of living creatures is impossible. Calculating culpability... unintentional. Administering punishment.*

Joe's array shattered like spun glass, and a backlash of mana drove into his heart.

Damage taken: 115!

Even though the damage taken wasn't all that extreme, the fact that it had happened so suddenly and unexpectedly—also bypassing his Exquisite Shell—almost caused Joe to stumble right into the pit with the zombie Dwarf. "That's... ow... another thing I'll need. A sorter or filter. I think I got it. A decagon, a ten-sided building with ten storage areas. A hole in the middle to drop living things out of it. A supercharged Ritual of Little Sisters Cleaning Service to sort by rarity, a ton of batteries to power everything, all of it laced with a permanent Aspect Array. Sounds good? Great, *break*! Go team!"

He didn't want to waste the free experience the monster offered, so he pulled out three Ritual Orbs and set them to slamming into the trapped undead. That was slow going, so all six eventually came out, and Joe used them like a giant hammer, all moving together to hit at roughly the same time. That caused three hundred points of damage per strike, also known as *too slow*! On the next descent, Joe activated Cone of Cold as well, dealing a total of over five hundred on hit damage.

The creature tried to escape the pit, but every lunge upward only made the walls of garbage sink down, sending it tumbling away from Joe. This reaffirmed the human's decision that he really *liked* having the high ground, and he resolved to keep it as much as possible in the future.

As the orbs started striking out of sync in their one-sided assault, Joe adjusted them slightly. The attack was as fun to watch as it was to carry out, so Joe didn't worry too much about how long it was taking. He tossed in a Dark Lightning Strike to hurry things along whenever possible. Over the next thirty seconds, the monster's health dropped rapidly. Joe had Corify activate on what he hoped was the last hit. It wasn't, but he managed to deal another eight hundred damage over the next five seconds—another Cone of Cold activated—and the Zombie went from undead to dead-dead.

You have defeated a monster that was over ten levels higher than you! Bonus experience has been granted! Experience gained: 777!

Joe stared at the notification, then the defeated creature, then the notification again. "I didn't even think about that until right now, but the only reason it would have been here is because the ritual drew it in due to the level difference between us. I... do I need to leave?"

He rushed to summit a tall slag pile and scanned around. As far as he could tell, no other monsters were currently approaching him. "Okay... that was a fluke. Everything is fine for now, but I need to remember that I'm here for a reason. Everything else can wait until I'm in a safe location. I need to bring *power* to the upcoming fight."

"I can start here." Joe looked down at the pile of slag he was standing on, and his mana pool that had refilled over the last few seconds. "But first... gotta check to see if that Zombie dropped a Core."

CHAPTER FIFTY-TWO

Joe staggered out of the landfill just over a day later, remembering to use Lay on Hands only thanks to the 'bleeding' notification that kept popping up. His vision was swimming; the last day had been a constant grind that tested him immensely, but the profit was certainly worth the effort.

He had managed to reduce things in the landfill for almost twenty-two hours straight, his improved constitution allowing him to ignore sleep for more than a *week* if he wanted to do so. He had managed almost thirty reductions an hour, which meant his mana pool had refilled six hundred and sixty times. At that point, he had made a sizable dent in the area, and his actions were drawing attention from the more powerful inhabitants of the landfill.

The zombies had come one at a time, at first, but eventually, one of them broke through while he was distracted. It didn't go after Joe directly, as he had expected; it had charged directly at the Ritual of Quarantine and smashed it until the ritual shattered. Then it had *howled*, and a wave of lower-level undead had flooded through the landfill toward him. Joe had no choice but to run, *jump*, flee for his life. He had managed to escape, but by that time, he was near the walls and decided that it was a good time to leave.

Just before he had stepped out, a sneak attack struck him and demolished his Exquisite Shell, sending Joe reeling and bleeding into the streets of the capital. Now that he had escaped, he looked around for the door so he could use it in the future. Once again, the entrance to the landfill was nowhere to be seen, and he couldn't risk opening the door and letting Zombies through... so he didn't go out of his way to learn how to open it.

Joe sat in the small puddle of his rapidly vanishing blood— thanks being given to that magnificent Neutrality Aura once again—and perused the increases from the last day of grinding.

Strength, dexterity, constitution +3!
Intelligence, wisdom, perception +4!
Luck +5!
Class experience gained: 1,200 (Reductionist)
Mend (Journeyman II)
Lay on Hands (Journeyman II).
Neutrality Aura (Student VIII).
Retaliation of Shadows (Journeyman III).
Exquisite Shell (Student V).
Dark Lightning Strike (Apprentice VIII).
Mana Manipulation (Student VIII). It looks like you found an effective training program!
Coalescence (Student IX). Finally flushed out all that stagnant mana! Bet you feel better, don't you?
Battle Meditation (Novice VIII)
Assisted Ritual Orb Usage (Beginner I)
Knowledge (Beginner VI)
Architectural Lore (Beginner III)

"Stagnant mana? I really need to figure out what that means." Joe stared at the messages and once more swore to himself that he wouldn't be taking on any more quests after this war. At least, not until he had gotten sick of gaining all the skills and stats he could grab. His gathered aspect list was equally impressive; he had been able to make and partially fill both a Unique and Rare Aspect Jar, but a sound tore his attention away before he could open the itemized inventory and cackle over the hundreds of thousands of collected aspects.

Boots. Metal boots that were marching in time.

The sound was distant, but that just meant that there were so many that the rhythm was resounding even here. That could only mean one thing: the battle was starting, and he, the person who had sparked the war and was responsible for its success, was late.

"Does overmorrow mean three days or *two* days? I thought I had three!" He hopped to his feet and fought through the fatigue, sprinting along the roads until he caught sight of the flowing river of silver that was the Legion on the move.

Message available! Send a message to friends list contact? Yes / No.

"What?" By the time Joe recognized the notification, it was already cancelled.

Friend list member out of Line of Sight!

"Who was that, then?" Joe shook off his confusion and ran for a series of Legionnaires that had a black trim on their armor: the sign of an Officer. Getting closer drew unwanted attention to him, and a few soldiers even drew steel and pointed it at him. "Candidate Joe reporting! I'm looking for Major General Havoc!"

The various weaponry was pulled back, and one Dwarf grimaced as she replied to him, "The Major General is part of the advance force. That… fine example of what not to do to make political friends… will either be right at the front, or already digging into Gramma's Shoe by the time the remainder of the Legion approaches. Please use caution, Candidate Bro."

"Thanks, Officer Dudette." Joe slammed an open palm on her paulron and turned to run. He needed to get ahead of all the marching soldiers if he was going to get a Ritual of Argus active on the person that was likely *the* most important figure that had joined the war effort. In his haste, he didn't catch the pink tinge that colored the cheeks under the flowing auburn mustache of the Dwarf he was taking with.

"I can't believe *Joe* knew *my* name!" Dudette breathed in a deep, gravelly whisper. "If we win this... I can't imagine he'd be any less famous than Havoc himself!"

The human had no idea the effect that he was having on the Dwarves around him. If he had... he would have been utterly uncomfortable. The bearded Dwarves looked on in admiration and slight jealousy: *they* wanted to be the ones to incite a full-on assault! The mustachioed ones looked at Joe with gazes wavering between interest and self-doubt. Joe was *hairless*. Though he might soon have a reputation worthy of capturing the attention of the Oligarchy, he was a human, hairless as a child, and a *mage*. For most of them, those factors snuffed the ember of interest that formed when he was mentioned... but only for *most*.

Running at top speed was the only way Joe could slowly make his way past the miles-spanning troop formation. No one laughed as he panted along; no one commented that he was out of position. There was only one thing on the minds of the Legion: the Elves had invaded their home. Their monument to what was once the matriarch of all the Dwarven Clans. Even now, a day away at marching speed, they could see the plumes of black ash that rose from the volcano; the benefit of a flat plane of existence.

Half the day later, Joe was starting to flag. He saw one Legionnaire with a bright red mustache that he had been leapfrogging for almost ten minutes. Joe would see her passing him, put in more effort and get ahead, but then she would slowly and inexorably catch up to him and march forward. Joe had been giving her so much side-eye that she was starting to look at him with a nervous expression whenever she got ahead. Finally, Joe thought of a solution to his current problem. "Mate! I need a jolt, *Over-caffeinate!*"

The small elemental bubbled onto his white robe and gave

him a searching glance. Joe blushed lightly, "No, I haven't made a special cup yet, but the next time I'm forging in a safe area, I will! Promise."

Mate bubbled happily and extended tendrils of pure caffeine out of its body, appearing to become a delicious version of a sea urchin. The iridescent tendrils swooped around and dug into Joe, and a moment later he shot forward at a speed he hadn't gotten *close* to all day. For the next ten minutes, he sprinted past the marching formation, laughing wildly the whole way.

Then he remembered why the ability was mainly used in a pinch, and not as a travel booster. When the buff expired, his stats were temporarily reduced by thirty percent, and continuing to run made him want to puke. That nasty side effect didn't last too long, thanks to Neutrality Aura, but it was still a pain. Joe was hoping that the Legion would bunker down and sleep soon, but as the day wore on and darkness settled over the plain, they showed no signs of stopping or slowing down.

The final straw was when the red-haired Dwarf caught up to him again.

"That's *it*, I need to move faster." Joe was getting crabby and annoyed from the constant exertion and several days of no sleep. His stamina was flickering between empty and a *lil* bit full, but what else did he have? "Full mana bar. Gotta. Figure out. How to cheat!"

Skipping was fine, and used a speck of mana at a time, but he was a *Master* Jumper! He should be able to cross vast distances, shoot into the sky, leap through open areas like a gazelle! Joe stopped running and let his stamina build up a little. He was slightly embarrassed that he would be testing this next to the Legion, but he couldn't go off in the distance right now. Not only was this the most direct route to Gramma's Shoe, the Legion was also dealing with all the threats that dared to come close to them. If Joe wandered off, he was going to be moving even slower.

After catching his breath, he started sprinting again, but

this time as soon as he got to his top speed, he shifted down and *jumped*, pouring mana into his legs. He hadn't really tested the limits of his body, especially not like this, yet he wasn't totally surprised when his leap carried him a full thirty feet forward before he touched down again. Only his high skill levels in both Jump and Aerial Acrobatics kept his feet under him, though he stumbled before moving forward to do it again.

On the third attempt, it got *easy*. Joe landed and went again, seeing a notification that made him smile.

Through a special action, you have managed to generate a skill!

Skill gained: Leap (Master 0). At the cost of 8% total stamina and 7% total mana pool, you are able to leap forward at great speed.

You have managed to generate a skill by using three other skills in a combined fashion. (Jump, Aerial Acrobatics, and Jump Around). As you created all of these skills with no system help or guidance, you have the option to instantly and freely combine these and the newly generated skill 'Leap', along with three ranks in Mana Manipulation, to create a higher-ranked skill.

No more details are available. If you choose not to combine the skills, you may still do so at a later date. Note: each person can only combine a skill in this manner once. If you wish to use other self-guided skills, please make sure to say 'no'.

Combine (Jump, Aerial Acrobatics, Jump Around, Leap, and 3 ranks of Mana Manipulation) into higher rarity skill? Yes / No.

"Not what I was expecting, but I'm still happy to see that happening..." Joe looked at the options, hesitating before hitting 'yes'. These skills represented his only Master ranked abilities, and letting them go was... tough. "I need to remember what I was told. Not every skill can get into the Master ranks, and, well, I've seen no movement with this one. Maybe a higher rank will let me reach the Grandmaster ranks someday."

Joe had been continuing to move, his body practically on autopilot as he played around with his movement. Thus, he didn't think much before accepting the changes, and he was in the air when he did so. He crashed to the ground painfully as the skills vanished and reformed into a new, more potent version.

Exquisite Shell: 9,782/9,842

Guild (The Wanderers) bonus from having a Mastered skill has been lost!

Skill decrease: Mana Manipulation (Student V).

Skill combination successful! New skill gained: Omnivault.

Omnivault (Expert VII). The ground has never been your friend. You have only ever seen it as something you must use as a launch pad to reach greater heights. Now, you are getting ever closer to a higher form of movement! You can now jump upward Strength/10 feet directly upward from a standstill, or leap forward (Strength/10)*3 feet forward while moving. Your sense of balance in the air is unsurpassed. Each empowered leap now costs 1x% stamina and 2x% mana, where x is each consecutive leap. At double the x cost, you may leap or jump a single additional time while still in the air. 'Consecutive' is considered any jumping or leaping within 3 seconds of the previous one.

That had been a lot of changes in an overly fast time, but Joe was amazed by the implications of the skill, as well as how he received it. "I can combine only a certain amount of *ranks* of a skill? That's… game changing! How many possible skills *are* there? Oh, I can't *wait* to try this."

But he did have to wait. Almost four minutes, to be exact, since he wanted a full stamina bar when he started trying out the new skill. As soon as it peaked, he took a running start and vaulted into the air, travelling forty-three feet in a beautiful parabolic arc. At the top of the leap, he somersaulted perfectly. At the end, he smoothly transitioned into a second leap forward. After eight total leaps, traveling three hundred and fifty feet in practically the blink of an eye, Joe collapsed to the ground and started dry heaving.

"Mana… gone… *already?*" He gasped for air, staring in shock at his mana bar. "Eight vaults cost… four *thousand* eight hundred and eighty-seven mana?"

His dreams of bounding through the open plains vanished

like fog on a hot day. "There's *gotta* be a way this is usable. I…
right! Okay, let's try this again."

Joe waited a few minutes to be back in peak shape, snarled
viciously at a familiar red-mustached Dwarf, then started
running and leaping again. This time when he landed, he ran
for a few seconds before leaping again. "*Ha-hahh*! Non-consecu-
tive. One hundred thirty five mana per leap, each time. My
mana regen can handle that. Time to get a *jump* on catching
Havoc."

CHAPTER FIFTY-THREE

Joe had been getting some overly-wide smiles from the Legion as he got closer to the front of the line. He was sure that they were waiting for a chance to 'broaden his horizons' by whaling on him for annoying them so thoroughly, but they would just need to wait their turn.

The Reductionist internally admitted that he might have been going overboard with his new skill, but there was something so *freeing* about shooting through the air in a perfectly controlled motion. This had naturally led to him angling his leaps so that he arced over the formation, springing back and forth. It only made him a *little* slower, but it had made people chuckle. A few had even halfheartedly taken swings at him as he went over, but even the most angry Legionnaire only grumbled quietly. One of the great things about living in a 'nice' society; no one wanted to call you out for non-harmful silliness.

Joe could finally see Havoc's outline, just as the sun was starting to rise. He knew it was the Dwarf he sought only because the Major General's voice was reverberating across the open space as he shouted at the advance party that was with him. The Dwarf was encased in a massive golem, which sported four spinning drills on each hand—each of which also spun—and had overly bulky pistons for elbows.

"Are ya *ready*, Dwarves?" Havoc howled at his troops; their reply was almost incoherent screaming.

"Aye, aye, Major General!"

Havoc slammed his construct's left 'fist' into the mountain, sending a spray of torn-out stone flying into the air. The other fist came down as that one retracted. "I can't *hear* you!"

"Aye, aye, Major General!"

"Ohhh!" The fists started moving four times as fast as they pulverized the rocky surface. "Elves in a bunker, under this rock!"

"War crimes, war crimes!"

"What will we do, when we pull them on *top*?" Havoc bellowed as rock chips flew everywhere.

"War crimes, war crimes!"

"Is bloodshed and razing something you wish?"

"War crimes, war crimes!"

"Then come over here, and gut 'em like a fish!"

"War crimes, war crimes!"

"Ready?" Havoc popped out of the golem as it vanished into the tunnel it was rapidly digging, and he no longer needed to manually control it. "War crimes, war crimes…"

"War crimes, war crimes!"

"War cri~imes…! Here we go~o!" Havoc screeched as the golem broke through and a wash of hot air blasted from the tunnel. The Dwarves flooded in, following his charge, and Joe sputtered to a stop; knowing he was too late to be helpful to that first wave.

For one thing, the ritual he planned to use was at the Expert rank, and he would need a few hours of work to get it ready. Still, most of the leadership was near the middle or end of the formation, and he was hopeful that he could have it ready before they arrived.

Joe moved out of the way and got to work as another breach point was established, allowing the Legion to hopefully flank the hidden fort when the tunnel was completed. He got to work right away, setting up a Field Array and reducing the top layer of stone—entirely Trash Aspects—to make the area perfectly level. Next came the difficult part: creating an Expert ranked ritual diagram. As per usual, the circles from Novice to Journeyman were fairly straightforward to create. When it came time for the final circle, Joe began struggling mightily.

"I need this to *spin*, abyss it!" Joe sighed as he scowled at the interlocking sympathetic links that connected the Novice circle to the Journeyman circle. "Where's a good gyroscope when you need it? Well... I've seen rituals that are free-floating, so why can't I do that? *How* would I do that, though?"

The answer was not forthcoming, and Joe grumpily *almost* gave up. "What if I just draw it out? I've already seen that sometimes the ritual circles will form out of energy and lift out of the ground. Why did I never think of that before? Every time I have put it on something that was going to rotate, it was a ritual that I wanted to use long-term. Maybe most of the time, I don't even need to do that!"

Hoping that his assumption was correct, Joe pulled out an aspect jar that was shining with a dark indigo light. Adding the jar to the array *very* carefully, he held out a hand and allowed the dark flames to waft out of the jar and coalesce into a beautiful quill. He added embellishment after embellishment, hoping to make a truly *unique* inscriber.

Joe gripped the ethereal inscriber, hoping it wouldn't blow up in his face. It seemed that he had succeeded, and after patting himself on the back, he quickly checked how many aspects he had to work with.

Unique aspects: 1,719 split between proper and improper storage devices.

Natural Unique Aspect (Uncommon) Jar: 1,224/2,150 Unique aspects. Current rate of collection: 4 Unique aspects per hour.

Natural Unique Aspect (Unique) Jar: 193/9,558 Unique aspects. Current rate of collection: 7 Unique aspects per hour.

"The rest of the flames are in my codpiece, huh? Should I

think about spreading them out among a few friends?" he hummed out loud, getting a reaction right away from someone he hadn't seen approaching.

"You should see an alchemist or a healer if that's the case, human." Surprised, Joe turned regard the Dwarf walking toward him, an Officer with a raven-dark mustache. He saluted, and the Dwarf nodded in reply. "At ease, Candidate. I'm Major Infraction. I'm here because I've heard some troubling reports on your activities. Then I get here, and you're talking about spreading fire from your nethers, and I'm worried for entirely different reasons."

"That's not... I can explain this *really* easily..." Joe mumbled with a beet-red face.

"Why not go over why you're making a giant magical circle out in the open?" Major Infraction demanded, not a hint of mirth on her face. "I'm happy to explain that magic makes my soldiers nervous. They might have to fight it, or *think* about it, and I don't like my Legion to think; I like them to *act*."

"That's a terrible shame." Joe sketched the very first symbol carefully, letting the Unique indigo flames travel along the Field Array and into his inscriber, then onto the smooth surface of the stone. "Taking the thinking out of your soldiers and only letting it be done by the most powerful of your people... it makes the powerful into cowards and soldiers into fools."

"You dare insult the *Legion*? The very Oligarchy itself?" Major Infraction glowered darkly, and a few Dwarves outfitted in an armor style that Joe hadn't seen before walked forward to flank her. The Dwarven guards were covered from head to toe, not a single part of their hair or skin showing. "I'll have you torn apart *twice* for those words!"

The Dwarves around her moved smoothly and perfectly in sync, which tipped Joe off to what they were. "Oh? You're a necromancer? You practice on your own troops? I didn't think that was allowed."

"No fear at all?" Major Infraction grinned, breaking her stoic expression for the first time, and the undead at her side stopped closing in on Joe. "It isn't allowed. Unless, of course, you earn your position by using the forbidden magics for the glory of the Dwarven Oligarchy. Then you get named based on your deeds. I broke the rules. Almost all of them, when I could. Hence my moniker. Now, what are you doing?"

"Setting up a counter to Elven illusions. I need to make sure it gets to the people that most need it, but I don't even know who that would be, except myself and Major General Havoc." Joe traced the next symbol on the ground carefully, but it wasn't enough: he made a slight error. The aspect flame burst from that symbol and consumed itself *and* the one Joe had already made. "Oh, great. Now I don't get a chance to make *corrections?*"

"Just be glad it didn't cascade downward and take the whole magic circle." The Major commented dryly, indicating that there was some personal experience in that statement. "Higher order materials have more catastrophic effects in direct proportion to their position on the rarity charts. You're Candidate *Joe*, then? Hairless, magical, insufferable... yup. You fit the description."

"*Hey!*"

"No backtalk; you don't have the rank for it. Yet." She chuckled, waved, and a few undead walked off. "I'll gather a few Majors and above that are willing to participate. Need anything else?"

"Now that you mention it..." Joe cracked a lopsided grin. "A protection detail would be lovely. I was *educated* on what a failed ritual can do recently, and I wouldn't like to blow away half the mountain. At least, the half with the Dwarves on it. Oh, and anyone that can channel large quantities of mana. I'll need help with this one."

Joe refocused on his ritual circle, needing *far* longer than he'd estimated to finish it. He looked up only once, finding an entire platoon arrayed around him, before turning his eyes to the ritual once more. By the time he finished the sixth circle— the Expert circle—the day was almost half over. "Okay... that one was a lot more... *intense* than I expected."

No mistakes allowed meant perfection was mandatory on the first attempt. Luckily, he was working with an actual diagram instead of going by memory, else he would have had to start over and over. Joe decided then and there to create his own personal grimoire; he needed notes, helpful hints, and tricks! These dry schematics were useful, but... not his style. "Who's ready to power this puppy up?"

The platoon around him stayed silent, but Major Infraction took a step forward and shouted at the Legion that was still queued up to delve into the volcano. "Anyone who can't use mana is a weakling!"

"What?"

"Dude! Did you hear what Major Dudette just said about you?"

"*Bro*! She was *totally* talking about you, I can totally use the mana. I use the mana all the *time!*"

A veritable flood of volunteers came over and got into position, as directed by Joe. The Major introduced Joe to the commanders that were good candidates for illusion breakers, but they had no characteristics that made Joe remember them. Most were 'Bros' or 'Dudettes', Legion members that had become high-ranking through years of service instead of accessing the Officer track.

Joe started arranging them, getting each of the one hundred and twenty-seven conscri—*volunteers*, to stand where he needed them. After they were organized in the correct positions, he placed his hand into the initial start point of the ritual and allowed an influx of mana to-

You are unconscious! Calculating... time remaining: 30... 29...

CHAPTER FIFTY-FOUR

When Joe woke up, he wasn't feeling... good. In fact, he was feeling pretty ragged. Blood was soaking his white robes—currently dyed red—and a terrible headache was situated right between his eyes. He lumbered to his feet and rubbed his grainy eyes. "What in the *abyss* happened?"

He looked around, discovering that all the Dwarves that had joined him were little more than mincemeat contained by armor. The sight made him gag, and he stumbled back in horror. The only people in the area that weren't destroyed were the ones that hadn't participated. Joe slapped his status screen open and read over the notifications.

Attempting to start ritual!

Caution! Mana requirements cannot be fulfilled with the current cadre of mana donors! Ensure that you have enough for stage two!

Ritual stage one activating... ritual expansion has been completed! Mana requirements not fulfilled. Ritual is pausing. Please ensure mana requirements are prepared for stage two before resuming!

"Nothing in here about what happened... were we attacked?" Joe looked frantically at the... armor that surrounded him, then down at the ritual. All that remained was the initial, central Novice ring. His eyes widened, and he frantically looked for what had destroyed… "Wait. Ritual expansion? *Paused?* What does that mean?"

Major Infraction stepped toward him with a weapon in each hand, yet past the bluster, Joe could see a hesitation to come closer to him shining through. "Joe! Candidate, you just killed over a hundred-"

"Not *now*, Major!" Joe barked at her, his hoarse voice laced with frustration and anger. He wasn't immune to the grisly sight. A failed activation had never done something like *this*. "What happened? Where is my ritual?"

Silence reigned for a moment, the only sounds echoing down from the tunnels that had been carved into Gramma's Shoe, or the distant thunder of more Legion reinforcements closing in. Then one of the people that had been selected for an Eye of Argus stepped forward. "Reporting, Teamkiller Bro! Those fancy circles started rotating, then raced off into the distance. They became bigger as they moved, which I'm pretty sure breaks the law of conservation of-"

"They moved?" Joe stared the Dwarf down until the words stopped. Even as he started realizing what that meant, Joe was running toward the sound of incoming troops. "They didn't break, they just *moved*? No! They *expanded*!"

It didn't take long for him to reach the next ritual circle, it was about eleven meters from the Novice circle to this one. Just as he had hoped, it wasn't broken. As the notification had stated, it was *paused*. He stepped on the circle, and a strange thing happened.

He got feedback.

Ritual of Argus: Beginner Circle. Current requirements: filled.

He stepped over it, and a dark glow—which he hadn't even originally noticed —vanished. Joe kept going, reaching the next circle after travelling seventeen meters. "Okay, they're arranged out in prime distances. Next one should be… eleven, seventeen… twenty-three meters if the pattern follows."

Ritual of Argus: Apprentice Circle. Current requirements: Not filled.

This time the circle hadn't lit up, making Joe nod. He couldn't supply a circle this large by himself; he had known that was going to be the case. Right now, what he really needed was a truckload of charged mana batteries. Were ley lines a thing? Could he tap into them if they were? The sound of metal-shod boots on stone became louder, and he glanced up to see more troops arriving. "No batteries... but this might work."

He rushed over to the front of the column and body-blocked them from moving forward. "Legion! I have a change order!"

They came to a halt as his Candidacy impacted them. The platoon sergeant stepped forward and hollered at Joe, "Get the *abyss* out of the way! I heard that we're authorized for war crimes today!"

"*War crimes!*" The Dwarves shouted, heat appearing in their tired eyes.

Joe walked over to the platoon sergeant, took three Ritual Orbs out, and hit the Dwarf with them and a Dark Lightning Strike all at the same time. With the pure constitution score that the Dwarf had, it was Joe's equivalent to punching him in the face. "I said there was a *change order*! This operation was put into play by *me*, and the success of the Dwarven Oligarchy is relying on my orders being *followed*. Follow your orders, or are *you* going to take the blame for the Elves overrunning this position?"

Not waiting for a reply, and wanting to keep the Dwarves confused—which was unfortunately a little too easy—Joe directed the Dwarves to split by highest mana pool and take a position on the nearest ritual circle. The entire platoon fit onto the Beginner circle, but the circle had only lit up when there were at least half of them on it.

"Split this unit; a quarter of you follow me. As for you, *sergeant*, get on the road and get all of the reinforcements onto these circles until I tell you to stop!" Joe sent the glowering Dwarf away, then started populating the next circle. It took a few minutes before the next contingent arrived, and his ears caught a familiar conversation after a dull **thud** resounded through the area.

"-or are *you* going to take the blame for the Elves overrunning this position?" The sergeant's voice reached Joe's ears. He laughed that his own confusing argument was being used again, but he wasn't about to complain. Joe started directing the Dwarves into position as they arrived. The Apprentice circle took twice as long to reach the 'fulfilled' condition, and he lost count of the troops needed to fill the Student and Journeyman areas. By the time the Expert circle was filled, an unbroken line of Dwarves trailed off into the distance in both directions.

Joe watched the uncomfortable Dwarves shifting slightly, their chest plates scraping against the armor of the person in front of them. The circle was glowing, but he knew he needed to hurry. If something didn't change soon, his orders would lose their potency and the Dwarves would wander off before they missed the chance to fight. One small problem was that he was on the outside of the ritual, but it was only a *small* problem. He got a running start, hurdled over the line of Legionnaires, and landed in a sprint, repeating the acrobatics until he was standing at the center; the only person on the Novice circle.

Mana requirements fulfilled with the current cadre of mana donors! Ritual of Argus Stage Two is ready to activate!

Wasting no time, Joe activated the ritual with a chant and the first influx of mana. "Omnes videntes oculo. V videre. Si opus fuerit, his comedent!"

Ritual requires targeting mechanism.

The notification was unexpected, but Joe's eyes lit up after a moment of panic. He dug through his ring and found an item he had been saving, but forgotten about. "Use this Taglock!"

Targeting mechanism accepted.

The bright sun was hidden as darkness covered the land. Each of the literal thousands of Dwarves that Joe had forced to help cover the mana costs of the ritual cried out and slumped as the small amount of mana they had in them was drained away, circle by circle.

Novice circle: complete.

Beginner Circle: complete.

After this message, the Dwarves in that circle slumped to the ground, and cries of alarm rose in the Apprentice circle. Before anyone could react, the circle drained them as well. The circle completed, but Joe winced at the notification that appeared.

Apprentice Circle: complete. Stability compromised! Attempting to stabilize... failed.

Just as he read the last word, a *whumph* like fireworks exploding in the distance reached his ears. The Dwarves that fell were in a similar state to the ones that had helped with the stage one activation: nothing left but armor.

As each circle activated after that, Joe could do nothing but take a deep, shuddering breath. He was really, really wondering if allowing *five people* to ignore illusions was going to be worth the death he was causing to his own side.

Student Circle: complete.

Journeyman Circle: complete.

Expert Circle: complete. Stability is partially compromised! Attempting to stabilize... partial success!

Shouts of alarm, then disgust, reached a crescendo as roughly half of all the Dwarves standing on the Expert circle disintegrated into filthy armor. The remaining Dwarves were in the blast zone, abruptly covered in the gore of their closest comrades. Joe felt countless eyes on him, each glaring with fury and planning their revenge.

Then, one more gaze turned on him.

In the darkest area, directly above the center of the ritual circle, an eye snapped open in the sky. It seemed as large as the volcano they were standing on, and the slitted pupil focused in on Joe for a long moment, then shifted ever so slightly to the Taglock.

Ritual complete! Use of Taglock will apply an 'Eye of Argus' to up to five individuals! The effect will last up to seven days.

Reductionist class experience gained: 800.

Congratulations! You have reached Reductionist level two!

Bonus: all aspect and mana costs are when reducing items or recombining aspects into items are reduced by 10%!

"I... I have no idea what just happened." The eye in the sky went bye-bye, vanishing with a blink and windy sigh. Joe swept his eyes across the area with a horrified expression on his face. He closed his mouth and hoped that no one outright attacked him for what had just happened. "Stability? The only thing I've ever seen that can help with that is forging..."

"Deciding to get your war crimes out of the way early or something?" Major Infraction's words were pure ice as she leveled the accusation at him. At that point, Joe noticed that only a few Dwarves remained standing after being drained; none of which had participated in the ritual. All of the others were out cold, waiting for their mana to regenerate.

"Major Infraction... I have no idea what happened." Joe waved at the ritual diagrams. "This is the first time I've ever done something so large with my new crafting materials. I think that the magical matrix I used was designed with the original components in mind, and switching to a more pure form-"

"Just stop. You *abyssal* prove this was worth it, or I'll come after you with my personal forces." One of the people Major Infraction had nominated walked off in a huff, muttering to himself. "Stupid magic. Stupid human. I knew better than to get involved. Now I need to find clean underwear."

CHAPTER FIFTY-FIVE

"There is literally no chance that I am going to let you touch me with that thing." Major Infraction stated clearly. She was blocking Joe with a double row of undead, and the human was starting to get grumpy. "You take another step toward me, and I refuse to take responsibility for what I'll do to your corpse."

"Are you really afraid of a little needle prick?" Joe taunted her, finally resorting to childish insults to get a reaction. "Big bad *Major*, afraid of a little needle!"

"Your needle has *eyes* on it, Joe!" Major Infraction shouted at him. "You need to go to *prison*, not have access to the most important Officers in the Legion!"

"Only a few people died, and that was an accident." Joe argued with her, wondering if he should just try vaulting over the undead.

"A *few*?" She bellowed at him. Apparently, his thoughts must have been written on his face, because she warned him off right away, "You come near me, and I'll have a new undead guard by high tea. I'm not sure you *want* to gain the new experience of being undead, but by the abyss, I'll *make* it happen!"

"Fine! I'll go first!" Joe held out his arm, and gently poked the skin with the taglock.

Apply Eye of Argus to 'Joe'? Yes / No.

"Yes." Joe answered loudly, to make sure the nay-sayers could hear him using the magic. He needn't have worried, because in the next moment he was screaming in pain and horror as an eye appeared on the back of his hand. As soon as it did, the eye connected with his nerve endings and *burned* a new line of sight into Joe's brain. There were also... *emotions* that came through. Namely, displeasure.

The eye began to roll up Joe's arm, each movement disconnecting and reconnecting it again. The vision was like a strobe light in Joe's mind, and the pain and terrible migraine didn't stop until the eye had swirled around his neck and reached the back of Joe's head. Then a feeling of '*good*' came through, and the eye simply looked around with constant curiosity.

Joe stayed on the ground, not even remembering falling. He panted for a few minutes, then stood up and activated Neutrality Aura. The blood that had dried on him all the way back at the start of the ritual began vanishing, and the new lines from tears and vomit promptly dissipated. "Ugh... see? Major? N-nothing to it."

"That's a *hard* no from me." She was backing away, keeping the undead in a line to make sure Joe couldn't get closer.

"I'd start it on the back of your head!" Joe challenged her reputation one final time, hoping that he could inform her how important this would be to everyone involved. "What, now you can't deal with pain? You *sure* that's what you want your troops to know about you?"

That stopped her cold, and the undead stepped aside as she marched toward him. "Why are you doing this, *Candidate*? Are you *sure* you need me as an enemy?"

"No." Joe swallowed when he realized that her troops were moving to surround him, this time not as a test. "I *am* certain that I need you as an ally. You control all of the undead, right? That means that they attack what *you* tell them to attack. If the Elves can subvert *you*, that means we will have a powerful enemy against our side that we can't do anything to contain. I know it might never have been an issue for you before, but Havoc told me that they have a new illusion focus; something everyone thought was only theoretical. Are you willing to take the risk of the disease when the cure is *right here*?"

He held up the Taglock, and Major Infraction fumed before turning around. Joe thought she was going to storm off, but instead she only lifted her helmet to expose her head. "Do it. Know that you will never repay me for this."

"Success is its own reward, Major." Joe jabbed the Taglock forward as he stated the mantra of the Dwarven Oligarchy. An eye oozed off of it and grew in size, consuming the Major's flesh until it had created a lovely eye socket for itself. Through the entire process, the Dwarf didn't even flinch.

"That's... it?" She turned and rolled all three eyes at him. "What kind of a puny constitution do you have in that frail body? I'm assigning you an escort if you're planning on joining this battle. Captain! Get over here!"

Another Dwarf ran over, and Joe saw something that confused him. Half of the teal-colored mustache on her face was ragged, as if it had gotten caught in a door and yanked out. The Major pointed at the Captain. "Joe, this Is Captain Cleavage. Her axe skills are unparalleled. As an example, she's able to cleave through *three* Hammer Beasts with a single blow. She will be escorting you, so make sure she can *see*."

The Major walked away, and Joe looked at the Captain. "Captain... Cleavage. Um. Okay. Do you accept that assignment? I'll admit I've been feeling a little exposed, and a teammate would be pretty helpful."

"I look forward to impressing you with my reach. Always ensure you are *behind* me; anyone who can clearly see my cleavage is slain by it," she stoically informed him. A double-bladed axe was strapped to her back, the sharp portion extending over her head and the shaft almost dragging on the ground as she walked. "I'm actually looking forward to having eyes in the back of my head, so let's do this."

"*An* eye." Joe told her, getting no response. "Not... it's not *eyes.*"

Already unsure of his new companion, Joe poked the Taglock into the back of her head, and an eye grew to full size before locking on him. He moved around, but the eye only watched him. "How are you controlling where it looks?"

"I've had practice focusing." Joe paused at her words, but... he wasn't sure if he had just been insulted. It was hard to tell, with Dwarven culture being what it was.

After looking around for the other people that were *supposed* to be getting an eye and not finding them, Joe realized that all the troops and leaders had entered the tunnels already. More reinforcements had arrived, yet the tunnels obviously hadn't widened; the line was starting to slow. Joe waved at the Captain, and they hurried to the front of the queued-up warriors. Though they got a few dirty looks—only noticeable thanks to the eyes watching behind them—no one questioned their right to be there.

The tunnels themselves were straight and sharp, lined with broken volcanic stone and obsidian. Brushing against them meant a sure way to take terrain damage, which slowed the Legion ever further. Forced to follow the path and wait, they could only move forward at a non-enhanced human's running speed; far slower than most of these Dwarves even usually bothered to *walk*. Though the mountain was massive, thanks to hundreds of years of volcanic eruptions and growth, the tunnel eventually widened out into a sight Joe was familiar with.

They had entered the cavern.

The hollowed-out space was illuminated by the lava flows and dancing lights, which allowed Joe to see the raging war that he had walked in on. Hulking earth elementals slammed hammers of stone onto golems and automatons; spells and arrows fought for air supremacy with crossbow and ballista bolts; and the walls of the fort were being reduced to rubble by hammers, while simultaneously being repaired by mages specializing in earth spells.

"Our troops are being pushed back," Captain Cleave—as Joe forced himself to think of her—summed up the situation succinctly. "Perhaps if they had been getting constant reinforcements, they would have had the opportunity to penetrate the defenses of the fortress."

Joe let the eye on his head turn to look at her, meeting the single eye staring at him. That made him feel slightly sick, so he 'looked' away. "I strongly feel that this was the right thing to do."

"I hope we can learn the truth of the matter together, and study it after surviving this battle." She blithely stated, forcing Joe to take a deep, calming breath. Before he could retort, a howl rolled through the cavern. Joe had never heard such fury in a single statement, but he knew the voice. Major General Havoc was on the warpath.

"You want to *retreat*? You… filthy *cowards*!"

CHAPTER FIFTY-SIX

Havoc was *not* having fun. His troops weren't *listening* to him. If they needed to die so that Francine would get out here, then they would *die*. His shouts were so loud that even the war itself could not stifle the echoes that rang through the cavern. "Traitors, every one of you! I... this isn't going to happen! *Not again*! I don't need troops. I *told* them I didn't need troops! I warned them... I warned you *all*!

A silver orb appeared in his hands, and he crushed it with a single squeeze. In an instant, his form was obscured by a dense cloud of silver smoke. The people around him noticed what he was doing and screamed, turning to run immediately. Only the fastest of them, the ones that had been furthest away, managed to escape from the area of effect. The smoke climbed the wall, reaching the parapets after only a few moments.

Screams came from within the smoke, but they were different from the screams of a wounded person. These were more... concerned? Not pained, at least. It was the sound of someone waking from a nightmare only to find that the dream was, in fact, reality. When the smoke vanished, the people that had been caught in it were nowhere to be seen. The wall that had been holding them back was also gone, a massive breach revealing that the first layer of defense had been broken.

All of the stone composing the wall around the breach was slowly vanishing, so slowly that no one but Joe really thought much of it. He was seeing everything from as far away as it was possible to see, but his architectural senses were tingling. That thing that Havoc had used, it was a weapon. He knew it was; he just wasn't sure what it *did*. One thing he *did* know was that whatever he was seeing wasn't the end of the effect, and that using that hole as a point of entry wasn't an option. He took a step forward and was slapped with a buff.

You have entered a raid area! All experience gain has been paused, and will only be calculated at the end of the raid, or when leaving the raid area.

The Lord of Slaughter stands with you! -30% sensation of pain. 25% damage dealt with melee weapons. 10% reduced damage taken from all sources.

"At least I know that Havoc is still alive in there." Joe grumpily charged forward, joining the flowing silver-clad troops as his adopted group of soldiers entered the fray. Almost a kilometer of space had been cleared from the outer wall to the fort, and people and *things* were fighting for every inch of that space. Charging through wasn't an option, and Joe didn't think that trying to be fancy and jumping over people would end well. Certainly not with the sheer number of projectiles in the air.

The stone of the ground was scorched, and the interior of the volcano was actually *increasing* in temperature from all the plasma that was coming into being. He hurried forward, planning to join at the flanks, but Captain Cleave was suddenly in front of him, shoving him back and pulling her axe into her hands. A twist and a pull, and the stone elementals in front of them fell to rubble. She glanced back at Joe. "Stay *behind* me."

"Don't get hit by my spells," Joe shot back, starting to get annoyed by his sudden babysitter. He was trying to remember why he accepted a partner; he had forgotten that it was so *restricting*. One of his orbs popped into his hand, and he tossed it forward. Just before it hit, Cone of Cold came into effect. The orb struck the elemental and left cracks at the point of impact, then the spell washed over the line of elementals; evidently it was extra effective against the stony foes in this high-temperature arena.

The subsequent hits from the Dwarves caused extra damage to the brittle defenders, and their line was broken in the next moment. The elementals that had been caught and surrounded were demolished, and the troops moved forward more than a dozen feet as a whole in under a minute. Captain Cleave nodded approvingly at Joe. "More of that would be exceedingly welcome."

"Cooldowns." Joe tried to stay salty, but he was as susceptible to praise as the next person. Checking that no Dwarves would be caught in the area of effect, he let out an Acid Spray to start weakening the hulking defenders.

Just after the liquid settled, Joe was knocked to the side as a dozen automatons pounded through the area and into the rocky defenders. It was a strange dichotomy of the natural world fighting the artificial, but it quickly devolved into a stalemate. The automatons were more directly powerful, and were designed specifically to fight this foe, but the elementals didn't need an outside power source to keep fighting. The automatons could only last so long before needing a fresh core, but in that time they inflicted massive casualties.

Then they couldn't move.

Elementals surged forward, slamming into the powering-down metal and reducing it to scrap with heavy blows. Incensed, the elementals turned their stony gazes on the Dwarves and rumbled forward like a landslide. They met a wall of blunt weapons; even the Dwarves that used edged weapons knew better than to attempt cutting these foes. Swords were replaced with rebar-looking weapons—perhaps weighted training blades?

Dwarf after Dwarf was crushed beneath huge arms, feet, or even a defeated elemental falling on top of them. For a few minutes, Joe was worried that they were going to be pushed back by the behemoths, but for every Dwarf that fell, two would enter the fray. He didn't need to turn around to see that a new tunnel had connected; now they were being reinforced fifty percent faster.

Joe had truly underestimated the resolve the Dwarves had, the fury that they were holding in their hearts for having their ancient memorial site intruded upon. Not a single tear was shed for the fallen. There was only grim resolve and deadly intent. The elementals would move, or *be* moved. A light strobed within the cavern, and a swath of the Legion stopped attacking; worse, they stopped *defending*.

Illusion ignored: Fae Beckoning. Eye of Argus grants immunity to illusions!

"Snap out of it, soldiers!" Joe bellowed in the face of an auburn mustached Officer, who was standing there with a dreamy smile showing through the gaps of her helm. There was no reply, so he whacked her with a Ritual Orb. The damage registered, and she backhanded the empty air; making him extra happy that he had hit her at range. That gave him an idea, "Pain does the trick?"

He cast Dark Lightning Strike at an elemental, and the splash damage washed over the nearby Dwarves. They came back to themselves with a vengeance, and Joe hurried to stand near them. His three standard buffs were in place, meaning anyone within five feet of him would slowly heal over time.

The next hour was a grind of healing, attacking, working to keep people out of mental traps, and hardcore survival. Somehow, the pressure on them was waning, even though they were getting closer and closer to the actual fort. At the same time, the illusions were becoming more potent, more frequent, and harder for people to resist.

At one point, Joe noticed that Major Infraction was looking at him—yet another benefit of the Eye of Argus was that it let him know when people were looking at *him*—when Joe's head snapped around so that they could lock eyes, she simply nodded at him with resignation in her gaze.

"Like your people always say, Major… success is it's own reward," he chuckled to himself. Joe was almost to the wall of the fort when a notification appeared, one that had happened earlier.

Message available! Send a message to friends list contact? Yes / No.

"What?" Joe selected 'yes', asking the empty air, "Who is this?"

The message sent, and a moment later a strangled cry of surprise reached his ear. It… it wasn't human. Joe's Eye of Argus locked on the position emitting the sound, and he watched as the tip of a reptile's head vanished, leaving behind unmoving fingertips. The rest of the person was buried under a half-dozen boulders; this was clearly the end of an important battle. It took a moment, but he finally understood what was happening. Joe rushed to the boulders and touched the finger-tips, allowing Lay on Hands to flow into the only portion he could touch.

The fingers spasmed with renewed feeling, their owner clearly in fresh pain. Joe turned to search for the nearest Dwarves, screaming for assistance. They ignored him at first, until Captain Cleavage stepped forward and slammed her axe into one of the boulders, shearing it off the pile. A Bro walked over. "Yo, guys, no one can fix that mess. I saw Pokey-Bro get squashed. He's human; he'll come back."

"Get these *off* him." Joe's voice was furiously quiet, and he forced Mend and Lay on Hands into the fingers as fast as he could manage. The Dwarf shrugged and helped the Captain with the rocks. Joe tried to help as well, but even with his high stats, the magical rocks were simply too heavy for him to budge. His eyes flashed with an idea, and he slapped the rocks with a touch of mana.

Item: Elemental Stone (Dead). Aspect-

He ignored the rest, dumping mana into the Ritual of Reduction that was engraved in his very being. The first rock he had touched vanished, then he healed, and allowed his mana to come back. He reduced... and a mangled body was revealed. "Lay on Hands!"

After that heal, the face warped back into a recognizable one with a sickening popping of facial bones. "Jaxon! What the *abyss* happened?"

The man couldn't speak; it appeared that he was still unconscious. Joe pumped more healing into him, making sure to do as much as possible so that his friend would awaken to a healthy body. It didn't take long. As soon as his health passed an unknown threshold, Jaxon came up swinging. It was always concerning to see how the man stood, as if he were being *dragged* into the air by an outside force.

Then Jaxon calmed, too fast for it to be natural. He stared up at the ceiling, his standard smile becoming creepier over the next few seconds. Joe pulled out his Taglock, jabbing it into the back of his friend's head. "There ya go, buddy. Now that illusion can't get you."

"Joe?" Jaxon slapped at his own head at the sudden pain, more arriving as he poked his new eye. "Ow! What? What illusion? I was just reveling in the feel of my bones being complete once more, and you poked me! Also! It's *very* nice to see you again. So... what's new? Been doing anything fun? Oh, thanks for the *eye*! I can see so many people *smiling* at me! Hello!"

"Who are you assigned to, Jaxon?" Joe tried to get the man to focus, which was hard, since it wasn't Joe's strong suit either.

Jaxon waved at the pile of rocks, "Oh, his day is off to a rocky start. I told him he needed to be boulder, and he took it literally! When I got over here, he was destroyed, and I had to charge those earth elementals with aggregated assault."

"Wind spirits," The Captain stated, getting a strange look from both of the humans.

"Oh. Right. The whole 'call them by their weakness' thing." Jaxon stepped forward and tried to shake her hand. "Hi, I'm Jaxon. I was in Joe's party on Midgard, and I'll fight you if you took my spot on his team."

"I'm his escort, not a party member. Though, I am thinking that I might want the chance to prove my skills and travel with him," the Dwarf admitted cheerfully, limbering up with a swing of her axe.

"Joe!" Jaxon turned scandalized eyes on his party leader. "An *escort*? Now?"

"Not like that." Joe shut him down as fast as possible. He turned and started toward the slowly disintegrating walls. "Both of you follow me. There're Elves to boot out of the Shoe."

CHAPTER FIFTY-SEVEN

With the flood of reinforcements continuing, the war was swinging heavily in favor of the Dwarves. The Elves had no chance to bring in more people, as the travel point became restricted right after they were invaded. After all, if the Dwarves had easy access to Elven territory, they could use it just as well as the Elves had.

As far as Joe could see behind him, silver-clad Legionnaires were pushing forward. They had spread out to fully encapsulate the fort and were rapidly defeating the remaining defenders. Victory was assured; it was only a matter of time.

Joe pushed the last distance to the wall, far too close for comfort to the breach made by Havoc. That area was still uninhabited, and at first, he thought that it had just been out of either fear or respect for what Havoc had done. Then he noticed that Dwarves were dumping boulders from the elementals into the strange, colorless region, and the magical material was just… melting away.

Then a hand pushed up through the floor, and the colorless zone receded toward the center; not fully, just enough to be noticeable. The hand pushed on the floor, and a hulking golem pulled itself up and ran into the fort. Screams and insults soon followed, but they were too faint for Joe to understand. Captain Cleave studied the new creation and shook her head. "I truly wonder who authorized the weapons of mass destruction. I do not envy the Elves this chance to study a Grandmaster Gole-mancer's work up close and personal."

"You know what that is?" Joe glanced at the uncomfortable Dwarf, and her mustache quivered as she tried to provide the proper reply.

"Only what history has told me of this effect," she slowly admitted. They had a few minutes until they were able to rejoin combat; a new hole had been made, and the fight was ongoing. Still, a foothold needed to be established before they could sweep through the space. "Major General Havoc was the first known Micro-Golemancer in Dwarven history. He studied what was once forbidden knowledge and learned to apply it to his own work. That 'smoke' is actually hundreds of thousands of golems too small for the eye to see."

"He made *nanites*?" Jaxon enthusiastically chimed in. "How extraordinary! That was far away with science. Magic is just so... forward thinking! I'll need to *adjust* my perspective!

"I know not what 'nanites' are." The Dwarf shook her head. "So long as these golems have material, they will build up and deploy war golems over time. The better the materials provided, the more potent the war golem will become. It will take *any* material; do not let it touch you."

"So..." Joe's brow furrowed as he realized that he may have had a misunderstanding with the Dwarf when they were first discussing tactics to deploy against the Elves. "He *didn't* unleash a spell on them that destroyed their vegetation?"

"No. He cast an area spell. The rest, as far as I know, came from applying his studies of a forbidden art and applying it to his craft as a golemancer. A ritual is something similar to what you did outside to give me this eye, so it was not that." The Captain gestured at the back of her head.

"A *lovely* color, by the way." Jaxon's voice was filled with sincerity as he stared into her singular eye.

"If that was a ritual, then I can say with full certainty that he did *not* use a ritual even a single time. He had his golems eat everything in the material world, and then replicate themselves. Eventually they were more numerous than the grains of dirt in the plains of Jotunheim." The Dwarf shuddered at the terrible image in her mind. "The havoc that he created by destroying hundreds of kilometers to defeat a few mere fortresses... his name, and the accompanying shame, has haunted him ever since."

"Traitors... he shouted something about traitors. Did his troops turn against him at that time?" Joe recalled how Havoc had reacted when he first started this fight in the volcano.

"They did," Captain Cleave nodded sadly. "It was their treachery that led to the death of Francine the Stabilizer deep in enemy territory. When he learned of her death and loss from the rolls, the Ledger of Souls, he vowed to trust no one ever again."

Jaxon pushed for more when she remained silent for too long. "...And then?"

"Then? Then he never did. He holds no love for the Dwarven Oligarchy, but he needs their resources in order to wage his personal war against the Elven Theocracy." Cleave shrugged, her armor jangling heavily. "I can only be glad that he is on our side, and I will be terrified if I need to stand in front of him on the field of battle."

"Who was Francine to him?" Joe was suddenly desperate to know who this mystery figure was that held such a large portion of his mentor's attention.

His question had to be ignored, for at that moment, the interior defenses were broken. The Legion drained into the opening, and Joe's party was swept along with the tide. Once more, he was seeing familiar territory, though it was in much worse shape than the first time he had come through. The interior of the fort was burning, and most of the buildings at the edge were rubble. The merchants where he had window shopped, and the streets that he had walked, had only the barest resemblance to that which had once stood.

Huge footprints had torn the ground apart, and flashes of light still raged deeper within the fortress. The roaring of voices, clashing of weapons, and energetic detonation of spells dropped Joe's mind into an almost fugue state, where the only thing that mattered was getting deeper into the fortress. They needed to capture this place to ensure the safety of the capital, as well as to be able to respawn or even grow their forces.

"To the Guardian!" A voice rose above the others, and the people not actively engaged in combat roared their approval. With every step, Joe trod upon fallen Dwarves, but even more Elves. He looked down at them, expecting to feel sorrow for the fallen, but even in death their faces were smug and seemed to be laughing at him. The combat moved along the shattered streets of the major fort, slowly closing in on the massive plant that nearly brushed the ceiling of the volcano.

Joe planned to go with them, to tear the plant out by the roots along with the others, but that seemed... more like a... *compulsion* than anything else. Not for him, as he was immune to illusions, but when he tried to get the attention of the Dwarves around them, he was brushed off. They only had eyes for the great plant; everything else was secondary. "Jaxon!"

"Yes, down with greenery and vegetables! Let's cheese that broccoli!" Jaxon finished his inspiring speech, getting roaring approval before turning to Joe. "You needed something?"

"Jaxon, Cleave, come with me. This isn't right. This was too easy. They knew we were coming, so why didn't they do something about it?" Joe veered off the road, heading for the crystal tree that was still flashing with an intense light.

"You think this was too easy?" The Dwarf sounded *shocked*. "Breaking into a volcano, fighting a true horde of Wind Spirits, and toppling a major fort? I... I look forward to the opportunity of seeing what you consider a *hard* fight."

"We're a pretty big deal." Jaxon wrapped his arm around

her shoulder, helping to guide her toward the building Joe had zeroed in on. "Did you ever hear why Joe got exiled from Midgard? He killed... like... a couple hundred thousand people over and over? I think he's wearing white clothes so people don't think of him as a dark person. Turning over a new leaf, and all that. Hey! If we are in the Shoe, and this place is hot and painful, does that mean Gramma's ankle is inflamed?"

"Not *now*, Jaxon." Joe stepped through the unguarded illusion of a door, entering into the cavernous room filled with foci, stabilizers, and as it turned out: Elves. He came to a screeching halt as they all turned to stare at him. Jaxon and Cleave stepped through, a similar reaction of panic crossing the Dwarf's face, while Jaxon waved chipperly.

"Hello! Have you heard the benefits of chiropractic services? I'd be more than happy to hold a seminar, perhaps be on whatever panel it is you're watching?"

CHAPTER FIFTY-EIGHT

Four Ritual Orbs popped out in front of Joe, and he double-checked that his Exquisite Shell was at full power. He was about to leap back and out of the building, when he realized that not a single Elf had made a move on them, nor cried out. Peering closer, he could see that their normal smug expressions were gone, replaced with a strange hollow stare that he had only seen in the most drastic of battles.

Captain Cleave hissed in a sharp breath, her hand jabbing forward to point out the thick layer of 'smoke' that swirled around their feet. "They're golems! Don't move."

Joe felt sick, but forced himself to stay still. "You really meant it when you told me that it can use *any* material, huh?"

"I try to use every word to maximize my truthfulness," Captain Cleave stated in a hushed tone. "They have not attacked us yet, which I take as a good sign, but I don't know why-"

"Francine, *please* just listen to reason!" Havoc's cataclysmically loud voice shattered the unnatural stillness of the area. "If I kill you here, you'll lose so many more levels than you would if I got you into the capital first!"

"You *still* think you can kill me, you old monster?" A too-familiar Elven voice snapped back, followed with a ray of multi-colored light that caused spots to break out all over Joe's vision. "I've been breaking chunks off you since we got started!"

"I just don't want you to *suffer* more than you need to, Francine." Havoc's voice was almost laughter. "You need to suffer, don't get me wrong, but when you're back where you belong, we can finally-"

"I. Am. *Elfreeda*!" Each of the words were followed by blasts of lightning that seemed to come from the walls of the building itself. Havoc came into view with the light show, his appearance so grotesque that Joe was almost sick once more.

"For now, Francine. For now." Havoc's face had been pulled and stretched until it was almost flat. His defining features were affixed in the center of the chest of a huge golem, so large that Joe had initially mistaken it for the nearest wall; it put the Guardian of a minor fort to shame. A hand swept through the air too fast for Joe to see, but a bright firefly dodged it and sent another light burst at the golem that Havoc had turned into. "Why not give in? There's no escape from here; I've ensured that."

The 'firefly' resolved into the flying form of Elfreeda; they were just so far away that she seemed tiny. "*You* ensured that? Ha!"

The stark laughter felt like a gut-punch to Joe. He *knew* that this had been a trap. The Elf continued a sudden monologue, "This building is failing, thanks to *your* minion. What do you think happens next, Dwarf? You think the Prismatic Evergreen will simply shatter and have no *repercussions*? The main force of the *entire Legion* is within this hollow space, with only one thing holding back every. Single. Volcanic eruption... that should have occurred over the last few years! Every bit of fire, lava, and pressure that mounted as we grew this place from the crystal seed!"

That did seem to impact Havoc, but instead of putting fear in his heart, his flat smile widened fractionally. "Isn't it so good to speak with each other again? I have so many stories to tell you! What an *eventful* half century it has been, Francine."

"Stop saying that name! It means *nothing* to me!" She flew backward, the air shifting in the colossal space. Lightning rained down on her outstretched hands, and the room dimmed as every spectrum of light was drained into the area in front of her. "Let me tell you what is going to happen, *Havoc!*"

"You die, the building shatters." Havoc recited calmly, his uncaring words ensuring that the Elf fell deeper into despair. "The energy that had been going into sustaining this tree is diverted into the outer walls, closing them and ensuring that nothing can escape the impending volcanic eruption. The Legion dies. You die. I die. We died in an Elven fort, and this one will be fully destroyed, meaning we all come back at the nearest major Elven fort. As Elves."

"That's right! Even if you manage to capture the fort, the eruption will... destroy it and make sure it becomes an... Elven fort again." Her words slowed as she realized that Havoc didn't appear concerned at all. "Why aren't you trying to stop me?"

"I'm just... I'm so happy that we get to die together, and come *back* together." Havoc's words sent a chill down the spine of everyone hearing them. "Together again as my greatest enemy is better than a lifetime apart as the most honorable race. Success... it is truly its own reward, Francine."

"You're up to something, and I won't let you do it. What- ever it is." The spell in front of Elfreeda shifted slightly, condensing and firing as a finger-thick beam. It pierced right through the Havoc-golem, right above the bridge of his nose. It exited his back, and swept upward like a sword slicing through butter.

"Feel better?" Havoc's ability to speak after being almost cleanly sliced in half made Joe feel like he was in a horror movie. The two sides started melding back together, and Havoc continued speaking as if nothing had happened. He took slow, careful steps toward the flying Elf. "I replaced my brain *years* ago. It was *such* an imperfect memory storage device."

"But… your path forward would have been…!" Elfreeda's voice was frantic as she tried to think of a way to destroy him. Her face stilled, and shifted in a way that Joe could understand clearly. She had *decided* on something.

"The path of the Sage was closed to me, but all that needs to happen is a single death and resurrection to reopen it. Sure, I can't progress, but a Sage already stands on the first rank of GoleMaster. Enchanter, too. Everyone thinks it would be empty, since it is such a hard path… but no. Of course, there is always a final trial that keeps them from progressing."

Joe was yanked closer as Havoc blasted forward, the movement of such a huge body at that speed causing an implosion of air in the enclosed space. Havoc appeared again next to Elfreeda, slapping her out of the air and into the ground. To the credit of the powerful building, she simply bounced and skidded along instead of breaking through the crystal flooring. War golems in the shape of her once-people swarmed over her, and the smoke in the area concentrated until it had all coalesced on her.

For a long, *long* moment, Joe thought it was over. Then the Prismatic Evergreen itself intervened, and a perfect column of light stretched from the base to the crown of the room, centered on Elfreeda. Every light-generating element seemed to be a part of the column. Fire, lightning, radiation, *anything* that made light was a part of the torrent. An eruption followed a fusion reaction, until finally, the light turned soft and Elfreeda stepped out, in pristine health and garb. Her clothes, skin, and eyes had been bleached by the light, creating an albino effect that could only be matched by a snowman.

"Oh? That's a one-time effect, I'm sure. Too bad, You might have enjoyed the life of a golem. Until we reached the capital, of course." Havoc's voice was still soft and oddly cajoling. "I suppose you'll just have to lose the levels, then."

Havoc loomed above Elfreeda, his fists hammering down to end her. They impacted a dome of light, and she gasped in pain. With a push, the dome stabilized and her hands began flying into different seals and positions. "This cannot happen. You seem to think that you'd survive mentally as an Elf... there must be something you know."

"That's... *no*, Francine!" Havoc was studying her hands, and his face shifted to reveal a terrible fury. An additional set of arms grew out of the top of the golem, blades affixed to the ends instead of fists. All four appendages flailed against the protective dome, and after the first few... cracks began to appear.

"This will delay the eruption, and force your people to perish in a panic instead of swiftly, but so be it. Your mind cannot be trusted, as an enemy *or* ally!" Francine's words seemed ritualistic, as if she were chanting instead of speaking. Her voice was an edict, a proclamation that a king would be hard pressed to match in tone or authority. "Your people have been chanting their thirst for war crimes? *Fine*! Let them *taste* a war crime, starting with you!"

"*Francine*! Don't you *dare*!" Havoc's weapons landed, and a chunk of the dome shattered. He focused in on that spot even as she completed the spell. "Francine! *You listen to Daddy!*"

All around them, energy was pulled from the Prismatic Evergreen and siphoned into a massive spell circle that centered under the golem. The building began to break down as it was cannablized to feed the spell, but Havoc never stopped slamming the dome protecting the alabaster Elf. She didn't seem to mind at all. "*Forbidden Art Resplendent Trap: Nostrum of Progressive Eradication!*"

All movement stopped. All sounds halted. Black lines appeared over the entirety of Havoc's body, but rapidly flowed toward his face. "Good bye, Havoc. A thousand years in a mental illusion, introspection without stimulation, will either fix your broken mind or grind it away to nothing. Either way... fortress command, imprison target upon death."

Elfreeda stood fully erect, allowing the final shards of her protective dome to fizzle out of existence. "Time to end this war. I've been looking forward to a large influx of troops, and the promised rewards will bring my research to the heights I've been dreaming of for *years*. Sure, the loss of the shapers and their research into environmental energy supplies was a blow, but I'll have all the time in Eternium to get it right when the Dwarves are gone. I'd ask if you had any last words, but-"

"Oof. That smarts." Havoc's raspy voice was Elfreeda's only warning before his blades came down and sliced her apart. He stared down at the slain Elf, tears already flowing down his face. "I'll be with you soon, sweetheart. Daddy's coming to save you."

CHAPTER FIFTY-NINE

"Thanks for the save, Joe. A thousand subjective years of sensory deprivation isn't something I was looking forward to experiencing again." Havoc couldn't turn his eyes from her, but he didn't need to; he simply sighed his next words. The eye on the back of his head studied his mentee and the bloody needle he was holding in his hand. "How'd you sneak over to me?"

"Choppy movements." Joe informed him quietly, doing his best not to stimulate the mammoth golem he had vaulted onto. "Pretended I was one of the things your gas got at."

"Yeah. Hard to get limbs to articulate correctly if you don't do it by hand." A pocket opened up on the side of Havoc's ribs. "You mind?"

Joe grabbed the log-sized cigar and got it in front of the… Dwarf. It lit itself, grew legs and scuttled up to Havoc's lips. He took a long pull and sighed out the smoke. "I'm gonna detonate pretty soon. My Core is overloading as we speak."

"I know." Joe could see the telltale lights emanating from his chest whenever Havoc opened his mouth or eyes. "I'm thinking fast might be the way to go, for both of us."

"True; by now the walls are sealed…" Havoc took another

deep inhale. "This place is going to be a disaster area of monumental proportions."

There was silence for a few long seconds. Then Havoc continued, "They'll blame you, ya know. For the loss. The core of the Legion, gone just like that. The Elven tide will sweep across the plane, and no one will be able to stop them. Ugh. Alfenheim. What an ugly name. Still, what can you do?"

"What a great pep talk," Joe deadpanned, moving over to check Elfreeda's body. She had on a spatial ring, and he almost gagged at the sheer wealth it contained. Metals, Cores, herbs... enough rare resources that it could have rivaled the yearly income of the Netherlands before Eternium became a thing. "At least I'll have some seed money."

"You should give that to the Elves." Havoc chuckled at Joe's glare. "What? Just looking out for the people I'm gonna have to join."

Joe couldn't help but laugh at that. The Dwarf-golem's lips twitched, and he sighed darkly. "Too bad about those shapers. That's what they call their scientist, 'cause they 'shape' the natural world. I would have loved to know how they managed to turn an entire volcano into an abyssal *power supply*. Some kind of geothermal exchange? Oh, the things I could have done with that."

The room shook, and ragged cheering could be heard through the new holes in the crystal walls around them. "There goes the Guardian. Time's about up for me, Joe. See you on... the other side. You should run. Elfreeda used so much power in here... that *had* to have bought you some time. Enjoy the last few hours you have before the Dwarven Oligarchy turns on you."

Joe nodded and turned, sprinting toward the exit. Havoc watched him go with his third eye, his main two still focused on Elfreeda's corpse. A Dwarf and another human joined the escape, and Havoc made sure they were out before he took one last pull of his cigar.

Then he relaxed.

Crystals reverberated as the explosion finished the Prismatic Evergreen, and the magically expanded space collapsed. Joe stood outside of the building as it fell, looking over a notification he had been hoping not to see.

The Lord of Slaughter has fallen!

"Now... now what?" Captain Cleave swallowed deeply as the cavern went dark, only lit by the flowing lava.

"Now? *I* have an idea what we could do." Joe paused and reached for his codpiece. Captain Cleavage's eyes widened and she blushed under her teal mustache. Then a long-forgotten suitcase appeared in Joe's hands, and he owned it for the first time. "Research. We have a volcano to tame."

"A *shoe* to tie up!" Jaxon offered with excitement.

"Jaxon..." There were no words that Joe could use to describe his frustration at not being able to make a quip or insult to use against the gregarious chiropractor. He stalled, thinking that perhaps he could turn the conversation into banter, but the moment had passed. Jaxon chuckled as Joe awkwardly tried to move into new territory. "I just can't with you right now."

"I need to save this place. An enclosed volcano, far from anyone else, where my research would be useful as well as protected? If I capture this place, get control of it, I can *finally* get away from the demands on my time and focus for a while." Joe's eyes were bright as he looked for a place to start going over the documents he was holding. "Of course, that all depends on what's in here. I'm really hoping that this was what High Priestess Embertank was talking about, and Tatum was giving me a not-very-subtle hint."

Luckily, Joe knew a building nearby that had a perfect table for this sort of thing. He had wiped out a handful of Elves there, after all. It almost felt heretical to walk into the conference room and place the briefcase in the same place he had first picked it up. The Reductionist sat in the bloodstained chair, and started working even as his aura cleaned the room up. As his work proceeded, Officers started to filter in to ask him questions or see what was going on. In almost no time flat, the oversized conference room became an impromptu command center.

"Ten hours left, Joe, and that's on the generous side," Major Infraction's voice snapped Joe out of his concentration, and he glared at her. "Then this place reaches the moon."

"Constant updates about the *time* are really not going to help, Major." Joe turned back to his notes and continued scribbling furiously. "We have both an advantage and a disadvantage. According to the notes left behind, they started by transporting a crystal seed here, and it eventually drained this cavern of lava to make it what it is now. But-"

"Magma, we're underground." Jaxon interjected cheerfully. "Almost literally in the flames."

Joe's quill quivered as he worked to keep his hands away from Jaxon's neck. "Thank you, *Jaxon*. We can work with a building that simply maintains this place. Something that drains and directs the lava. I just don't know what it should be."

"Joe." The Major met his eyes. "*Anything* is amazing. A lava-proof shack? The best thing I have ever heard of. It means we get to *live*, remember? This place will be under your control if you save it, you know. Any Candidate that takes a major fort is given their first acquisition to run. Got anything extra nice for you that you have plans for? Something that would work?"

Joe looked at the briefcase, which was actually a storage device that could only hold various forms of paper. "I... might. The problem is, I don't know if we have the time to make it happen. Or the resources."

"Tell me what you need. I'll make the logistics happen." The Dwarf promised grimly.

"I need mana. Lots of it, and repeatedly. I need to set up a ritual, and I need *everyone* in the entire volcano to be on board with getting it going. Start getting people into circles now." Joe's words made the Major go pale, but she nodded stiffly. "Also, all of the Guardian, and any parts of the Prismatic Evergreen that you can get. Pile them as close together as possible."

"As you say... Candidate." The Major saluted him, much to his surprise, and marched off, already shouting orders.

"You're so *cool*, Joe. Can you sign my chest?" Jaxon lifted his shirt to tease his friend. Joe slapped the exposed ribs, getting a yelp from Jaxon as his skin turned red instantly.

"Handprint. *Kinda* like a signature," Joe laughed as he pulled out a folded paper and laid it out over the entirety of the circular table. "Look at this with me, and pretend you understand it. I need someone to bounce ideas off of. This is an alchemy building, and as far as I can tell... this was their backup plan if the Prismatic Evergreen failed to produce the results they were looking for."

"Oh! So you already have a building that will save us all?" Jaxon wiped his forehead. "Thank goodness. I was trying to stay positive, but I was getting pretty freaked out there, Joe. You know-"

"It's Artifact-ranked," Joe stated heavily, his head spinning at what he was planning to do. "I have ten hours to have it *ready*, which means I can only draw the ritual and hope that everything goes smoothly. That's an *Artifact* building, and an Artifact blueprint, that I'm trying to build with a *student-ranked* ritual. I don't know if I *can* make this building by using this ritual, but I literally have no choice. Thanks to Elfreeda, I at least have the Core I need for the building itself."

Joe raised a hand that was holding a Core too bright to look at, even with his hand fully wrapped around it.

You have found a Master Core (Artifact/Immaculate)! Absorb it for 14,927 experience?

Joe dismissed the prompt with a bitter mental shove.

"Hmmm." Jaxon rubbed his chin and tapped at the blueprint. "I see, what if you..."

Joe stared at the man as he trailed off. "What if I *what*, Jaxon?"

"Huh? Oh. No idea." Jaxon shrugged and stepped away. "You told me to pretend I understood."

Having half-stood in excitement, Joe collapsed back into his chair. "I changed my mind. Go tell the Major that I need items or material at the Artifact rarity and lower to make this happen. *Anything* will suffice."

Jaxon walked out, and Joe got to work. It didn't take a terribly long time for him to finish the ritual perfectly, but then the 'fun' started. He began encapsulating the massive blueprint in the ritual diagram, transferring the data from the blueprint to the ritual. For six hours he worked at it, and at the end it was all... glowing grey?

All except one small part that was black. Joe looked at the blueprint and the ritual side by side, finding that there was a single small line that he had thought was an eyelash on the blueprint. He connected that line on his blueprint, and the entire thing flashed gold. "Oh! Tatum! I can see truth and falsehood again!"

That skill had faded pretty slowly after Tatum had been locked away, but it *had* eventually vanished. Now, it was back in full force, and it couldn't have had better timing. The ritual was as ready as it could be; all that remained was to obtain the building materials. He stood and hurried out to the site they had chosen for the building, but blinked at the changes in the area. The buildings that had been destroyed were all vanishing, leaving huge piles of building materials behind. Joe hadn't thought it would be an option, but he diverted his gaze to the space where the Prismatic Evergreen had stood, and gaped at the stacks of crystal that were under guard.

It appeared that Major Infraction had anticipated his desire to have an important building constructed in the best protected area of the fort, because Joe had needed to vault over ring after ring of Legionnaires as he approached the space. He located the Dwarf in question right away; she was arguing with another bearded Officer that Joe didn't recognize.

"I gave the order to *dig*, Major! Why are these soldiers just standing around?" The bearded Dwarf was bellowing in her face, but the Major didn't flinch.

"The success or failure of this mission is resting entirely on the shoulders of Candidate Joe, and he needs these troops and materials," she calmly stated, the words hollow. It seemed she had been repeating them over and over.

"Then *where* is the Candidate? I have some *choice* words for him! These resources belong to the *Dwarven Oligarchy*, not some-"

"If you want to live, stop trying to line your pockets," Joe ordered the Dwarf as he breezed past him and immediately started setting a Field Array around the first pile of crystals. It solidified as the Dwarf sputtered, and Joe sent a touch of mana to test the material cost.

Item: Approximately 10 cubic meters of Artifact and below material. Reduction value: unknown. Total mass: 410 pounds of material. Reduction cost: 14,062.5 mana per second. Estimated reduction time required: 5 seconds.

Joe almost choked as he read the cost and time requirements. Then he was grabbed roughly and spun around, meeting the Dwarf face-to-face. He had seen him coming thanks to the Eye of Argus, but had been too stunned to react. "Human, I am *General* Information, and you will not insult me by-"

"Sir, we have only a few hours until we all blow our top. How about *you* wait until then to do it?" Joe cut off the General before he could continue. "I read the Elven shaper's notes, sir. The walls of the Shoe are being reinforced by a backup enchantment that had been included in the Prismatic Evergreen. In the case of a malfunction, the excess energy would seal the walls and hold this place together until the pressure became too much and it detonated. It was intended both as an escape device *and* deadman's failsafe."

"Why are you telling me-"

"You have loyal troops digging. They've made no progress." Joe's words weren't a question: he would have been doing the same thing in the General's position. "More digging won't help.

What *will* help is bringing every mana-rich Dwarf here, right now, to help me make the solution."

The General tried to stare Joe down, but the human turned and only let the eye on his head play that game. There was no eyelid on that eye, so it would win for sure. Joe narrowed the size of the Field Array, repeating until he squeezed it down to the smallest size that it would allow him to cover.

Item: Approximately .5 cubic meters of Artifact and below material.

Reduction value: unknown. Total mass: 20.5 pounds of material.

Reduction cost: 14,062.5 mana per second. Estimated reduction time required: 1 second.

No matter what he did to shrink the size of the array, the estimated time stayed at a minimum of one second. At six thousand seven hundred and eighty-eight mana in his personal mana pool, he could supply half of it himself if needed; but would rather not. The General seemed to make up his mind, and it appeared Joe had succeeded. A handful of Dwarves came forward, but they were all heavily decorated Officers, including Major Infraction.

Joe made the array glow red where they needed to touch it, and soon they began reducing the crystals one by one.

Nearly two hours later, they all had bags under their eyes and were shaking from fatigue. Joe checked his aspect list with trembling eyes, and found that they finally had enough. All of the crystal, all the Guardian, and a few Artifacts that had been forcibly 'donated' by the disgruntled Officers had resulted in...

Aspects gathered
Trash: 187,252
Damaged: 105,594
Common: 100,267
Uncommon: 92,300
Rare: 62,284
Special: 100 (Zombified). 1521 (Anima). 111 (Molten) 4,891 (Crystalline)
Unique: 19,428

Artifact: 10,357
Legendary: 0
Mythical: 0

Core energy: 5,498/5,498 (Rare-ranked Core)

"We made it above ten thousand," Joe stated with relief, his words getting a cheer from the exhausted Officers. His follow-up stifled their excitement. "Now we can start on the dangerous part!"

The Dwarven Legion was in position. The materials were ready. The area was secure. Joe pulled out the Architect's Fury and placed it on the ground, then set a Field Array around it. He wasn't exactly certain how this would work, or how long it would work for, but he hoped that having the array in place would be beneficial.

He gazed around the area, at all the faces filled with hope as they looked at him, and steeled his resolve. It was do or die, and the heat was rising. Literally. Joe glanced up and saw that the top of the volcano was bright: the stone was starting to melt.

"Let's go." Joe placed his hand on the ritual and injected mana. The ritual lit up and started glowing with energy. He linked his Codpiece of Holding to the Array, then every standard aspect jar he had. After a long moment, he almost decided against any special aspects. The only one with enough quantity to be effective was the Crystalline aspect, but he didn't know how that would impact this design. He didn't have time to get this wrong, but it had seemed *really* important that the tree that had once stood on this spot be made of crystal.

Joe could only hope he would have enough; desperately, he added it to the mix.

He and practically the entire Legion that remained in the volcano were lifted into the air as the ritual began. Everyone was held in place, and soon, the gyroscopic effect began. Aspects began flowing from Joe into the array, so many and so fast that it looked like he was using a flamethrower to outline a building.

The first thing that materialized was a wire-thin framework of the brightest neon orange that Joe had ever seen; figuratively, the essence of the color orange. That thin wire stretched into more and more filaments; the only comparison Joe could think of was the capillary system of a body. It reached every point of the structure but was so delicate that it was practically invisible in places.

Joe could have screamed in joy when the flames shifted from orange to a deep indigo: the Artifact aspects had been accepted without a warning message. The Unique aspects flowed over and around the orange, shifting the glaring color into a starry blob that thickened and grew. The nerve system, if Joe continued the analogy. From indigo to light blue, then silver, then white. Finally different colors of grey, and two messages appeared. One was an easily completable task, while the other almost made Joe panic.

Please assign a Core for the structure's usage.

Please assign the focus for the structure. (Artifact or greater).

Joe opened his hand, and the Master Core appeared in his fingers. It was pulled into the building a mote of light at a time, a slow but constant stream of power. It gave him a moment to think, and he realized that there was only one thing that would work... one thing that would be a perfect fit.

"Use the Morovian-metal cauldron." Joe allowed the cauldron to appear, and it hung in the air, unsuspended by anything. Then it was pulled into the building, and vanished. Up until that point, the building had been a shapeless, formless blob of interwoven colors. With the Core and the cauldron added, it began shifting, twisting, and growing. Starting at the base, pure white marble stairs extended in a pentagram around the lowest area.

At each of the five corners, an obelisk of dense obsidian shot upward, nearly impaling the people on the lowest ritual Circle. A ring appeared on the side of the spire, facing the center of the structure, and from each ring grew a thick chain. The chains clattered down until they reached the ground, then flowed inward along with newly forming marble, creating a perfectly level surface. The ground stopped moving, leaving a triangular space where the natural ground could be seen.

Each of the chains snaked over to the ground and joined together. Once they were all linked, a thick... harpoon? A harpoon was formed. It lifted into the air, higher, higher... then slammed down into the ground, penetrating deeply and being forced further down by the jingling chains. A gout of lava geysered into the air, somehow being captured and forced into a shape by the magic of the ritual.

The lava continued to flow upward, spinning, *spinning*, and hardening into a multi-hued, inverted pyramid. The pyramid itself was filled with all sorts of material directly from the lava itself; everything from quartz, to diamond, and any metal that Joe could think of was present. Each chain retracted, and a dull thud echoed from the interior as they all went taut. The pyramid came down, cracking the perfect floor underneath with the pointed tip. All of the marble dropped away, allowing lava to boil upward until it reached a certain height; then it seemed to stop and form a shifting, superheated plane. Only a small walkway of pure-white marble remained, a path that led into a door that was forming on the side of the pyramid.

The ritual began to falter and finally finished.

Congratulations! You have successfully built 'Pharaoh's Pyramid of Panaceas'. Your chance of adding an additional effect did not activate.

Rituarchitect class experience gained: 3,000!

Reductionist class experience gained: 1,600!

Joe, one of the only people still on their feet after the powerful draining of the ritual, could barely wait to run up and inspect the building. As he got closer, he could see a huge column of lava extending into the base of the sphere, as well as what appeared to be invisible pipes pumping lava through the exterior of the sphere itself.

As he walked up to it, he realized that there was no heat

coming off of the building's exterior. He stepped up onto the stairs, climbing to the top and peering into the lava below. Joe reached out a hand, only to find that it was blocked by perfectly clear glass. Joe could only thank the crystalline aspects for that, as the original flooring was supposed to remain marble. He drew closer to the first wall and found that the entire structure was coated in the same smooth, clear surface. That didn't bother him, but when he walked to the door, his heart sank.

Caution! The Pharaoh's Pyramid of Panaceas does not recognize you as its user. Only a Master Alchemist or above may enter and claim this building. Any efforts to enter the building otherwise will be met with hostility.

Jaxon came up next to Joe and got the same message, then patted Joe on the back to make him feel better. "Welp. At least the volcano is calming down! Let's go get a coffee and catch up. Since you think you're gonna own this place, maybe you could put in a good word for me and transfer me into your unit? I hear there are health benefits to living in a sauna."

EPILOGUE

Getting out of Gramma's Shoe was simple after the walls had stopped being magically reinforced. Between the Dwarves and the automatons, several tunnels were rapidly constructed. Technically, they did not *need* the tunnels; as soon as they had captured the major fort and stopped the impending eruption, the option for rapid transit became available.

Most of the Officers took that option, but the rank-and-file had to go back the long way. Control of the fortress had been immediately foisted onto Joe, much to his consternation. Luckily, Captain Cleavage had stayed behind to teach him how to activate the respawning functionality. *Then* Joe understood why everyone else left as quickly as they could.

"This is… *insane.*" Joe looked at the numbers arrayed before him in horror. The sheer cost to respawn everyone was going to drain every bit of the resources that he had gained from Elfreeda's ring. Joe had no idea how each nation managed to bring back its fighters and recover its losses, and he *especially* had no idea how they had done it for several hundred years.

Even so, it was incredibly satisfying to look at the 'Ledger of Souls' and see Major General Havoc appear as an option to bring back. It appeared that Elfreeda's order to capture him instead of letting him die had failed. The thought made Joe shudder; their side had almost lost Havoc. However, before Joe made the mistake of bringing him back without good news to tell him, he looked further and found the only name that he had been truly scared that he would not see. "*There* you are, *Francine*. How about that? Havoc was right."

Resources poured from his new spatial device and into the open air, and after a long moment, his mentor appeared in front of him. The Dwarf's eyes were closed, and remained that way until a large cigar found a way into his hand. He took a deep pull from it. "*Celestials*, I hope I'm not an Elf."

Joe couldn't hold it in anymore; he started laughing, nearly falling over as tears streamed from his eyes. He reached up to touch them, wondering why his face was so wet. He tried to force some words out and failed, until he looked up and saw that Havoc was preparing to 'help' Joe get himself under control. That sobered the human up instantly. "Major General. Are you ready?"

"For what, human? Disappointment? From you? Always." Havoc took another deep pull on his cigar. "Although... to be fair, you surprised me a few times now. What have you got up your sleeve this time? Where are we right now, the capital?"

The human did not answer him, instead selecting the next name off the rolls and allowing only a slight wince to escape as all the beautiful resources vanished forever. A new Dwarf that Joe had never seen before took shape, coalescing into a blonde mustached body... a Dwarf with long hair. She was nobility as well? Her eyes popped open, a brilliant green that exactly matched Havoc's. Her deep voice echoed into the absolutely silent room, the confusion evident. "Where am I? What happened...? We were just about to finish the campaign... *I overslept!*"

Before she could panic any further, her gaze swept through the room and landed on Major General Havoc, who was trembling and staring at her with wide eyes. His cigar fell to the ground, quickly standing up and snuffing itself out. "*Dad? What happened to you? Did you get hit by an aging spell? Your beard...! Who set your beard on fire?*"

That was all she could get out before Havoc had enveloped her in a hug and swept her into the air. "My... my little love. I've been so lost without you. I..."

The pressure behind his thick lenses mounted too much, and tears spilled out. Tiny wiper blades appeared and washed the front, but couldn't clean the source. Havoc's top hat dropped off his head and landed on the floor, revealing wild white-blond hair. "I'll never lose you again, Francine. I'm so sorry I left you all alone."

"You're freaking me out." The startled Dwarf held Havoc tightly as she realized what must have happened. "Fifty years? I... I can't imagine what you've gone through. But I'm here now, and you'll never have to worry about losing me again."

Joe decided it was time to leave the room, and quietly let the family reunion run its course. His task was complete, all the troops—Elven and Dwarven—that had perished in the assault were back as Dwarves, so all that remained was to reap the rewards. He looked through the flood of messages that had poured in as soon as the raid officially ended, then at his status sheet.

You are considered the main contributor to the destruction and capture of a major fort. Experience gained: 50,000. Reputation gained with the Legion: 1,000. Reputation gained with the Dwarven Oligarchy: 500.

Quest complete: Ranker. After review, your Candidacy has been accepted. Your preliminary rank in Dwarven society has been set to 'Major General'.

Major accomplishments as a Candidate:

1. *Bringing access to the Deities back to the Dwarven Oligarchy.*
2. *Granting an option for a Grandmaster to advance into the Sage ranks in two disciplines (Smithing, Enchanting).*

3. *Applying a buff to various Officers that arguably saved the lives of thousands of Dwarves, as well as the Officers themselves on 15 occasions.*
4. *Rebutting an invasion.*
5. *Recapturing a national memorial landmark.*
6. *Rescuing 8,891 Legionnaires from an ambush.*
7. *Capturing a hidden major fort.*
8. *Building an Artifact-ranked Alchemy workshop for the usage of the Dwarven Oligarchy.*

Pending review, your rewards will be as follows: Noble title (Major General). You have completed a task, or created something that benefited the Dwarven Oligarchy as a whole. In addition to your rank, you will gain 5000 reputation with the Dwarven Council, a small homestead, a command of your own, immunity from past crimes, and a large plot of land to do with as you will. Report to General Court-Martial to receive rewards.

Plot of land determined as: Gramma's Shoe.

Welcome back to level 21!

Name: Joe 'Tatum's Chosen Legend' Class: Reductionist
Profession I: Arcanologist (Max)
Profession II: Ritualistic Alchemist (1/20)
Profession III: None
Character Level: 21 Exp: 240,559 Exp to next level: 12,441
Rituarchitect Level: 10 Exp: 45,000 Exp debt: 6,590
Reductionist Level: 2 Exp: 4,636 Exp to next level: 1,364
Hit Points: 1,864/1,864
Mana: 6,788/6,788
Mana regen: 52.7/sec
Stamina: 1,524/1,524
Stamina regen: 6.46/sec

Characteristic: Raw score

Strength: 146
Dexterity: 146
Constitution: 142
Intelligence: 152
Wisdom: 133
Dark Charisma: 100
Perception: 137
Luck: 79
Karmic Luck: 11

"I... I *did* it! I can finally bunker down and forget the world for a few months!" Joe was almost screaming from joy as he browsed the changes that had occurred since he had landed on this new Zone. Now he had a chunk of land to develop however he wanted, and he could barely wait. "That's okay, though! No more deadlines, no more quests from random places. All I'm going to do for the next... I don't even know how long... is turn this major fort into the most powerful outpost for the Dwarven Oligarchy, and the most *awesome* base for The Wanderer's Guild when they eventually catch up to me. Can I grind to my skills, train myself, and-"

"Joe! Get your rear over here!" Havoc shouted at him, poking his head out of the door to the one of only two buildings in the entire fort. "We have a war to plan! We're going to pay those elves back triple for daring to-"

"Nah..."

"Excuse *me?*" Havoc was taken aback by Joe's noncommittal answer.

"Havoc, all I want to do is spend some time putting my fort together and getting more powerful on my own. I don't want to have to-" Joe was cut off by a rude snort from the Dwarf.

"Did I say we have to charge in right *now*, screaming like chickens? No! I said we have a war to plan! If the plan is to wait for a while, that's a stupid plan, but at least it's a plan." Havoc smiled as he watched Joe slump. "Still got it. Listen, failing to plan is planning to fail. I'm here for you. I can never repay you for what you have done for me. But I'm going to try. Get in here, and let's map out your future."

"I want base building and skill grinding for the foreseeable future!" Joe demanded petulantly. "Oh! How about we get a-"

"See, this is *exactly* what I'm talking about!" Havoc grabbed Joe's shoulders and shook him. Joe hadn't even seen him cross the distance. "You're all over the place! A leader needs to be focused!"

"With me by your side, my *Apprentice...*" Havoc's acceptance made stars appear in Joe's eyes. Then his 'human culture class' teachings came along and ruined it all, making Joe run into the building just to make it stop. "You're gonna be drawn to more success than a moth going up Inflame!"

ABOUT DAKOTA KROUT

Author of the best-selling Divine Dungeon, Completionist Chronicles, and Full Murderhobo series, Dakota Krout was chosen as Audible's top 5 fantasy pick of 2017, has been a top 10 bestseller on Audible, and top 15 bestseller on Amazon.

He draws on his experience in the military to create vast terrains and intricate systems, and his history in programming and information technology helps him bring a logical aspect to both his writing and his company while giving him a unique perspective for future challenges.

"Publishing my stories has been an incredible blessing thus far, and I hope to keep you entertained for years to come!" -Dakota

Connect with Dakota:
MountaindalePress.com
Patreon.com/DakotaKrout
Facebook.com/TheDivineDungeon
Twitter.com/DakotaKrout
Discord.gg/8vjzGA5

ABOUT MOUNTAINDALE PRESS

Dakota and Danielle Krout, a husband and wife team, strive to create as well as publish excellent fantasy and science fiction novels. Self-publishing *The Divine Dungeon: Dungeon Born* in 2016 transformed their careers from Dakota's military and programming background and Danielle's Ph.D. in pharmacology to President and CEO, respectively, of a small press. Their goal is to share their success with other authors and provide captivating fiction to readers with the purpose of solidifying Mountaindale Press as the place 'Where Fantasy Transforms Reality.'

Connect with Mountaindale Press:
MountaindalePress.com
Facebook.com/MountaindalePress
Twitter.com/_Mountaindale
Instagram.com/MountaindalePress

MOUNTAINDALE PRESS TITLES
GameLit and LitRPG

The Completionist Chronicles,
The Divine Dungeon, and
Full Murderhobo by Dakota Krout

King's League by Jason Anspach and J.N. Chaney

A Touch of Power by Jay Boyce

Red Mage and
Farming Livia by Xander Boyce

Space Seasons by Dawn Chapman

Ether Collapse and
Ether Flows by Ryan DeBruyn

Bloodgames by Christian J. Gilliland

Threads of Fate by Michael Head

Wolfman Warlock by James Hunter and Dakota Krout

Axe Druid and
Mephisto's Magic Online by Christopher Johns

Skeleton in Space by Andries Louws

Chronicles of Ethan by John L. Monk

Pixel Dust and
Necrotic Apocalypse by David Petrie

Henchman by Carl Stubblefield

Artorian's Archives by Dennis Vanderkerken and Dakota Krout